Armageddon!

Before Hamilton could reply, a flash appeared at their right side, though it was much less intense than the first one. In quick succession came two more to the left. "My God!" Hamilton said in a tone indicating more awe than horror. "That's probably Cincinnati or the army depot in Lexington, and God knows what else. It's actually happened. They've finally gone and done it!"

Soldier of Fortune books from Tor

BULLET CREEK
THE COUNTERFEIT HOSTAGE
THE CULT CRUSHERS
DEADLY ISLAND
DOORGUNNER
FADED TATTOOS
THE FOUR CONDITIONS
FREEDOM BIRD
THE HARANI TRAIL
A HUNGER FOR HEROES
JADED BY CHOICE
THE LAST 48 HOURS
MACCAT
MacGONIGAL'S RAID
MacGONIGAL'S WAY
MISSING BY CHOICE
NATURE OF THE BEAST
THE OCTOBER LETTERS
SHUTTLE SHOWDOWN
STRIKER ONE DOWN
VALLEY OF PERIL
THE WARGAMER
THE WAY TO THE NORTH

SOLDIER OF FORTUNE MAGAZINE PRESENTS:

ED MANN

FIRST ANGEL

TOR®

A TOM DOHERTY ASSOCIATES BOOK
NEW YORK

FIRST ANGEL

Copyright © 1988 by The Omega Group, Ltd.

A TOR Book
Published by Tom Doherty Associates, Inc.
49 West 24 Street
New York, NY 10010

ISBN: 0-812-51229-4   Can. ISBN: 0-812-51230-8

Library of Congress Catalog Card Number: 88-51003

First edition: February 1989

Printed in the United States of America

0 9 8 7 6 5 4 3 2 1

To Charlene.

Special thanks to Leon Driskell
and Bob Maples for their help
with this book.

Ah, love, let us be true
To one another! for the world, which seems
To lie before us like a land of dreams,
So various, so beautiful, so new,
Hath really neither joy, nor love, nor light,
Nor certitude, nor peace, nor help for pain;
And we are here as on a darkling plain
Swept with confused alarms of struggle and flight,
Where ignorant armies clash by night.

—Matthew Arnold, "Dover Beach," 1867

PART ONE

But this I say, Brethren,
the time is short: . . .
for the fashion of this
world passeth away.

—1 Corinthians, 7:29–31

THURSDAY, MAY 16th:
The Day Before

John Robert Hamilton burrowed deeper into his bed covers. The sounds from the master bath, where Roseanna was showering, pulled him semiconscious into the pale morning light, though the cool spring air made him unwilling to wrench himself from the snug cocoon of sheets and thin blanket.

But his eyes opened of their own volition. His gaze drifted around the room, from the carved twin spires of the four-poster's footboard, to Roseanna's brocade-covered jewelry box on the dresser, to the white ruffled curtains billowing lazily before the open window. He took comfort in the bedroom's familiarity and began to remember that today was another that would be very different from the kind of days to which he was accustomed. Instead of a pin-striped suit, he would dress today in a camouflaged, battle-dress uniform of the United States Army.

Last week, Thursday, he had been at the dinner table when the phone call came. . . .

"Major Hamilton, please."

"Speaking." His stomach muscles tensed involuntarily as he recognized Lieutenant Colonel Mallory's voice. He didn't often receive phone calls on National Guard business at home. Given the international crisis that had been developing, however, he had expected eventually to hear what the voice on the line was about to say to him.

"This is Bob Mallory, Jack. I'm afraid it's really hit the fan. We've been mobilized. I got word about fifteen minutes ago. You're to report tomorrow at 0730 to the armory. You'll be given further instructions as to the mobilization timetable then."

"I don't suppose this is a bad joke." Hamilton tried to feign humor.

Mallory chuckled humorlessly. "You know better than that. According to the recall roster here, I see you have to call Mattingly and Simpson, and I have four more calls to make. I guess I'll see you bright and early in the morning."

"Yes, sir."

"Jack?" Mallory said before Hamilton had cradled the receiver.

"Yes, sir?"

"Ain't this a bitch?"

"You better believe it. See you tomorrow."

When Hamilton returned to the table, his son and daughter, sensing a profound change, looked at him curiously. Roseanna looked at him, too, but she didn't have to be told. Suddenly he had little appetite for the roast chicken and baked potatoes on his plate.

Friday, after a night of fitful sleep, Jack Hamilton left home, not for his office at First Fidelity Bank, but, as ordered, for the armory.

As he drove down the expressway that morning, delayed by the usual rush-hour traffic, Hamilton could no more help looking at the neat array of bombers off to his left than the average motorist can help pausing to rubberneck at an accident in the other lane. Strategic Air Command crews and aircraft had been dispersed across the nation during the rising tensions of the past several weeks.

Standiford Field was not a major air facility, at least not when compared to really large facilities around the country, such as Atlanta International Airport, or Lambert Field at St. Louis. But it did service adequately the needs of Louisville, Kentucky, and its metropolitan area of one million. And its runways were longer than the eight thousand feet the SAC bombers required. The dispersion concept permitted SAC to get its bombers away from the heavily targeted SAC bases—all the eggs out of the same basket.

Hamilton observed the airmen milling around the green-and-tan camouflaged aircraft that seemed like so many mottled birds of prey. He couldn't determine at this distance whether the men were part of SAC crews or support personnel from the air guard facility. Their nonchalant pace was, however, some comfort to him. He arrived quickly at the Crittenden Drive North exit, and he proceeded on to the armory.

The 149th Armored Brigade, 35th Infantry Division (Mechanized) was headquartered at the Fairgrounds Armory, perched on the edge of the sprawling Kentucky Fair and Exposition Center and nearly within sight of the airport. "The Kentucky Brigade" comprised approximately 4,500 officers and enlisted personnel spread across the state, and it represented about 60 percent of the Kentucky National Guard. As Hamilton pulled into the parking lot, he could see other key personnel arriving. A few officers stood outside the armory, engaged in animated conversation. Bobby Lawford walked up to his car.

Major Robert Longstreet Lawford, at six feet two inches, with the well-maintained figure of a former college halfback, was one of only two officers on the brigade staff with combat experience in Vietnam. With a Bronze Star and two Purple Hearts, he was the closest thing to a combat hero in the brigade headquarters. The fact that "he'd been there," and Hamilton had not, always made Hamilton feel at a disadvantage. "Good morning there, S-2. How about an intelligence report?" Lawford drawled, smiling broadly.

"Beats me, Bob. I only know what I read in the newspaper." Hamilton grinned and reached back into his car for his briefcase.

"I thought you'd have the latest scoop from the National Security Council by now," Lawford chuckled.

"Just what *do* they put in that Munfordville water, anyway?" Hamilton said as he slapped the taller Lawford on the back and walked with him into the armory.

More often than not, being the S-2, the Brigade Intelligence Officer, meant that Hamilton received information that was no more confidential than the news the public was fed by the media. At the 9:00 A.M. briefing, a team of army personnel from Fort Knox told him not much more about the rapidly deteriorating situation in the Middle East than he had read in the newspaper or watched on the CBS Evening News, all well-known current events.

The ayatollahs in Iran had lost control of the country after the Ayatollah Khomeini was finally gathered to his fathers. A revolt based on popular discontent with the serious economic malaise that had gripped the country since the Shah's departure finally, after much bloodshed, bore fruit. Although conservatives and leftists alike joined the rebellion, the leftist extremists maneuvered themselves into key positions of power, helped, without doubt, by the covert machinations of the Soviet KGB. The leftists had barely grasped power when Iraq, seething from the results of the earlier conflict with Iran and now seeing the opportunity to settle an old score, broke the armistice and launched an invasion once again.

Much of Iran's oil-rich southwestern provinces passed quickly into Iraqi control. Due to dissension and rebellion of conservative elements in the Iranian Army caused by dissatisfaction with the unstable leftist government, it appeared to most Western observers that Iran was in danger of losing control of much of its petroleum production capability. Oil supplies to Western Europe and Japan, as well as to the Third World, were, at least temporarily, drastically diminished.

The tottering leftist government, its political back against the wall, played its trump card and issued a public invitation to the Soviet Union to intervene. The Soviets, more interested in Iranian oil and a warm-water port like Chahbahar on the Persian Gulf than in Iraqi friendship, responded quickly and efficiently.

Within twenty-four hours, the vanguard units of the Soviet army made initial contact with the Iraqis. Within forty-eight hours, lightly equipped Soviet forces had been airlifted forward and were engaging the Iraqis at several key points.

The usual burst of diplomatic commmuniqués from Washington followed disclosure of Iran's request to the Soviets. The president gave up on private efforts to defuse the situation when initial press reports disclosed that the first Soviet units had arrived in Iran.

The United Nations, as usual, failed to act, and within hours of the first news of Soviet combat deployment, the United States issued a warning that it was considering using the Rapid Deployment Force to meet the Soviet presence and to restore stability to the area. The Soviets ignored the warning.

Within two days, thirty thousand Soviet troops had crossed the Soviet-Iranian border, and there were no indications that the movement of Soviet troops and equipment would cease.

The young Soviet leaders in power after the passing of Gorbachev, Andropov, and Brezhnev were not about to suffer a loss of face like that after the Cuban missile crisis. Not sharing their predecessors' memories of Russian suffering in World War II, they were emboldened to play the situation to its limit, with what more cautious observers considered an inadequate appreciation of the possible consequences. Pleas from conservative Iranian rebels for American intervention had little effect on the Kremlin leaders.

Within ten days of the invasion, Washington moved. The RDF's 82d Airborne spearheaded the operation at three Iraqi airfields, and was greeted by enthusiastic Iraqi support. Elements of the 2d Marine Division followed in short order. The president proclaimed the presence of the U.S. forces as a peacekeeping mission, suggested a bilateral withdrawal of both superpowers, and issued public orders to his commanders in the field not to force contact with the advancing Russians.

The president's actions met with an initial surge of domestic support, but antiwar sentiment began growing as each new day brought Soviet forces closer to American positions. Assurances from Washington that the matter would never reach "nuclear proportions" allayed the fears of most Americans, and the matter was perceived by most citizens as a relatively "low-risk" test of will.

From the time the first troops arrived in Iran, however, it was apparent that the American forces were at a considerable disadvantage. Sea lines and air routes half a world long made the movement of men and equipment a logistical nightmare. One round trip of one giant C-5A cargo plane equaled one tank on the ground in the Middle East. By contrast, the movement of Soviet equipment on the Iranian highways was quick and unimpeded. The Soviet equivalent of the Red Ball Express had proven extremely effective. The situation with the Soviet air force was parallel.

The mobilization of National Guard and Reserve units reflected the realization in Washington that if the United States did not intend to allow Iran and its oil to fall permanently into Soviet hands, an all-out military effort, or at least the appearance of such, would have to be made. With no draft in place, and the fact that it would take several crucial months to implement the new Selective Service System and provide the first draftees to their units, the National Guard and Reserve forces were the only alternatives to which Washington could quickly turn to augment the nation's military muscle and indicate the strength of America's resolve.

The mobilization timetables were well known in advance. Just how well these schedules for the massive movement of troops and equipment would *actually* work was completely unknown. Only day-to-day monitoring of the timetables' successes would give any indication of the actual deployment date. Indeed, none of the briefing officers had any idea as yet where the 149th or the 35th Mech would be sent.

As the briefing ended, it became obvious to Hamilton that he was not going to learn where he was going or when he was to leave, only that he should be *prepared* to leave, perhaps in seven days, and that deployment would be to an unspecified destination for an unspecified period. As he walked out, Lawford looked at him, rolled his eyes, and grinned. "Learn a lot?"

"Oh sure," Hamilton replied. "I think they call this 'stand by to stand by.'"

The clatter of a deodorant can bouncing across the bathroom floor jarred Jack Hamilton back to the present. Roseanna cracked open the bathroom door and peered out sheepishly at him. "Are you awake?"

"Guess," he said, rolling over, stretching his muscular frame across the sheets. Racquetball did wonders for a man in his late thirties.

She came toward the bed, dropped her towel, and slid under the covers. She pressed her warm, moist body against him and ran her fingers across his chest. "Sorry," she said, "but you had to get up in five minutes, anyway."

"It's okay. I was already half awake. I was just thinking about everything."

Her fingers began to play with the thick, dark hair on his chest. "Sweetheart, it's seemed as if you were just putting on your uniform in the morning and going to work, and not much else has been different for the past week. Almost as if you were still working at the bank every day. I'm not sure how I will handle it when you really have to go off to this godawful war."

"Maybe not war. Maybe we'll just warm an army brigade's seat at Fort Hood." He really didn't believe it, though.

She straddled his abdomen and sat upright, with one knee at the side of each of his hips, her heavy breasts swaying slightly. She ran her fingers through her damp auburn hair and pulled it back down her neck. "I think I liked this National Guard business a lot better when it was one weekend a month."

"Me, too," he replied, pulling her to him and rolling her onto the bed. He gently pressed his lips against hers. He pulled off his bedclothes and moved between her firm thighs, embracing Roseanna in search of unison with her.

For both of them, if only briefly, the war in Iran did not exist.

The staff meeting that morning made it increasingly clear to Hamilton that someone had pushed the "mobilization button" before anyone had figured out that the timetable was not going to function with the clockwork precision that had been hoped for.

As the meeting finally broke up, Hamilton let out a sigh of relief. It sometimes seemed to him that lengthy staff meetings were the only reason the army existed. He stretched his back, and approached Lieutenant Colonel Mallory, the brigade XO, a middle-aged accountant in "real life," with an excessive fondness for an ever-present pipeful of aromatic smoking tobacco. "Sir, the S-2 section is about as ready as I can get it. Our equipment is ready to be loaded, and I'm about up to here with these so-called situation reports, which are twenty-four hours behind the six o'clock news. Do you mind if I sneak off to the bank for a couple of hours? I left a lot of loose ends there, and I'd like to take care of a few of them if I could."

"No problem, Jack," Mallory replied, tapping the bowl of his pipe in an ashtray on a nearby table. "I know exactly what you mean about the situation here, but try to stay near a phone in case the totally unexpected happens and someone finally decides what to do with us. Given the way things are crumbling over there, who knows what will happen next?"

The situation, as Mallory had put it, *was* crumbling. The news the evening before had carried reports of yet more

Iraqi and rebel Iranian army reversals; the Soviet and Socialist Iranian steamroller continued to push on toward the American forces at the Iranian-Iraqi border. On everyone's mind was the question of whether a latter-day Dunkirk was in the making for the American forces, when and if the Soviets made contact.

Hamilton waited for an opportune moment to make his exit; he didn't want everyone to see him wandering off to his car. Nevertheless, as he ducked out to the parking lot with more than a little spring to his step, it occurred to him that rank did have its privileges.

"Hi, soldier!" chimed Stephanie, the ever-so-cheerful blond receptionist, as Hamilton left the elevator on what until a few days before had been his floor. First Fidelity didn't pay Stephanie for her intelligence. Her large breasts had impressed the bank's personnel director, just as they had impressed the numerous callers in Hamilton's department every day for the past three years. Some of the male customers wouldn't think of taking their business elsewhere and foregoing the opportunity to look down what was considered the most exciting décolletage in downtown Louisville. Hamilton was always amused at the number of bank executives who found it necessary to call on him personally rather than pick up the phone and give up the opportunity to pass by Stephanie's desk and engage in brief chitchat. According to the grapevine, a couple of them had engaged in more than repartee with her.

"I thought you were supposed to be defending your country." She mocked a little-girl tone.

"*Our* country," he corrected. "But even John Wayne took a break every now and then."

"From the sound of the news, we need John Wayne now more than ever. Did you hear the latest? The man on the radio said an Iraqi division was overrun last night, and some of the rebel Iranian units were completely destroyed. Can you believe this situation?"

The news brought an immediate frown, but he didn't stop to discuss the matter.

As he rounded the corner and started into his old office, he caught Jim Rutledge in the process of rearranging the furniture in the place that, until a few days before, had been his private domain. Looking to the door, he noticed that the sign saying John R. Hamilton had been removed. The one below it, which said Vice-President in Charge of Commercial Loans, remained untouched.

With Hamilton's call-up, Rutledge had jumped five years in service at the bank. Hamilton had never particularly cared for this cocky subordinate, and despite his best efforts he found himself resenting Rutledge for his unexpected and hasty promotion. Startled by Hamilton's unannounced appearance, Rutledge grinned like an eight-year-old caught with his hand in the cookie jar.

Hamilton smiled wryly. "Christ, Jim! You could have at least waited a decent period before you desecrated the place. Don't you have any respect for the recently departed?"

"You caught me right in the act, good buddy. Have a seat and make yourself at home. I think you're familiar enough with the place. How in the hell did you get the time to come down here and harass me? I thought you'd be halfway to Khuzistan or some such place by now."

"You know the army—hurry up and wait. Nobody still knows how soon we'll be leaving or where we'll be going," he said, gazing out the broad expanse of glass toward the river. He walked to the window, looking down several stories at the activity below. The river barges moved along at their usual snail's pace. Two hundred school children were just starting out on the *Belle of Louisville* from the Fourth Street wharf for an end-of-the-school-year steamboat ride up the Ohio River. Traffic moved without hesitation through Spaghetti Junction's layered ramps at the intersection of I-64 and I-65. Good grief! he thought, these people act as if they don't know that there's likely to be a war at any minute.

With his tone growing more serious Rutledge said, "Jack, maybe I shouldn't ask this. I mean, after all, we never have been all that close. But you seem really worried about the war and all, leaving your family and everything behind."

"Yeah. Really worried." Still staring out the window, Hamilton continued. "This war business in the past has always been one where Johnny would go marching off to war with the assurance that he was fighting for Mom and apple pie most of the time, and that Mom and everyone else back home would be safe during the war. No matter what happened to Johnny, his family would be safe, secure, and provided-for back home. Well, that's not the case now. It's sort of like asking a volunteer fireman to come and put out the fire at city hall when his own house is ready to burst into flames." He said nothing for a few seconds. "Who knows how soon before the Bomb is used?"

"Aw, c'mon, Jack." Rutledge swiveled around in his chair. "The president wouldn't use the Big One until Russian soldiers were molesting his daughter on the White House lawn. The guy doesn't have the balls. Besides, everything out of Washington sticks to this peacekeeping mission line. How many times in the past month have you heard State Department or Pentagon people promising to handle this thing by conventional means only?"

"Maybe. But it could just be that this sort of talk keeps a lid on the protest movement, which has grown large enough as it is. It seems more obvious to me all the time that if the fighting starts, the troops over there aren't going to stop the Russians conventionally, and the chances for the use of at least tactical nuclear weapons seems to grow daily. It seems to be the only option we have left. Considering that we've sat fat, dumb, and happy for twenty years while the Russians outspent us on defense two to one, it'll be no surprise if we get steamrolled over there," said Hamilton.

"Spoken like a true military man," grinned Rutledge. "We'll never use the Bomb. Iran and all the oil in the world can go straight to hell, but we'll never use nuclear weapons to save it. They've always been a bluff, if you want my opinion, and as a bluff they were useless unless we acted as if we really would use them. The 'big secret,' Jack, is that we'll never use them, and especially not for a few oil fields in Iran. Armageddon this *ain't*."

Hamilton looked directly at the man, and then remembered why he had never really liked him. "After Iran, what? Are you absolutely sure that the Russians won't look further south to the other Persian Gulf states? A lot of those sheikhs are biting their nails down past the cuticle right now, hoping some rebel group doesn't make a play for power and invite the Kremlin into *their* socialist struggle. I wish I could be as confident as you are. It would certainly make leaving Roseanna and the kids here a lot easier if I didn't have to worry about the war over there escalating to one where the whole country becomes a goddam battlefield." Hamilton turned his gaze once again out the window.

Rutledge leaned back and cocked his feet up on the desk. "Trust me on this, fella. It'll never happen. You're looking at those people down there. Do they think it will happen? Hell no, and it *won't*. You can bank on it."

And with that the two moved together and commenced going through a stack of files lying in the In basket Rutledge had inherited from Hamilton. Hamilton plucked from the stack the recent appraisal on the Carlisle Harbor Condominium project, an important and very large new condominium development proposed for the city's affluent East End.

But as Hamilton studied the details of the report, his mind was still set on Iran and the nuclear ogre.

The phone rang in Kurt Rogers' office. As he was the only one nearby, his secretary being on vacation, he grabbed the receiver as soon as he could free one of his hands from the coffee mug and the files he was carrying.

"Regal Real Estate."

"Siegfried? Have you heard the news this morning?"

Rogers immediately recognized the voice of Larry Jackson, who still referred to him occasionally by his college football nickname, from the days when he and his brother, Travis, had been known as the Mad Norsemen. The nickname was related to his striking Nordic features, due no doubt to his Norwegian mother, and though Rogers' football days had ended more than a decade ago, the name still seemed to fit.

"Christ Almighty! The Russians are kicking ass over there, Kurt. I'm really beginning to get nervous, old buddy. I mean, it would really be a kick in the old petoot after we've sunk all this money, time, and effort into it, and we just sat here and waited for the Russkies to drop a silver bullet right on top of us. I've been talking to George and Jerry, and they're kinda nervous in the service, too. What's your thinking?"

Rogers dropped the files he was carrying onto the credenza next to the stack of new listings that he had made in the past month, and he groped for a chair. He sat down and leaned back, cocking his long legs up on one corner of the mahogany desk. He actually enjoyed immensely these opportunities to advise Larry and the others in the group. Larry in particular usually needed advice on one thing or another. "I don't think you should be too concerned yet, Larry. A lot more will have to happen before I start heading out. Things are slow here in the office now, since there are a lot more sellers than buyers. But things are probably going to pick up soon. And Josh is still in school for a while. I just can't pick up and get out to the country without taking these things into consideration."

To the average Louisvillian, "the country" was any place outside Jefferson County. To Rogers' group, it had a very special meaning. "The country" for Kurt, Larry, and several others was a special place along the meandering course of the Rolling Fork River in the rich bottomland of Marion County, sixty-odd miles to the southeast of Louisville on the fringe of the bluegrass area. Located there was a farm of approximately two hundred and fifty acres, well removed from any well-traveled road. They called it the Aerie.

Kurt, Larry, Travis, and George Anderson had purchased the place three years before from a college friend who had gone "back to the earth" for several years before giving up and returning to the comforts of the city. They had paid what most considered an above-the-market price, but what was sensible to Kurt and the others was quite different from what was sensible to everyone else.

The farm offered a location that was out of the way but at the same time not too remote. It was fertile and cleared for the most part, at least those parts suitable for crops. The buildings were sound and sat clustered on a knoll which gave anyone a good field of observation of all that took place in the flat river bottomland that spread out around it. With its diverse livestock, fruit trees, wind-powered generator, photovoltaic solar panels, and deep well, it was a very acceptable refuge. It met their consensus as to what a survivalist retreat should be.

Kurt's group had formed due to common mistrust of the economic system's stability, a dissatisfaction with the dependency of the average individual on a fragile, technologically based society, and a general feeling of anxiety over the continuing international tensions between the United States and the Soviet Union.

There was no formal leader of the group, as conditions—

so far at least—had not required one; nor were there any bylaws. However, the fact that Kurt, Larry, George, and Travis owned the farm in partnership, and the other families in gathered and living there were friends or relatives of the four, made them the dominant decision-makers for the loose coalition. Travis's transfer had taken him out of the picture now, and of the three college fraternity brothers who remained, Kurt was most often looked to for his opinions as to how group decisions should be made.

Continuing, Rogers said, "Things *might* be getting out of hand, but I'm going to watch and wait a little more."

There was a silence from the other end, and finally Larry said, "I don't know. Maybe I'm just too antsy. Sometimes when I'm not thinking very straight I think that after investing so much money in food, medical supplies, guns, and all the other survival gear out there it would be a damned shame for a catastrophe not to happen and for all of it to go to waste. Sort of like a race-car builder who never gets to take his new racer around the track."

"Larry Jackson, I think you're right when you say you don't think you're thinking very straight," replied Rogers, stopping briefly to sip at his coffee. "What we've been doing is building a lifeboat out there. Should the ship of state, you might say, hit an iceberg, we have our own little lifeboat to take off in. But when all is said and done, fellow, nobody in the lifeboat will have wanted to set out too soon bouncing around needlessly if he'd been given the choice of staying aboard a warm and comfortable cruise liner—"

"On the other hand," Larry interrupted, "you've got to launch the lifeboat before the ship starts its deathroll."

"Touché. But I don't think we're near that point yet. I'll keep listening to the radio for developments, and I suggest that you do the same."

"Okay, ol' buddy, but I've still got the jitters. By the way, Billy got a few acres of corn planted on that high ground last week, but with all this wet weather this spring, it'll be a while before it'll be dry enough to plant most of the bottomland. I'll talk to you later." With that he hung up.

Rogers slowly placed the phone back on the hook, continuing to think about the conversation. Was he frittering away precious time? he wondered.

He didn't want to be like those religious fanatics who

every so often trek out to some mountaintop to await Jesus' Second Coming. On the other hand, he didn't want to wait in Sodom until it was too late. The parallel to the situation of the Jews who stayed in Nazi Germany didn't escape him, either. But Josh did have to finish the school year. And he did have several real estate prospects he hated to walk out on right now. Besides, the plans and specifications on that house Duke Droppelman wanted him to build sat there squarely in the center of his desk, luring his attention back to business matters.

From the FM radio across the desk, the hourly news carried the lead story of the Soviet advance to a point only fifty kilometers from the American positions, as well as reports of further Iraqi setbacks. Placing his feet against the corner of the desk and stretching his large frame back in the chair, he stared out the window at the neat row of marigolds and thought, I wonder what old Lot would have done in my place?

Charlie Brighton sat in his office at city hall, looking at the stack of pink "While You Were Out" memos piled in front of him. The local civil defense director was quite sought after lately. He and his assistants at the joint city-county agency did their best to answer the inquiries that had bombarded the office in the past few weeks. Suddenly he was the most popular man in local government. The paper had done a feature on him, and a couple of the televisions had sent crews by to interview the retired Marine Corps warrant officer.

Yes, the Office of Disaster and Emergency Services—a more "with-it" name than Civil Defense Office, had gotten more attention in the past few weeks than it had in the preceding ten years. Suddenly he had immediate entrée to people with whom, just a couple of months ago, he had had to make appointments days in advance. Although the local citizenry were still only moderately concerned, at least some of the politicians had "gotten religion," even with the continued assurances of the White House on the nuclear question. It helped that the war still appeared to be contained in the Iranian theater. Even if U.S. and Soviet forces should meet, it would likely remain so—if Washington could be believed.

The mayor had seen him three times at length last week alone. The county judge executive had him practically locked in his office all afternoon just yesterday. The picture Charlie gave did not sit well with either of them. After years as local government's stepchild, with barely enough money appropriated, as Charlie saw it, to provide for his own letterhead and postage stamps, Brighton's program was terribly inadequate. An emergency command center was in place in city hall, a network of sirens did cover most of the populated areas of the county, and there was a sketchy, *very* sketchy, plan for evacuation of the city. But as to fallout shelters and provisions for food and water, Brighton's cupboard was bare. The mayor's chief administrative aide, Tom O'Hara, was aghast when Brighton first informed him of the situation.

"You mean there's nothing in those shelters we have? Not even water?" he had asked incredulously.

"Not a thing," Brighton had told him as bluntly as he could, relishing the effect on O'Hara.

"Then what the hell happened to it?" demanded O'Hara with a boyish petulance, though he was well beyond the *boyish* stage, despite the occasional reference to him by admirers and detractors alike as the mayor's fair-haired boy.

"It was all taken out in the seventies, Tom. Most of it was spoiled or spoiling," said Mayor Don Burns. "Twenty years old for the most part—just spoiled or spoiling," he repeated.

O'Hara stood up, straightened his tie and the center line of the pin-striped vest that accented the lines of his trim physique, and began pacing around the room. "Good grief! What the hell do we do now if we need it?" O'Hara was as exasperated by his display of ignorance about the situation in front of Burns as he was about the situation itself. Brighton, it seemed, had very clearly embarrassed him. It wasn't the first time.

"It looks as though we do without," Burns observed, reclining in his chair, a posture that only served to flatten his double chin across his neck.

"There's going to be hell to pay with the public when and if things get hotter in Iran. If the 'great unwashed' finally look around and figure out that the government can do little or nothing for them, it could get rather ugly . . ." It seemed that O'Hara was talking more to himself than to the others.

The mayor snapped him out of it, interjecting, "The 'great unwashed,' as you call them, will obviously be looking for scalps whenever there are problems or annoyances which inconvenience them. This whole goddam area has been one where nobody really gave a damn one way or the other. Given the choice here of a quarter mile of asphalt or a hundred thousand dollars more in civil defense expenditures, there's no contest.

"Government people, me included, understand that and respond accordingly. You start talking about spending money on civil defense, and the peace freaks scream you're planning a war. Bishops start condemning you from the pulpit, and college students bombard the newspapers with 'bitch letters' to the editor. To keep from getting labeled prowar, you have to keep your mouth shut if you value your political hide. I'm as guilty as the next in this regard, but beating my breast and shouting 'mea culpa' from the top of city hall won't help us out now."

The mayor spun in his chair and poured himself a glass of water from the insulated decanter on his credenza. He took several gulps from it before continuing. "There's no money coming from the feds immediately, and we sure don't have any money locally to make even a dent in the problem. I suppose at this point it's sort of like being without homeowner's insurance and not having the money to pay the premium. You just pray that it doesn't storm too hard . . ."

Brighton shifted from the reverie of that unsettling meeting and glanced across his desk, picking up a few of the pink messages from the large stack before him. He sorted them into piles: one for immediate action, one for "get to it later" types, and a third for those to which he had no intention of responding. Two from O'Hara fell somewhere between the last two categories.

With the soothing words flowing daily from Washington, only a minority of the population was interested in civil defense measures. Their fervor, however, approached the religious, and their numbers were growing. But even this minority of interested and concerned people was enough to overwhelm Brighton's small staff. When inquiries from this group were added to the number of worried-but-not-necessarily-frantic callers, the demands placed on the office rose to a Herculean level.

A million things needed to be done. Who knew how much time was really left in which to do them? Oh, well, he thought, what was it that the Chinese say? Something about a journey of a thousand miles beginning with the first step?

And after all, maybe he was overreacting to the situation.

Jack Hamilton sat at the evening dinner table with his family. As usual he had already shed his uniform for a comfortable polo shirt and a pair of cotton-twill trousers. Kip, his twelve-year-old son, and Jennifer, his ten-year-old daughter, were arguing over which television show they would watch on the "good" television set that night. "Neither of you is watching anything unless you keep quiet and let your dad and me enjoy our meal," interrupted Roseanna. Turning to her husband, who seemed to be wrapped in thought, she asked, "Jack, what are you thinking about so intensely?"

"The human condition, the fate of the earth, the war in Iran, you name it. But most of all, you and the kids," he said, still staring at his plate.

"You mean leaving us here?"

"Exactly. I don't like the idea of going off in a few days to some godforsaken stretch of Iranian desert, or Texas desert for that matter, when all hell could break loose at any moment, and the war could really escalate."

"Don't worry, sweetheart. The kids and I are perfectly capable of managing."

Hamilton's tone stiffened as he replied. "Don't let me offend your feminist sensibilities, dear, but for the kind of situation I'm talking about, you and the kids are definitely *not* equipped to manage."

"What does *ex-ca-late* mean, Daddy?"

"It means it's time to finish your vegetables and get upstairs and do your homework, princess," he said, dismissing her question. With that, Hamilton excused himself and went into the family room. He sat down in his favorite chair in front of the television and began reading the evening paper. He was flipping through the advertising supplements when the *CBS Evening News* came on. Dan Rather began briskly,

Good evening. Just moments ago, following closely the news that Soviet Backfire bombers conducted devastating firebomb raids on Baghdad today, killing thousands, the State Department issued an ominous statement: Unless the Soviet advance is halted, and the Soviet Union disengages itself from the Iranian-Iraqi conflict, the U.S. will take action that could result in, quote, the gravest of consequences, unquote. The statement further indicates that the U.S. is examining its options in employing, and I quote, "whatever force is necessary to restore peace and stability in Iran." For more on the story of this dramatic public announcement and what these new developments will mean to future developments in the Middle East, we go live to Joseph Cambron, who is standing by at the State Department . . .

Christ! Hamilton thought, this is really getting serious. He looked over his shoulder and saw Roseanna watching silently from the other room, her arms folded across her chest.

Finally, she said, "What does this mean, Jack?" as she walked closer to the set.

"It means anything could happen. Sit down, will you?" He shifted his position so that he could look directly into her eyes. What he was about to propose would take good eye contact. "What do you say to our taking Kip and Jennifer out to Cliff's for a few days? I mean, just long enough to see how this mess in Iran is going to develop." He spoke softly, but with such resolution as to leave no doubt as to his seriousness.

"And what? Leave you here? No way. Besides, the kids are still in school. We can't just jump up and run off without considering that."

"Listen," he said as he leaned closer to her to make his point, "I don't think you appreciate how serious that last bit of news was. Given the usual diplomatic terms used in describing these matters, it means that the situation is deteriorating rapidly."

"You mean that you think they're at the point of using H-bombs or something?" she said, wrinkling her brow at the thought.

"Maybe not, at least not immediately. But small nuclear devices, tactical nuclear weapons on the battlefield—

perhaps. It seems at this point to be the only way of stopping the Russians. Unless we decide to let them have Iran, and then probably the whole Persian Gulf, the only option left is the nuclear option. But once it's used, who knows where it will stop?" He spoke with such deep concern that she recoiled at the implication.

She stood up and began to pace the room as his words sank in. Walking up to the bookcase, she grabbed at a figurine and started running her fingers up and down it. "Nuclear *option*?" she mimicked. "And you defend this unbelievable madness?"

"It doesn't matter a hill of beans whether I defend it or not. I'm just analyzing the situation like a doctor would analyze a disease." There wasn't a trace of emotion in his voice.

"You really think it will spread and bombs will be dropped here? Why in the world would the Russians want to bomb Louisville?"

"With seven to eight thousand strategic warheads to use, should it turn into an 'all-out' war, they have to put them to use somewhere. Ordinarily, Louisville would be considered a Class II target, like any other manufacturing and transportation center. But with those SAC bombers sitting out at Standiford Field, it becomes Class I. The Russians are going to take out anything that can hurt them as soon as possible, and you can bet your sweet fanny that those bombers were picked up by Russian satellites very quickly after their arrival."

Maybe it was true, she thought. And maybe other people had the same fears now. On the way home from the university, where she had been working on her thesis, she had noticed an unusual number of campers and cars pulling rental trailers on this weekday. One car in particular was pulling a trailer overloaded with a strange combination of camping equipment and household goods and the trailer was fishtailing dangerously. She had passed it very carefully, silently cursing the driver for his stupidity.

She put the figurine back in its place. "But if the situation was that serious, don't you think that the president would tell us so that people could do something?"

"Not really. Did Kennedy tell the American public to get out of the cities during the Cuban missile crisis? It may be similar to a gunfight in the Westerns. If one guy starts unbuttoning his coat so as to get his holster clear, the other guy is just as likely to shoot first. Same thing here. We start evacuating our cities and the Russians just might go ahead and hit us first. What they used to call in Vietnam a preemptive first strike. The president sitting there with his finger on the button, figuratively at least, may decide that he could save millions of lives by ordering an evacuation before a nuclear exchange occurs, but by ordering an evacuation, he may insure that the bombs actually do drop."

His words had hit home with her, but she still had a few reservations. "Are you suggesting that we leave tonight?"

"No, but I would like to start getting things ready. Then we'll be able to leave quickly once we decide to go. Let's just act like we're reacting to what we might call in the army 'a warning order.'"

"Well, I suppose just getting things together can't hurt anything," she said.

They began to compile a list of what the kids would need. Without seeking her agreement, Hamilton added the children's winter clothing and, as an afterthought, pulled down from the bedroom closet the old Luger his father had brought back from Normandy. After fishing around for a few seconds, he located what remained of the box of shells from his abortive attempt the previous summer to teach Roseanna how to shoot the pistol.

With the children's help, they amassed a huge stack of clothing and other items on the living room floor. The children had been most cooperative at the thought of an early start on the weekend at the expense of school.

"Why don't we go tomorrow morning?" Kip asked.

"Why not tonight?" Jennifer squealed with delight.

"It's not certain we're going anywhere at all," Roseanna replied. "This is just in case we decide to go."

"But why are we taking all this winter stuff to the farm now?" Kip asked. He looked quizzically at some of the items his father had pulled out of the spare closet.

"Just in case we decide to stay longer than we had intended, son."

"Oh, Dad, be *real!*" Kip muttered as he walked into the next room.

Roseanna paused from sorting the clothes in front of her and looked Hamilton straight in the eyes. "I wish it weren't real," she said softly.

"Hello?"

"Cliff, what's going on out there?" Hamilton said as cheerfully as he could manage.

"About the same as usual, Jack," replied his brother, recognizing the voice. "I was able to squeeze in planting another hundred acres of corn last week before the rains hit again. Everybody down here is really behind with all of this wet weather. People are even starting to be worried about what an early frost could do to us. Haven't had to worry about that kind of a problem for a while."

"Sold any livestock lately?" Jack asked, trying to extend the chitchat a while before getting to the real business of his call.

"Yeah, the market was up a little, so I sold a few head of cattle last week, but no hogs lately. I'll have a check on the way for your share soon."

Cliff Hamilton. City boy turned farmer. Cliff was two years younger than Jack, though two inches taller at six feet one inch, and quite a bit heavier. Early in his teens, Cliff became interested in farming on the summer vacations he and Jack had spent on Uncle Charles and Aunt Susan's farm. The two were a childless couple, considerably older than the boys' parents, and they were always glad to have the boys for company. As it turned out, Cliff became serious about the matter, and went off to college to study agriculture at the University of Kentucky.

When Uncle Charles and Aunt Susan died four years ago in an automobile collision with a local young redneck who had two prior drunk-driving convictions, Cliff and Jack unexpectedly found themselves the new owners of the six-hundred-acre farm. Cliff took over the day-to-day operation of the farm, and Jack collected a share of the profits.

For Jack, the farm was a profitable enterprise that period-ically served as a pleasant diversion from the hustle of the city. His kids enjoyed frolicking in the hayloft and fishing in the lake as much as he and Cliff had when they were younger. Jennifer loved collecting eggs, and Kip felt like a real grownup when Cliff allowed him to sit beside him on the tractor when he plowed. Roseanna, being a strictly city-bred girl, wasn't fond of the farm, but she didn't resist the frequent trips because they meant so much to the children.

"What's the deal, soldier? Any news on when you're leaving?" Cliff asked, trying too hard to maintain a casual tone.

"No word, yet," said Hamilton. After pausing a few seconds, he asked, "Cliff, Roseanna and the kids might be coming out for a few days. We don't really know for sure yet. Do you and Marge have anything planned?"

"Nothing special. Same as usual." His tone grew more serious in response to his brother's worried voice. "Does this have anything to do with the news tonight?"

"Yeah, exactly with that."

"Well, what about you? What are you gonna be doing?"

"Exactly what I'm doing now. Going to the armory each day and wasting time until we get our deployment orders," Jack replied. "I might be down with Roseanna and the kids tomorrow or the next day, depending on how things are going. I just don't know yet."

"We'll be here, brother."

"Kurt!" the excited voice on the other end of the line exclaimed before Rogers had even had a chance to speak. "Did you catch the evening news a few minutes ago?"

It was Larry again. Rogers had been hunting for his own phone list.

"Yeah, I heard. I guess this is good enough for me. I was just about to start phoning everyone right now. I don't know how the others will feel, but I expect to be out there tonight. How about you?"

"I'm three minutes from hitting the road. Dana and the kids are just waiting for me to lock up. I'll see you out there, old buddy," replied Jackson.

"Right. See you there," and with that Rogers hung up. That Larry was something, he thought. His voice had been almost dripping with excitement.

Rogers looked at the list and started his calls. On the first two he got no answer. Could they have left already, he wondered? The next two answered and indicated that they were in the process of leaving. Rick O'Connell said he was taking the family out right away, but that he would have to go back to work the next day.

"I think that might be unwise considering everything, Rick. Are you sure you shouldn't stay down there for a few days to see how this thing is developing?"

"My vacation's used up, and I can't just walk out on my job, Kurt. Hell, I'm only four years away from retirement. Besides, I can always change my mind if things get any hotter. For now, Jerry can take care of Kitty and Missy. He's eighteen and thinks he can handle anything and everything." O'Connell chuckled, but his pride in his son was evident.

"You're right about him being able to handle the situation, Rick. I'll see you down there tonight, but I still think you should give it some more thought."

Rogers continued with his efforts. He even tried to call Travis in California. He got only the answering machine, but went ahead and left a message anyway. He wound up contacting seven families, six of whom had indicated that they were moving to the farm that night. Not bad. Not bad at all. He had always wondered whether the group would really work together when the time came. This cohesiveness made him feel very much better about the whole situation.

Cohesiveness had always been a primary concern, and for that reason, Larry, George, and Kurt had drawn on family members in the beginning because of the inherently stronger bonds. The old adage about blood being thicker than water was not lost on the three. This idea had met with partial success. Larry had recruited a brother, Dan Jackson, and George had recruited a sister, Jean Godfrey, with her family, and a cousin, Bob Rose, with his family.

Kurt's brother, Travis, had been an active and important member in the beginning, but a new job in California had ended his involvement the preceding year. The group sorely missed his drive and ability. He still retained his ownership interest in the farm, as he said, "Just in case . . ."

Also added were Michael Mulloy, an ex-army mechanic, and Jerry Mazurkis, an electrical engineer. Skills such as these would be precious should the economy and social order break down for whatever reason.

Skills of a different nature were represented by Joe and Jackie Olsen. They were what the group jokingly referred to as reformed hippies. As flower children of the sixties and early seventies, they had spent several years on a large commune in Tennessee. In doing so, they had accumulated skills in self-sufficient living which the group hoped to be able to use, should the time come when they were ever needed. As a manager of a fast-food franchise now, Joe was culturally light-years removed from his hippie days, thereby giving rise to the "reformed" label. However, he still had a distaste for the weapons on which the group placed such an important emphasis.

It was the consensus that should a breakdown occur, the odds were very high that no family would be safe from the depradations of less-well-prepared survivors without the willingness and ability to use firearms in self-defense. To that end, each member was encouraged to acquire weapons of various types, to become familiar with their operation, and to develop a high degree of expertise in their use. Those, like Travis Rogers, with military and marksmanship experience, had conducted extensive training, so that now, even the most reluctant women in the group had acquired a respectable level of skill, as well as a high level of confidence in their ability to protect themselves and their families.

For Rogers' group, Rule One had always been Keep a Low Profile. Their particular social arrangement had already caused enough curiosity among the local people. The group's "cover" was that they were just friends of the owners of the farm, and that they enjoyed the fishing and camping there. Since the place was removed from the secondary roads, and the farm's manager, Billy Finan, was tight-lipped about the group's purpose, the curiosity had gone no further.

Kurt was replacing the phone list in a table drawer when Josh entered the room with a bagful of things he wanted to take with him. At thirteen he wasn't quite old enough to seriously question his father's involvement in the group. It had never occurred to him that others might consider his father a kook. Since his mother had died a few months ago, he had become all the more dependent on Kurt, whom he idolized.

"How about these, Dad? Can I take these?"

Rogers looked at his son and remembered again how he had felt trapped into marrying Laura in college when she had told him that a baby was on the way. As it had turned out, the years of warmth and love he had shared with Laura and the pride he now took in Josh made him feel that he wouldn't have had it any other way. "Son, you know you won't be needing that skateboard. There's not enough hard surface down there to use it. The other stuff you have is okay," he responded. "Now let's see how soon we can get on the road."

As the boy walked away, Rogers reflected on the fact that all his plans were finally coming to fruition. Thank God things for Josh were so much better than they had been for himself and his brother during an earlier crisis. He would never let himself become that vulnerable again. Never. *Ever.* . . .

CUBA BLOCKADE SET AT 9 A.M. TODAY: THANT'S HELP SOUGHT TO AVERT CLASH

From AP and UPI Dispatches

Washington, Oct. 23—President John F. Kennedy Tuesday ordered a blockade clamped on deliveries of offensive arms to Cuba effective at 9 A.M., eastern standard (Louisville) time, Wednesday.

Soviet vessels bound for the Communist-ruled island steamed toward a United States armada posted to enforce the quarantine—and a possible Cold War showdown on the high seas. . . .

SOVIET CALLS U.S. ACTION WAR STEP
Military Preparedness Is Ordered

By Preston Grover
Associated Press

Moscow, Oct. 23—Denouncing the United States arms quarantine against Cuba as a step toward world thermonuclear war, the Soviet Union Tuesday ordered its armed forces into a state of combat readiness.

Forces of the Warsaw Pact—Communist counterpart of the North Atlantic Treaty Organization—followed suit.

The orders for military preparedness came after the Soviet Government issued "a serious warning" over the action ordered by President John F. Kennedy against Cuba Monday night. . . .

RUSSIAN CALLS FOR AVERTING ATOMIC WAR
Says Soviet Will Make No Reckless
Decisions, But Will Act On 'Piracy'

Moscow, Oct. 24 (AP)—Premier Nikita S. Khrushchev, calling for a summit meeting, urged Wednesday that the United States stay its hand in the Cuban crisis to quench the threat of thermonuclear war. . . .

FRENCH MILITARY PUT ON ALERT

Paris, Oct. 25 (UPI)—Because of the Cuban crisis, the French armed forces Thursday went on no. 2 alert orders, the final stage before general mobilization. . . .

SOVIETS RUSHING CUBAN MISSILE WORK, DEFYING KENNEDY'S WARNING TO HALT

Washington, Oct. 26 (AP)—The White House reported late Friday that the Russians are continuing rapid development of their Cuban missile sites.

"The activity at these sites apparently is directed at achieving a full operational capability as soon as possible," the statement said. . . .

Mom?
Yes, Kurt.
Are we really gonna have a war?
I hope not. Now you and Travis get in bed.
But everyone's worried a lot, aren't they?
Yes, I'm sure they are. I know I am.
What are we gonna do if there is one?
I'm not sure.
We'll take care of you. Right, Travis?
Right, Kurt. Don't worry, Mom. But I still wish Dad were here.
Me, too, Travis.
Can Russian missiles reach Louisville, Mom?
I expect they can.
I wish we weren't here right now. I wish we were back in Wisconsin.
Well, Russian missiles and bombers can probably reach Wisconsin, too.
Where can we go then?
I don't know. I don't think we really have anywhere

we can go. I guess we'll just stay put and hope for the best.

Do we have enough food?

I'll try fighting the lines at the supermarket again tomorrow, Kurt. But for now, you boys just go to sleep. You're going to be very tired at school tomorrow.

Good night, Mom.

Good night, boys.

I love you, Mom.

I love you both.

The two set to work, and within a half hour, due to Kurt's prior planning, the car, trailer, and motorcycle were loaded and ready to go. Kurt went to each window and placed nails in the previously drilled holes in the wooden frames, which would prevent anyone from smashing in the window and opening it by simply unlocking the latch. He then stepped outside and locked the door with the double deadbolt lock, thinking that the extra steps wouldn't stop the bastards (whoever "the bastards" were), but that it would surely slow them down a bit.

He had locked that door a thousand times before, that door with the contrary lock that had to be just right before the bolt would pass and secure it properly. But tonight it seemed different. There was a sense of finality about it, as if he had crossed a barrier or passed a milestone, much the way he'd felt the day he left his college campus with his diploma tucked away in his suitcase, or the day a short time later when he had driven to the church and married Laura. There was a sense of passage, from which there seemed to be no return, and a feeling that things, for better or worse, would never be quite the same.

As he started to open the door of the Bronco, he stopped and looked at the house, which was dimly illuminated by the streetlight across the way. He thought of all the times he had enjoyed there with Laura and Josh. It was still difficult at times to realize that she was gone.

Sometimes he would roll over at night expecting to touch her before he realized that she was not there, and never would be there again, no matter how much he wished.

He tried to shake the melancholy by jumping briskly behind the wheel. "Ready, Josh?" he said with a wistful smile on his face. He looked at the boy and saw the very image of himself at thirteen, with thick blond hair and piercing blue eyes.

"Ready, Dad."

"Then let's move on down the road!" he said, trying to affect a cheerful tone and snap himself back to the problem at hand.

When Kurt hit the ignition, the big V-8 came to life. The meticulously restored '72 Bronco purred like a tomcat in front of an open hearth. The Bronco and trailer moved slowly down the driveway. Once Rogers cleared the subdivision, it was a short hop to the interstate. Then father and son were cruising southward in the darkness toward Marion County, leaving the city's lights and—Kurt hoped—its dangers far behind.

Charlie Brighton popped the top on another Budweiser. An hour and a half had passed since Dan Rather's unsettling announcement. Charlie's dark eyebrows were joined in irritation as he sat in the overstuffed chair in his living room with his two sons, Charlie Junior and Rick. He ignored the comment from his wife about the effect his increased beer consumption was having lately on his waistline—just as Charlie Junior ignored Brighton's request that he stop tossing the football to Rick because he might knock over a lamp.

Three beer cans littered the floor around the chair, but he had no intention of picking them up any time soon. The evening news had sent him into depression, and he had been arguing with himself for the past half hour as to what he should do. He knew that a simple phone call could be made, and those expedient fallout shelter plans from the Federal Emergency Management Agency could be in the paper tomorrow, along with the recommended routes for evacuation of the city under the plan drawn up by his staff over the past couple of weeks. The plans for quickly improvised fallout shelters were in the hands of hundreds hell, he thought, probably a thousand or more of the civil defense directors around the country.

The problem was that no one had published the plans in a major newspaper, the purpose for which the layouts had been originally designed. Though Brighton's office, like others, had provided copies of the plans to anyone who asked for them, there was considerable pressure not to publish them. All of this was in keeping with the official line that the use of nuclear weapons was not an "option" to be used in dealing with the situation in Iran. Since the Russians were doing quite nicely, thank you, without them, by deduction it then followed that nuclear war was not to be.

What bothered Charlie was that all of this stuff about nuclear weapons not being an "option" had been said for the most part when the war wasn't going quite so badly for the "good guys" and when the immediate loss of the bulk of Iranian oil to permanent Russian control did not seem to be a likely possibility. All that had changed in the past few days. Maybe now America was starting to bite its nails.

Nevertheless, no one up the chain had suggested publication of the plans, simply because of the public uproar their appearance was likely to create. Insiders opined that the antiwar protests of the sixties and seventies would pale in comparison to what was likely to result from public disclosure or merely acknowledgment that nuclear weapons were being given even passing consideration.

As if to drive the point home, on the same newscast Brighton had been watching earlier, there had been the story about the planned march on Washington for the coming weekend. Organizers were boasting that a half-million people would take part. The camera had panned the three hundred or so protesters then marching in front of the White House. From the "bleeped" soundtrack, it was still discernible that they were chanting the familiar battlecry of the latter-day successors to the Yippies: "Two, Four, Six, Eight! Fuck the Oil! It's Not Too Late!" All these people needed—and, for that matter a considerable and more respectable portion of the American public—was the specter of nuclear war being brought closer to reality by publication of what would be interpreted as plans to fight a nuclear war. Then all hell would break loose.

The other side of the coin, however, was the nagging worry Charlie had about what would happen if the public didn't know how to protect itself if a nuclear war actually came about. Countless thousands locally, and tens of millions of lives nationally, hung in the balance. It caused him no small amount of agony that he had it within his power to influence the matter.

Still there were the heavy political considerations. Good sense told him to run the matter past the mayor for approval. Past experience told him that the idea would probably be axed if he did so.

To hell with it, he thought, the beer getting the upper hand. Like they used to say in the Marine Corps, no guts, no glory.

He strode into the kitchen and grabbed the phone, fishing John Poppe's phone number from his wallet. He stared at the number for a few moments, making sure that this was exactly what he should be doing, and then he dialed. If he didn't act now, there might not be enough time later.

"Hello?" answered a male voice at the other end.

"John," Brighton said, recognizing Poppe's raspy voice, "Charlie Brighton here. I need you to exert a little influence down at the paper. Is there any way that those expedient fallout shelter plans we sent you a few weeks ago can be printed in tomorrow's edition?"

"Good grief, Charlie! You sure know how to push an old Kiwanian's friendship to the limit. Do you know how much time is left before our deadline tonight? Besides, has this been approved up the line at city hall?"

"Just got a call from the mayor himself, John. Highest priority," Brighton said, lying through his teeth. "You know how tense the situation is getting to be in Iran. The mayor wants the information out and in the hands of as many people as possible as fast as possible. Just send the bill through the usual channels."

"Well, all right, but I'm going to have to go back down there myself to insure that there aren't any hitches. It'll have to be reduced in size, though. No way we can carry the diagrams and pictures full-sized on this short notice," he said. "But Charlie, is it really that serious? Otherwise, wild horses couldn't get me down there tonight."

"It's serious enough, John, and I'd appreciate anything you can do to help. Thanks, fella," Brighton said, and then he hung up.

It took Charlie Brighton a little longer to fall asleep than usual that night. But when he did, he slept sounder than he had in weeks.

* * *

Kurt Rogers and his son arrived at the entrance to The Aerie at about ten o'clock that evening. The Bronco eased slowly off the narrow asphalt road onto the gravel road. Rogers carefully avoided cutting the turn too sharply and damaging the side of the camper trailer he was pulling. The rig was a real beauty. A self-contained home away from home, it had cost Kurt a considerable dent in his commissions the previous year. He guided his vehicle down the five hundred yards to Billy Finan's home and the collection of barns and outbuildings which served as the focal point for the farm's activities.

As Kurt drove toward Finan's home, he passed the two-hundred-foot-high limestone cliff that had inspired Laura to give the farm its name. He continued past the rows of fruit trees and grapevines, which just the year before had begun to produce really sizable crops. Kurt passed several vehicles. One of the cars and a Winnebago motor home he recognized as belonging to the Mulloys, a family he had been unable to contact by phone. Either someone else had gotten in touch with them, or they had been already on their way down here, he thought.

The farm was a very typical one for this part of the country, its size about average, and it contained nothing which to the casual observer would seem very suspicious. Finan's home was a rambling frame house built in the twenties. There was the obligatory tobacco barn which any farmer in central Kentucky would need to house his tobacco for curing, another barn for livestock and storage of hay and feed, and several miscellaneous outbuildings and sheds of one sort or another.

Even the natural gas well that heated the farmhouse was not particularly unusual. Drilling for oil that lay in shallow deposits around the area was quite common. Some wells paid off, some didn't. And many that didn't occasionally produced a free source of natural gas to the landowners long after the drilling rigs and their crews had departed.

There was also nothing unusual about the large new metal "pole barn," as it was referred to, which sat near the Finan house, except perhaps for its large size. Given the advances in lightweight construction technology, most farmers were opting for metal barns supported by poles set in concrete for reasons of economy of construction and low maintenance costs. As many would say, it just made dollars and "sense."

What was unusual about the farm, as many of the local people who happened to make calls on Billy saw it, was the unusual diversity of livestock and crops grown on it. The farm had not only beef cattle, it had dairy cattle and even goats. Rabbit cages were in one corner of the farmyard, and the chickens and geese were very numerous. A very large garden was usually planted in the summer as well. All of this seemed unusual to the nearby farmers, most of whom were accustomed to buying their milk, eggs, and vegetables at the supermarkets in Lebanon, the county seat. After all, the money in these parts was made mostly in beef cattle, hogs, corn, soybeans, and tobacco. The other things didn't seem worthwhile bothering with.

Billy, of course, explained the situation by saying that these Louisville people wanted the animals and such for their kids, and it was they who took care of that huge garden in the summer. "Hell," he would say, "if they want to waste money on all those other things instead of putting the farm into producing the kinds of things that will turn a profit, it's their farm. You know how those city people are, anyway." This was a plausible enough explanation to allay the curiosity of most of the people around there, because they *did* know how those city people were—more money than sense.

"Kurt! We made it!"

It was Larry Jackson jogging up to the Bronco and opening the door while pushing the dark heavy-rimmed glasses back up to the bridge of his nose. Larry was beaming and he gave Rogers a good-natured slap on the shoulder as he and Josh got out and stretched. Kurt looked around and saw that several others were walking up to him. "You all look familiar. Have I seen any of you here before?" he said, grinning.

"Did you have any problems on the way down?" George Anderson asked. George was a portly man, a little under five feet nine inches in height with a medium-length beard. If there was any man on earth other than his brother Kurt would trust more with his wallet and checkbook—or his sister if he had one—Kurt didn't know who it was.

"No serious problems, just a little traffic backup south of Shepherdsville. Some guy with an overloaded rental trailer lost it and spilled his load all over two lanes. It took ten to twenty minutes to get around it and to get moving again." Rogers looked around at the people gathered around him.

There were three he didn't recognize, and this bothered him. Probably friends or relatives who'd been invited along at the last minute with little thought or outright indifference to the meticulous planning that had gone into predicting the group's needs.

Rogers looked down at George's side and saw a .45 caliber automatic in its holster. "You guys expecting an Indian attack tonight? Maybe there's something I ought to know?"

Anderson grinned sheepishly. "Aw, Kurt, you know how it is. I just feel a little more secure with it. Sort of a security blanket for insecure times. But come on. Let's look at the barn."

Together they walked into the pole barn. Each side of the barn was lined with rooms that ran the length of the barn. Each family in the group had its name on the door of its room. Several of the rooms were open and Kurt could see into them. Mike Mulloy was in the first one. He was opening up a case of food and inspecting the cans for signs of rust. He greeted Rogers and continued, preoccupied with his task.

Jean Godfrey was in the next room. She and her daughter were folding wool blankets and replacing them in their plastic bags with new mothballs. Kurt saw two Ruger Mini-14 semiautomatic rifles on the table in different states of disassembly. The odor of bore cleaner and lubricant drifted into the hallway.

Jerry O'Connell was in the room on the opposite side of the broad hallway. He was trying to light a Coleman lantern when he glanced up and saw Kurt. "Hi, Kurt," he said with a somber tone to his voice.

"Hello, Jerry. Where's your dad?"

"Already left. He went on back to Louisville. God. I wish I could have talked him out of it. But you know about his job and all. He said he couldn't just throw away his job security on a long shot. Jesus, if this nuclear stuff is such a long shot, what's everybody doing out here, anyway?"

"Probably just wasting our time," Rogers said reassuringly. "You didn't see half of Louisville on the road tonight, did you? We're probably just the ones who overreacted, right?"

"I hope so," the boy replied, as he turned and went back to tinkering with the mantle of the lamp.

As George and Kurt continued down the hall, George said softly to Rogers, "You really believe what you said?"

Rogers shot a glance over his shoulder. "Do you think I would be here if I did?"

The two proceeded past other rooms to the end of the building, where roll upon roll of barbed wire was stacked. Rogers bent down and pulled at the handle recessed into the thick concrete floor. With both hands in position he grunted and pulled the door upward and to the side. He put a barrier in place to prevent someone from stumbling into the hole, and then the two men descended.

At the bottom of the ladder, Rogers flipped the switch. The lights from the reinforced concrete ceiling flooded the room lined with narrow bunks along two walls. A small, very small, latrine at the far end of the room balanced the minikitchen at the other end. One wall was lined with shelves holding cans of dehydrated food.

Along a section of the wall opposite, upon knotty-pine shelves, buckled and warped, was one of the farm's most valuable assets, its library.

Cascading down the wall, competing for shelf space and prominence, the titles seemed at first merely a riot of color and confusion.

A closer inspection revealed the care and thought involved in their selection. Along the bottom ran dozens of back issues of *Mother Earth News, Organic Gardening,* and *American Survival Guide Magazine.* Above, a hundred titles and more competed for attention—*The Encyclopedia of Organic Gardening, Practical Beekeeping, The Next Whole Earth Catalog, Producing Your Own Power, Electrical Wiring, Survival Family, Carpentry Made Simple, Raising Poultry the Modern Way . . .*

Of particular prominence in the center were two tattered copies of Cresson Kearny's *Nuclear War Survival Skills.* Flanking them, Bruce Clayton's *Life after Doomsday* and Mel Tappan's *Survival Guns* stood guard. These were followed by several dog-eared Army manuals on everything from the M-16 A1 rifle to the Browning .50 caliber machine gun.

Just to the left, *Kentucky Country Cooking* laid crossways atop *Making the Best of Basics, The Betty Crocker Cookbook,* and *Old-Fashioned Recipe Book.*

Five Acres and Independence was sandwiched between

Modern Firearms and Ragnar Benson's *The Survival Retreat.* Nearby, *The Well Body Book* yielded to the *Lippincott Manual of Nursing Practice, Emergency War Surgery, Where There Is No Doctor,* and *Handbook of First Aid and Emergency Care.*

Other shelves held an *Encyclopedia Britannica* and *The World Book Encyclopedia.* Nearby were three hundred paperback novels of various types. Just below them were two shelves of textbooks, manuals, and a dozen or so games for children, from Monopoly and Risk to Chutes and Ladders and Candyland. Two chess sets in ragged and worn boxes were also there. As Rogers looked about the room, everything appeared to be in order.

Rogers walked over to the air pump. He switched the pump to the on position, and checked the battery to see if it was properly charged. The needle pointed to the green portion of the meter. He hit the switch to the generator outside and heard the "whoosh" from the nearby vent that was reminiscent of his car's air conditioning system. He shut off the unit, and then tried it manually. "How about the photovoltaic panels?"

"They're ready to go anytime," responded Anderson. "No need to take them out of their protective casings till necessary."

Rogers reached into a cabinet and pulled out a radiation detection meter from its shelf, checked it, and then returned it to its place. He put his hands on his hips and, with a strong sense of satisfaction, slowly surveyed the room again. As George started up the ladder, Rogers said, "Insurance."

"Beg your pardon?" said Anderson, stopping on the second rung.

"I said 'insurance.' This whole thing is like insurance that you or I might buy for the times when things go wrong. Only this kind of insurance doesn't pay off double indemnity or lump sum in any kind of negotiable currency. It's for when money is worthless. Maybe in this day and age it's the smartest kind, but it's the kind few others have."

The two continued up the ladder and then out into the cool night air. The clear sky sparkled with the lights of thousands of stars, and the sounds of what seemed to be an equal number of contented insects added a steady rhythm to the evening. Finally, Anderson looked at Rogers and said, "Insurance, maybe. But I just think of this place as my *ark.*"

Kurt looked at Josh as he sat with two of the families in the group roasting marshmallows around a campfire, and he contemplated Anderson's words. Slowly he turned toward Anderson and looked him straight in the eyes. "George, I never really thought about it quite like that, but you're right."

His eyes drifted back to his son and the others around the fire, but his mind was on what George had said.

An ark, he thought. And the thought warmed him.

Near the village of Tatishchevo, not far from the banks of the Volga River and two hundred miles north of Volgograd, formerly Stalingrad, two officers of the Strategic Rocket Forces stood watch in their subterranean command center. From the capsule about ten times the size of a modern high-rise elevator, behind a blast door weighing several tons, these men controlled the operation of a dozen SS-19 intercontinental ballistic missiles.

All around the command center lay steel-and-concrete silos sunk forty meters below the mud of the late Russian spring. At the bottom of each vault, below concrete doors weighing a hundred tons, was one cigar-shaped missile, approximately eighty-eight feet long and eight feet wide. Along the green sides of each missile were the bold scarlet letters "CCCP."

Sheathed atop each missile were several nuclear devices. On command they could travel several thousand miles across the polar icecap and, within thirty minutes, lay waste to a significant portion of the military-industrial capacity of the enemy of the proletariat.

The lieutenant on duty was a twenty-two-year-old Ukrainian career soldier, Stefan Shchevchenko. The captain, Ivan Kharkov, a Great Russian, was twenty-eight years old and a career officer as well. Neither of them was particularly hostile to the United States of America—at least not in a very emotional way. And neither had ever been closer to combat than the occasional newsreel footage of the socialist military victories carried nightly on Soviet television. They were not combat soldiers, merely technicians.

"Coffee, Captain?" Shchevchenko inquired after pouring a cup for himself.

"No, Comrade," Kharkov replied. "I'm afraid our Third World political considerations have prevailed, and the quality of the brew we've been getting has suffered fiercely."

Shchevchenko winced as he took his first sip. "Yes, sir, but then it is better than nothing." He paused, watching the steam rise from his cup, then said, "It would appear that matters are becoming more serious in Iran, sir. Do you believe that we will come to the point where we will actually launch our birds?"

Kharkov slowly shook his head. "I'm afraid I can't answer that, Stefan."

"More and more, I find myself wondering what I will do if that phone on the wall actually rings."

"It's simple, Stefan. You'll do your duty."

"Of course, sir," he quickly responded. "I just meant how I would feel *inside*." He took another sip. "You've been at this business for quite a while, Captain. Do you ever wonder where our missiles are destined? A bomber base? A missile silo? Or maybe a city, say, in California?"

"Of course, Stefan. When you punch in the codes you can't help but wonder."

"Codes do make it simpler. Cleaner. I guess it's better that way."

Kharkov looked at the blinking console in front of him, and nodded. "*Da*, Comrade. Much better."

FRIDAY, MAY 17th:
The First Day

There was quite a reception waiting for Charlie Brighton at city hall the next morning. One of his assistants met him at the door of his office and told him that the mayor and O'Hara were awaiting his arrival and wanted to see him in O'Hara's office as soon as he came in. Though it really wasn't necessary, the look on the assistant's face warned him exactly what awaited.

"Come in, Mr. Brighton," O'Hara said sternly, just as Brighton turned the corner into O'Hara's office. "We've some things to talk about." O'Hara sat comfortably in the large leather swivel chair behind his massive walnut desk. His body language indicated a casual mood. The firmly clenched jaw indicated just the opposite. The mayor, radiating hostility, sat in the large wingback chair to one side of the desk.

Behind the desk was a wall lined with pictures, diplomas and mementos of O'Hara's past. College achievements, business-group membership certificates, and assorted photographs and letters of appreciation comprised what O'Hara often unabashedly referred to in his lighter moments as "The Tom O'Hara Hall of Fame." Were Brighton to have been objective about the matter, the collection really did indicate a rather impressive list of achievements for a man in his mid-thirties.

Perhaps it was the extent of O'Hara's success that elicited such pronounced ill will between the two. O'Hara was a handsome man of a comfortable upbringing, good education, and excellent family and political connections, who had found early success as a "man of affairs," and who was generally regarded as being about to use his position as a springboard to higher places. He was now poised for a position of real power in the next election, possibly even the mayor's office or Congress.

Brighton was a man of a very much more modest and rough-and-tumble background, who had found it necessary early in life to scramble for everything he received, despite what was in its own way equal talent, and obviously broader experience.

Brighton despised the charm the younger O'Hara exuded when confronted with people who pressed vehement demands on the city. His articulate and seductive manner could defuse the most explosive situation or disarm and dissuade all but the most irate complainant seeking redress of grievances, real or imagined. But what irritated Brighton most was that it seemed to him as if O'Hara's interest in the problems before him was more feigned than genuine. To Brighton's structured, apolitical mind, which saw things always as either black or white and was not the least bit concerned with or sympathetic to the considerations and expediencies attendant to elected public office, this was purely manipulative and, therefore, disgusting.

On O'Hara's part, it was Brighton's obvious lack of deference and equally obvious disdain for so many of the things O'Hara felt were important that engendered in him reciprocal hostility. Brighton had earned his practical experience far from any ivy-covered graduate school or fraternity house. His knowledge came from the streets and from whatever military training he could pick up along the way. But, though Brighton had no diploma or academic credentials of any import, O'Hara often felt an unwelcomed sense of insecurity when dealing with him.

As is often the case, the contempt such men bear for each other is as natural as that between cat and dog.

Brighton now strode into the room and sat down at the chair positioned midway between the two men. There was an uncomfortably long pause, and then the mayor said very slowly, "You son of a bitch." After waiting for the greeting to sink in, he proceeded. "Do you have any idea of just what you've done? We're being bombarded on every phone line by frantic callers wanting to know if the crap in the paper means we're going to be nuked. Hell, they're even calling in on the tax receiver's line asking to transfer the call! And I suppose all those hysterical idiots out there in the lobby didn't escape your attention!"

It was true. He'd had to take a detour to a side entrance to get into the office, and every line on the phone sitting on O'Hara's desk was lit. Brighton looked the mayor squarely in the eyes and said, "Mr. Mayor, what about our last conversation when you indicated—"

"To hell with our last conversation. Besides, that was between you and me, as one professional to another. The only way we've prevented mass hysteria in this country so far is by assurances from the top on down that this business with the Russians won't get out of hand. And this newspaper stuff of yours—at least for my little part of the country —just blew those assurances straight to hell. I'm in the middle of a lunatic asylum right now, and I owe it all to you!"

O'Hara interrupted. "Did you notice the number of people getting on the road this morning, Brighton? On my way in I couldn't *believe* the number of people who were in their driveways and who were stuffing their cars with everything but the kitchen sink. If we're in the 'middle of a lunatic asylum,' as the Mayor calls it, the edges are expanding rapidly as these people head out to God knows where."

The mayor shot back, "But *our* Mr. Brighton never considered what he was doing to these people by inciting them to run away from their jobs and go who knows where for God knows how long." Jumping to his feet, he jabbed at the desk repeatedly with his index finger to make his point. "Do you think I'm unconcerned about all of this? I'm fifty years old with a wife and three teenagers, and I'm as concerned as the next guy. But dammit to hell, Charlie, you don't scream 'fire' in a crowded theater!"

"Even when the theater really is on fire?" Brighton replied softly, unintimidated by the outburst. "My decision to print those plans was a moral one, and it is one I'll live with whatever the consequences. You can always take any step you gentlemen feel is appropriate, but I think I can assume that this is it for me." Brighton got up and started for the door.

"Wait a minute," said the mayor, his mood—or at least his tone—obviously shifting. "I never said you were being fired."

Brighton stopped halfway out the office and turned to eye him suspiciously. The mayor let out a deep sigh, and after a few seconds of silence, he said in a more conciliatory tone, "Charlie, I'm stuck between a rock and a hard place. I understand somewhat the considerations prompting you to act as you did, but you've got to understand my position. For now, regardless of how I feel or how Tom or anyone else might feel, the most important thing is to defuse this situation. If you'll agree to help me and to go public with a statement saying there's no reason for alarm, and that the whole thing was a result of poor communications with the paper, then we'll forget the whole matter."

"Think about it," O'Hara added. "You'll help convince people that we haven't *all* come unglued down here, and you'll still have a job. It's the pragmatic thing to do without a doubt. And in a job like ours, the pragmatic approach is the *only* approach."

Brighton looked first at the mayor, and then at O'Hara. After a few seconds, he said simply, "I'm sorry, gentlemen.

If *you* want to take the moral responsibility for lying to all those people out there about just how serious all of this can get, you go ahead and lie to them—*if*, and I repeat, *if* you can live with the consequences. But me? I just can't do that."

The mayor leaned back in his chair. His eyes turned to O'Hara, and he silently nodded. O'Hara looked at the mayor for a moment, and then he glowered at Brighton. "Then consider yourself fired. You've got fifteen minutes to get your things together, and then I want you out of this building."

Brighton turned and walked swiftly from the room without a word, and then straight to his office. With five minutes to spare he said his good-byes to the people in his office, and with a handful of personal possessions he left through the side door of the building to the parking lot. As he strode across the asphalt, there was a bounce to his step that hadn't been there in years.

As he got in his car he began to make mental notes of the things he must do to prepare for his family's departure from the city. South, maybe. A friend's cabin at Nolin Lake sounded nice.

As his car passed Jefferson Square, his eyes drifted over to the fresh spring greenery, and he thought, God it's good to be alive!

And though Brighton failed to notice, Tom O'Hara, disgusted now, and standing at his office window, watched him until he could be seen no more.

Kurt Rogers stumbled from his bed into the camper trailer's bathroom, squinting from the light pouring in the windows. He stared at himself in the mirror, hair tousled, a day's growth of stubble sprouting from his jaw. More than a few of the whiskers were a disturbing gray. He stuck out his tongue and examined it in the mirror. Hell must look like this with the lights out, he thought.

He reached for the toothbrush and toothpaste and began to give his teeth and gums a good brushing. As he did so, he looked around the corner and out to the small combination sleeper-sofa on which Josh still slept.

Josh began to stir, partly because of the gargling sounds from the bathroom, and partly because of the continuous yelps from an excited spaniel outside. "Morning, son," Rogers said as he emerged from the bathroom still smacking his lips from the brushing. "How about some grub?"

"What've we got?" his son asked, with one eye barely open.

"You name it—pancakes, waffles, cereal, eggs. What do you want?"

"Eggs," he said simply, and then he withdrew under the sheets again. From under the covers there came a muffled "And bacon."

"Eggs and bacon it is then, partner." Kurt was already in a good mood and it was getting better. He quickly whipped together a breakfast of eggs and bacon for the two of them, and even added some instant buttermilk biscuits.

Since Laura's death, he found it necessary to do many things he had previously avoided. Breakfast was one of them. Before, if it couldn't be cooked in a toaster or poured from a teakettle or coffeepot, he didn't have the time or wouldn't make the time for it in the morning. But now, his sense of responsibility to Josh had forced him to begin doing many things to which he had been unaccustomed. Though they were time-consuming, the extra concerns helped form a deeper bond between him and his son.

A knock came at the door, and Rogers peered out and saw George Anderson with Larry Jackson. "Come in, come in," he said, "but I'm afraid you're about five minutes too late. The grub's gone."

The two entered and sat on the sofa bed. Kurt handed them both cups of coffee.

"You haven't been listening to the radio, have you?" Anderson asked. Rogers shook his head. "The *Courier-Journal* carried a big spread on improvised fallout shelter plans this morning. Together with the announcement about that warning to the Russians last night, the whole thing has caused quite an uproar."

"No kidding?" Rogers replied. "Was this fallout shelter thing a national or local effort?"

"Just local I heard. Hell, they can't even get anyone at city hall to comment on it so far. But it sure has stirred up a lot of people, according to the radio," Anderson said. "Oh well, enough of this. The reason we're here is to see if you'd join in helping us set out a vegetable garden. The ground over there is just about right. We need something to keep everybody occupied if we're going to be sitting around here for a while. And if we make this a community effort, we can get out one helluva garden really fast. What do you say?"

"Sounds great. Anybody checked with Billy to see about preparing that ground for us with the tractor?"

"He's on his way down, now," Jackson replied, rising to his feet.

"Great then. Let's see how many we can get interested." So far, so good, Rogers thought. This was the way it was supposed to go. Just like they had planned it from the beginning that first weekend they had all trekked down to the farm. . . .

"Okay, people. Listen up! Go ahead, Travis."

"Well, here we are, just sitting here contemplating what in hell motivated us to drag our butts down here today from Louisville." Travis looked at the assemblage around the campfire. He could see he had their full attention. "What about you, Dan? What brought you down here?"

"Because I want to live a long and healthy life, and I want the same for my family. That's about it in a nutshell. I'm damned worried about the nuclear arms race, and I'm also worried about the economy."

"Good enough. And how about you, Dana?"

"Because Larry dragged me here," Dana Jackson replied. Her response brought sympathetic chuckles from several of the other women present.

Jerry Mazurkis stepped forward to the campfire. "I'll tell you what brought me down here," he said. "I'm sick and tired of being a pawn of the MAD policy."

"The what?" came a response.

"The MAD policy. Mutually Assured Destruction. Didn't you know that's our country's nuclear policy? It's suppose to be that the Russians won't dare attack our population because we'll attack their population. We're all just hostages, and it makes me sick. I want a way out of this arrangement for me and my family."

"Good enough," Kurt replied. "Anybody else?"

Mike Mulloy stood up. "I feel like Jerry. I'm just as concerned about going along like a sheep to the slaughter with the rest of the flock. If I'm going to die, I want to go out kicking, spitting in the devil's eye."

"So how are you going to make sure that you don't have

to spit in that devil's eye, as you call it, in the first place?" Travis replied.

There was no immediate response. Finally, Larry Jackson said, "Guns and ammunition. Because when the time comes, you'll sure need it to protect yourself from those who didn't have the brains to prepare in advance."

"Sure, guns are necessary," responded Travis. "But I'll tell you this. It's not as much what kind of gun you have that will insure your survival in the long run, it's what you have up here," he said, pointing to his head. "You have to have a survivor's mentality and not be inclined to go belly up at the first bit of adversity. And you've got to possess the skills and knowledge to make it in a 'brave new world.'"

Jackson was persistent. "But one of those skills *is* handling a gun." He wiped his glasses and put them on again.

Kurt smiled patronizingly at Larry. "Okay, but before you get too eager for a firefight to defend your family and property, remember that the best way to survive a fight is to avoid one. No matter how big a badass you become, Larry, old boy, there's gonna be some badass out there who's *badder*."

Several of those present joined in the laughter at Kurt's last remark. Dana Jackson didn't. "I think you're all nuts. Some of you are just aching for the chance to shoot it out with someone."

"Dana," Travis replied, "I've already done that, compliments of the United States Army. But if I've learned one thing in the past few years, it's that you've got to depend on your buddies in a tight situation. That's the way it was in 'Nam. Forming that bond with others is very important, whether it's with the members of a rifle platoon or with survivors after a nuclear holocaust. And while we work together for a common purpose, we need to develop certain skills. I expect that I can take care of the firearms training that Larry talks so much about. But just as importantly, Joe and Jackie can teach how to plant green beans, broccoli, squash, and such. And Mike here can teach how to rebuild a carburetor and how to operate a still to produce alcohol for fuel. That's what we're talking about. Bonding for self-defense, and bonding for meeting life's daily needs, if there ever comes a time when it's necessary to do it that way."

Kurt turned to Dana. "Maybe the government takes care of most people from cradle to grave, Dana, but we just figure that unless we do something about it now, given the way things in the world have been going, we all might wind up in that grave sooner than we expected."

"I still think the answer is to work to end this arms race and try to find some way to insure a lasting world peace," she replied.

"Sure," Jean Godfrey, Anderson's sister, added, "but world peace requires both sides to do their part. As far as I'm concerned, I don't see the Russians agreeing to do their part, and I wouldn't trust them even if they said they would."

"If you ask me, most of you are paranoid." It was Nick Townsend, a schoolteacher friend of Larry Jackson's who had come down that day under halfhearted protest, and only to put an end to Larry's incessant preaching on the subject.

Kurt grinned. "Maybe. But like that little saying goes, 'I may be paranoid, but that doesn't mean that the bastards aren't out to get me.'" Several of the listeners chuckled at his remark. "Everyone here will have to admit that we've lived under the threat of thermonuclear war for all or at least most of our lives. Is it really paranoid to want to remove some of the danger of that threat?"

Townsend shook his head vehemently and gestured broadly with one of his arms. "Okay, okay. But what about all this stuff about a 'nuclear winter' that you keep hearing about in the media? You know, where all that stuff is blasted into the atmosphere by the explosion, the sun is blotted out and temperatures drop, and then everything freezes up. Wouldn't that make the whole idea of this place here kind of pointless?"

A few heads slowly nodded in agreement, but no one spoke immediately.

"No," George Anderson finally responded. "Especially not if you also think it's very important to prepare for serious economic problems caused by such things as runaway inflation, huge national debts, and the like. I'm personally more worried about what will happen after the economic breakdown which I expect in the next few years than I am about going to war with the Russians.

"But as far as this nuclear winter concept is concerned, there's considerable scientific opinion that indicates that the whole concept is very exaggerated. And who says any nuclear war has to be an all-out nuclear war? I've read quite a bit, and I know that there are several scenarios that are considered realistic. Like strikes against strategic weapons and command-and-control networks, to strikes against military-industrial capabilities, to full-scale strikes against everything—including population centers. Lots of informed people say that an all-out nuclear war is unlikely because neither side wants the other to reciprocate against the other's civilian targets. Hell, the most likely nuclear threat is probably from some Libyan terrorist group or the like getting hold of a single weapon and doing God knows what with it."

"That's right, George," Travis added. "And how can anyone accurately predict that a 'nuclear winter' will happen after a nuclear war, given so many variables that would be involved, when they can't even predict next week's weather with any accuracy? Even if they're right, though, it's just one more scenario to prepare for if you've got a proper survivor's attitude . . ."

That was the way it had been at the first big gathering at the farm. Rogers wondered now how it would all work out.

As Jack Hamilton arrived at the armory that day, he was still nursing the cup of coffee that served as his breakfast. He and Roseanna had been up late the preceding night after taking care of the packing of all the items on the hastily compiled list. Since space in the car and on the rooftop rack was limited, as much time had been spent determining what did not need to be taken as deciding what did. Jack rejected many items because he knew that they would be available at Cliff's. All in all, he was satisfied with the result.

He pulled into the parking lot as three staff officers prepared to board the Huey helicopter that was landing on the helipad. Several boxes and crates were offloaded, and the helicopter was quickly airborne before Hamilton could make it into the building. He grabbed his cap and braced himself against the rush of fine gravel and dust from the prop wash, and he grinned at the misfortune of an NCO who had grabbed at his cap a half-second too late, and was now scurrying frantically after it across the asphalt.

He checked in and looked at the several messages awaiting him at his office. A newspaper one of the enlisted clerks was reading caught his eye. The item that grabbed his attention was not the lead story on page one of the dramatic increase of tensions from the Soviet successes and the U.S. diplomatic response, but the style and layout of the pictures and diagrams of the feature on the special supplement's front page. He knew immediately from across the room that they were governmental in origin. Upon closer inspection, his suspicions were confirmed: they were fallout shelter plans.

Specialist Fourth Class Riley Nugent, the befreckled driver of the section's armored personnel carrier, could not remain oblivious to Hamilton's presence over his right shoulder. "You wanna read this section, sir?" he said, handing the paper to Hamilton. Nugent had been in the National Guard for three years, and he had always tried his best to stay on the good side of any officer. It just made sense. Hell, he thought, if giving Hamilton the goddam paper would increase, however slightly, his chances of getting recommended for promotion, it was worth sucking up to an officer every now and then. Besides, as slow as things were expected to be in his section today, he would have plenty of time to read it later.

Hamilton accepted the paper with a preoccupied "thank you" and walked over and sat down at his desk. He studied the plans quickly, wondering if their publication was tied to last night's news developments. Was it Washington's way of easing the public into a new perspective on the war without actually having to admit anything?

Over the radio on Nugent's desk came the hourly news, with word that a new Russian assault had begun against the Iraqi forces in the vicinity of the Shatt al Arab—Hamilton did not catch the exact name of the place. Another news item mentioned that an American AWACS surveillance plane had mysteriously crashed in the Persian Gulf the previous night. The Pentagon was thus far refusing to release details on the incident. The fallout shelter plans and news items did nothing to ease Hamilton's anxiety.

At ten-thirty, an enlisted clerk poked his head into Hamilton's office and told Hamilton that there was a staff meeting at four o'clock that afternoon. Hamilton acknowledged the messenger, and his eyes drifted away from the report he was reading, back to the newspaper on Nugent's desk. Slowly he stood up and peered out the window. After a few minutes he said audibly, but to no one in particular, "Screw it," and left the room.

Nugent looked over to Master Sergeant Tom Mattingly, the section's slightly paunchy senior enlisted man. Nugent rolled his eyes toward the ceiling and, obviously in reaction to Hamilton's peculiar departure, said simply, "Officers."

"Get back to your work and mind your own business," Mattingly shot back. Nevertheless, he too found Hamilton's behavior a bit strange.

Hamilton found Mallory in his office concluding a conversation with the brigade operations officer. Hamilton poked his head in and said, "Got a minute, sir?"

"Sure, come on in. I was just about to come by and see you anyway. It looks like we'll be getting some news on deployment soon. We got a packet just a little while ago, and the colonel has been in with the general ever since. The only word out of that office so far is that there will be a briefing at four o'clock for all staff officers."

"Great," Hamilton replied, but his tone was without a hint of any real satisfaction with the new development. "What I wanted to see you about was whether you would have any objection to my slipping out and taking my wife and kids out to Bardstown. I don't think it would hurt a thing for her to be down there for a few days, considering the situation."

"All things considered, I guess you're right. I discussed the same thing with Carol last night after the evening news, but the only relative we have outside Louisville is a cousin she can't stand who lives in Corydon. Go ahead, but be sure to be back before the briefing."

Hamilton excused himself quickly and bounded up the steps to his office. He met Mattingly and immediately related the situation to him.

"How about me coming along, sir? I've got a sister out south of Bardstown, and I think Mary Beth would be willing to go out there for awhile until it's clear how this thing is going. She's been awfully worried about all of this."

"No problem. Is your wife going to be needing your car? We can have Nugent follow us in the quarter-ton, and leave our own cars out there."

"That's a good idea, Major. My truck out there really needs some engine work, and since Mary Beth will be wanting the car, I wouldn't want to drive back with that engine the way it is. If we keep this quiet, we won't get our ass in the wringer for using the jeep."

Hamilton laughed and said, "I'll meet you at the main entrance to the Bashford Manor Mall at one o'clock. Now let's get out of here."

Tom O'Hara's office was bathed in shadows. He sat at his desk, ideas bouncing around his mind like popcorn in a popper. He had drawn the drapes tightly and the only illumination came from the track lighting, which cast pools of light across certain parts of the room. An adjustment to the rheostat switch brought the lighting down to a very low level, and made it somewhat difficult for him to read the cryptic notes he had scribbled on the legal pad in the middle of his desk. Considering his mood, the trade-off was worth it.

What a mess he had before him. There were a hundred and fifty people milling around outside the entrance to city hall demanding to know whether they should evacuate, dig in, or simply go about their business. Effective steps would have to be taken to convince them and hosts of others across the city that Mayor Burns had not received some "secret" communication from the president and that the public was not being left out while the mayor and his family were being safely sequestered in some secret government blast shelter.

Burns, for his part, had appropriately decided to cancel his appointments outside the office so as to appear to be steady at the helm throughout the day. The old business-as-usual approach.

Since early morning, the federal boys had been screaming all the way from Washington. They hinted with all of the subtlety of a velvet hammer that unless the public reaction was controlled, and controlled damned quickly, certain discretionary federal monies might become unavailable for certain local programs in the near future.

However, what really bothered O'Hara about this whole ruckus was the impact it might have on him personally. Maybe only a few people remembered it right now, but it had been O'Hara who had gone to bat in getting Brighton his job in the first place. Though he did not know Brighton personally, a call from a retired major general who was active in local civic matters and an active participant in local party politics had insured O'Hara's support for the man. It seemed a small favor that might produce handsome dividends in the future.

Most of O'Hara's adult life had been like that. Every decision and every activity had been calculated to produce dividends for the future. That was the way the game was played. As he saw it, he was no different than anyone else.

He had dutifully joined the junior business groups, the civic groups, and the charitable organizations early in his career. He met people, shook hands, and remembered names. He, as well as most of these other people were "getting around," "making contacts," and "getting their names known." The ostensible purposes of the organizations were merely a facade to obscure the fact that the involvement of O'Hara and his counterparts was only for the purpose of advancing themselves. The higher the office in the organization, the greater the personal visibility for the officeholder.

For him, the political campaigns were similar. In the beginning he had licked enough envelopes in the mass mailings to reach to the moon and back, and all for candidates for whom he couldn't have cared less. Most of the others, in his opinion, were doing the same. Oh, they would say the right things in public—talk about the good of the community and the party—yet all the while be cementing contacts, memorizing names, ingratiating themselves with those higher up the ladder in hopes of political appointments, fat personal service contracts, or simply entrée to the successful candidate's office later in order to feather their own special interest's nest.

The starving lawyers, the union leaders, the insurance brokers, the minority community activists. Consolidating and advancing their positions. Selfish goals which taken together resulted in the common good, or so they said. Or did these selfish goals merely lead to equally selfish results?

He advanced through the political organizing committees, the numerous campaign staffs. He learned to ignore the merits of the party's candidate. What was more important was retaining or advancing his position of prominence. That the candidate was an idiot was unimportant as long as he was *our* idiot. People would remember O'Hara in a year or so because of all of his efforts, and all of the IOU's he had created along the way would be called in.

Burns, a mellow, father-figure to the community, was a heavy delegator who took little pleasure in the day-to-day details of his office. He trusted O'Hara's judgment, and was content to let O'Hara wield most of the power—as long as Burns got the credit.

O'Hara always kept his finger on the pulse of the community in doing so. Throughout his time at city hall he had known where the public's interests lay, knew what they wanted to hear. He was always prepared to jump right out and lead the parade, once he found out which way it was headed.

O'Hara would never be called a True Believer in any cause. The art of compromise on any issue was the key to success in this game, and that he knew oh so well. The only thing he truly believed in was himself. Or Cathy.

He had never tried to bullshit Cathy. They had always been totally honest with one another. She served as his conscience and kept some of his excesses in check. He truly loved her and now, within a few months, they would be a real family. All of his political activity and her interest in her two boutiques had meant there had been little time for children, though they had always talked about the idea. Now, they both had reached an age where the ticking of the biological clock meant that it was put-up-or-shut-up time. He looked forward with immense pleasure to being a father. Besides, being a good family man was great for his political image. Thus was the world according to O'Hara.

Now the problem was how to deal with the Brighton mess. As he tapped his pencil on the desk pad, he decided to grab the proverbial bull by the proverbial horns and meet the press people head-on. Jenkins, Mayor Burns's press aide, had cautioned him about the matter, but going head-on with the press people and appearing to be the epitome of tranquility and reason would look good—very good—on the evening news. Besides, he needed to increase his media exposure anyway.

Thousands of voters would see him as a man who could keep his head in a crisis. And if things didn't come off quite as well as he would like, then maybe it would test the worth of the old political boss's adage, "I don't care what you say about me as long as you spell my name right." After all,

O'Hara mused, few politicians ever failed by underestimating the intelligence of the American public.

Captain Anatoli Tupolev's Yankee Class nuclear submarine of the Soviet Red Banner Fleet glided silently nine hundred feet below the surface of the Atlantic Ocean, three hundred miles off the coast of Virginia. An hour earlier, a Very-Low-Frequency radio communication to Tupolev had eliminated the previous month's tedium, and now the crew worked feverishly in checking and rechecking the launch system. Tupolev's submarine carried sixteen SS-N-18 missiles aft of the conning tower.

The 500-foot-long vessel closed the gap to the Virginia shore at the ponderous rate of 10 knots in order to avoid detection by patrolling P-3 Orion aircraft and the numerous surface ASW vessels. As Tupolev expected, his crewman performed their duties quickly, flawlessly and by the numbers, just as they had done a hundred times in practice.

Tupolev had trained his men well. And now, everything was in order.

Hamilton exited from the unusually crowded Watterson Expressway at the Newburg Road North ramp and punched a button on his car radio to find something more interesting than the golden oldie—Barry McGuire's "Eve of Destruction"—that the loudmouthed, wise-ass deejay was playing for the fourth time that morning. The button brought him to the middle of a newscast on WHAS, a station that until a few years ago had promoted itself as being "RADIO-ACTIVE." For some strange reason, the station management had decided that current conditions made this promo somewhat out of step.

... and the dust is still settling at city hall after this morning's firing of Charles Brighton. Mayor Burns issued a statement calling the firing lamentable but necessary in the face of such a serious violation of city policies and procedures. Aide Tom O'Hara had this to say: "There's absolutely *nothing*, I repeat nothing, to be read into the publication of those plans. Nothing to be alarmed about whatsoever. We have had absolutely no communication from anyone in Washington that would cause us to believe that the situation in the Persian Gulf would require this sort of preparation. Mr. Brighton apparently got a little too wrapped up in his job, and has been under a great deal of pressure these past few weeks. Obviously he couldn't handle it.

"I have asked the City Law Department to consider civil proceedings against him to recover the printing expenses which the city has incurred because of Mr. Brighton's outrageous and irresponsible actions. For now, I strongly encourage the public to do as I and the mayor will be doing, and that is to go about business as usual."

The reporter continued:

But only last week the opinion around city hall was quite a bit different. Brighton, who had been thrust into a position of some prominence by international developments, seemed to enjoy the unswerving confidence of Mayor Burns.

He talked freely in an interview with this reporter about the fears of at least some of the public that matters were growing more serious daily.

". . . Mr. Brighton, how is your office handling the numbers of people seeking or demanding nuclear defense information?"

"Well, of course, we don't have enough personnel to handle everyone as well as we'd like, but then we're keeping our heads above water. Although there has been a tremendous increase of those wanting information and answers, the simple fact is that these people represent a small minority of the community. But that's only because the Iranian situation hasn't gotten that scary for most people yet."

There was an obvious interruption where the tape had been spliced in editing, and the reporter's voice began again.

"But if an evacuation were ordered, what advice would you give people?"

"Well, frankly, I'd tell them that they should have been prepared long before that order was given. But in any event, I'd tell them to take lots of clothing, all types of it, since they may be away from home much longer than they might imagine. Bedding would be important. Every bit of food they can transport is vital, and enough utensils to prepare the food would be very important. And don't forget medical and sanitation supplies, and tools like shovels, axes, hammers, nails, and things for constructing fallout shelters.

"There are a lot of other things, too many to mention here. We have some pamphlets on this subject, and they are free to the public."

"Speaking of those pamphlets, Mr. Brighton, I noticed that they requested people not to take firearms with them."

"That's right."

"Is that your feeling also?"

"I didn't write these pamphlets . . ."

The reporter continued.

That was Charles Brighton just last week. And today, while refusing to be interviewed on tape, he maintained that he did what was warranted under the circumstances.

And the efforts of city hall to the contrary, it is obvious that many people have reacted strongly to the announcement from Washington last night and the appearance of the plans in the paper this morning. A check with supermarkets in the local area shows that an unusual number of shoppers are making large food purchases. Several managers have indicated that business has never been better. Limits have been placed on purchases of many items, and this has resulted in flaring tempers and, in a few cases, physical violence. Business at banks and automatic teller machines appears to be brisk.

And finally, a check with the local police departments shows that the level of traffic out of the city has increased noticeably as many of the people have taken the situation seriously enough to do something about it. Back to you, Rob.

Thanks for that special report, Dan. And now in other news . . .

Hamilton stabbed at the button again. Bruce Springsteen and "Born in the U.S.A." Now that was more like it.

When Hamilton pulled into his driveway, it was just past eleven o'clock. The streets in his quiet neighborhood were all but abandoned. He called out for Roseanna when he entered the house, but got no response. He continued through to the patio where he found her with her sister, Chris. Together they were lying out in the sun soaking up some of the rays on this beautiful late spring day. Hamilton's arrival was a surprise, and both of them began adjusting swimsuit straps to cover areas that were a little overexposed. The fact that Chris didn't move quite as quickly as one might have expected in such a situation only served as an example of how different the two women really were.

Roseanna, a former high school teacher, conservative in outlook and tastes, was in many ways a mirror image of her sister, who was five years her junior. Roseanna had deep auburn hair, and as the commercials sometimes referred to women with large breasts, she was "full-figured," though she could still slip comfortably into a size-seven dress. While not introverted, she was not exceptionally gregarious. She was a perfect mother, as Hamilton saw it. As a lover, she was a "10." The muted sexuality she displayed publicly did not reveal the depth of her sensual nature.

Chris, on the other hand, was blond, taking after her father's side of the family. She was slender and athletic, looking always as if she should have a tennis racquet in one hand. She was well satisfied with her figure, and chose clothes to accent it. A string bikini was *de rigeur* for anything having to do with sun or water.

Chris loved to party, and she loved the "good times." A nurse in constant contact with doctors and male patients at her hospital, she had a very—no, extremely—active social life. Chris loved men, and she went through them the way a hypochondriac goes through bottles of pills.

To Chris's way of thinking, however, she didn't have "affairs," she had "relationships." No one had affairs any more, she would say. Chris had had three "serious" relationships in the past few years—which resulted in living-together arrangements—and four other "casual" relationships, which consisted of several weekend trips together, in the past year alone.

For Christine Marie Whittington, it was life in the fast lane, charge cards to the credit limits, and to hell with anyone who didn't like it. At twenty-eight years of age, Chris had successfully avoided the night shift, pregnancy, and herpes—in the reverse order of their importance to her.

As Hamilton approached, Chris stood up and exclaimed, "We've caught ourselves a peeper, Roseanna." She adjusted the fabric of the bikini bottom she was almost wearing, and her teeth flashed sunlight at him.

"It's a little more serious than that," Hamilton replied brusquely. "Roseanna, I think its time to get down to Cliff's and I don't think we should waste any time." He was using his Mr. No-Nonsense tone.

"Okay," Roseanna replied, sensing the urgency in his voice, and realizing that it was pointless to argue. "I've been talking to Chris about it, and she was saying she might come with us. Well," she said, turning to her sister, "what do you say?"

"How soon?" She was not really ready to towel off the suntan oil which she had just spread over herself so liberally, but realizing Roseanna's reluctance to go at all, she decided it might make the trip more interesting and bearable for her sister if they could spend the time together. With Chris's vacation not over until Monday, and her weekend trip to the lake canceled because of what's-his-name's being stuck at the office on his "big deal," she had nothing better to do anyway. She just hoped Marge wouldn't give her any trouble.

"I want to be on the road at a quarter till one so we can meet another fellow at Bashford Manor. Roseanna, you can keep the car out there, and I'll come back in a jeep." Hamilton said all of this as businesslike as possible, to convey the seriousness and nonnegotiability of the matter.

"Okay," responded Chris, "I'll be back at twelve-thirty after I've thrown a few things together." She grabbed her beach jacket and glided past him to her car on long, suntanned legs, leaving behind air perfumed with Chloe and Coppertone. As she was about to open the door, she tossed her head to the side, sending her windswept blond hair over her shoulders, and then cocked her hand upon her left hip. "But what about Mom and Dad?"

"Forget it, Chris," Hamilton replied. "Roseanna mentioned it to them last night. They'll probably leave if and when they see the contrails of Russian bombers in the sky. Don't waste your time."

Chris frowned. "Well, I suppose you're right." She slid into her Pontiac Trans-Am, whipped out the driveway, and disappeared down the block.

Hamilton turned toward Roseanna and patted her on the behind. "I'll start loading the car if you'll get into something a little less exciting and walk over and meet the kids at school," he said.

An hour later the car was loaded and Hamilton was making some adjustments to the car roof rack. He turned to see Martin Healey, his next door neighbor, lumbering across the lawn like a Macy's Parade balloon run amok. Healey was a fairly successful restauranteur. His girth often caused Hamilton to wonder who ate more at Healey's restaurant, the owner or the customers.

"Good afternoon, neighbor. Have you come to give me a hand?" Hamilton asked. The greeting was without any genuine good humor. The two had had several "discussions" in the past over the behavior in the neighborhood of Healey's children, both of whom Hamilton regarded as unmitigated brats.

"Are you heading for the hills, too?" Healey asked with a slightly sarcastic ring to his voice.

Hamilton gave up any attempt at congeniality, and replied coldly, "Not quite that far, just taking my family to the farm for a few days."

Healey shook his head, looked skyward, and with a patronizing smile replied, "You know I just can't believe it. I mean, all those people I saw on the way home heading out. You guys know no one's going to use the Bomb. Christ, they haven't yet! The Russians are bound to pull up short before they run into our guys. Anyway, who'd want to live in a world after a nuclear war? If the time ever comes, Ol' Marty will just run out, look up into the sky and wait to get evaporated!"

"I'm holding that thought, Marty," Hamilton replied. He then paused for a few seconds. "But what if you don't get *evaporated*, Marty? What if you just get blinded, horribly burned and mutilated, and just wishing you were dead, Marty?" he said with his voice rising in anger. "And what about your kids? Will they appreciate your making that same decision for them because you were too stupid to do anything for them, such as getting them the hell out of the goddam target area? No, Marty. When the time comes, you'll *claw* for every day of survival just like everyone else.

Your flippant attitude is just a cop-out for your doing nothing now, and your doing nothing now will only reduce your chances of *clawing* successfully later!"

Hamilton turned his back on Healey and continued to work. Healey bristled at the words and his nostrils flared, but he said nothing as he stalked back across his yard and into his house.

Fran Fitzgerald put temptation aside and decided not to have that breakfast roll with her midmorning cup of coffee. Middle-age spread was not going to get to her any more than it had already, and she hoped to be ten pounds lighter in another few weeks. *If* she could stay on her diet, that is. She sat down at the kitchen table and separated the various sections of the *Courier-Journal*, and as she did so, her attention was immediately drawn to a special section.

"THESE ARE PLANS FOR EXPEDIENT FALLOUT SHELTERS," the bold headline began. "Save These Plans —They May Save Your Life." The unexpected appearance of the section added to its dramatic effect upon her, and an immediate frown came to her brow as she nervously began scanning the multitude of diagrams and pictures on the pages.

"Car Over Trench," "Door-Covered Trench Shelter," "Tilt-Up-Doors and Earth," read various diagrams. She scanned the information on water purification, sanitation, and shelter supplies. The impact was very disturbing. Was this connected with the news last night? No one had said anything about the possibility of nuclear war over this thing in Iran. In fact, it was obvious from the beginning that there was great emphasis in playing down the idea. But the situation seemed to be changing. The forty-five-year-old mother of three didn't particularly care for it.

She thought about her weekend plans. The family had been planning on visiting her sister near Nashville, and Ken was supposed to be home around twelve o'clock to help with the packing after taking care of some yard work.

Her husband ran the most popular gas station in St. Matthews, an eastern section of the Louisville area, and he could leave work whenever necessary. His employees didn't just pump gas, they hustled to the pump, and customers liked that. No car left the station without clean windshields and if the customer preferred, an oil and radiator check. The best part was that Ken Fitzgerald's assistant manager could handle the three employees on duty during most days without him.

Fran put the paper down after a few minutes and stared outside to the backyard. Something deep within her said something was very wrong—something ominous. Something dreadful.

Oh sure, she had had feelings like this before and sometimes they turned out to mean something, and sometimes not. Ken used to kid her about them. But he hadn't said a thing about them since the day her mother had died and she'd known about it across the many miles. When she demanded that he pull over and let her call her parents' home, the only person with whom she had been able to speak was a next door neighbor who was just about to lock up the house. Her father had left with the paramedics, who were working continuously all the way to the hospital, trying without success to revive her mother.

Today, the feelings were equally strong, and after a few minutes' reflection, she decided to start packing early. When her husband walked in two hours later, she had everything laid out and ready to be loaded into the car.

"Well, it looks like you got a head start," he said as he washed his hands at the sink.

"Yes, and the sooner we get on the road, the better. Look at this," she said, briskly opening the paper and spreading it out across the table.

He studied the plans for a few seconds before responding. "Yeah, I heard about this. It seems to have a lot of people worried. People have been lining up at the pumps all morning, many of them getting out of town. Business has been great! Had to put a ten-gallon limit on each customer." Fran said nothing but continued to stare at him. He looked at her and then said defensively, "So?"

"So I think it's time we got on the road to Rosie's, and the sooner the better. The kids will be home from school in an hour and a half, and I want to be ready to go out the door as soon as they get here."

"Aw, c'mon, Fran. The news on the radio this morning said that this stuff was printed only because one of the bureaucrats down there flipped his cork or something.

There's nothing more to it than that," he replied in a tone that was just a little too patronizing.

"Listen, Kenneth Allen Fitzgerald, if the situation is bad enough to cause the people responsible for these matters to flip out, as you call it, then it's surely bad enough to get us on the road for the weekend two hours early. Maybe Sunday afternoon, when it's time to come home, I'll feel differently, but now my feelings are strong, and they're telling me to leave, and to leave *now*."

Ken Fitzgerald inhaled deeply, and then exhaled slowly. Those "feelings" again, he thought. Sometimes that woman's feelings were enough to drive him nuts. Still, there *was* the time her mother died, and the other time when Melanie broke her arm on the camping trip. What the hell. The yard work could wait until Monday night anyway, he thought. "Okay," he said, "if it'll make you happy, we'll be ready to go by two-thirty.

"Women!" he muttered.

Although Jack Hamilton and most others in Louisville were unaware of the situation, U.S. forces had been at DEFCON-1, that is Defense Readiness Condition 1, the maximum state of force readiness, for two hours. Ominous events that morning, of which most outside the military establishment were unaware, were then occurring along the Tigris River in Iraq, and east of the Fulda Gap in Germany.

The Program 647L satellites, as the successors to the MIDAS satellite program of the 1970s were known, were being monitored with white-knuckled intensity. Each of the three $150 million, 22-foot-long satellites was positioned approximately 22,000 miles above the planet. This placement was necessary in order to permit them to orbit precisely at the same rate as the earth's rotation, thereby remaining stationary over one spot above the earth's surface.

Each satellite's mission was to search for the infrared energy which would be generated by the telltale plume of a Soviet missile launch within the observation field of the satellite's telescope. Within less than a minute after a missile launch, information would be transmitted to two readout stations, one at Aurora, Colorado, outside Denver, and the other at Nurrungar, Australia.

The data would be appropriately processed at these places, then forwarded to the National Military Command Center (NMCC) at the Pentagon, and the alternate command center buried deep within Raven Rock Mountain, Pennsylvania. For obvious reasons, Raven Rock Mountain, after the first hour of a nuclear war, was expected to be where control of the U.S. response to any nuclear exchange would shift.

The same information would also be forwarded to the Strategic Air Command facilities in a large complex known as The Hole at Offutt Air Force Base in Omaha, Nebraska, and the North American Aerospace Defense Command (NORAD) facility at Cheyenne Mountain, Colorado, below fourteen hundred feet of Rocky Mountain granite.

After the report from the Program 647L satellites, any missile launch would be confirmed by the Tactical Air Command's Ballistic Missile Early Warning System (BMEWS) radar facilities in Thule, Greenland; Clear, Alaska; and Fylingdales, England. The composite BMEWS radar fans, using Over-the-Horizon Backscatter radars, would provide a three-thousand-mile radar range, completely covering the northern approaches to North America.

At each of the command centers, dozens of men and women sat this day in cavernous, dimly lit rooms before consoles, videoscreens and telephone switchboards, ready to summon information from sensors and computers. This technology made it possible to evaluate and assess any missile launch deemed to be on what in the jargon was called a "threat azimuth." The state of the art was so advanced that the precise destination of each incoming missile could be determined and depicted visually on large display screens, showing its trajectory superimposed on a map of the country, as well as a time-to-impact. All of this could be determined well before each missile reached the continental limits of the United States, or at least quickly after the release of one of its warheads. At some point an "appropriate" U.S. response could then be recommended up the chain of command to the commander in chief, at the White House or elsewhere, hopefully in time to be useful.

Although rehearsals and exercises had been conducted often enough in the past, never had any of the men and women on duty this day been involved in any previous situation which actually placed them in a DEFCON-1 status. The sweat on the palms and fingers that pressed the buttons and answered the telephones at these command posts around the country was an altogether unusual and profoundly unwelcome experience.

Regardless, the pistol was cocked.

Hamilton arrived with his family at the shopping mall parking lot exactly on time. As he pulled in, he frowned with puzzlement when he did not find Mattingly waiting for him. His concern disappeared a few seconds later as Mattingly pulled into the lot, followed closely by Nugent. The three drivers then headed south without further delay.

Hamilton didn't think the extra traffic unusual for the first few miles. Bardstown Road was heavily traveled most of the day. This was Friday afternoon, anyway. Roseanna involved him in continuous conversation, and it took him a few miles before it occured to him that the traffic was not tapering off as it should. He had cleared Fern Creek and was just short of Mount Washington when it finally dawned on him that most of these people were probably leaving the city for the same reason he was. They were worried. Damned worried.

Over Kip's protest, Hamilton punched a button on the cassette player and they traveled to the accompaniment of Beethoven's Ninth Symphony and Bach's *Brandenburg* Concertos. The weather was nearly perfect, and his spirits were lifted as he put each additional mile between his family and Louisville.

They continued across the Salt River into Spencer County and on to High Grove and Nelson County. The countryside was bursting with the vigor of spring. Along the way in many places, trees with their seasonal attire newly in place formed dense canopies over the road. An excursion in the country along this highway seemed to take the traveler past history at each turn.

Still visible in places along the road were stone walls of native limestone, the product of antebellum slave labor. Built without a speck of mortar, they were being slowly lost as the elements took their toll. Unfortunately, the skills needed to rebuild them, with precious few exceptions, had died with the people who so carefully fitted each stone in place. Like others who have things that should be cherished and fail to realize their value before it is too late, farmers each year replaced a little more of the deteriorating limestone walls with barbed wire fences.

Black wooden tobacco barns constantly greeted Hamilton's "convoy." It was obvious how much the agricultural economy in this part of the country depended on the "golden leaf," burley tobacco. The fields in which each of the plants would be carefully set by hand were still bare. The wet weather that had delayed the planting of corn and soybeans had created problems for tobacco as well.

Hamilton's favorite stretch of U.S. 31 E was that part where the horse farms were. Thoroughbreds and saddlebreds grazed unconcernedly behind white wooden fences as the rest of the world passed by. Newborn colts frolicked on wobbly legs as their mothers quietly consumed prime Kentucky bluegrass to produce the milk for the youngsters' next meal.

Past the horse farms and the old mansion a little further down the road, Hamilton was delayed briefly by the state highway crew that was spot-patching some of the damage wrought by the winter's fury. Hamilton noticed the overweight flagman with dirty blond hair who was leaning, arms folded across his massive chest, against a speed limit sign. Again the question of how many people were really worried about the international situation and just what it might mean to them passed through Hamilton's mind. Judging by the traffic, a large number had begun to worry and were doing something about it. But what about this fellow whose bulging stomach strained at his belt, Hamilton wondered. Did this guy think much about the war as he stood their passively? Did he think about anything in particular? Did he *think?*

Hamilton's progress thereafter was uninterrupted until he neared Bardstown. On the outskirts of the town he glanced at the large, newly painted sign. Welcome to Historic Bardstown, it proclaimed. Pop. 5,512. Founded 1780. Sister City of Billom, France. Underneath a smaller sign read, Bardstown, Kentucky—One of *U.S. News and World Report's* Ten Great Places to Live in the United States.

Hamilton continued past the town's ugly-but-functional

National Guard armory. He saw ten or twelve enlisted men out in the motor pool working under the hoods of several vehicles parked near the building. A large sign in front of the armory proudly announced: Battery C, 2nd Bn (155mm SP), 138th Field Artillery. Though the feeling was common throughout the other units, this one, even more than others in the Kentucky Army National Guard, had reason to be worried about the future developments in the war. When Charlie Battery was called up in '68, several of the local boys came back from Vietnam the hard way after the unit's firebase was overrun one terrible night. CBS News later estimated that Bardstown, Kentucky had suffered more casualties per capita than any other community in the United States.

Traffic was heavy as Hamilton approached the center of town. Bardstown was accustomed to a continuous parade of out-of-town visitors, but this was obviously more than the usual summer tourist crowd.

Hamilton proceeded slowly past Federal, Victorian, and Greek Revival homes whose owners had marked them with small, ornate, black metal signs. Circa 1838, Circa 1809, Circa 1850 the signs read in succession as he passed down the street. Bardstown was deservedly proud of its history, and it did far more than most places to protect it.

In the center of the town square stood the courthouse on the spot where Confederates had camped during a raid through the state in 1862. Across from the courthouse Talbott Tavern stood proudly—since 1789, its sign clearly and smugly informed any observer. The inn's food and drink had been good enough for Abe Lincoln, Henry Clay, James Fenimore Cooper, and Louis Philippe of France. Today it was more than adequate for the unusually heavy number of out-of-towners.

Hamilton passed the state park where Federal Hill, made famous to the world by Stephen Foster as "My Old Kentucky Home," stood in antebellum elegance. He noticed that the driveways and parking areas were jammed. Were the crowds tourists, or were these people merely looking for a place to rest before heading elsewhere in their flight from the city? And where would they go, anyway?

Hamilton was able to clear Bardstown without further delay. Mattingly turned off at the McDonald's Restaurant after indicating that he and Nugent would pick up Hamilton on the way back. Hamilton then proceeded unimpeded to the farm and safety.

He felt better already. Lots better.

Hamilton pulled onto the narrow road leading the three hundred yards or so to the turnoff for the farm. Ahead of him was a gentle rise. On top of it was what seemed a picture postcard of the American heartland. From this distance the Hamilton farm had almost a pristine beauty, as if its barns, silos and grain bins perched above the surrounding cropland and pasture land had been placed for visual effect rather than function. This, of course, was not the case. His Uncle Charles had been a practical man, and Cliff's improvements were just as practical and economical.

Perched on the other side of the small hill was Reuben and Clara Cissell's farm, an equally well maintained and prosperous-looking place. By their appearance, both farms told any knowledgeable observer that the owners were people who knew how to reap a respectable living from the soil even in times which were not especially favorable for American farmers.

Jack drove slowly up the road, glancing at the white wooden fences lining each side. These expensive indulgences added little in the way of security for the cattle, but they had considerable visual appeal. The fences were departures from the usual practical approach of Cliff and Reuben, but Jack loved them.

To his left was the Hamilton family cemetery. In the shade of two gnarled, time-ravaged oak trees, enclosed by walls of hand-fitted Kentucky limestone, five generations had found their final resting places. Although the use of family burial plots had fallen out of favor since great grandfather Sam Hamilton's time, the little cemetery continued to receive the care and attention it deserved.

Hamilton pulled over to one side of the narrow road to allow an oncoming pickup truck to pass. The driver waved, as was common for people in central Kentucky. Each might not know the other, but greetings were exchanged, regardless. Hamilton did not recognize the driver, but he was accustomed to seeing local farmers stopping by to talk to

Cliff. Often it was just to "swap lies," and on other occasions it was to sound out Cliff on some idea or method Cliff was using.

As Jack drew closer to the house, he saw Cliff standing beside the barn. Near him was a large tractor-trailer rig, and atop the low-boy trailer was a large Caterpillar bulldozer. Hamilton honked the horn, and Cliff turned from his conversation with the driver of the tractor-trailer and waved.

"Hey, fella!" shouted Cliff, walking quickly up to the car. "Who are these three good-looking women you've got with you?"

Jennifer giggled, and she and Kip jumped out of the car and ran up to their uncle. "You really think I'm good-looking, Uncle Cliff?"

He lifted her up above his head and exclaimed, "Why you're the best-looking niece I've got!" He threw back his head and laughed heartily. It did not dawn on Jennifer that she was Cliff's only niece.

"We brought company, Cliff. I hope you don't mind. It was a spur-of-the-moment thing," Jack said, gesturing toward Chris.

Cliff looked at Chris and smiled. "Of course not." What else could he say? But if the truth were known, Cliff would very much have preferred that Chris had not come. He and Marge had only seen her four or five times since Jack and Roseanna had been married. And although Marge refused to admit it, he knew that there were some lingering feelings of jealousy toward the woman. Chris was the sort of woman who would flirt unconsciously even when she had no interest in a man. It was simply her nature.

Cliff's reaction at their first meeting had been, as Marge saw it, to give Chris far too much attention, and there had been hell to pay later. Things had been better on later occasions, a word to the wise being more than sufficient. But Cliff still suspected that Marge watched him closely when he was around Chris. All too closely.

"What's with the dozer?" Jack asked, pointing at the rig as he got out of the car.

"I thought we'd go ahead with the new pond. Larry Horton will be out here tomorrow morning to start working. But c'mon in and let's find Marge. She'll be glad to see all of you."

Jack was ready to return to Louisville when Mattingly and Nugent rolled up in the jeep. Hamilton hugged Roseanna, and when he was sure the car obscured Mattingly's view, he slid his hands around her buttocks, giving them a playful squeeze as he kissed her. She abruptly pushed him away and quickly looked over her shoulder to see whether anyone had seen his roaming hands. "Jack!" she exclaimed, "I'm trying to be serious!"

Hamilton looked at her, raised his eyebrows, and in his best tongue-in-cheek fashion said, "But madam, I *was* being serious!" He then pecked her on the lips and got in the jeep. "Listen, I'll call you tonight. I'll probably be back out tomorrow night. Don't worry about a thing." As the jeep backed up, then stopped as Nugent placed it into forward gear, Hamilton refused to show any hint of concern, knowing that it would be much easier on Roseanna for him to maintain the appearance that all was well. He gave her a slight wave as their eyes met one last time, and the jeep lurched forward and accelerated down the road back to Louisville.

As Hamilton returned to the city, he could not hear the radio news bulletin which interrupted regularly scheduled programming that afternoon to announce that a naval destroyer, the U.S.S. *Luce*, had sunk as a result of a collision with a Soviet destroyer whose purpose had been to harass American naval forces operating in the Persian Gulf. And Hamilton didn't hear the second, and equally ominous, portion of the broadcast that reported large Soviet troop movements near the East German border, which the Pentagon refused to confirm or deny.

And, of course, even the radio announcer that day could not hear the Klaxon horns sounding at precisely that moment at nineteen Strategic Air Command bases and assorted dispersal airfields around the country, or the call to general quarters on thirty-two fleet ballistic-missile submarines around the world.

This was not a case where ignorance could be described as bliss.

PART TWO

For, behold, the day cometh,
that shall burn as an oven; and
all the proud, yea, and all that
do wickedly, shall be stubble;
and the day that cometh shall
burn them up, saith the Lord of
hosts, that it shall leave them
neither root nor branch.

—Malachi, 4:1–6

Bart Sanders pulled his patrol car slowly out of the Fourth District police station parking lot in Louisville's West End and took another sip from the coffee cup he was holding with his free right hand. He had just returned to work that day, and now he was getting back to the old routine of his patrol duties.

The week away had been a good one for himself, his wife, and their four-year-old daughter. He had gotten in some good fishing, and his freezer held the proof.

For Sanders there was no more enjoyable pleasure than the pursuit of newly active spring bass at Kentucky Lake, except of course the pursuit of his wife at Kentucky Lake. The week had given him ample opportunity for both.

But now, that was behind him. He was back on the beat and had more pressing matters with which to concern himself. His eyes drifted over to Southwick, the large public housing area known as "the projects." The sprawling brick complex served as a warehouse for a large number of the city's lower class.

Preschool children ran about most of the buildings, and at the corner several older black teenagers stood watching the gyrations of a young man engaged in a frenetic effort at break dancing, his Third World ballet. The youths spotted Sanders approaching, and they eyed him suspiciously, but said nothing as his car passed. In this part of the city, people were accustomed to the continuous presence of the Man. That Sanders was also black meant little.

Just sit on the doorstep of one of the housing units, and not more than ten minutes would pass, or so it seemed, without someone walking by packing a walkie-talkie. With all its social problems, unemployment, and violent crime, the measures utilized to deal with these matters made the projects the closest things to police states in the entire community.

At the next corner, two young men were passing a joint back and forth when one of them spotted Sanders. The one who had just taken a long drag before he noticed the patrol car quickly pulled the joint behind him and cupped it in his hand. He tried to appear nonchalant as he dropped the joint to the ground. Slowly, very slowly, he exhaled and watched Sanders pass by. Fuck it, Sanders thought as he gave the two a second glance over his shoulder. If he tried to run down and bust every kid smoking pot in the projects, he would be standing around juvenile court for the rest of his natural life. There were a helluva lot more serious things to worry about.

Sharonda Tyson leaned against a stone wall on another part of Eighteenth Street. She was tired and dejected. After sauntering down Dixie Highway to St. Catherine Street and back four times in the last three hours, she hadn't had a bit of luck. She had expected the new dress with its plunging neckline to cause her johns to form lines, but that hadn't been the case.

Sharonda looked down at her baby-doll heels and at the slinky material of her dress, which fluttered gently in the warm breeze. Her firm breasts strained against the material leaving no doubt as to the size and dimensions of her nipples—which was exactly what she intended. Any passing motorist would know exactly what Sharonda was selling. In the last year, she had learned very well how to package the merchandise.

Though she had been arrested twice and was looking at serious time in the county jail on her next bust, she had found a reasonably lucrative supplement to her state welfare check for herself and Latosha, her fourteen-month-old daughter. She was, one might say, upwardly nubile.

Hell, she thought, nobody else would take care of her if she didn't help herself. That no-good son of a bitch, Lamont. Running off to Detroit just when she was due to deliver. At eighteen and with no education, she was unprepared, or at least not inclined, to earn a living any other way.

The shift would be changing soon down at the distillery, she thought. Rush hour meant better prospects.

As Major John Robert Hamilton said good-bye to his wife and family, a Soviet SS-19 missile, which had, until a few minutes before, sat undisturbed for a very long time in its concrete-and-steel lair, reached an altitude of 80,000 feet above sea level. As it climbed, it moved toward its target, or rather, targets, at ever-increasing speed.

The first stage completed its work and then tumbled back to earth after explosive charges blew apart its connecting bolts. The second stage did its part in propelling the business end of the missile toward its destination until the on-board digital computer of the complex guidance system "told" the rocket to shut down after calculations as to speed and trajectory indicated that the missile was directly on course, and that it could fly unaided to its targets.

After the booster rockets shut down, the shroud covering the warheads fell away and the payload and booster stage separated. Sheer momentum now carried the payload toward the target at twenty times the speed of sound.

Before the halfway point between the launch site and its ultimate destination, the post-boost vehicle commenced a process of steering, braking, and accelerating to position the six warheads on the MIRV, that is, the Multiple Independently targeted Re-entry Vehicle. By using its small retro-rockets, it backed away, releasing one warhead, then another, at the rate of two per minute until all warheads were released and on their way to separate targets.

Major Hamilton was, of course, oblivious to these events, as were all but a most insignificant number of the planet's population. At about the point Hamilton pulled out of Bardstown, the last warhead separated from the post-boost vehicle. It continued on its trajectory to arrive with amazing accuracy at, or at least very close to, its intended target.

Midafternoon found Sharonda Tyson, the Fitzgerald family, and Tom O'Hara in very different parts of Louisville.

Sharonda had just made herself comfortable, leaning once again on one of the stone walls along Eighteenth Street, when a station wagon driven by a balding, middle-aged man in a business suit passed by on the other side of the street. His attention was firmly riveted on her. Sharonda's eyes lit up immediately, and she waved vigorously at him. "Hey! Mistah! Hey!"

Suddenly, Sharonda noticed a girl a hundred feet down the other side of the street doing the same. Damn! she thought. Now where did that bitch come from?

The station wagon continued on until it reached the parking lot of a used furniture store, and then it turned around and headed back. Sharonda pulled at her dress, straightening it and adjusting the spaghetti shoulder straps. She fidgeted with anticipation as the car passed by her competition. "Come to mama," she whispered. This looks like an easy twenty dollars, maybe more, she thought.

The car stopped directly in front of her and the rather nervous driver leaned over and cracked the window a couple of inches on the passenger's side. He kept the door locked, however. Sharonda leaned over and placed her hands on her knees. "You looking for somethin' special, Mistah?" she asked, making sure that the driver got as good a look as possible down her substantial cleavage.

The man's eyes fixed immediately on her bulging breasts, and he tried without success to find his voice. He then glanced nervously up and down the street for anyone who might be watching. Finally, he stammered, "Uh, sure, uh, honey. But it, uh, depends on what you're selling . . ."

His clumsy approach irritated her. "Got no time to bullshit, man. You wanna date or not?"

The man suddenly gave a start and slid behind the wheel, pulling rapidly away. Sharonda fell back quickly and caught her balance before looking to see what had caused such a drastic reaction. Bart Sanders was pulling up in his patrol car, and he was motioning with his index finger for her to come to him.

"Aw, man!" Sharonda cried, flinging her hand to her side in disgust. "I don't believe this!" As she walked slowly toward him, she made no effort to hide her contempt. She silently mouthed the words "motherfucker," and as she reached Sanders' car, she said, "What you want? I didn't do nothin'."

"Sharonda," he replied, matter-of-factly, 'Loitering for the Purpose of Prostitution' is still 'something,' even on Eighteenth Street."

Sharonda clenched her fists in disgust, "Man, what you mean I'm . . ."

Tom O'Hara was on the back nine with Jim Mulhall and two of Mulhall's friends, Ed Robertson and Larry O'Neill. When Jim had invited O'Hara to Hurstbourne Country Club for a round of golf, it didn't take O'Hara two seconds to decide to get away from the looney bin for the rest of the afternoon. Thank God it was Friday, O'Hara thought.

What a nut house Louisville's city hall had been that morning. All those people down there expecting the world to end because Brighton had taken it upon himself to put all of that fallout crap in the newspaper. And then there was that bit on the news about the big Russian drive from Iran into Iraq. Even more people were coming in after that. As the mayor's chief aide, O'Hara had done what he could to handle the problem, but even the president's public assurances that the situation was under control had little effect.

Regardless, O'Hara considered this something for the new civil defense director to worry about. The sunlight, fresh air, and good company beat all to hell the insanity that prevailed around city hall.

His host, Jim Mulhall, was a man in his early sixties. He had begun forty years earlier with a battered Ford pickup truck, an honorable discharge from the Seabees, and a driving ambition to make it as a building contractor. Now a millionaire several times over, he enjoyed several lucrative construction contracts with the city. He liked to maintain good relations with anyone in the mayor's office; inviting O'Hara for a round of golf was nothing out of the ordinary.

For O'Hara, maintaining good relations with a potentially large contributor to a future campaign was nothing out of the ordinary, either.

Mulhall had just finished making a putt when he said, "You know, Tom, I don't mind telling you—even if you don't want to hear it—that I have a little of these war jitters myself. Here I am shooting my best game in a month of Sundays, but in the back of my mind I'm wondering whether I should be at the grocery buying food, or maybe just getting the hell out of town."

"Not you, too," O'Hara replied. "I never thought you of all people would start talking like this. You've got a lifestyle most people only dream about. Can you imagine how it would be after a nuclear war? Nobody in their right mind would want to live in a world that awful. I'm sure I wouldn't want my kids growing up wondering where food was going to come from, one meal to the next. By the way, did I tell you that Cathy is going to have twins? Got the word Monday."

Mulhall placed his putter back in the bag. "Congratulations on the twins, Tom. It's about time you and Cathy got around to that sort of stuff. But back to your point, I sure don't relish the thought of life under those circumstances. It's just that I'd like the option of trying it. And remember this, as long as there is any hope left at all, the living never really envy the dead. Anybody who tries to tell you that is blowing smoke up your ass. Last year, when I lay in that coronary care unit, tubes running in and out of me every which way, I never stopped hoping and, yes, praying for one more day, no matter how bad it got. Just how many Jews at Auschwitz asked to jump to the head of the line?"

O'Hara noticed that his right shoe felt a bit loose and he knelt down beside the golf cart to tie the lace. "I understand what you're saying, Jim. But you've got to agree that . . ."

By three-thirty that afternoon, the Fitzgerald family had been inching along in the traffic for one hour. The prospect for improvement did not seem to be immediate. The Watterson Expressway was at its worst, and I-65 was just as bad. This wasn't just Friday afternoon traffic. It wasn't even rush hour yet. Ken Fitzgerald gritted his teeth as he looked around at the nuts he imagined were running for the hills. The thought of placing a sign on his car, reading "I AM NOT A NUT. I'M ONLY GOING TO VISIT MY SISTER-IN-LAW," brought a sardonic grin to his face. How in hell did Fran get him out in this mess? he wondered.

He looked over and noticed a couple of four-wheel-drive vehicles cutting onto the grassy median, quickly passing cars and trucks stalled in the southbound lanes. More four-wheel-drive vehicles appeared, seemingly from nowhere, and did likewise. Then, in the best monkey-see-monkey-do fashion, several cars and vans joined in, only to become quickly bogged down in the soggy depressions in the median strip, blocking passage for everyone.

Ahead, several men succeeded in pushing a stalled vehicle off the asphalt to the grassy shoulder. Probably out of gas like so many others, Fitzgerald thought. As the traffic once again inched ahead, one car attempting to dart through the newly cleared hole sideswiped another. Both vehicles came to an abrupt halt. The drivers sprang from their cars, and a fight quickly ensued. Traffic was again at a standstill until a third driver, brandishing a pistol, leaped from his car and forced the first two men back into their automobiles. Traffic started moving slowly, once again.

"Goddam!" Fitzgerald muttered uneasily, as the danger of a shooting in front of him passed. "This is a circus."

Fran grimaced. She knew that he was silently holding her accountable for having made him a part of all of this. "Melanie," she said, "will you reach in the cooler and hand your father another drink?"

Ken accepted the Coke, and then punched a button on the radio. ". . . that was Patti LaBelle and 'New Attitude.' And now for . . . Jesus Christ! What's this? . . . Is this for real?"

A split second later there was a loud, familiar tone lasting several seconds, and it caused Ken and Fran to tense immediately. "This is the Emergency Broadcast System. This is *not* a test . . ."

Ken squeezed the can of Coke so hard that the sides buckled abruptly and sent much of the drink spewing into the air. Ken looked at Fran and said, "Now just what the hell is . . ."

Sharonda Tyson, Fran and Ken Fitzgerald, and Tom O'Hara never finished their conversations that Friday. As they spoke, a gasp came simultaneously to their lips and, perhaps, to the lips of a hundred thousand others. The unearthly dazzle of a nuclear detonation several thousand feet above Louisville suddenly started the city on a slide to damnation.

Hotter than the core of the sun, the nuclear chain reaction released massive quantities of radiation and heat that flashed across the city at the speed of light. The dragon's breath of the bomb's thermal effect vaporized the people and buildings on the University of Louisville's Belknap Campus, just to the southeast of Ground Zero, and incinerated the unfortunate souls caught in the open thousands of yards beyond.

The air at the epicenter was compacted to an astounding degree. It rushed outward as a supremely compressed, granite-hard wall of air, a wind of steel.

Buildings nearest the epicenter convulsed and simply disappeared, leaving little evidence to prove that they had ever existed at all. Further away, it was as if the giant, angry hand of a nuclear beast had reached down and cleared the tabletop of the urban landscape. Homes, businesses and schools collapsed and disintegrated in the shock wave's wake.

In the downtown area, the glass-box, high-rise office towers reeled and shuddered mightily as the shock wave roared past. Their glass facades burst into millions of crystalline shards, the shrapnel dicing and slicing the occupants, who for the most part were already seared from the heat and light. The bridges across the Ohio River to the Indiana shore buckled and groaned as the blast wave slammed into them at the speed of sound. Finally, one by one, they dropped to the boiling, churning water below.

The shock wave rolled like a megaforce hurricane across the remainder of the stricken city, completely decimating the horse barns and majestic twin spires of Churchill Downs, and crushing the Brigade Headquarters and the surprised Guardsmen inside. As the shock wave fanned out, it uprooted trees, pinwheeled cars and trucks, and scattered pedestrians as if they were so many dry leaves in a late November wind.

Fortunately, fallout was negligible because the high altitude of the detonation meant that no contaminated soil or debris were sucked or blown into the atmosphere. But in the twenty-five-square-mile area of destruction around Ground Zero, almost everyone was a casualty on this clear, warm spring day.

At city hall, the last thing Mayor Don Burns saw as he sat at his desk, trying to figure out why his telephone had suddenly stopped working, was the major portion of his ceiling hurtling downward.

As for Sharonda Tyson, as she reached for the door of Bart Sanders' car, the flash first seared the pattern of her new dress onto her skin, and then nearly evaporated it before she even fell to the ground. The speed with which she died was, in the purely clinical and unhumanistic sense, awesome. Her suffering and the suffering of Bart Sanders was terrible but, mercifully, brief.

The shock wave that followed violently flung Sharonda and Sanders two hundred feet down Eighteenth Street. A few minutes after the detonation, very little of the patrol car remained except twisted, molten slag.

Fran Fitzgerald's family was more fortunate. Considerably removed from the detonation and heading away from the city, no one in the family was looking toward the blast. Ken and Michael received second-degree burns along exposed portions of their necks and upper arms, but their injuries were not life-threatening.

Tom O'Hara, too, was fortunate, in a way. The golf cart protected him from the flash, and by flattening himself to the ground, he was able to avoid injury as the greatly diminished shock wave rolled across Louisville's suburbs.

With his ears still ringing as if from a gong, he numbly looked around him, and then crawled over to Mulhall. The man lay on his back, with first- and second-degree burns on his face and arms, clutching at his chest in what seemed to be the final stages of a coronary attack. Just as O'Hara reached him, Mulhall gave a long sigh and his eyes rolled upward. O'Hara quickly checked for a pulse. Nothing.

Still in shock, O'Hara drew himself unsteadily to his feet and looked around. A strange shiver raced up his spine as he watched Robertson and O'Neill running away without pausing even briefly to check on Mulhall or himself. What in God's name had happened?

He turned back toward the city and was struck dumb by the sight of the rising, roiling mushroom cloud. His jaw went slack. He wanted to cry. He couldn't. Suddenly, he thought about Cathy, his wife. *Sweet Jesus, no!*

He started walking, staggering as if drunk, toward the clubhouse parking lot. He slowly picked up the pace to a jog, and then to a full run.

He had to get home, he thought again and again. *Home.*

Earlier, Hamilton's jeep had cruised slowly down Stephen Foster Avenue in Bardstown. He had little choice. The street was choked with cars bearing Louisville license plates, and the sidewalks were crammed with people milling about.

On North Third Street, he looked into the dozen or so retail stores along the town's main drag. It was as if the merchants were conducting a fire sale. People stood in line to get into a couple of stores, and outside the drugstore a middle-aged man Hamilton recognized as the manager argued heatedly with several people trying to force their way into the packed building.

Hamilton was amazed at how the crowds had mushroomed since he'd passed through town less than an hour before. They seemed to have no sense of purpose. It was as if these people had fled Louisville for safety, but once they had arrived at this place of relative safety, the next question seemed to be, "What the hell do we do now?"

As the jeep cleared the center of town, the northbound traffic thinned out. Approaching Kentucky Home Square, the small shopping center at the town's northern limits, Hamilton saw a parking lot that reminded him of the Christmas-season crowds in the shopping malls around Louisville. But here there was a difference.

Camper trailers, pickups, and motor homes were scattered across the asphalt. People sat outside and many poked at barbecue grills beside the awnings they had erected for protection from the sun. "Holy shit, Major!" Nugent exclaimed, "it looks like a goddam RV park, or maybe like a Cambodian refugee camp with Winnebagos!"

"Nugent, turn left at the light. We'll hit the interstate just past Bernheim Forest. It'll get us back to the armory in better time," Hamilton said. After a short delay at the traffic light, the jeep was clear of Bardstown.

A few miles down the road Nugent leaned over to Hamilton and said sheepishly, "Gonna need some gas, Major."

Before Hamilton had a chance to respond, Mattingly cried, "You knucklehead, if you had done the maintenance on this thing yesterday, it would have been topped off before we left."

The traffic was extremely heavy on Highway 245. A broad, two-lane road with wide gravel shoulders, its improvement a few years before had been a significant addition to the county. The fearful drivers traveled much too fast and much too close together now. Some were even passing others by going around them on the gravel shoulders.

God, this is insane! thought Hamilton. He had seen two near misses and one minor collision in the past five miles. He felt as if he were in a strange demolition derby whose rules had been eliminated.

Ahead was a small food market with self-service pumps, and the jeep slowed. After waiting for a fleeting gap in the oncoming traffic, the jeep darted across the road and pulled up to the pumps.

Mattingly and Hamilton walked into the store as Nugent began filling the tank. "Damn him!" said Mattingly. "If he had taken care of that yesterday, we wouldn't be paying for gas now out of our own pockets."

Hamilton walked up to a cooler and pulled a small bottle of orange juice from the shelf. He looked at the snack cakes on the nearby display, but nothing looked good, so he took a place behind Mattingly in the checkout line. Nugent, who by now had finished gassing the jeep, got into line behind Hamilton carrying three Moon Pies, two packages of Twinkies, and a six-pack of RC Cola.

When Nugent noticed Hamilton looking at his selections, he said simply. "Survival rations." Hamilton looked back toward the checker, shaking his head in disbelief.

A split-second later there was a blinding flash to the north. Everyone flinched involuntarily and turned away. Like the sun, the light was so bright that the eye refused to focus on it.

"Jesus Christ!" Hamilton cried, "there goes Louisville!" and then he yelled for everyone to hit the floor. A woman screamed shrilly. For the few seconds it took for the intense light from the fireball to fade, Hamilton was not certain whether he had control of his bladder.

Hamilton looked around him and saw many people spread-eagled. Most of them were pale—just as he certainly was. Several were trembling almost convulsively. The smell of someone's recently evacuated bowels permeated the air.

"Listen to me!" Hamilton yelled. "Cover your head, get your feet toward the door, and stay down! The shock-wave will be here soon!" Most of the people did exactly as he said, looking for anyone who gave the impression of knowing what he was doing, as this army officer did.

Across the thirty-five miles or so from Louisville, the shock wave raced at the speed of sound. It made any sonic boom seem like a small firecracker set off in the distance. Although the store was far out of the area of serious blast effects, when the report of the explosion hit, it was nearly deafening. Glass shook violently, then cracked from top to bottom. Cans fell from shelves onto the prone figures on the floor. Fissures appeared immediately in the wall plaster.

When the wave passed, Hamilton and most of the others, still awestruck, walked hesitantly outside. Hamilton, Mattingly, and Nugent stared together in silence as the churning mushroom cloud rose to the north.

Finally, Nugent whispered, "Ho-o-ly shit."

"Sweet Mother of God," responded Mattingly in equally subdued tones. "It was probably an air burst. The Russians would surely have used an airburst on a city. Right, Major?"

Before Hamilton could reply, a flash appeared at their right side, though it was much less intense than the first one. In quick succession came two more to their left. "My God!" Hamilton said in a tone indicating more awe than horror. "That's probably Cincinnati or the army depot in Lexington, and Gods knows what else. It's actually happened. They've finally gone and done it!" Hamilton felt as if he were watching a surreal summer thunderstorm move across the landscape. The three stood mesmerized by the preternatural light show. Artificial auroras surged, faded, then surged again with greens, yellows, and purples splashed across the heavens. Never before had anyone seen anything like it.

Then for the first time, as if a curtain had been lifted in front of him, Hamilton became aware of the carnage and confusion around him. Strewn about the road were numerous vehicles that had collided. Other vehicles had simply stalled. One woman was on the ground beside her car, screaming loudly. Hamilton looked around and saw several other people running frantically about.

"Oh, God! I'm blind, I'm blind!" the woman on the ground cried, sobbing uncontrollably. Pulling himself together, Hamilton walked quickly to her as a man who appeared to be her husband placed his arms around her. "Listen," Hamilton said, trying to use his most reassuring tone, "it's not as bad as it seems. It's not permanent. It's just like a flashbulb from a camera. Most likely you'll be good as new in a few hours." True or not, it seemed to help the woman. When he stood up, the woman seemed to be getting a firmer grip on herself.

Hamilton then noticed two men attempting to extract a pinned driver from an overturned pickup truck. He walked quickly to the truck and grabbed at the door the two were trying to force open. "What happened to everybody? Flash blindness? The shock wave?"

The man nearest him responded, "Not me, at least. I didn't even have a chance to look at it before my power went out and I lost control of my car. One second it was driving fine and the next minute nothing. I plowed into the end of this guy before I could muscle the wheel over to go around him. My power steering just went out like *that*. Of course, that big flash didn't help any."

Hamilton got the door open and reached in to check the driver lying crumpled on the ceiling of his truck. "We're not going to be able to do anything for this guy." He turned around and looked up and down the road. He could see at least twenty stalled cars and trucks. A few were now starting to move.

"Electromagnetic pulse," Hamilton said as Mattingly jogged quickly to him.

"Sure as hell was," Mattingly replied. "Can you believe all these cars and trucks are now just a bunch of goddam paperweights? A lot of good they'll be for anything else."

The other man who had been helping the dead driver stepped closer. "Wh-what the hell is this pulse thing you're talking about?"

"A release of radioactive particles and rays. Like a strong radio signal from the explosion. You can kiss your transistor radios, electric lines, and data circuits goody-bye," said Mattingly.

It was true. The diodes, transistors, and integrated circuits in the electronic ignitions and all those "black boxes" in the late-model cars were fried by a megawatt power surge through units designed to function in the milliwatt range.

Hamilton wondered whether the microchip was the Achilles heel of modern civilization.

The second man thought about Mattingly's comments, and he was puzzled. "But why are some of these cars working?"

"Simple," Hamilton replied quickly. "They're older models with contact points and coils and no black boxes controlling the engine." Turning to Mattingly, he said, "C'mon, we've got to get the hell out of here. Let's try the jeep. We've got to get back to our families."

Together they jogged back to the jeep where Nugent was already nervously waiting. Mattingly signaled Nugent to get in the back and jumped behind the wheel. "Thank God," he muttered when the engine kicked over.

As the jeep was nearing the main road, the man who had been asking the questions ran up to the vehicle waving his arms desperately. "Can you guys give me and my family a lift?"

Hamilton looked at the woman and little girl quickly running up behind him. With only a slight pause he responded, "Okay, but hurry!"

The three squeezed into the jeep and held their luggage out each side. As the jeep moved forward, the man said, "Rick Sheridan. Pleased to meet you. Don't care a helluva lot for the circumstances, though."

Hamilton looked over his shoulder. "Jack Hamilton. Likewise."

Once on the highway, the jeep quickly picked up speed. The little girl squirmed into a more comfortable position and said, "What happened in Louisville, Mommy?"

No one responded immediately, so she asked again.

Finally her mother looked at her. Emotion was evident in her voice. "We're trying not to think about it, sweetheart." The child looked puzzled, but remained quiet.

Mattingly picked his way down the road around the stalled cars. Most of the people in the cars still operable, to their credit, seemed to be doing whatever they could to help those left without transportation. However, it was obvious that the ratio was too great and that many would find it necessary to walk or to hitch a ride with others who might pass. Several were trying to flag down the jeep despite the fact that it already carried too many passengers. The army jeep seemed to represent the government and, therefore, authority. This seemed to make many of the stranded motorists more aggressive.

Mattingly swerved twice in rapid succession to avoid hitting people rushing toward the jeep. Both times he nearly lost control. One woman standing beside a middle-aged man bent down, scooped up a rock and then threw it at the jeep as it passed, hitting the hood. "Stop, you son of a bitch!" she screamed in frustration. "You're the army! You're supposed to help!"

Hamilton looked back over his shoulder and said softly, "I've got a family, lady. They come first."

They continued uninterrupted to Bardstown. When they reached the shopping center, Hamilton directed Mattingly to turn left.

"But that's toward Louisville, sir!" Nugent exclaimed.

"We're going down to the battery," Hamilton said, and Mattingly proceeded to the National Guard armory on the outskirts of town.

As they pulled in, several guardsmen were crammed in a couple of cars pulling out of the parking lot, and one cargo truck loaded to the limit with soldiers was leaving the motor pool.

Hamilton jumped out before the jeep made a complete halt, and he quickly jogged into the building, straight for the Orderly Room. When he entered, the battery first sergeant was rummaging frantically through some manuals in front of him, and a second lieutenant, a red-haired young man in his early twenties, was just slamming a phone down in anger. "Damn!" he said. "Still out!"

"And it's going to be out for a long time to come, Lieutenant."

Startled by the unannounced visitor, the lieutenant replied, "Jesus, sir! Where did you come from?"

"I'm Major Hamilton, the Brigade S-2. For all I know I may be all that's left of Brigade Headquarters, considering where that bomb probably detonated."

The young man wrinkled his forehead at Hamilton's words. "Then I suppose Captain Farley is dead if that's the case. He went there for a meeting. And Lieutenant Fischer is with a detail of men at Fort Knox. Goddam! The world's just turned to shit!"

"Your battalion headquarters may be gone as well. One of those flashes could well have been Lexington or the army depot being hit."

The lieutenant slumped in his chair, trying hard to cope. In an effort to snap himself out of the beginning of a serious depression, he said, "Ted Ackerson, sir, and this is First Sergeant Johnson." The three shook hands quickly.

"Listen," said Hamilton, "I don't want to waste any more time than necessary. What's with your people?"

Ackerson stammered a bit and then said, "Sir, well, we, uh, didn't know exactly how soon this would be over, so we . . ."

"How are you going to get in touch with them?" interrupted Hamilton, anticipating the response.

"Well, we told them we'd come after them after any fallout that might hit us had passed," Ackerson replied defensively. "We know where they all live."

"Fine. You couldn't have kept them here at gunpoint anyway. Since we're chewing up precious time, I suggest that we all get the hell away from here and back to our own families until we see about this fallout situation. I suggest you take your radiacmeters home with you, and when conditions are safe to come out, start rounding up your men. I'll be at my brother's place. You know Cliff Hamilton by any chance?" Hamilton started for the door and the other two followed.

"You're Cliff's brother?" Johnson replied. "Well, if that's so, I'll be proud to serve under you." Hamilton jumped into the jeep where Mattingly, Nugent, and the Sheridan family were waiting, and he waved back to Johnson to acknowledge the compliment. With a wave from his other hand, he signaled Mattingly to move out.

Hamilton's jeep sped up the narrow road to the farm. Roseanna ran down to meet it, and when Hamilton stepped out, she threw her arms around him. "Darling," she cried, "I was scared to death for you!" She squeezed him even more tightly. "Mom . . . and Dad . . ." she said softly, tears rolling down her cheeks.

"I know, sweetheart. I know." He tried to think how to assure her that her parents were out of danger, but nothing convincing came to mind. Turning to the Sheridans, he said, "This is Rick and Linda Sheridan, and their daughter, Rebecca. They'll be staying for a while." He turned to Mattingly and Nugent. "I'll come after you when they let me know it's safe to come out."

That was all Mattingly needed. Without more than a nod, he spun the jeep around and headed back to the highway.

Cliff came running up and Hamilton introduced him to his newest uninvited guests. "Listen," Hamilton said, "we have a lot to do, and maybe not much time. There's no way of telling how soon fallout could be here."

"What are we gonna do? All try to crowd into that small root cellar?" Cliff asked, incredulous.

"No. The best thing we have going for us is that barn. All we have to do is reinforce the floor, spread a helluva lot of dirt on it, and take that dozer and push up dirt to close off the lower level from the outside. Anybody have a better idea?"

No one did. The group set to work in carrying out the plan. The task before them was one which might have taken several days of careful planning and execution in normal times. But time was a luxury now. Hamilton barked orders as a drill instructor might to new recruits. There was no time for courtesies.

The effort was made immensely easier by the bulldozer and, of course, the old barn. Built shortly before the turn of the century by Jack's great grandfather, Samuel Hamilton, it was a classic example of nineteenth-century agricultural and construction craftsmanship. It had three levels. The first level, made of stone, was below ground on three sides and opened outward to the hillside on the fourth. The second level, resting on great timber joists, appeared even with the ground when viewed from the farmhouse. At the third level, an immense hayloft held enough hay to supply the needs of the farm's livestock for months, regardless of the time of year.

Oak and poplar beams, fitted in joints as solid now as they were the day they were set over three generations earlier, gave the feeling of strength and permanence. This structure stood for durability and stability, and in silent counterpoint its presence mocked and shamed the no-deposit-no-return society around it.

But now, Jack Hamilton and the others were working frenetically to adapt the barn to a purpose Great-Grandfather Sam Hamilton would have never foreseen and probably would never have understood. Cliff worked skillfully with the bulldozer and pushed mounds of dirt up to the barn's lower level to close it off from the outside. More dirt was pushed carefully to the barn's entrance on the main floor, and as quickly as possible, Jack, Rick and Kip shoveled the dirt across a section of the wooden floor to a depth of about twelve inches. Taking no chances, Jack found some additional shoring material and he placed it at critical points below the floor.

"Goddam, Jack!" Cliff exclaimed when he jumped down from the dozer and looked at the dirt piled high on the barn floor. "Uncle Charles always said Great Grandpa Sam wanted this barn to last forever, and I'm sure glad he didn't skimp when he built it."

Marge, Roseanna, and Chris hurriedly collected large quantities of food and brought them to the shelter. They stored water in any container available. Marge hurriedly located bedding, extra clothes, and a couple of old kerosene lamps. Acting on Hamilton's request, Rick Sheridan removed the small light bulbs and the batteries from every car and truck, and then took them to the shelter.

The last task to be completed was rounding up the livestock. Cliff made quick and tough decisions on which livestock would go into the extra space in the barn's lower level. Bloodlines and breeding potential influenced his decisions, but he did not ignore the simple fact that two small heifers could be crowded into one mature cow's space, and several small pigs could be herded into one mature sow's space. Quantity had to come before quality.

Throughout the effort, Jack Hamilton raced as if to get to safety off a doomed ship, never knowing just how much time remained. Every few minutes he checked for the settling of telltale specks of gray dust. Thank God for that bulldozer, he thought more than once. In two hours, the work was done.

As everyone settled into the new surroundings that evening, there was little conversation at first. The physical efforts had taken their toll, and there was immeasurable concern and worry about friends and relatives in Louisville —and about the expected fallout.

Marge and Cliff immediately set down their personal items in one corner of the shelter. Acting every bit the lady of the house, Marge presented Rick and Linda with their pillows and blankets, and then directed them to another corner. They followed without question.

"Just how safe are we in here, Jack?" Roseanna asked as she handed him a Pepsi, already a little too warm for his liking. The others, sitting around the room, separated from the animals by a very thick wall of stone, looked to him for the answer. After all, military men were supposed to know something about this nuclear stuff, weren't they?

"Safe enough, I suppose. Fallout's not going to come in like a gas and poison us. It'll come down in heavy dust particles initially, particles that've been contaminated with radioactive material from a bomb's surface or near-surface burst. That's one reason Louisville won't pose too much of a problem for us—it was probably an airburst. Prevailing winds would probably send most of it to the northeast anyway."

He reached to a toolbox and picked up a pair of pliers. He grabbed the domelight Sheridan had removed from Cliff's pickup and began to strip the coating from a wire he intended to connect to a car battery.

"It sounds almost like Mount St. Helens and all of that volcanic ash," Chris said.

"In a surface burst, exactly. If the bomb hits the earth and blasts stuff into the air, it drifts downwind and settles. If not, there's not much of a radiation problem away from the immediate area, thank God," responded Hamilton. "I didn't have a helluva lot of time to explain what we were doing or why we were doing it today, but basically I was trying to get as much insulation, you might call it, between us and any fallout that might drift our way. The density of the material between us and the fallout is what matters most. I think we did well enough, and I'm not saying that just to make everyone feel good."

"But what about all those people out there who don't have places like this? Will they all die?" Roseanna asked, thinking, without saying so, of her parents.

Hamilton shook his head slowly. "If you're talking about the ones who survived the blast, you're asking me about something I can't begin to answer. There may be little or no fallout in some areas. If the Russians hit the cities to the west with aerial bursts, there won't be any fallout here except from the strikes on things like missile silos or command posts. Unfortunately, the Minute Man silos in Missouri were probably hit and will probably send fallout toward us. Of course, the great distance means that most of it will fall to earth before it ever gets here. Slight wind changes could send the debris north or south of us. But there are so many variables, who knows?" He finally made the connection on the little dome light. It came to life and added a surprising amount of illumination to the room. Hamilton looked at his handiwork and said, "*Fiat lux.*"

"But will those people out there die if the fallout does come?" Marge persisted.

"I'm sure that many, very many will. But anyone able to dig a trench and place wooden doors across it with dirt mounded on top can have a functional fallout shelter. Anyone who read the paper this morning would know this. It wouldn't be perfect, but it could save their lives. Besides, there are lots of buildings around, even out here in the country, and these buildings can give a lot of protection with a little work. You're sitting in one. It's not hopeless for those people out there, it's just that they will have to make the best of a bad situation—correction—very bad situation."

"What about the livestock?" Cliff asked.

"Just as with people, it all depends on the level of fallout," his brother responded. "Just putting them in a barn with a filled hayloft above them will help. Those bales of hay will stop quite a bit of the radiation."

As Jack spoke, Cliff tinkered with a transistor radio. When Jack finished, Cliff said, "We might find out something about what's happening out there if I could get this damned radio to work." He shook it vigorously in disgust.

"Are the batteries any good?"

"I just replaced them two weeks ago, and I haven't used them since," he responded. "Been running it on house current."

"Then forget it," Jack said. "The transistors were fried by

the same pulse that knocked out the lights and everything else."

Just then they heard a "hello" from someone in the distance. "That's Reuben," said Cliff. "Hello, Reuben! We're down here!"

After a few seconds, Reuben Cissell came lumbering down the ladder, followed by his wife, Clara. The mental and physical strain of the day had taken a toll that he could have ignored twenty years before. But even Reuben's bearish frame was not immune to the physiological changes of late middle age and the accompanying entry into the no-man's-land between muscle and fat. "Is there any room in the inn?" he asked, trying to catch his breath.

"You know there is, Reuben. Where the hell have you been? Marge went over to find you two hours ago," Cliff said.

"Me and Clara just walked six miles to get here. We was comin' back from her sister's place in Lebanon when' my truck just plumb broke down after that damned flash. So we just got out and walked."

"Before you come any further, Reuben," Hamilton said, "was there any dust settling out there?" He held up a strong flashlight and looked to see if any obvious particles had settled on Reuben's clothing.

"Not that I noticed, why?"

"We don't need any fallout contamination brought in here," Hamilton replied. "Better slip out of those clothes, wash off the exposed areas of your skin, and slip into a set of the extra clothes here. The same for you, Clara. We'll put your old clothes outside."

Reuben's ordinarily gruff demeanor was shaken. "Lord! Talk like that scares me, but I'll do as you say."

"Roseanna, grab that blanket over there and we'll make a makeshift change area here. The rest of you might as well get settled in. We're going to be here for a while," said Hamilton.

"Just how long *are* we likely to be in here?" Reuben asked.

"It depends. If the attacks continue, who knows? But if the only fallout we have to worry about is that coming from the attacks today, then we'll probably be able to come out after a couple of weeks, given standard fallout decay rates."

"Two weeks!" Marge exclaimed. The subtle glance she

shot Chris and the expression accompanying it made clear to Hamilton that the enmity she bore Chris was alive and was likely to surface soon in these close quarters.

Though it took some time for many at The Aerie to collect themselves after the initial flash on the horizon, they vigorously commenced carrying out their plan. Kurt and Larry dismounted the Kawasaki motorcycle from the back of Kurt's trailer, and Rogers took off on it to help round up the cattle that had been earmarked for the livestock shelter. Others did likewise with the chickens, goats, ducks, and hogs.

In a hill on the southern side of the farm, a small cave ran back two hundred feet through the Kentucky limestone. Though it was not large, a man of average height could walk erect through a hundred feet of it. The small stream which trickled through it made it too damp for human comfort, however, and this was the main reason the group had built the pole barn with its special "foundation." For the livestock, however, it was a reasonable and inexpensive alternative.

The cave had been provisioned with stores of feed, and two teenage boys volunteered to stay in it and care for the animals. A partially sandbagged entrance protected the animals in front.

After a half hour of effort, the animals were inside, and Rogers and several others headed back to the barn. When he walked up to several members who were talking nervously among themselves he said, "Everybody go ahead and take the potassium iodide pills."

The outsider whose appearance on the farm had irritated Rogers the night before asked, "The what?"

"Potassium iodide. It will saturate your thyroid so that it can't store any radioactive iodine that could be harmful later. We're probably safe enough from fallout in that shelter in any event. But just in case it's heavier than expected, taking those pills could make a significant difference."

As more of the group appeared around Rogers' camper, he continued. "I recommend that everybody stay close by and watch those radiacmeters. There's no point getting down to that shelter before we have to. We'll be sick of the damned place before this is over, I expect." He added with a sigh, "I need a beer."

Josh had been listening attentively to his father, and in response he went into the trailer and came out with a Coors in his hand and gave it to Kurt. "But what about Louisville, Dad? I mean, is it just *gone*?"

"Son, I'm afraid a direct hit would have destroyed a good portion of the city, and given the accuracy of missiles now, there's no reason to assume that the Russians didn't hit what they were aiming for," Rogers said, placing his hand on his son's shoulder. "One bomb, even a very large one, wouldn't have wiped out Louisville, but I expect many thousands of people were killed, son. I'd be lying if I told you otherwise."

Josh looked to the ground. "Jeez," he said slowly, "all my friends . . . and our home, Dad. What about our home?"

"I really have no idea. But you're getting to be a young man now, so I'm sure you can keep a stiff upper lip. I know it's difficult, though."

Kurt's expression of confidence helped diminish the boy's despondency. He sat down slowly on a camp stool beside the trailer door and contented himself with listening to the adults talking. Nevertheless, he couldn't help noticing the effects of his father's words on Jerry O'Connell, who was standing at the edge of the group. He realized that Jerry's father had probably been on the job in Louisville when the bomb detonated. Even from this distance he could see tears welling up in Jerry's eyes.

George Anderson walked up to the gathering, buckling the pistol belt around his bulging but firm waistline. "Two radiacmeters are working now and Bob and Jerry are watching them constantly. So far we've got nothing, but don't anyone wander off. Just hang loose around here, if anybody *can* hang loose at a time like this. When the light starts fading, the meters will probably pick up any fallout before you can see it."

Rogers sank to the step of his trailer. Through his mind raced images of what he imagined had occurred in Louisville, and what he imagined his brother Travis out in California might be going through. God help him, he thought. Dejectedly, he looked toward George Anderson, and drained the last few drops from his can of Coors. "George, I really think I'm gonna be needing another beer."

Tom O'Hara was still in a semidaze. When he arrived at his BMW in the club parking lot, he found that it wouldn't start even after several attempts.

While he continued his efforts with the ignition, a frail, elderly man in a new, but ill-fitting red polo shirt, white trousers and robin's-egg-blue golf hat leaned against the new Cadillac Coupe de Ville next to O'Hara's car and sobbed uncontrollably. And though he did not ask for any assistance, the man's eyes begged for help, or at least guidance.

O'Hara, however, had no time. Not for this man or anyone else. He was still half numb himself, and after giving up on his car, he struck off on foot. Alternately walking and jogging to his home in the Highlands, he began to regain some of his composure.

As he drew nearer, he noticed that the level of destruction appeared to increase. Homes sagged a little more with each block he passed, and the number of secondary fires seemed greater. Impromptu bucket brigades had formed near occasional streams and swimming pools as people came together to fight the spreading fires. Looting was in progress in a couple of areas.

On one street O'Hara passed he saw a woman whose home was missing a substantial portion of its roof. Every pane of glass in the house seemed shattered. The woman sang to herself and swept furiously at the debris scattered across her driveway. She had a detached, faraway air about her, and she obviously needed help. O'Hara didn't care. He was obsessed. He had to get back to *his* home and to *Cathy*, no matter what was happening to the rest of the world.

When O'Hara finally arrived at his street, Hilltop, just off Lexington Road near Cherokee Park, his reaction was one of horror. The houses were a shambles, two were afire, and debris was strewn everywhere.

After running to his home, a spacious Colonial two-story, he pulled up short, panting and gasping for breath, and stared numbly. The roof was buckled. Most of the paint on two sides of the house was blistered and peeling. The leaves on the large oak trees in the front yard were wilted and limp.

O'Hara stumbled to the front door and groped in his pockets for his keys. He realized then that he had left his entire key chain in the ignition of his car. To hell with it, he thought, and he walked over and crawled through the picture window, now minus its glass.

The Barrett's house across the street burned fiercely out of control and helped illuminate the room. Furniture was askew. The drapes hung in tatters. Shards from the windows were embedded in the plaster on the other side of the room.

O'Hara called out hesitantly for Cathy. He got no response. He was near the point of mental and physical exhaustion, but turned around and crawled out the window. His wife's boutique was a couple of miles away at most.

If he hurried, he could get there before it was completely dark. Several neighbors called out to him for help in fighting the blaze at the Barrett house. He turned away and began running to the heart of the battleground his city had become. As far as O'Hara was concerned, whether every house on the street burned was no damned concern of his.

When O'Hara finally arrived at Cathy's boutique on Bardstown Road near Bonnycastle Avenue, the building's appearance caused him to feel as if the bottom had fallen from his stomach. The destruction was much greater in this area. The buildings that were not actually flattened had suffered massive structural damage. The ceiling of the boutique had fallen in places. Heavy beams were scattered throughout. Racks of clothes lay helter-skelter. The front windows had blown inward, shredding the body of a person who could be identified only as male. The corpse seemed to float in a pool of coagulating blood.

Up and down the street several people moved in front of the buildings whose facades had hemorrhaged onto the pavement. A fire from the explosion of a leaking natural gas line burned ever brighter. "Dear God, somebody help me!" came a cry from within the rubble of a shop a few doors down, and a couple of teenage boys worked feverishly trying to extricate the victim as the fire inched closer. Another boy, totally unconcerned, proceeded down the street carrying in his arms a freshly acquired color television.

O'Hara forced aside the debris at the front of the store and then stepped over it. He called out for Cathy. He heard nothing. Was she here, or had he missed her as she was returning home? *That's it*! he thought. *She's on her way home*!

Then from the darkness at the back of the store, he heard a groan. With animal-like ferocity, manicured fingers more accustomed to jotting notes with a gold-filled Cross pen tore at the debris. Finally, O'Hara found his wife unconscious beneath the rubble.

O'Hara strained his eyes to examine her in the pale light. He found no puncture wounds or serious bleeding. His trembling hands paused gently on her abdomen as he thought of the twins she carried. He felt movement, thank God. Yet despite the lack of outward injuries, it was obvious that Cathy had been seriously hurt.

"It's okay, Cathy. We're going to make it!" *Dear sweet Jesus*, he thought, *don't let her die*!

As gently as possible, he picked her up and carried her outside to the street. With no ambulances running and with thousands upon thousands needing medical attention, it was obvious that if he didn't get Cathy to the hospital, she wouldn't get there at all. He laid her down on the sidewalk and contemplated his options.

St. Anthony's Hospital was the closest of the city's hospitals, but he felt certain that it must be in an area of even greater carnage. So his mind began to consider, and then dismiss, ways to get his wife to treatment at Baptist Hospital East, which seemed to be the better alternative. Her pregnancy, however, seriously complicated the matter.

O'Hara studied the rubble around him. An idea slowly came to him.

He quickly walked over to the debris at the front of the boutique and picked up two loose pine studs. From further back in the rubble he retrieved a decorative tapestry and brought it to the sidewalk.

He looked down the street and saw an ancient, overturned Volkswagen bus. A cheery yellow face and the hand-painted greeting on its side advised him to have a nice day. Just beyond the VW, he spotted a pickup truck with a camper-top. A hunch told him the truck was his best bet. He jogged over to it, peered in the back, and saw an army footlocker.

He tried to open the camper-top's rear door, but found it locked. Pulling a length of angle iron from the debris, he smashed the rear window and removed the footlocker. Luck was with him. Upon opening it, he found a rope and flashlight, whose batteries, though weak, were serviceable.

Returning to the studs and tapestry, O'Hara quickly constructed a makeshift stretcher and harness that made it possible for him to drag the litter behind him like an Indian travois. He carefully placed Cathy upon the stretcher, and twenty minutes after his arrival, O'Hara was on his way, pulling his wife on the improvised litter, looking for medical treatment.

Within this period, however, new fires had spread rapidly about the area, illuminating the streets with a brilliant orange glow almost as intense as daylight. Great blasts of hot air and cinders from the nuclear maelstrom assaulted him at every step. All along his route to the hospital, a cacophony of explosions, screams, and appeals for help by the damned met him on every block, almost as if he were on the poet Virgil's tour of hell.

The city's death rattle had clearly begun.

Through streets littered with fallen telephone poles, uprooted trees, overturned automobiles, and occasional corpses, O'Hara marched, gasping and laboring, his mouth coated with a heavy, phlegmy slime. He passed people in all manner of disarray and hysteria. Continuous cries of pain, anger and desperation met him on his meandering course through the rubble.

Hosts of survivors with myriad physical grotesqueries confronted him. They reached out to someone—anyone—hoping for assistance, aid, or comfort. Still he marched.

And as he marched through the mass grave that had once been his city, he saw that just as men had done from the earliest of times when they first organized and raised weapons in anger, even now on this, a nuclear battlefield, the living picked among the dead.

"Hang on, Cathy! We'll be at the hospital in no time!" he repeated a dozen times. And just as often he thought, *Dear God, don't let her die*!

At one point a fiftyish-looking, obese man with burned skin hanging from his face and arms, shoeless and clad only in torn and bloody boxer shorts, walked zombie-like directly down the street. As he walked he repeated over and over, "Jesus, Mary, and Joseph. Jesus, Mary and Joseph." He would have walked directly into O'Hara had O'Hara not stepped aside at the last second.

Further on, a young woman, perhaps in her twenties, dabbed carefully with a wet cloth at the burns on two young children in the yard in front of a collapsed home. One of them lay supine on a blanket shaking uncontrollably with chills, and the other, his hair singed and face blistered, sat upright staring blankly, either too numb or in too much pain to cry. Although he could not be sure, he noticed that the two children might well have been twins. O'Hara continued his march.

"We're gonna make it, Cathy," he gasped. *Oh God, please help her!*

Despite the endless array of injuries of every conceivable description, among the most bizarre were those received by two teenage girls who had, perhaps, cut school that afternoon to take advantage of one of their first opportunities to sunbathe in the warm spring sun. Etched on their nude bodies were the patterns of their swimsuits. The dark material had absorbed more of the heat from the bomb's flash, and had transferred it to the skin underneath, leaving horrid imprints. The girls walked grimly and silently past O'Hara on their way to the hospital, totally unconcerned about their nakedness.

A little further down the street he passed a church day-care center in flames. The children had escaped unscathed from the building, perhaps having been in the basement when the shock wave passed. They now stood nearby, confused, helpless, and terrified as the flames consumed the structure. Two dozen of the preschoolers seemed to be crying out, bleating in unison for mothers who, if they were still alive, were undoubtedly trying to fight their way across the city to them.

After a tortuous journey through the debris-clogged streets of a city gone mad, O'Hara finally made it to the hospital. Dry saliva caked his mouth, and blood from the rope's heavy abrasions soaked his shirt. Though the litter had helped him considerably in carrying Cathy, the physical effort was clearly beyond anything he had ever endured in his entire life.

The scene that met his eyes upon his arrival, however, stopped him cold. The hospital seemed an island among a sea of dead and dying. The numbers seeking treatment had completely overwhelmed the precious few medical professionals who had remained at, or who had returned to, the hospital.

The suffering about O'Hara was a nightmare. All across the grassy lawn around the hospital, victim after victim cried out for assistance. Moaning, groaning, mewling, screaming. A din of pain and suffering.

The lights from Baptist Hospital East's emergency generators provided some illumination to the area otherwise lit only by the orange-black sky of the burning city and the beams of hundreds of flashlights and gas lanterns of family members and friends who attended to the injured. His nostrils were assaulted by a combination of vomit, excrement, and Coleman lantern fuel. He fought a strong gagging reflex. The panorama of pain and suffering, of compound, comminuted fractures, lacerations, and burns was more than O'Hara could absorb.

Several aides, orderlies, and volunteer stretcher bearers moved through the crowd with the injured. Like O'Hara's, many of the stretchers had been improvised from whatever materials were available.

O'Hara removed the tight harness from throbbing shoulders which felt like bloody pulp. He sank to the ground and patted Cathy's hand, saying, "I'll be right back, sweetheart. I'll get a doctor, just you wait," as if she might be going somewhere.

O'Hara spotted a middle-aged man in a business suit walking hurriedly through the crowd with a small black leather medical bag in his hand. O'Hara wobbled after him.

Finally catching up with the man, O'Hara gripped his arm firmly.

"Let go of my arm!" the man cried, his teeth clenched.

"You're a doctor, right?"

"Yes, I am and I have to get to O.R. Now let me go!"

"But my wife needs help badly. For God's sake, Doctor, *please!*"

"I'm sorry. I'll see her when they bring her in. I can't treat people out here."

O'Hara stiffened and his face turned granite. "Do you know who the fuck you're talking to? I'm Tom O'Hara!"

A puzzled expression came to the doctor's face. "Is that supposed to mean something to me?"

"Goddam it! I'm Don Burns's right-hand man, and if my wife doesn't get treated—and treated now—I'll have your *ass* when this is over!"

"*Now I remember*," the man sneered. "You're the sonofabitch on the radio who told everybody there was nothing to worry about this morning. Well, get the fuck out of my way. I've got a lot of people who listened to you waiting for what help I can give them." He broke free of O'Hara's grasp and started for the hospital.

O'Hara grabbed at the man and attempted to stop him once again. An unexpected roundhouse punch sent O'Hara rolling to the ground, and then to painless darkness.

When O'Hara regained consciousness, the scene around him had not changed. He made it to his feet, and looked about, totally disoriented. Then he panicked. He couldn't remember where he'd left Cathy.

O'Hara stumbled through the crowd that stretched outward as far as he could see. Most people were indifferent to his problem, or too preoccupied with their own difficulties to pay any attention to O'Hara. Others, mostly the injured, pulled at his pants legs or shirt, begging for help.

After what might have been a half hour's frantic search O'Hara once again found Cathy. She was lying there just as he had left her. He bent down and lovingly brushed at her blood-soaked hair, tears of relief welling up in his eyes. His voice cracked as he said, "The doctor's on the way, honey."

Dear God, don't let her die! She's done nothing to deserve this! Just grant me this. And if you won't do it for me, then do it for her. If it will help, take me, God! Take me instead of her!

Finally realizing that it could take days for Cathy to receive attention, and sensing that the skies threatened rain, he reluctantly decided to take his wife home for the night.

The rain began as O'Hara arrived at the house. He unharnessed himself and reached down to check on Cathy. Her skin was unnaturally cold. He quickly checked again. And the awful realization hit home. O'Hara slumped to the steps and sat immobile, tears rolling down his cheeks, mixing with the rain. He stared numbly into the subsiding flames of the house across the street.

This can't be real. Dear God, how could you let this happen? Cathy never did anything to deserve this. And the babies. Why them, God? Why? Why . . . ?

As he sat there in the depths of despair and bewilderment at the day's events and his terrible loss, he was aroused by sounds emanating from the house. O'Hara immediately froze and waited for a moment to identify the noise. Again he heard something—or someone.

Though well past the point of exhaustion, he summoned from some untapped reservoir the strength to hoist himself through the picture window, and he glided silently, as if on cat's paws, into the kitchen.

He paused again, and after a moment, heard someone coming up the basement steps. O'Hara groped in the darkness, but he could not find anything that might serve as a weapon before the intruder was through the door.

From the reflected glare of a large dry-cell lantern in one of the intruder's hands, O'Hara saw a man of about forty years of age holding two large bags of groceries. In one of his hands, O'Hara saw a very large Bowie-style hunting knife.

"What the hell do you think you're doing with that?" O'Hara hissed.

The stranger drew up short, startled by the unanticipated presence of someone else in the home. He quickly got control of himself, however, and said slowly to O'Hara, who now stood between him and the side door of the house, "Things are going to be tough for a while, friend, and I need this stuff as much as you do. You can either get out of my way, or I can go right out over the top of you." He punctuated his words with flicks of the knife.

The intruder's words galvanized O'Hara. He lunged to the wall beside the stove and grabbed the small fire extinguisher. In an instant he had it ready and blasted his surprised adversary in the face.

The man reeled backward and dropped the sacks, sending the canned goods bobbling across the floor. O'Hara snatched away the knife, and in a heartbeat, he plunged the knife into the blinded man's ribs. The stranger immediately crumpled to the floor. O'Hara followed, wildly plunging the knife again and again into the man's chest and abdomen. Chest! Abdomen! Chest! Abdomen! each blow coming harder than the last.

O'Hara did not remember how many times he actually stabbed the man. There was too much satisfaction in venting his rage and pain on this person who would dare violate the sanctity of his home, who would now dare take from O'Hara the very essentials of life.

After finally satiating his need for reprisal, O'Hara slumped against the door, drenched in blood like a butcher at a packing house. For some strange reason he glanced at the Rolex on his wrist. Twelve o'clock midnight.

Finally, after a few minutes without moving, he pulled himself slowly to his feet. He went to the front door, unbolted it, and brought Cathy's body inside to the relative protection of the basement, reverently spreading a blanket over her. This done, he mercifully lapsed into a comalike sleep beside her.

Black Friday had ended.

Saturday, May 18th: The Second Day

O'Hara awoke about midmorning. The pale imitation of sunlight shone through the basement window on his face. After rolling over and wriggling about to avoid the gray glare, he peered through eyes still half pasted together from sleep. He stared at his odd surroundings, and for a few seconds was completely disoriented. As he extended his leg, he touched the stiff body of Cathy lying under the blanket— and then it all came back to him.

Unfortunately, the nightmare had been real.

O'Hara sat up and took inventory of himself. The shoulders of his shirt were soaked with blood from the rope's bite. His hands and forearms were also caked with blood, and the remainder of his clothing was spattered heavily with the red-brown evidence of the incident in the kitchen.

He slowly stood up and stretched his arms and legs. He felt as if a steamroller had passed over him. Though his trim athletic frame would ordinarily have been described as fit, muscles and tendons more accustomed to sitting behind a desk for the better part of each day were now telling him in the most painful way that the physical exertions of the previous night were beyond their limits.

O'Hara looked at his wife stretched out before him. He did not have the courage to touch her, or even to lift the blanket from her just now. He trudged haltingly up the steps. God, how he ached all over.

Sprawled across the kitchen floor among the cans of food was his adversary of the previous night. The man's glassy-gray eyes seemed frozen. His face had a matching gray, waxy appearance. A stiff tongue bulged from the corner of his mouth. Until yesterday, O'Hara had never seen a dead person outside a funeral home. This corpse lying in the coagulating muck was a far cry from the "dead" people he had seen on television and in the movies. The entire kitchen stank of blood and emptied bowels. He stepped carefully so as not to get any of the mess on his shoes.

Out the window, O'Hara could see the dark pall that hung low over the city from the countless fires his nostrils told him must still be raging. The Barrett house across the street was now only a mound of smoking coals and ashes. Fortunately, the fire had not communicated to the adjacent homes.

As O'Hara turned and passed the dead man again, he paused to examine him more closely. He noticed a wedding ring on the man's left hand. He squatted down and rolled the man over just enough to pull the wallet from his trousers. Opening the wallet, he found several credit cards —MasterCard, Visa, American Express—an AAA Club membership card, a Lion's Club membership card and a healthy supply of business cards identifying him as the district manager for Prudential Life Insurance.

He examined the wallet's contents as if they were lab specimens. He studied a picture of the dead man with his wife and three children—a daughter, perhaps ten, a son, maybe eight, and another daughter, maybe five. Suddenly, it hit him. My God. He recognized these kids. They lived a block down the street. The Hoffmans. Or was it the Hauptmans? He had passed them dozens of times in his car. The picture was a couple of years old, but it was the same kids. They were, O'Hara thought, still waiting for their father to return to them. He wondered if they were even now praying for his safety.

So this was why the intruder had been so determined to risk his life for a couple of sacks of canned goods, he thought. Yet he had been prepared to preserve his own family at the expense of the survival of the family whose home he was robbing. The bastard.

But as O'Hara continued to study the photograph, he slowly concluded what it had all meant there in the kitchen last night, and what it would probably mean to him and to everyone else in the months ahead: survival of the fittest. Hoffman knew it last night. And now O'Hara knew it.

From this day forward, he determined, Tom O'Hara could count on no one but himself. Not his friends. Not his God. No one.

O'Hara rose to his feet. No longer interested in its contents, he dropped the wallet on the dead man's chest.

Through his mind there suddenly passed for the first time a concern about fallout. Radioactive poison could be doing terrible but unsensed damage to him at that very moment, for all he knew. He could be marked for an early death already. But then, you could see fallout coming down, couldn't you? He wasn't sure.

He quickly turned and went back into the living room and found Friday morning's newspaper. He thumbed rapidly through it and found the section that had been added, compliments of Charlie Brighton. He took it downstairs with him and studied it for a few minutes. One plan, in particular, looked feasible.

From his workshop, O'Hara pulled two sawhorses over to a corner of the basement. Returning to the workshop, he located an old door, which he then brought out and placed across the sawhorses. Nearby were several boxes of books from his study. Cathy had asked him to remove them a couple of days earlier to permit her to turn the study into a nursery for the twins. Atop the door he stacked the books as high as he thought prudent, and then he continued stacking books around the floor on the sides so as to create walls on a boxlike house, a cocoon of books.

O'Hara then went to the water heater in the corner, drained enough water to fill the plastic milk jug he found on a nearby shelf, and put the water and a few cans of food in his shelter. All was ready—except one thing that could not wait.

Summoning all the courage within him, O'Hara carried Cathy's stiff body outside. After a half hour's effort, he had a shallow grave prepared for her in the backyard, and he reverently placed her body in it. He paused for a minute and said his last farewell to her. He considered saying a suitable prayer, but decided against it. With hot tears painting his cheeks, he tenderly kissed her on the forehead, and slowly closed the grave. Dear Cathy would know well enough what to say to her Creator when she saw Him. As for O'Hara, he had nothing to say to Him at all. Not now. Not ever.

Returning inside, he grabbed an old canvas tarp from his workshop, wrapped up the dead man's body, and carried it outside to the street as if he were carrying out so much garbage. Besides not wanting to spend the time and effort to bury the intruder, the thought of burying him near Cathy reminded him too much of a cemetery plot for husband and wife.

O'Hara returned downstairs to his shelter and crawled in. He had no idea how long he would remain there. He had no idea how long radiation would persist—if indeed there were any radiation. Maybe he would be dead in three days, or maybe the fallout had blown in another direction. For now, however, he would simply stay here for as long as he could tolerate the confinement, protected, as it were, by the likes of William Shakespeare, John Steinbeck, James Michener, and Ayn Rand.

As the hours grew into days, Tom O'Hara left his shelter only to draw more water from the water heater and to relieve himself. During the period of silence and darkness, the events of that terrible day and awful night raced through his memory, careening through the corridors of his mind. The vivid images carried him down in an emotional tailspin, down a swirling vortex to a moral and emotional abyss at the ragged edges of his soul, as he relived the events over and over again.

"If you want to take the moral responsibility for lying to all those people out there . . . you go ahead and lie to them . . . if you can live with the consequences. . . ."

"Nothing to be alarmed about whatsoever. . . ."

"Tom, are you ready for this? Maybe you'd better sit down. Dr. Spalding says we're going to have twins!"

"We're gonna make it, Cathy! We're gonna make it!"

"You're the sonofabitch on the radio who told everyone there was nothing to worry about. . . ."

Slowly, out of the emotional maelstrom, O'Hara found a way to deal with the events, and, in particular, the incident in the kitchen that night. In doing so, he resolved how he would change to meet the world which now ran amok.

F. Thomas O'Hara, like the society of which he had been a part, was no more. They were both gone, and, quite possibly, would never return. He would adapt to his new environment, or he would die. And goddam it, *he* wasn't going to die. At least not for a very long time.

What this decision would mean to O'Hara and to the rest of the world would only be seen when he emerged in the days after Armageddon.

PART THREE

O brave new world,
That has such people in't!

—Shakespeare
The Tempest, V, i

FRIDAY, MAY 31st:
The Fifteenth Day

"Anybody home?" came the voice from a distance, barely audible to Hamilton as he sat on his makeshift bed.

He bolted to his feet, and yelled, "Yeah! We're in here!" He scrambled up the ladder and poked his head outside the barn. He found Lieutenant Ackerson and a driver standing beside a jeep in front of the farmhouse. Hamilton immediately began walking toward them, enjoying the opportunity to stretch his legs after that godawful period of tedium and inactivity.

He looked about him. The sky was a heavy gray and the temperature cool. Nevertheless, it was hardly the sort of change to the weather that he and others had worried about—so far at least.

"What's the situation?" he asked, thankful to see someone—anyone—other than those with whom he had been confined for the last two weeks or so.

"All clear, sir," Ackerson said as he saluted Hamilton, "or at least clear enough. We never did get that much fallout around here. Could have been the winds, and it could have been that there weren't that many surface bursts. Whatever it was, it means that we're in pretty good condition. We have some residual radiation at one tenth rad per hour. Given the fact that both sides have been trying to blow the planet away, it's not so bad."

Rubbing at the two weeks' accumulation of stubble on his face, Hamilton responded, "If that's the case, I'd still want everyone not to overdo it, but there's no reason we couldn't get out of these damned holes for necessary work. Got any news on the war?"

"Yes, sir, but it's not good," replied Ackerson. "From the limited facts we've been able to pick up at this point, Louisville, Lexington, and Indianapolis were all hit badly on Black Friday. There's a lot of conflict from the stories people are telling as they come straggling in, but it seems clear that Frankfort and state headquarters were untouched by anything except the fallout. Regardless, we haven't had any contact with anyone in authority at state level so far."

"But what about the Russians? What kind of damage did we do to them? I sure hope the bastards paid for this."

"It looks like both sides let 'er rip, if some of the reports we've heard are accurate. There were initial reports of tactical nuclear weapons being used against the Russians after they crossed the Iraqi border. I would ordinarily have assumed that it would have been us using them since we couldn't have stopped them any other way, but one story going around has it that the Iraqis got hold of a couple of nuclear devices on the black market, like Colonel Khaddafy did awhile back, and then used them on the Russian 'infidels' who had sold out to the Iranians for a few barrels of oil. The result did not sit particularly well with 'Ivan,' whatever the source of the bombs was, and all hell broke loose. No matter who used them, the Russians apparently thought *we* had nuked them, or maybe had given them to the Iraqis, and that was enough."

"And what about around the country?"

"From the minimal news that's available, we took a real shellacking. Washington and several major cities were hit, or so I've heard, as well as most worthwhile military targets. Whatever's left of much of Europe is supposed to be in Russian hands," Ackerson said, his tone growing more serious. "People who have survived are still dug in in many places, waiting for the fallout in their areas to drop off. We were just a helluva lot luckier than most."

"So we're down to a tenth of a rad an hour now?" Hamilton was trying to assimilate the information he was receiving from Ackerson.

"Yes, sir, and that's very acceptable, at least when you consider the circumstances. It's decreasing by the hour, but the meters are being continuously monitored. Should the winds shift and radiation levels start increasing, we'll know immediately. Why, we could still get another salvo from the Russians, since there's no word about any armistice. Maybe both sides are just licking their wounds between rounds."

"What's the situation in Bardstown?" Hamilton asked,

shifting the conversation to what was expected to be his most immediate concern in the next few weeks.

"I was only there briefly before coming out here, sir, but it's not so good now, and apparently it's getting worse," responded Ackerson. "Not only are there still all those people who came out before the bomb hit, but it looks like there's an avalanche of new arrivals who have come out from the city. Probably trying to get away from the target area in case there's a second attack. Many of them are injured, and most of them have brought precious little with them, just what they could carry on their backs, or push or pull in a cart or the like. There are so goddam many city people . . ." Ackerson cut short his words, and then turned a bright crimson as he remembered who his listener was. "Sorry, sir, I, well, I just meant that . . ."

Hamilton shot him a withering glance. "I know *exactly* what you meant, Lieutenant." The muscles in his neck tensed noticeably as he glared at the young man. "I want to clean up here first, and then I want to go into town to check on the situation. Can you get a vehicle back out here in four hours or so?"

"No problem, sir," replied Ackerson, glad that the subject of the conversation had shifted.

"Good. Then I'll take care of several things here, and see you later." Without waiting for a reply, he turned and walked briskly back to the barn. Ackerson saluted awkwardly and departed with his driver. Roseanna, Cliff, and Chris were standing at the barn door as he returned.

"Well?" Roseanna said.

"It's safe enough to come out for necessary things, although it would be better to sleep here and to stay inside for periods when we're not occupied. Given the amount of work before us, those idle periods will be brief, I expect. We made out very well on the fallout business, though. That lieutenant just confirmed what I already knew. If we had had all that much radiation, the less protected cattle and hogs would all be dead by now. As it is, we only lost those that were completely unprotected." Hamilton then began to fill in the group on the national situation.

After hearing all that Hamilton had to tell them, Chris said, "I ought to see about getting to the hospital. I expect that they are overrun by now. Those 'goddam city people' your lieutenant friend was complaining about will probably be needing lots of medical attention."

"I'm sure you're right," replied Hamilton. He placed the sleeve of his shirt to his face, and then wrinkled his nose in an exaggerated fashion. "I suggest that a quick trip inside the house to the bathtub would be in order. If we take turns running inside, it shouldn't take long. Cliff, how about the two of us heating some water so everyone can get rid of the godawful grime of the past couple of weeks."

"I'm with you, brother!"

"Oh, God!" cried Chris. "My kingdom for a few inches of warm water! I've never felt this dirty in my whole life!" The prospect of escaping Marge's company seemed equally delightful.

"I'll call the others out for a stretch," said Cliff, "and then we'll get started on that water. We'll have ourselves a regular bucket brigade."

After heating and carrying several barrels of water to fill and refill the two bathtubs in the house several times, Hamilton was among the last to have his opportunity to soak away the grit and grime acquired during the confinement. The activity gave him the opportunity to reflect on the period that had been as difficult as any he had ever experienced.

Anxiety about the intensity of the danger outside, and the intolerable boredom in that lower room had been very wearing on him. After three days of cabin fever, Cliff made a dash to the house, and returned with an armful of paperback novels, playing cards, and games. The books helped for a while, but even as Hamilton strained by the light of the dim kerosene lamp to read of fictional characters in faraway places, the dominant question in his mind was whether these characters, or at least their real-life counterparts, were still alive and whether these places still existed. In a way, it was like the old movies he would see on television when he was younger, and then wonder whether any of the actors were still alive. The thoughts took the pleasure out of the escapism the books might otherwise have provided.

But now, all that was past, and there was much that needed to be done.

Hamilton came into the bathroom with the last two five-gallon buckets of warm water just as Roseanna was finishing with Jennifer's hair. "There you go, young lady. Now you be a good girl and go back to the barn. It's *my* turn now," Roseanna said. As Jennifer picked up her soiled clothes and left, Hamilton poured the water into the tub.

"Don't hog the tub for two hours, Cleopatra," he said, smiling. I'll be back with some more for myself just as quickly as I can get it hot enough."

He was out of the house when suddenly he stopped, turned around, and went back to the bathroom. He threw open the door, catching Roseanna nude.

She quickly yanked a pair of slacks to her chest. "What are you doing?" she asked after she realized who it was who had burst in on her.

"Well, we're the only people in the place now, and it just occurred to me that there is great wisdom in the old adage, 'Save water. Shower with a friend.' How about it?"

"John Robert Hamilton, you horny bastard! Don't you think I know what you're up to?" she said with mock determination. She glanced quickly out into the hallway to make sure that everyone else had returned to the barn.

"After two weeks in the Black Hole of Calcutta, ma'm, you might as well give up. You'll need an army to protect your virtue."

After quickly doffing his own clothes, he slid into the tub with Roseanna. "It may be a tight fit in here," he said, "but I expect this is going to be the best bath either of us has ever had."

As the warm water produced its relaxing effects, both of them sank back, enjoying the opportunity to be alone together for the first time since the attack. "Sweetheart, how is anyone ever going to deal with all of those people in Bardstown," she asked, slowly sponging her forearm as she lay back.

"That's a very good question. The situation is bound to be a mess like none anyone has ever seen before. I expect that food, or at least, the kind of food most people are used to, will be in short supply pretty fast. Keeping law and order under these circumstances is going to be damned hard."

"But surely there's enough food on these farms for months."

Working the soap to a lather between his hands, Hamilton put the bar down and began running the lather up and down her leg. "I can't say there isn't. But probably not the kind of food that will satisfy many people. There'll be a shortage of vegetables, since farmers around here generally grow vegetables for their own needs only, and not much more. Most of the stuff we eat comes from California and Arizona and such places. You can forget all of that now. And seeds will be in short supply for filling the gap. Regardless, it will take several weeks for most vegetable crops to be harvested, and then with what there is, there will be no way other than by drying to preserve much of the harvest. Even Marge has to buy new rubber rings each year for her canning, with what little she does. If the electricity isn't restored, freezing is out also. So with much of the livestock being dead, people are going to get used to eating wheat, corn, soybeans, and whatever else they can come across."

"But what about all that stuff you used to hear about the surpluses. I mean, where is all that cheese and nonfat dry milk and such?"

"This country may still have lots of it, but is sure isn't anywhere near enough to do us any good. I expect that all the surplus grain, cheese, and other things that Uncle Sam has been storing will be sitting right where it has been and won't be seen around here. Transportation problems will be too damned great. Maybe somebody should have thought about that before, but there's not much we can do about it now. But to hell with food," he said as he slipped his hand very slowly up between her thighs to the thick, auburn hair between them. "Who wants to talk about grain and cheese at a time like this? Let's talk about something a little more personal, which we haven't been able to talk about for the last two weeks."

After some maneuvering, he was able to pull her gently up on top of his thighs. He cupped her breast in his hand and kissed her. Roseanna responded by pressing herself against his chest, letting her hands wander up and down his back, arousing him even further.

Hamilton had been right. It really was the best bath either of them ever had.

What seemed to be the sound of human activity nearby caused O'Hara to peer out between the books to the basement room. Did this sound mean that it was safe to come out now? He wondered whether he should risk the exposure and make contact with this person who might have knowledge of the situation.

It didn't take him long to resolve the question in the affirmative. He really wasn't sure how many days he had been in his self-imposed confinement. The days seemed to blur together when he was at the peak of his emotional roller-coaster ride. Slowly, as he came back to complete, or at least more complete control of himself, he became more and more oriented to time and the passage of each day. O'Hara "guestimated" that it was now twelve to fifteen days after the blast, though he could not be sure.

He considered each day that passed without any obvious signs of radiation sickness a victory. He had heard that the faster the first signs appeared, the worse the chances were of recovery. So far, so good. What he could be very sure of now, however, was that he could not stand confinement much longer.

O'Hara shoved a box of books aside and hesitantly emerged. He stood up and arched his back, stretching muscles that had been unused for too long. Slowly, he mounted the steps and looked out the kitchen window to determine the source of the noise that had aroused him. A neighbor, Joe Klinger, along with his fifteen-year-old son, was standing in his backyard and cutting wood.

After considering whether it was a good idea to go out and talk with Klinger, O'Hara finally opened the door and walked outside, squinting and holding up his hand to shield his eyes from the unaccustomed brightness.

"Tom!" Klinger exclaimed as he stopped in the middle of a thrust with a bow saw. "We gave you up for dead!" Klinger, a pale, hatchetfaced man around forty-five, walked over to the fence separating the two yards. His son followed. "We figured that you were probably dead like so many others around here. A lot of people came straggling in within a day or so after it happened, but the others—well, I guess that they won't ever be coming back."

"I made it. I've been holed up in the basement. I was worried about the fallout," O'Hara replied in a dull monotone.

"As far as anyone has been able to find out, there hasn't

been too much radiation from the blast here. At least that's what somebody said. What we got was mostly the stuff drifting in from the west. We've been keeping to the basement, though. No use in taking unnecessary risks. Kevin and I came out to cut a few pieces of firewood. We've been cooking on the Franklin stove in the family room downstairs. This wood's too green and not worth a crap, but it'll burn if you put it with enough kindling. Unfortunately, the kindling is from the new bedroom furniture we just bought." Realizing that O'Hara had not mentioned Cathy, Klinger asked, "Tom, where's Cathy?"

"Dead." O'Hara's response was terse and without any apparent emotion.

"Aw, Jesus, Tom. I'm really sorry." Klinger placed his hand on his son's shoulder and said softly, "I guess we were damned lucky, although I'm still awfully worried about my brothers and their families. No way to find out now . . ."

"Have you been coming out very often?" O'Hara interrupted, refusing to let the conversation dwell on the loss of loved ones, his or anyone else's.

"Only a few times before this. Like you, I guess, we didn't want to take any extra chances on this radiation. Maybe we shouldn't even be here now. I don't know if the guy we talked to before knew what he was talking about. With the radio not working, we can't be certain. But God, Tom, I really am sorry about Cathy."

O'Hara looked silently about the neighborhood in a matter-of-fact way, slowly taking inventory of the damage. The trees appeared lifeless with their leaves shriveled and dried. The buckled roofs, blistered walls, and smashed window panes gave the neighborhood a curious ghost town effect that would have been completely unimaginable just two weeks before. "Have there been any problems other than the fallout?"

Klinger turned to his son. "Kevin, go on over there and finish cutting that piece of wood." After the boy was out of earshot, he said, "Tom, there's a dead guy wrapped in a tarp out by the street. At least what's left of him. Christ, the guy's cut up like you wouldn't believe. No nuclear bomb did *that*, I can tell you."

"Really?"

"Yeah. I haven't told any of the family yet. No need to

have them any more worried. I also think I heard three gunshots last night. Did you?"

O'Hara shook his head in response. "Well, anyway," continued Klinger, "I'm pretty sure that they were gunshots. This morning I heard what might've been another one, but I'm less sure about that one. Not very likely that it was a car backfiring. Very few cars are moving around. Could be we're in for serious problems if this is a preview of coming attractions. Some people are sure to be getting desperate for food in the next few days, if they aren't already. We're okay though, we—"

Klinger stopped short as he sensed for the first time that the man standing before him was very different from the neighbor he had known just two weeks before. The cold detachment and aloofness were not typical of him at all. Of course, it was probably just the loss of Cathy, but the change in O'Hara compelled him to draw up short as a person might when he entered a room and first noticed that something familiar was missing, though he could not be sure exactly what it was. Whatever was missing in O'Hara, however, made Klinger feel as if he would be well-advised to withdraw. "Aw, listen," Klinger said. "We've got to get going. Kevin, grab those logs there and come on." Looking back at O'Hara, though trying to hide his suspicion, he said, "We'll see you in a few days or so. It'll probably be safe to come out for good, assuming, God forbid, that we don't get hit with another nuke. And again, I'm really sorry to hear about Cathy. She was such a nice woman, a really wonderful human being."

Klinger and his son returned to their house quickly. As he entered the door, Klinger turned to watch O'Hara walk slowly back to his house. Something very strange here, Klinger thought. Strange, indeed.

O'Hara walked into his kitchen and sat down at the table. He began to consider the situation before him. With the food in the refrigerator and freezer spoiled, he had perhaps another week to ten days' supply of food in the house. Cathy had been a mediocre cook at best, and other than meats and frozen foods, they had never made a practice of keeping large quantities of food at home. As he considered where he might find food in the future, he decided that the city wasn't the place to be when there was a food shortage, and there surely would be a food shortage now. The stains on the kitchen floor from the incident that first night were an indication to him of what the future might mean to those who had food and those who didn't.

It became clear that his city was a complex, and in the end, a very vulnerable society where people had lived and worked to provide their needs only indirectly. Like most of its inhabitants, he had worked for cash and exchanged the cash for goods and commodities. And one of the most important of these was food. This city now, or what was left of it, would now be producing precious little food or providing the few opportunities to earn anything of value to exchange for it. The prospect of trying to grow sufficient food in his small yard was absurd, and the likelihood of protecting it from others was probably equally absurd. Whereas before, in his city, he had perceived himself master of all he surveyed, now he felt as vulnerable as anyone—more so, perhaps. And Klinger's remark about another nuke coming wasn't lost on him, either.

O'Hara walked into the dining room still preoccupied with his problem. He looked to the street and saw two men and a woman standing on the lawn four houses away deep in conversation. Apparently they weren't overly concerned about fallout. Maybe like Klinger had said, there wasn't that much of it. The pack of five or six neighborhood dogs running down the street was certainly oblivious to any danger. How long had they been outside?

O'Hara turned from the window and came to a decision. He went quickly downstairs and pulled from a closet an old pack frame that he had not used for five years. In the next half hour he found a sleeping bag, a canteen, as much food as he could carry in the pack, and several miscellaneous articles he felt might be useful. Chief among them was the intruder's large Bowie knife.

After getting everything in order, O'Hara looked in the bathroom commode's tank, but decided he didn't like the looks of the water. He went downstairs again, drained more of the water heater's contents and carried it upstairs to the bathroom where he took a sponge bath, removing the stench from himself as well as he could.

He reached into the medicine cabinet and grabbed a can of shaving cream. He squirted out a gob of lather and smeared it over the heavy stubble that was just beginning to have the makings of a nice beard.

Suddenly, he stopped. He stared at himself in the mirror. After a minute's contemplation of the strange man's reflection, he thought better of the idea and rinsed off the shaving cream.

Walking to the bedroom, he passed the framed poster Cathy had given him on his birthday over a decade earlier. Two naked lovers stood silhouetted on a beach, staring at the sunrise. The caption, though dated and clichéed, was right. The first day of the rest of his life.

Once in the bedroom, he glanced briefly at the wedding pictures of Cathy and himself atop the chest of drawers. A dried carnation was taped to the glass in the frame. To the side was a picture of Cathy he had taken at Montego Bay, and before it was a favorite shell she had brought back with her. He thought for a moment and then slipped the shell into his pocket.

He pulled from the closet his twelve-gauge Remington 870 pump shotgun, which he hadn't used since that duck-hunting trip to Western Kentucky a few years ago. After rummaging around the shelves in the closet, he found the box of no. 4 shotgun shells. This was a start, he thought. It occurred to him that if the intruder the first night had come this well armed, *he* might be lying down there in the workshop now instead of that fellow.

O'Hara took the gun out to his garage where he had another small workbench set up.

He took apart the shotgun and removed the wooden plug from the tubular magazine. The plug had limited the gun to three shells, keeping it in compliance with the state game laws. He now wanted five shells in that Remington at all times. There would be no legal limit in this new world.

Next he placed the thirty-inch, full-choke barrel in the jaws of the small vise. He picked up a hacksaw from the bench and replaced the worn blade in it. He carefully placed the saw to the richly blued barrel of the fine sporting arm and began. The cold, sharp teeth rhythmically cut and devoured the gray steel beneath.

After considerable effort, O'Hara finally cut the barrel to a deadly twenty inches in length, cylinder bore. O'Hara wouldn't be hunting ducks any more.

He then reassembled and loaded the weapon. He rapidly ejected the shells, checking for malfunctions. It worked perfectly.

As the shells hit the floor one after the other, he caught a glimpse of himself in the mirror of an old vanity standing against the far wall of the garage. O'Hara reloaded, and then paused for a moment to consider his image in the mirror.

He stared at the man before him. Snug-fitting denims, cotton open-necked shirt, hunting vest, leather high-topped boots—and deadly weapon in hand.

As if in response to some silent command, he suddenly brought the shotgun to waist level, and began jacking shells in and out of the chamber, pointing the weapon directly at the reflection.

After ejecting the last round, he scooped up the shells on the floor and replaced them in the magazine. When he exited the garage, he suddenly spun around and fired a blast through the mirror. The ounce-and-a-half of lead shot crashed through it, shattering the image into a thousand pieces of crystalline shrapnel. The wall behind exploded into the yard beyond in a shower of lead, splinters, and shards of glass.

O'Hara strode forcefully from the garage into the house. He placed his pack on his back, stepped outside, and struck off at a determined pace, not once bothering to look back.

As O'Hara headed out toward the country, one thought dominated him. No matter what the future held, he would be a *survivor*. And at all costs.

Hamilton and Chris were ready to go by the time the jeep rolled up in front of the house. They hopped in and were quickly on their way to town for the first time since the attack. Hamilton looked around him as he traveled, just as a person might after returning home from a lengthy trip out of town or an extended stay in the hospital, more observant and sometimes more appreciative of that which is around him.

Until he arrived on the outskirts of town, there was nothing all that unusual about the appearance of things. There were a number of dead cattle along the way, and perhaps not as many birds or other wildlife as usual. This certainly bothered him. However, all things considered, there was little visible evidence around Bardstown that a cataclysmic event had taken place between two great super-powers trying to eradicate each other.

As Hamilton's jeep moved into Bardstown, it was obvi-ous that the little city was overrun and bursting at the seams. "Jesus, where are we going to stack all of these people," Hamilton said to no one in particular.

"I ain't got any idea, sir," the driver, Spec. 4th Class Dennis Cochran, responded. "They've already packed the schools and every church and public building in town. Lots of folks have taken in as many people as they can handle, but they still keep coming. The problem with taking people in is that then you feel responsible for seeing to it that they're fed, and there's only so much food. There's a limit you know, but what can you do, and how can you stop the flood of people?"

The young soldier was right. The crowds on the streets reminded Hamilton of the street festivals he had attended in Louisville. Surprisingly, Hamilton did not see on the faces of most of the people the desperation he'd anticipated. Most exhibited no outward sign of emotion that he could observe. Perhaps there was a feeling of being grateful for being alive after all they had come through. Regardless, he wondered just how long this state of relative calm would prevail.

Tapping the young driver on the soldier, Chris asked, "Are there a lot of badly injured people coming in?"

"Well, ma'am," Cochran said, as he swerved slightly to miss a rider on horseback, "it sure doesn't take many people to swamp that small hospital we've got, so you could say we've got way more than we can even come close to handling. On the other hand, we don't have nearly as many as you might expect. Maybe we're just getting the ones who were not too badly injured."

"That's probably it, Chris," Hamilton said. "I suppose it makes sense that most of the seriously injured will never be able to get far from the city. We're probably going to see those who were only on the fringes of the badly damaged areas. Most of these people were at worst only slightly injured or they wouldn't have made it this far. That's probably the ugly truth."

As the jeep pulled up to the armory, Hamilton hopped

out just as Ackerson was finishing up with the battery formation. The men in the formation exhibited a ragtag collection of uniforms and equipment. All too conscious of the appearance of the unit to this outsider, and especially to a senior officer, Ackerson walked up to Hamilton, saluted, smiled awkwardly, and said, "Battery C ready for duty, sir. Or at least part of it. I'm sure that things will improve." He shot a nervous glance at Chris and looked back at Hamilton for a response.

"What's your strength now, Lieutenant?" Hamilton asked, his eyes still on the men in formation.

"Sixty-seven, so far, Major." He added hastily. "But we've sent people out to round up the others." He then waited for an upbraiding that didn't come.

Hamilton turned to Chris after a moment. "Chris, this is Ted Ackerson. Ted, this is my sister-in-law, Chris." Without waiting for the usual courtesies, he continued. "Soldier, will you take Miss Whittington to the hospital?"

"Sir, I'll be glad to take her anywhere she wants to go," the young man said, beaming. With just enough time for Chris to nod to Ackerson and jump in the front seat, the vehicle was in motion.

As the two men began walking back into the armory, Johnson walked up to them. "First Sergeant," Hamilton said, "what's the condition of the troops?"

"Disorganized and loose as a goose, but we'll change that in short order. No obvious cases of radiation sickness at this point, sir. We gave the men a brief but sufficient rundown on how to protect themselves before we let 'em go after the bomb hit. It probably helped a lot. Believe it or not, I think I had their undivided attention for once. For the ones not here now, there's no way to know if they're sick from radiation, or just taking their own sweet time getting here."

As the three men entered the battery Orderly Room, Hamilton said, "We've got to make contact with the county judge and mayor as soon as possible. I'm sure that they'll be needing our help."

"The mayor has already been here, sir. I told him we'd get over to see him and Judge Spaulding around four o'clock. I hope that's alright with you."

"Fine. What's the status on rations and ammunition right now."

"Well, as far as the rations go," said Johnson, "we're helped a little by several extra cases that we squirreled away illegally after summer camp and weekend training at Fort Knox. I'd say that we're good for two weeks or so at half-rations, and then that's it. On the ammo, we've got our normal security ammunition, sir. But that's only about fifteen rounds for each weapon by our SOP. Of course, assuming that we don't have any serious crowd control problems that turn into riot situations, we'll be alright."

"That may be assuming too much, First Sergeant," replied Hamilton to the older, heavier man. "Let's go out here," he said motioning toward the door. "I want to look around this place."

Together the three walked into the drill hall and out to the motor park. Hamilton watched as several of the enlisted men checked the vehicles parked around the lot. He could feel their eyes on him. Field-grade officers were scarce around an artillery battery in normal times, and now with the arrival of this outsider especially under the present circumstances, he was even more of a curiosity. Although Hamilton couldn't determine who made the comment, he definitely heard someone around the vehicles remark, "Who the hell is that guy?"

"What's the situation with the battery's vehicles?" Hamilton said in a very measured and direct tone, knowing that fifteen sets of ears were probably straining to hear the conversation.

"Well, of course, the howitzers and armored personnel carriers have always been kept at Fort Knox where we do most of our training. So they're a mark-off now." Pausing, he added softly, "And so were the men who were with them." Ackerson cleared his throat and continued. "On the others we have here, there are no real problems other than a few batteries being down. These things don't have electronic ignitions, so they'll run fine."

"How about fuel?"

"That could be a problem, sir. We don't have enough to run things for very long," responded Johnson, "especially if we get involved in patrols around the county. Diesel fuel will be awfully hard to come by."

"Then I want you to make your first priority to be putting these men on the road as quickly as possible with a good siphoning hose in each vehicle. These roads here look like so many parking lots with stalled cars sitting everywhere. There's bound to be lots of gas still in them. If an owner does appear and give our people any trouble, tell them to give him a receipt for property that has been commandeered out of 'national necessity' or some such nonsense. If there's any threat of violence, though, tell the men to back off. I want as much fuel as possible in those storage tanks but I don't want any Guardsmen dead in the process. Anyway, it may be one helluva long time before we see a gasoline tanker truck pull into this place."

"Sir, with five jeeps and five trucks, we're not going to be doing much effective patrolling in a county this size, especially considering the population that's out there now," Johnson replied.

"True, but we'll just have to do the best we can. We may have to seize some automobiles that are still running before this situation improves. Lieutenant, I . . ."

Ackerson cut him off. "My friends usually call me Ted, Major." He smiled broadly trying to warm up to the man.

Hamilton responded coolly, "I think Lieutenant will do for now. Let's go back to the Orderly Room. We have several things to talk about before our meeting with the county judge and the others."

Oh shit, Ackerson thought to himself. That "goddam city people" remark was probably going to haunt him for quite a while.

"I'll take this lantern," the man said, placing the cheap imported kerosene lantern on the counter at Jarboe's Country Corner. He placed a ten dollar bill beside it.

"Keep your money, mister. It ain't gonna buy that lantern," replied "Boots" Jarboe, a sallow, chubby man whose hair was dyed an unnatural boot-polish black. His hair swept from one side of his head to the other in what appeared to be black noodles, a futile attempt to cover as much white scalp as possible. Boots never went outside without a hat on a windy day.

Christ! Jarboe thought. These city idiots still came rolling in here after they arrived in town, trying to throw around that green crap in exchange for good merchandise. Did they take him for a fool? He sure wasn't going to trade his goods for any paper money now.

He was damned lucky to have anything left, though. Why if he hadn't come down here and stayed in the store, he would probably have been like Walter Blandford down the road. Blandford was emptied out a couple of nights ago, and there wasn't one cop in Nelson County around to do anything about it, was there?

Nobody dared tamper with Boots Jarboe's property, though. A double-barrel, twelve-gauge shotgun has a way of commanding more respect for a person's property rights, he thought. And if that wasn't enough, the Colt Trooper in his belt would help.

The man with the lantern protested. "But the sticker says $8.99!"

"That was B.B.," Jarboe said smugly. "This is A.B."

"B.B., A.B.? What are you talking about?" the confused man whispered. Pushed to his limits by the developments of the past two weeks, and thrust now into strange territory, he was at once irritated by this further demonstration of his impotence, and yet still afraid of saying anything which might eliminate the chance of obtaining the lantern from the arrogant storekeeper.

"Before Bomb, and After Bomb." A slight smile began to appear slowly at the corners of Jarboe's mouth. "That paper money of yours won't buy you much after the bomb. The only place I can use that stuff is in my bathroom, mister. Make that the outhouse now."

The man across the counter studied Jarboe's smug countenance for several seconds. "Listen, my family and I just got here from Louisville. We need light since our flashlights are shot. I'll give you this ring for this lantern, the two gallons of fuel there, and that case of canned goods."

Jarboe paused for a second and then motioned. The man took the ring from his finger and handed it to Jarboe to examine. Not bad, Jarboe thought as he held the diamond-encrusted object up to the light. "Let me see the other one," he said, motioning to the man's other hand and starting to suck at some food caught between his teeth.

"But both of these rings are worth a thousand dollars!" The man protested in a mixture of exasperation and pain.

"Fine," Jarboe responded flatly. "Then go ahead and take this thousand dollars worth of lantern, kerosene and canned goods and we'll call it even. Remember, you can't light up much with those rings, and you sure can't eat 'em."

If looks could have killed, Jarboe would have been lying spread-eagled on the floor. Grudgingly, and with no effort to hide his contempt, the man slipped off the expensive wedding band from his left ring finger, paused for a moment, and then dropped it into Jarboe's outstretched palm. He picked up the items as soon as Jarboe placed them on the counter, and he quickly carried them out of the store, embarrassed and humiliated.

Jarboe watched him disappear down the road and then turned to reexamine his new acquisitions. He slipped them on his fingers and held them up to the light at arm's length. Maybe he could have gotten more for that stuff. Or maybe he should have refused to trade altogether. Like he'd said, he couldn't light up much with them and they sure wouldn't fill his belly.

But damn! he thought. They *were* awfully pretty.

Hamilton and Ackerson jogged from the jeep through the light rain to the courthouse which stood like an island in the center of the town square. Inside, they waded through the crowd seeking refuge from the weather. Almost every square foot of floor space was filled. After enjoying fresh air and freedom for the past five hours, Hamilton found the stench from the unbathed bodies nearly overpowering.

As Hamilton approached the office of Leon Spaulding, the county-judge executive who was the county's nearest equivalent of a mayor, fragments of conversation ricocheted toward him from the buzz of conversation within.

". . . no way we can handle 'em . . . shot him dead on the spot, he did . . . Who invited all of them here in the first place?"

When Hamilton crossed the threshhold, the conversation ceased immediately. A knot of people by the door sipped coffee from Styrofoam cups and eyed him carefully. A couple of them nodded at him silently and a couple of others stared at him from behind plastic smiles.

The walls around the room were lined with pictures of high school ball teams, some yellow and crinkled, others glossy and apparently quite recent. Civic club and American Legion certificates, walnut plaques, and mounted gavels covered the wall behind the massive, antique, African mahogany desk, and by the door were framed copies of the Declaration of Independence and Norman Rockwell's *Four Freedoms*.

A white-haired, potbellied man in a blue seersucker suit stood with his back to Hamilton, opening a window to ventilate the stench permeating the building. He turned around, pulled a crumpled red bandana from his pocket and wiped at his nose. "Wonderful thing, air conditioning. Going to take some getting used to doing without it."

When the man returned the bandana to his pocket, his eyes brightened when he saw Hamilton and Ackerson at the door, and he walked across the room, extending his hand. "Leon Spaulding, Major, uh, Hamilton is it?"

At the conference table sat the mayor, Bob Phillips, the county sheriff, Ralph Osborne, and two other men. Hamilton immediately sensed their curiosity and suspicion. Ackerson, a high school chemistry teacher and track coach, was a known quantity to these men, as had been the unfortunate Captain Chuck Farley.

Hamilton's connections, on the other hand, were too remote to permit him to be considered anything but one of those "goddam city people," as Ackerson had indiscreetly put it. Just one of the very people who were now overrunning the county. Their resentment hung heavily in the air. Nevertheless, Ackerson enthusiastically introduced Hamilton to the entire group.

After the formalities, Spaulding, a man with a certain grandfatherly air about him, began. "Gentlemen, we've got ourselves here the biggest catastrophe in American history, that's for sure. Thank God, around here at least, we're probably in better shape than most places in the country. Still, as anyone can readily see, the population of the county has exploded, and it certainly seems to be growing daily. We've not nearly enough places to house these people who we might as well call refugees, since that's what they are. The problem is that I have a great distaste for calling Americans refugees. That's always been a term used to describe foreigners, it seems, but I suppose we've got to call a spade a spade."

"Still kinda sticks in the craw," Bob Phillips drawled.

"Regardless of what we call these people," Spaulding continued, "we have to deal with them. Maybe we can try to set up some formal refugee centers instead of letting them throw together these shanty camps of theirs. Convincing them to listen will be difficult perhaps, but if we can't sweep back the sea, maybe we can at least influence the way the water is going."

Spaulding paused for a moment, as if gauging Hamilton's reaction. "Major, Mayor Phillips and I have been discussing this situation before you arrived, of course. You should know that we have around thirty peace officers from the various small departments around the country. With numbers like that, we both agree that we need your men to help maintain law and order. Unfortunately, our Army Reserve unit shipped out last week. I don't think it would be overly dramatic to say that you and your boys may be our 'thin green line.'"

Phillips added, "We all just thank the good Lord that you boys weren't already on your way to Iran—for your sakes and ours."

Spaulding nodded in agreement and continued. "But now we need to know what assets you have, and what you're willing to do."

Hamilton cleared his throat and his eyes darted to the other men at the table who seemed to be taking his measure. A piercing child's scream reverberated from the corridor, and the man nearest the door excused himself in order to deal with the disturbance.

"As you know, Judge, we're officially in federal service," Hamilton replied, "and frankly, I'm uncertain what we're technically supposed to do in this situation. Apparently the rules weren't written with this problem in mind. But since we've no orders to the contrary, I suppose we'll assist you as well as we can. The old rules and regulations don't seem to be very relevant now, anyway.

"But you should realize that our assets are very limited," he continued. "We have five quarter-ton jeeps, and five large cargo-type trucks. We have less than seventy enlisted men present for duty right now. In normal times all of this might be enough to handle most natural disaster situations, but considering the number of people we'll be dealing with, and considering the severity of the problems we're likely to encounter out there, we're quite frankly—if you'll excuse the expression—in a piss-poor position. I think it's important going in to be realistic about the situation."

Spaulding sat silently through Hamilton's words with the fingers of both hands steepled in front of his mouth, and then looked at Sheriff Ralph Osborne to his left, who said nothing. Spaulding looked back to Hamilton and responded, "I may not like it, but I agree with your assessment, Major. So what can we do to help make the best use of your people and equipment?"

"We'll need food and fuel for starters. We have efforts underway to locate enough fuel for the short term, but we'll need to keep our troops properly fed if they're to do a decent job."

Spaulding shifted his weight from one buttock to another, ran a hand through his wavy, white hair, and then replied, "We'll do the very best we can, Major. What next?"

Hamilton considered for a couple of seconds the condition attached to the judge's response, and then continued. "The sheriff and I should arrange to send our boys out with our radiacmeters to locate any hot spots around the county. Also, I expect we'll be needed on the burial details as more and more refugees who got lethal radiation doses die in the coming weeks. And of course, perhaps most importantly, we'll have to coordinate our security measures—patrols and so forth. We'll eliminate duplications and establish contingency plans. Okay, Sheriff?"

"Sure. I'll be happy to work with you, Major," said Ralph Osborne, a burly, red-faced man in his late forties. He paused for a moment and spat tobacco juice into a cola can that was minus most of its top, and continued, "Most of these people don't realize how tight things are going to be in the next few months. When things start getting really bad it'll be Katy-bar-the-door."

Ackerson joined in. "Judge, maybe I'm wrong, but it appears to me that we're in the eye of the storm right now."

Spaulding raised his eyebrows, puzzled. "Exactly what do you mean, Ted?"

"Well," Ackerson continued, "first you might say there was the pain and shock, and then after that passed, there came a release of immediate tension as people realized that they had actually survived and were in one piece, at least most of them out here. But supplies of everything from milk and bread to toilet paper will soon be awfully scarce. Irritation will probably give way to anger, and anger to desperation. Then God help us!"

"I disagree as to the level of violence, Ted," Spaulding replied. "Maybe we'll have one helluva time with the usual rowdies, but I'm hopeful that between the police and the Guard that we can take care of it. After all, we're Americans and we're civilized people. I think everyone out there will rise to the challenge and unite in this emergency by pulling together." Looking at Hamilton he asked, "Don't you agree, Major?"

Hamilton repressed the urge to tell Spaulding that if he thought that, then he was a goddamn fool. Instead, he pondered his response for a second in order to tell the man in a more diplomatic manner that he was out in left field. From the pictures, plaques, and certificates on the walls, however, it seemed obvious that the man was cut from the cloth of small-town America. Reorienting his perspective and attitudes would come very slowly. And an abrupt attempt to do so would probably not be well received.

Hamilton cleared his throat and finally said, "I hope you're right, Judge, for our sakes. But whenever people had problems in the past, whether from tornadoes, floods, or whatever, they've always had the assurance that if they just sat there and waited, the police, National Guard, or some rescue squad would work their way to them eventually. That's hardly the case now. People will be on their own. Those who *can* cope, will. Those who *can't*, well . . ."

"Now, now, Major," Spaulding interrupted, almost, it seemed, clucking, "I don't think there's any need for such pessimism so early." With a smile that was a little too patronizing, he asked, "Where's that 'can do' attitude you people in the army are supposed to have?"

"It's easier to have a 'can do' attitude when you're not betting your ass on the outcome." Hamilton immediately regretted the candor of his remark.

Spaulding's face broke into a scowl. Slowly, however, the scowl melted into a slight grin. "I suppose that it just depends on the odds, Major. It just depends on the odds."

With that, Spaulding rose from his chair, and it was

obvious to everyone that he considered the meeting ended. The others began to break away from the group and started moving toward the door.

Hamilton paused for a few minutes with the mayor and sheriff before walking with Ackerson out of the building into the light rain that continued to fall. A jeep and driver appeared at the front of the courthouse, and Hamilton and Ackerson were quickly on their way back to the armory.

"Well, what do you think, Major?"

"I think Spaulding is a good man, but I don't think he understands how grave the situation's likely to get in the next few weeks unless things are kept tightly under control and a few solutions to some overwhelming problems get worked out. I don't have any of the answers right now, either. But I think I can damned sure see the problems a lot better."

"Which problems in particular, sir?" Ackerson's curiosity was real, but so was his desire to appear solicitous of the senior officer's advice and counsel. Anything to mend the fence between the two.

The jeep was rolling out of the center of town now, passing a series of makeshift fallout shelters dug by refugees who had been unable to find anything better. Several families had somehow located large plastic sheets and tarps that they erected to shelter themselves from the rain, and they now stood or sat about in clusters under them. Others sat idly in automobiles parked haphazardly across lawns and open spaces.

One family placed the finishing touches on the little ditch around their tarp, trying to funnel the water away. Underneath the tarp, a glassy-eyed, elderly woman rocked slowly in a Kennedy rocker, gently stroking a black and white tabby cat in her lap. The cat was uninterested in the woman's affection. Its tail and jaws twitched, and its eyes were fixed on the family canary in the cage hung from the tarp's center pole.

Hamilton gestured to the people to his right. "We need to find homes for people like these. Living through the summer with plastic roofs over their heads to keep them dry is one thing. Getting through the winter is another. How in hell are they going to pull through all of this? They're too damned scared to go back to their homes, even if they're still standing. There's no way to know if the war is really over or whether this is just a lull."

"It's really going to take some doing to cope with these refugees, sir, and to get them going so that they aren't just waiting for handouts. After the food runs out, I hate to think about it."

"Maybe we'll sleep a little better tonight if we just *don't* think about it. We can't answer all of the problems the first day, I suppose. By the way, have you noticed the number of guns these people are carrying?"

The driver, who had been silent up to this point, said, "That's right, sir. It looks more like Dodge City than Bardstown. Like maybe people was expectin' to find Russians on the outskirts of town. Outside the army, I ain't never seen this many people with guns in my life."

"There have been a few shootings in the last two days, sir," Ackerson said. "Tempers got a little short and they involved squabbles over something stupid for the most part. Hope it's not a trend."

"*All* we need is for people to start settling scores with each other or shooting each other over a can of peas." As the jeep rolled up to the armory, Hamilton looked to the motor pool area and saw several men pouring the recently collected gasoline into containers.

Hamilton walked into the Orderly Room as Johnson was just sitting down at his desk. "How's everything going, First Sergeant?"

"We've made quite a dent in the gasoline problem, at least for awhile, sir. We've done really great so far. So we'll keep at it as long as possible. One of our boys did have a shotgun poked in his nose by a fellow who didn't appreciate our efforts, but our boys backed off and nothing came of it."

"Who was it?" inquired Ackerson.

"Caldwell, sir."

"Would have been a small loss, anyway."

Johnson smiled at Ackerson's remark and continued. "I've reemphasized to all of 'em about not risking any violence in getting the stuff, Major, so I think we'll be okay."

"Sounds good." Suddenly Hamilton became aware of a low-pitched, pulsating sound. The lack of automobile and truck traffic on the highway made the noise all the more obvious. Hamilton froze, as did the others, and listened intently to the sound growing constantly louder.

Finally, after a few seconds, Hamilton identified the "whop-whop" that could only mean one thing. "Hueys!" he exclaimed. He bounded for the door and then out to the parking lot where a group of enlisted men were frantically waving their arms.

On the horizon, Hamilton saw two National Guard Huey helicopters. They were about a half-mile away and two hundred feet off the ground, making a beeline for the armory. In a matter of seconds, all of the battery personnel were in front of the armory. No one wanted to miss the first contact with the outside world since Black Friday.

The two aircraft circled the armory once and then sat down gently on the grass in front of the building. A short, slight crew chief wearing an olive-drab flight suit and a fiberglass helmet jumped out, pausing only to say something to the pilot before walking up to Hamilton.

"Sgt. Skeeter Mulrooney, sir," he said, pulling off his glove, saluting and extending his hand. "We're glad to see you."

"You're glad to see *us*?" Hamilton exclaimed. He pumped the crew chief's hand enthusiastically, feeling very much like a lost explorer who had just been rescued.

After quickly completing their postflight shutdown procedures, the pilots were out of their aircraft, and the two groups walked toward each other. "Major Hamilton! I don't believe it! I honest to God figured that you were dead," cried the young captain.

"Terry Rockwell, you're a sight for sore eyes yourself!" Hamilton threw his arm around the man's shoulder. "What's all that stuff you guys have on those Hueys?"

"Well, we have a few 'care packages' aboard we figured you people might be able to use if you were still around. Atmosphere's all screwed up, making it hard to communicate on the few radios left. We've had to make the rounds to see where everybody is. State headquarters didn't know what to expect, and with only the Hueys still operational due to all these electronic problems, it's been slow going."

"Well, let's get in out of the drizzle and do some talking. First Sergeant, how about getting a detail together to get that stuff off the choppers? Terry, grab your boys and we'll get some coffee."

After they arrived in the Orderly Room and poured themselves coffee, Hamilton said, "Now what's been happening to the rest of the world? And don't leave out a detail because we're all starved for news."

"First," Rockwell said, "the war seems to be 'on hold.' There haven't been any nuclear detonations since the first Friday afternoon. But it was hot and heavy while it lasted. Reports, or at least accurate reports, are still sketchy, but it appears that the damage has been devastating in some areas, and has totally missed others. For example, Atlanta and St. Louis weren't touched, and neither were Cleveland and Memphis. Some of the big military posts were missed, too. Maybe they were all part of attack plans that were never carried out. Or maybe the problem was missile malfunction, or the bombers were shot down. Who knows? The extent of damage varies tremendously. Thank God the truce came quickly, but no one knows how long it will last.

"One explanation for the pattern of damage may just be that the Russians were aiming at military targets for the most part, and that some cities unfortunately fell into that category."

"Maybe like Louisville, with those bombers?" Hamilton suggested.

"Perhaps. Just a guess."

Rockwell paused and took a short sip of his coffee and then continued. "Though no one is publicly saying so, and this may just be speculation on my part, I expect that we got the short end of the stick with the Russians hitting us first. Most of the nerve centers of the country have been decimated according to the reports that have been received so far. New York is a mark-off, nothing's coming out of Washington, and communication with most other places is extremely limited. The main transmitters in Frankfort were supposed to be protected from the electromagnetic pulses, but the radio room's doors were wide open since no one got word of an impending attack.

"By the way, it seems that there was a high-altitude nuclear burst over the West Coast that created tremendous EMP damage in advance of the main attack. We still don't know if we didn't get one here because of some missile malfunction or for some other reason. Maybe the Russians have problems with Murphy's Law, too. We got one later, so that's all that matters. Just about all of our transistorized communications gear has been zapped."

"What's the president saying about the situation?"

"The president is dead," said Rockwell's copilot, Glen Childs.

"Aw, Christ!" Ackerson exclaimed. "He's been warning everyone about the Russians for thirty years, and he has to get it. I just hope some of those liberals up there got it as well. Maybe if one of 'em was standing beside him as the missiles came in, the president at least had the chance to turn to one of them and say, 'I told you so, asshole!'"

Ackerson's remark brought a wry grin to Rockwell's face. "Washington was one of the first to get it, and he was in the White House, according to what we got. Of course, now we'll probably never know exactly what was happening at that time. Anyway, the vice president, I mean the president now, is calling the shots from the Doomsday Plane. You know, that airborne command post. He's one place and then the other. I've also heard that he's spending time on the ground in some kind of armored transport that's real hush-hush."

"From everything you've been describing," Johnson drawled, "it sounds like what we had was what used to be called a limited nuclear war."

"I suppose any nuclear war you survive is a limited nuclear war." Rockwell took another sip from his coffee mug. "Nobody has said whether this lull is necessarily going to last for long. The word is that we shouldn't let our guard down for now."

"What's the situation around the state?" asked Hamilton.

"The Bluegrass Army Depot, Fort Knox, Fort Campbell, and of course, Louisville were hit. People are everywhere. You ought to have seen some of the towns we've seen so far. From the air it looks as if there are a hundred goddam rock concerts going on across the state, judging by the masses of people packed in these towns. We've had lots of reports of violence, and I mean some really nasty stuff. Lots of looting, as you might expect. It's getting more than a little scary, and that's why state headquarters wanted to get you more ammunition along with the rations. We made a delivery to

Springfield earlier this afternoon. You should have plenty of M-16 and machine-gun ammunition to hold you for a while. At least for any likely emergency."

"You can hang on to the .50 cal. ammunition," Johnson replied. "Our heavy machine guns were at Fort Knox with the howitzers and ammo carriers. They won't be doing us much good now."

"Speaking of Springfield," Ackerson said, "what's the situation over there? Is Hart handling things okay?"

"Bud's got the Service Battery in control so far, but he's only working with about 60 percent strength right now. Springfield is not as hard-pressed as Bardstown seems to be, but then it's a much smaller town. I just hope things stay cool, because I'm not sure how much they can handle."

"Well, what about the brigade headquarters in Louisville?" Hamilton asked, though he was almost certain of the answer.

"Gone, Major. Sorry to be the one to tell you. Nothing left but rubble in the whole area. About a fifth of the metropolitan area is that way. Damage around the city differs tremendously, though. By the way, just how in the hell did *you* get here?"

"I had just brought my family out here to the farm my brother and I own about four miles from here. I was on my way back when the bomb hit that afternoon." He paused and after a few seconds said, "Christ! The whole brigade headquarters. I can't say that I didn't expect it, but it's still a shock having you confirm it."

"Sorry to be the bearer of such bad tidings."

"Listen, Terry," Hamilton said. "What you said about seeing the situation from the air makes me think that it would be a good idea to do just that tomorrow, weather permitting. I'm sure that you're not going to be flying back tonight, right? So Ted can get hold of the county judge and sheriff right away, and we'll all go up in the morning to get a different perspective on the problem. Maybe it'll let the judge know the true size of the problem."

"Sounds like a great idea, sir," Ackerson replied. "We can sure see a lot more from the air in an hour than we can see running around in a jeep all day. I'll see about setting things up for 0900 if that's okay."

"Fine."

Just at that point, Mattingly and Nugent walked into the Orderly Room. "Well, I'll be damned!" Hamilton exclaimed. "They did finally find you two."

"Take it easy on me, sir," Mattingly said. "I've just been through two weeks of living hell."

"Well, I suppose we all have."

"But you didn't spend yours in a basement with Nugent," responded Mattingly. The group then broke into laughter. Nugent only looked about with a sheepish grin on his face, though it was obvious that he wasn't all that appreciative of the attention.

As the laughter subsided, Hamilton said, "I'll see that you two are filled in later, but for now, since everything is coming along well enough, I think I'm going to run back out to the farm to check on a few things."

Hamilton settled some details for the next morning's flight, and then walked out of the Orderly Room to the lobby where he saw the cases of rations and ammunition stacked neatly together and awaiting storage. Continuing out to the parking lot to the jeep and driver awaiting him, he thought that things just might be all right after all.

When he sat down in the jeep, he glanced at the Hueys sitting on the grass, their propeller blades seeming to droop sadly. For the first time he consciously noticed that the helicopters had light machine guns mounted at each door. This was something that he had rarely seen in the National Guard, and then only in special training exercises.

As the driver started the engine and pulled away, Hamilton's mind was fixed on the guns and what they might portend for the coming months. Slowly his feeling of well-being began to slip away.

Earlier that afternoon, when Chris got out of the jeep in front of Flaget Memorial Hospital, she could see that this nursing assignment would be like none she had ever experienced—or even imagined.

Bright tents mixed with shelters fabricated from everything from canvas to garbage-can liners covered the hospital grounds. Beneath them were the hosts of injured and ill seeking medical treatment. Cordoned off to one side, a long line of corpses covered with plastic awaited the attention of a burial detail. After pausing a moment to drink in the scene, Chris thanked Cochran, who had been falling all over himself to charm her during the trip. She then walked hesitantly past the fallout barriers erected at the entrance into the building.

At the desk immediately beyond the door, a harried, middle-aged woman with heavy bags under her eyes was arguing with a couple in their early twenties. "Your problem is not life-threatening at this point. The doctor told you that. You very well *could* have a fracture, dear, but there's no gangrene evident. It'll be several hours before anyone can see you. So if you'll keep that number you were given and go out to the lawn and wait, preferably in one of the fallout shelters, someone will eventually see you." It was clear that she had been through the routine too many times.

"But listen, lady. You gotta understand. My wife is in terrible pain. She's just gotta see a doctor *now*."

The older woman clenched her jaw for a second, squinted her eyes, and then said, "Next!" with a firmness and resolution that made obvious the futility of further protest.

Chris turned and looked at the knots of people scattered about the room. She sensed a mixture of hope, pain, grief, and despair. In the corner a woman helped a man who was vomiting into a pan held in front of him. His face was a muddy color, relieved by blotches of yellow. The missing tufts of hair made the radiation poisoning immediately obvious.

As Chris inched forward in the line, she heard the solemn tones of an aged voice. She turned and saw among the dozen or so people to her left an elderly woman speaking to a child of perhaps seven or eight. The woman sat on the floor rocking in a neurotic rhythm. She raised a gnarled, liver-spotted hand and shook her finger in the child's face. She seemed to look through the child, past the walls of the hospital to an inner world bounded only by the limits of her imagination. "This is all God's will! It's been written for two thousand years, and now it's finally come to pass! And there's nothing to be done about it. There's nothing *anyone* can do!"

As if to prove her point, she thrust her frail hand into the large bag at her side, and pulled from it a tattered Bible bound in imitation Moroccan leather. Quickly she thumbed the worn pages. She finally began reading from Revelations:

> . . . Now the seven angels who had the seven trumpets made ready to blow them.
>
> The first angel blew his trumpet and there followed hail and fire, mixed with blood, which fell on the earth; and a third of the earth was burnt up, and a third of the trees were burnt up, and all the green grass was burnt up.

"There's more," she said. "Just let me find it." Her finger leafed quickly through the pages as she looked determinedly for another passage. Finally, her eyes lit up, and she started reading once again:

> . . . Then I heard a loud voice from the temple telling the seven angels, "Go and pour out on the earth the seven bowls of the wrath of God. . . . The fourth angel poured his bowl on the sun, and it was allowed to scorch men with fire; men were scorched by the fierce heat, and they cursed the name of God who had power over these plagues, and they did not repent and give him glory.

The old woman pressed her wizened lips tightly together and nodded to herself, satisfied that she had made her point. "So you see, we've only just begun. The first angel has visited the wrath of God on us, but there is *more* to come."

She turned from the child and looked around the room until, finally, her dark, deep-set eyes met those of Chris. "Don't you see? It's just *begun*. It's all part of God's plan. And there's nothing anyone can do about it! Don't you *see*?"

Chris swallowed hard. A harsh "Next!" drew her attention. Her turn had come to speak with the middle-aged woman at the desk. Feeling rescued, she stepped forward.

"My name is Chris Whittington. I'm an RN. From the looks of things, you could use some help around here."

"Praise the Lord!" the woman exclaimed, rolling her eyes toward the ceiling. "Honey, you're exactly what the doctor ordered, if you know what I mean. Are you from Louisville?" The woman continued without waiting for a response. "It seems like Louisville must have lost most of its doctors and nurses and such. Maybe the bomb was too close to the hospitals. Maybe they just went somewhere else. Who knows? Regardless, we've got all of these people finding their way here but we don't have anywhere near enough medical help. You're only the fifth nurse to come in here in the last couple of days, but honey, we could use a hundred more. Why don't you go down here to the third door on the right after you turn the corner, and see Charge Nurse Miller. She'll see to it you're not idle for long."

Chris nodded and started away from the desk. The woman added, "And honey, don't be too put off with her immediately. She's like me. Her bark's worse than her bite. Next!"

Chris picked her way down the hall, moving past gurneys and stepping around the patients who took up most of the floor space. A middle-aged couple, apparently dissatisfied with the treatment and attention the teenager in one of the beds had received, argued violently with a nurse in one room. A tired but determined sheriff's deputy whisked past Chris as the protests of the woman reached a hysterical pitch.

In the next room Chris found two women who appeared to be engrossed with a patient's chart. They paid little attention to the disturbance, and Chris had the impression that the problem was one that had become commonplace. "Excuse me, but I'm looking for Charge Nurse Miller."

"What is it?" the older woman snapped.

"My name is Chris Whittington," she replied, undaunted. "I'm an RN and I'd like to help if you want me."

The older nurse said tersely, "Jill, see that she's taken to ward three, and see if you can find her a lab coat. Find out what experience she's had, and we'll figure out where to put her permanently later."

The woman started scribbling quickly on the chart, letting Chris know the interview was over.

Jill led Chris down the hall and up a flight of stairs. The two stopped at a nurses station on the second floor, and Jill handed Chris a white lab coat to put on over her street clothes. "You'll have to understand about Sylvia Miller," the woman said in a conciliatory tone. "She's almost at her wit's end. We all are. I've been getting by on four hours of sleep for the past three days, and I'm sure she's had less. There are so many people needing help that you never get a break. She was glad to see you but just too tired to say so."

"I'll have to take your word on that."

Chris was given as lengthy an orientation as possible and was soon working with patients crammed into a wing of the hospital designed to accommodate a tenth as many. Burn victims were the most serious problem. With antibiotics and topical dressings nearly depleted, the situation required triage.

Triage involved dividing mass casualties into three categories: those who would live anyway, those who would die anyway, and those for whom medical treatment would make a difference. With few treatment measures available, Chris found that far fewer victims were placed in the last category. She also found herself making many of the treatment decisions, simply because doctors were not always available to make them for her.

Chris had worked emergency rooms extensively in the past. At University Hospital, Louisville's charity hospital, she had seen the strings of shooting, knifing, and accident victims who would overwhelm the facility on hot summer weekends. The city's lower class had a way of perforating, puncturing, and pulverizing each other in rather remarkable numbers, and University Hospital was there to clean up the mess. But this, *this* was unlike anything in her experience.

Besides the burn victims, victims of radiation sickness were there in heavy numbers. Of these, most had failed to take adequate protective measures from the fallout, through either ignorance or the inability to locate shelter. They were paying the price now, with continuous diarrhea and vomiting. Some would recover, some would not, and with the great numbers needing antibiotics and transfusions, there was little Chris or anyone else in the hospital could do to influence the outcome.

The next category was that of the trauma victims who had received lacerations, fractures, or internal injuries as a result of the blast. A surprisingly high percentage of the victims seeking attention at the hospital would survive, simply because the more seriously injured victims would never be able to make their way from the city to Bardstown.

Chris found the injuries to the children hardest to handle. She had always avoided "pedes" simply because the suffering of children had bothered her emotionally. As a nurse she never became accustomed to the suffering around her, but with adults she had always been able to control her personal feelings. Not so with children.

The bomb that destroyed the city had not discriminated. Young and old alike had felt its fury. On a cot at the end of the hall lay a four-year-old girl as proof of this, and beside her sat her mother. The woman was brushing the little girl's hair when Chris approached and knelt at her side.

"How is she doing?" Chris asked, smiling as cheerfully as she could.

"Better, I think." If the woman was trying to hide the worry in her voice, she was not doing a very good job. "Her fever's down, and she's in less pain, but she's got a long way to go."

Chris looked at the little girl's chart. Fracture of the left femur, fractured ribs, and possible internal injuries. "How'd it happen?"

"She was playing outside and I was in the house. God, if I could only back up in time and take her place. I feel so helpless, so powerless, and she needs so much help." As the woman spoke she stroked the shoulder-length hair of the child, who was only half awake.

Chris looked about the hallway. "Is her father here?" As soon as the words were spoken, however, she regretted, like the woman, that she could not go back and withdraw the question.

"I begged him not to go to work," the woman replied, tears welling up in her eyes. "I told him we ought to leave Louisville. But he wouldn't hear of it because he said we had nowhere to go anyway. Now we're all alone out here in this godforsaken place, and I don't know what we're going to do."

Chris patted the woman on the hand and said assuringly, "I'm sure that things will be all right." She then rose and walked hurriedly down the ward.

Good God. Was this how it would be from now on?

SATURDAY, JUNE 1ST:
The Sixteenth Day

As scheduled, the county judge and sheriff, along with two county magistrates arrived at the armory for the flight the next morning. This was obviously going to be the next best thing to a trip to Disneyland for Judge Spaulding, Hamilton thought, as he watched the crew chief properly securing the seat belt around the excited man's waist. The excitement civilians got from flying in military aircraft or riding in armored vehicles had always amused Hamilton. Congressman or potential recruit, the experience seemed to bring out the little boy in every one of them.

The helo was quickly airborne and as soon as it had gained a couple of hundred feet in altitude, the nature and extent of the refugee problem, if it had not been obvious before, certainly became so now.

"My God, look at this place!" Spaulding exclaimed. "People are everywhere. What are we going to do with them?"

"That could very well be the Sixty-Four-Thousand-Dollar Question, Judge," Hamilton shouted over the engine's roar. He decided that the judge was getting a better grip on reality already.

The chopper continued over the town at an altitude of about two hundred feet. The reaction of many below was one of excitement, as most people were unaware of the arrival of the helicopters the previous night. Many people waved frantically at the evidence above them that the U.S. Army still existed and, therefore, the United States Government still existed. Others, however, reacted with what seemed to be almost hostility to this symbol of a government which had failed them in its most important role— the protection of the people. Nevertheless, to many of the

141

people on the ground, the helicopter might just as well have been Air Force One. Spaulding waved silently out the side of the chopper, as if he were the grand marshal of the Fourth of July parade.

At Hamilton's direction, the helo headed north after a couple of passes and out toward Nazareth College, the old Catholic girls' college. The campus grounds served now as a gathering place for refugees who were taking advantage of the many large buildings that had previously served as classrooms, dormitories, and athletic facilities. As the helicopter circled, what Hamilton estimated at four to five thousand people reacted just as those in Bardstown had.

Rockwell turned to Hamilton and asked over the roar of the engine whether Hamilton wanted to land. The intercom had gone out with the radios.

"We'd better not land," Hamilton shouted back to Rockwell. "I'm afraid with that crowd down there acting the way it is, we might get mobbed. We can come back later in a jeep and not take a chance on injuring someone or damaging equipment. Let's head for Bloomfield." Rockwell gave Hamilton a "thumbs up" signal, banked the chopper sharply, and headed away from the college.

"This is worse than I ever imagined," Ralph Osborne shouted to Hamilton after the helicopter left the old campus. He had been silent up to this point and was subdued as he watched the crowds in the distance. "Where in the hell is the food gonna come from to feed all these people? And what's gonna happen to them and to *us* if we don't get food to them?"

Hamilton did not respond. He was sure that every one of the passengers was searching for possible answers.

The chopper was quickly over Bloomfield. Bloomfield was teeming with people, and the creek that ran through the center of town was filled with refugees using the most readily available bathing and laundry facility in the town. As others scrubbed themselves in the middle of the stream, dozens lined the banks washing clothing on the rocks.

They flew on to New Haven, New Hope, and every crossroad in between. The situation was universal.

As the helicopter returned to the armory and landed, Hamilton and the others jumped out. Hamilton walked up to Rockwell's window and asked, "When can we expect to see you again?"

"Who knows, Major? We can't get back here very soon though. We've got one hell of an area to cover and flight time is limited. With the electronics in all of the Blackhawks being fried to a frizzle, the few Hueys that weren't already deployed out of state are the workhorses now. Besides, there's only a handful of pilots for those we do have. But we'll be able to let the people in Frankfort know what your situation is here, and that should help in making decisions on allocations. All I can say is that until you get orders to the contrary, the policy is to continue supporting the authorities here. You're the boss of the Guard assets here now, so I suppose you're on your own and should use your best judgment."

Hamilton patted Rockwell on the shoulder. "Well, we'll be waiting to see your shining face back here soon."

Rockwell smiled broadly, shot Hamilton a thumbs up and revved the engine as Hamilton stepped back. In a few seconds the crew chief jumped aboard and the helo lifted slowly, circled once, and headed off to the east, followed by the second chopper. As the two choppers grew smaller in the distance, Hamilton stood with his hands on his hips, feeling as if his lifeline to civilization was being severed.

His reverie was ended by the yelping of a pack of dogs running down the highway after a female apparently in heat. A great number of these former pets roamed the area now, runaways from masters who had brought them from the city, but who were no longer able to feed them properly. Their pack instincts were causing them to become real pests.

Hamilton was still watching the dogs when Ackerson and Spaulding walked up. "Lieutenant," Hamilton said, continuing to address Ackerson as "Lieutenant" rather than "Ted," more often than not when it was business that he had on his mind. "What do you have posted in the way of security?"

"What do you mean, sir?" Ackerson replied with a puzzled expression.

"I mean guards. A local security plan, Lieutenant."

"Well, sir, our people on the vehicles have rifles with

them and sixty rounds of ammunition per man. But other than that, the only person required to have a weapon on him is the man in the arms room. That's always been the unit SOP."

"This isn't *like* before. We've got a situation where we're sitting here with a large amount of arms and ammunition. Before we're out of the woods, given what we saw this morning, it may very well be that some people figure that they need these weapons more than we do. So don't take any chances. You and the first sergeant work out the arrangements, and report back to me with your proposal by noon."

"Yes, sir. I'll get right on it." Ackerson pivoted quickly and walked off looking for Johnson.

"Major," Spaulding said, stepping a little closer after Ackerson was out of earshot, "I didn't want to butt in while Ted was here, but do you really think things are likely to get that bad?"

"Judge, I'm pleasantly surprised that theft and violence have been as low as they've been so far, but I am awfully worried that the situation could change rapidly. There are just too many people to provide for. I'm afraid too many are going to do whatever is required to get by, and the consequences be damned."

Osborne walked up in the middle of Hamilton's response. "Major," he said, "there's plenty of food out there for a good while. The problem is getting the people who have it to part with it. A lot of farmers have been contributing a helluva lot of grain. But there's going to be a need for a lot more. We have to set up a distribution system and then figure out how to sweettalk these farmers into contributing a decent amount of food without a fight. I sure don't relish the prospect of a shootout with some ol' poor boy over the contents of his grain bin that he thinks he and his family need to feed themselves in the long haul."

"I agree," Hamilton replied, "But one of the packages that the chopper dropped off yesterday was filled with Order of Taking forms."

"Order of what?" Osborne asked.

"Order of Taking. We're supposed to give these to the owner when we find it necessary to seize anything for public use. You know, gasoline, a driveable car, food, and the like. The government will settle up later with the owner."

"How *much* later?"

"Good question. A real good question."

Ralph Osborne looked at Spaulding, and then shook his head slowly. "Major, if we try seizin' livestock or grain bins from people around here, we're gonna have a goddam civil war on our hands. Askin' for it is one thing. Takin' it is another. I've got some pretty strong feelings on this myself. The longer we try to do without those 'forms' the better off we'll all be. Persuasion is the best route."

"That sounds perfectly reasonable," Hamilton replied. "But now come the details."

PART FOUR

O war, thou son of hell . . . !

—Shakespeare
Henry VI, Part II, V, ii, 33

THURSDAY, JUNE 6th:
The Twenty-First Day

A shot rang out. The tall man with a butcher knife in his hand jerked back, clutched quickly at his chest, and dropped to the ground as the report reverberated across the meadow. The two other men, scruffy and dirty, threw themselves to the ground behind the freshly slaughtered heifer. They stared, terrified, at the man approaching them across the pasture with his bolt-action rifle held at the ready position. "D-d-on't shoot, mister! For God's sake, don't shoot! We give up and we ain't got no guns!" one of the men shouted.

"You sonsabitches!" cried the man behind the gun as he walked up to the young cow, now minus its two hindquarters. He motioned with the rifle barrel, and the two men on the ground hesitantly stood up. "What the hell do you think you're doing coming on to *my* property and killing *my* cattle?"

"We was hungry, that's all. We wouldn't have done it if we hadn't been desperate. We got ten people waiting for what we bring back, mister," the short man with bandy legs explained.

A moan from the wounded man reminded the three that he needed attention. "Is it all right if I take care of him? He's hurt pretty bad."

"All right, but don't try anything," replied the man with the gun, his resolution weakening somewhat when he saw firsthand the results of his marksmanship. As if he needed to justify himself to the two men standing before him, he said, "I worked all my life to build this place. I worked twelve and fourteen hours a day six, sometimes seven days a week. And I'll tell you this. It's not all going to go to hell because every jackleg from the city who decides to pass through here thinks he can kill one of my cattle. *Under-*

stand? I gotta wife and children to think about, too. Mess with me or my property again, and the two of you will get what he got. Now pick him up and get outta here."

As the two men struggled to pick up the wounded man, the rifleman's tone softened slightly. "There's a hospital in Bardstown, so I suggest that you get him over there."

There was no argument. With one of them at the wounded man's arms and shoulders and the other at his legs, they struggled to remove themselves and their friend from the scene as rapidly as possible.

The man with the gun stood by the dead cow and watched silently as the struggling men reached the gate to the pasture and passed off his property. "Don't come back!" he shouted to reemphasize the well-made point.

Around noon on Friday, the next day, Sheriff Osborne, Hamilton, and a deputy rode up to the farmhouse a few miles south of Bardstown. Hamilton had been in Osborne's office earlier, and he had accepted the offer to come and to observe. As the car approached the house, a man with a rifle came to the door to meet them.

Osborne and the deputy got out of the car and walked to the house. Osborne took off his sunglasses and pulled a hankerchief from his pocket, wiping it across his forehead. "Otis, you didn't by any chance use that thing on a fellow out here yesterday, did you?"

The man was small and in his mid-forties, with a deeply lined face due to long hours in the sun and longer hours into the night.

Several chickens pecked at the ground around the yard oblivious to the conversation, while three mongrel dogs that had barked wildly when the car had come up the hill were now watching intently from a discreet distance.

The buildings and farm equipment indicated that the man in front of the house was at best at a stalemate in his battle to wrench a living from the soil. Hamilton could see a little girl and boy pressing their noses to the window, curious at the men in front of the house and wondering just what they wanted with their father.

"Sheriff," the man said, "I caught them red-handed butcherin' one of my young heifers. That was the third one I lost in the past ten days. I figured I had to do something about it, or else me and my family pretty soon would be no better off than they were. It was as simple as that."

And just about as complex, too, Hamilton thought.

"Otis, you know the law don't allow you to go around putting bullet holes in people because they kill a cow."

"But it was my property, Sheriff, and they was trespassin'. I got my rights, too. Besides, this thing is only a .22, and I couldn't have hurt him that bad. He knew what he was doing when he tried to steal that meat, and he got what was comin' to him. Maybe he'll *think* next time."

"There may be no next time for him, Otis. He's at the hospital now, and he may not make it."

Almost by reflex Otis began to move the end of the rifle barrel toward the men in front of him. Osborne cut him off by saying firmly, "Now don't do anything dumb, Otis. We've known each other too many years to have us goin' at each other. Just come along peaceably and don't be causing any problems."

Otis stepped back and placed his rifle against the porch. His shoulders slumped and he placed his hand over his eyes. "Aw, Jesus, Ralph. What am I gonna do about Cissy and the kids? I can't just leave them like this. Not the way things are."

"I'll get somebody out to your brother's place and let him know," Osborne replied calmly.

Osborne gave the man time to say good-bye to his family, and without further protest, Otis got into the waiting car. The scene was not pleasant.

The three children cried and sobbed as their father was being led away. They could not understand what was happening to their father or what he could possibly have done to be treated like this. Hate burned in the oldest son's eyes, and his mother fought back tears while telling her son continuously that things would be all right.

When the car hit the main road and began to pick up speed, Otis turned to Osborne and said, "Tell me, Ralph. What's the difference if a man *shoots* another and kills him, or if he *steals* his food and starves him to death?"

No one answered him, and satisfied with the silence, the man sat quietly for the rest of the trip.

Hamilton pondered the man's question for the next few minutes. All of this was probably just the beginning, he thought. And Hamilton was right.

WEDNESDAY, JUNE 12TH:
The Twenty-Seventh Day

Boots Jarboe sat at the counter of his store. Merchandise had certainly been turning over rapidly in the last couple of weeks. Matches, toilet paper, "feminine care needs," as they were called, and garden seeds had been bought up, or rather, bartered for immediately. People without them would just have to make do without, he thought. Ammunition was still around. In fact, it had become a new coin of the realm. Jarboe had stopped taking money early on. He had taken gold, silver, and gems for a few days or so, but Jesus, after he had collected several mason jars of jewelry, silver coins and Krugerrands, people started to refuse to take the stuff back in trade from *him*.

He berated himself for quite some time after that for giving in to his old fascination with gold and diamonds. But could anyone blame him? After all, he'd been barely scratching out a living at his store when suddenly he found that these rings and stones he'd longed for all his life were suddenly being willingly traded by these dumbass city people for even the cheapest and most poorly made items in the store. When the world was beating a path to his door, how could he resist?

Now that the gold and gems weren't being accepted by his suppliers, such as they were, Jarboe had switched to bartering items or accepting such things as whiskey, medicine, pot, cigarettes, and ammunition in payment. Unlike a gold ring, ammunition had intrinsic value. You could not only buy things with ammunition, you could shoot things with ammunition, or if necessary under the circumstances, you could shoot the thing's owner. Now that was intrinsic *value*.

Jarboe walked over and started folding the wool blanket traded that morning by a young refugee woman. To seal the bargain, like two other young women that week, she had given Jarboe ten minutes alone with her in the back room. As Jarboe finished with the blanket, a man entered the store and Jarboe turned to him and said with a synthetic smile he forced to his face, "Can I help you, mister?"

The young man with stringy brown hair and a patchy beard reached around to his back and pulled out a large revolver, either a .357 or .44 magnum. Jarboe swallowed very hard. At least from *this* perspective, it was the largest handgun Jarboe had ever seen.

"Yeah, you can help me. I want a few things, and you might say that I left home without my American Express Card." The man motioned, and three other armed men darted into the store.

Quickly they set about loading things around the store, carrying them out to their car. Interestingly, they bypassed the food and went for the items that might have more barter value. Jarboe, meanwhile, eyed the double-barreled shotgun and the Colt Trooper lying on the shelf just below the counter.

One of the men walked quickly over to the large wooden box of loose .22 ammunition on the top of the counter. From his expression, it was apparent that the robber considered its sparkling contents a treasure trove. His eyes gleamed as he yelled to one of his companions about his discovery. Placing his pistol in his belt and picking up the box, he was on his way out to the car when through the doorway popped a teenage boy who was unaware of what was happening inside.

The sudden appearance of the young man startled the gunman watching Jarboe, and his attention was momentarily directed to the teenager who threw his hands up in the air.

Jarboe seized the opportunity. He lunged toward the shotgun. In an instant he fired a blast that lifted the first gunman off the floor. It hurled him across a rack of clothes through a glass display case, leaving him twitching in spasms among the shards on the floor. Jarboe turned and fired the second barrel toward the man who was diving behind a row of shelves. The blast caught him squarely in the side of the skull, removing a large portion of forehead and brain matter, dropping him, as if boneless, to the floor.

Jarboe quickly dropped the shotgun to the counter and

jammed his hand to the shelf below in search of the revolver. Panic caused him to fumble a split-second too long. Before he could bring the weapon to bear on the man with the box of ammunition, the man dropped the box, whose contents rolled across the floor like so many marbles, and fired two quick shots from his revolver.

The first shot caught Jarboe just below the solar plexus, and the second one smashed through the counter, striking him in the lower abdomen. Jarboe's knees buckled immediately, and he fell groaning to the floor.

As the fourth man ran back into the store with his shotgun, the man who'd shot Jarboe screamed, "Let's get the hell outta here!" and the two ran from the building. On his way out, the last man stopped, turned around, and to the teenager's horror, fired one shot into the boy's chest. The gunmen jumped into their car and sped away.

Jarboe lay on the floor, groaning and mewling behind the counter, racked with excruciating pain. As he listened to the car roar away, the blood quickly flowed from his shattered arteries, and he sank into merciful unconsciousness, then oblivion.

Later that night, halfway across the county, Billy Joe McCubbins sat on the porch of his home, completely ignorant of the day's events elsewhere. The night was as pleasant as he had a right to expect. The sunset had been spectacular. It seemed that the sunsets were always more colorful since the war started, and it was also noticeably cooler and more comfortable than usual for this time of year. Well, whatever.

He reflected on the situation that faced him now. With the seed and diesel fuel he had on hand when the war came, he had been able to get out a fair-sized crop of corn and soybeans, and he expected to be able to harvest it without too many problems if everything went as planned. This would certainly carry his family through the first winter. With the surplus, he expected to be able to trade for anything he needed. And that was definitely *needed*, as opposed to *wanted*.

If he could just keep the poachers away from his livestock, he had every expectation of making it through the crisis without too much sacrifice for Lorraine and the kids. Why

SOLDIER OF FORTUNE

INTRODUCTORY OFFER

9 issues for only $18.95

Save over 29% off the 1 year single copy price.*

☐ Payment enclosed (must accompany order)

☐ MasterCard ☐ VISA

Card # _____

Signature _____ Exp. Date _____

Name: _____

Address: _____

City: _____ State: _____ Zipcode: _____

*Savings based on 12 issue single copy price of $36.

Offer good in U.S. only. All other countries add $7.00 for additional postage. Please allow 6-8 weeks for delivery of first issue. Offer expires 12/31/88. U.S. funds only.

BUSINESS REPLY MAIL

FIRST CLASS   PERMIT NO. 8   MT. MORRIS, IL

POSTAGE WILL BE PAID BY ADDRESSEE

SOLDIER OF FORTUNE

P.O. Box 348

Mt. Morris, IL 61054-9984

when things returned a little more to normal, he thought, he might be in a better position than he could have imagined just a month ago.

Just then Billy Joe heard something down at the barn. Then he heard the geese start to squawk. Very slowly, he reached for the Winchester Model 97, twelve-gauge shotgun at his side, a bequest from his grandfather a few years ago. He got to his feet and slowly started down the sidewalk in a low crouch and worked his way along the fence to the barn.

He froze, huddled next to a large fence post, and listened intently to the sounds of the night. After three or four minutes he heard nothing more, except the rapid beating of his own heart. Finally, the geese quieted down.

With the caution and stealth of an experienced hunter, he moved slowly around the corner of the barn, and looked out across the barnyard. With no moonlight, he could see very little.

After a couple of minutes he finally decided that the noise must have come from a stray dog, or possibly a raccoon or fox, and he turned and walked back toward the house with his shotgun on his shoulder. McCubbins was about halfway to the house when several gunshots rang out, violently piercing the still night air. McCubbins was struck almost simultaneously by several bullets from the volley, and they picked him up and spun him in the air. He was dead before he hit the ground.

Billy Joe McCubbins's farm was the third farm to be visited by looters that night in Nelson County. The results elsewhere were the same.

SATURDAY, JUNE 15TH:
The Thirtieth Day

"Mom, when are we going to find something else to eat?" asked the little girl.

Fran Fitzgerald stroked her daughter's blond hair and said as cheerily as she could, "Melanie, I'm sure your father will be back soon, and who knows what all he'll be bringing?" That wasn't a lie, she thought, but it wasn't exactly something to take to the bank either. The prospects were dim of her husband finding very much for the family to eat. Despite the assurances Fran thought she had given her little girl, with that comprehension that adults often underestimate in young children, Melanie sensed the uncertainty of the response. Though she did not press her mother further, she resorted once again to sucking her thumb. Until a month ago she had not done this for over two years.

And what a month. The blast, finding shelter that afternoon, the long days and nights with that strange family in that basement near the Interstate. She and her family were very lucky to have come through it, and she was thankful to God that her family was still intact.

Fortunately, the burns Ken and Michael had received were not serious, and they had been able to avoid infection with the use of proper first-aid treatment. The family they had stayed with the first couple of weeks, Harvey and Joyce Titus and their four children, had been very kind in providing him with the best treatment possible under the circumstances. They were generous with their food for the first few days as well. But as time progressed, the food began to diminish, "cabin fever" began to take its toll, and relations began to cool. Their resentment was soon manifest with every spoonful of beef stew or bean soup that the Fitzgeralds ate.

154

Finally, on the sixteenth day, the matter came to a head when Harvey took Ken into the kitchen. He poured Ken a cup of instant coffee from the hot water he had heated on the Coleman camp stove that sat beside the useless Amana microwave. Ken had anticipated the conversation, but said nothing until he had given his host a chance to speak.

"Ken," Harvey began, as he set his coffee cup down and pulled his chair up to the table, "there's something we've gotta talk about. It ought to be clear that we've only a limited amount of food here, and that at the rate we're goin', within a couple of weeks we'll be completely out. Since people are movin' up and down the highway now, it seems safe enough to go outside, so—and I'm awfully sorry to have to say this—we're going to have to ask you to leave."

Fitzgerald did not immediately respond. Instead, he quietly studied Harvey's face. Harvey, a forty-two-year-old father of three, had not looked directly at him during the announcement, and he still continued to stare at the coffee mug he now held in rough and calloused hands. "Well," Fitzgerald finally replied, "I guess we can't complain about all the generosity you've shown us. I don't know what we'd have done without it. I'm sure we'll get by. It's just that I don't have any idea how right now. But that's not *your* problem, of course."

Harvey stiffened and snapped back defensively after the barb at the end of Ken's response. "You're right. It's *not* my problem. I got my wife and my kids to think about first, and I can't let their welfare be jeopardized by people I didn't even *know* two weeks ago!"

Fitzgerald held up his hands. "Hold on, Harvey, I'm not bitter. I really do understand," he said, lying. "I'll get our things together, and we'll try to be gone in an hour or so."

Very little more was said by either of the two families prior to the Fitzgeralds' departure. They made their awkward farewells and, as Ken had promised, his family was on its way south within the hour.

For the next two days the Fitzgeralds wandered without a sense of purpose down I-65 and the adjacent roads, along with hordes of refugees who carried their worldly possessions in everything from Samsonite luggage and shopping bags to army-surplus ruck sacks.

Ken and Fran talked with as many of the road people as possible in order to glean any information on the war, the fallout, and conditions in general to the south, especially Tennessee.

Late the second day, Ken heard of a place called Deatsville where, according to a teenager he met, there was supposed to be a trainload of food. The young man did indeed have a backpack filled with assorted canned goods he claimed he had obtained from the train. Since the food the Titus family had given the Fitzgeralds would soon be gone, the prospect of adding to their supplies was too good to pass up, especially since the young man had indicated that Deatsville was not far to the east of the interstate.

A two-hour walk took the Fitzgerald family to the little collection of homes, the railroad siding, and the distillery warehouses known as Deatsville. Just as the young man had said, the train, or at least part of it, sat on the tracks. The food, however, was long gone.

The Fitzgeralds learned that on Black Friday the train crew had hastily dropped most of the cars to speed their arrival at their original destination. In the process, Deatsville became the recipient of fifteen boxcars and assorted liquid transport cars, a few of which were loaded with shipments of canned goods from a midwestern cannery.

The godsend didn't last long. Local people descended upon the boxcars like flies to honey, hauling off by car- and truckloads the train's edible contents. What they didn't get, the refugees behind them got, and many of them hauled their finds to the nearby distillery warehouses, most of which had been empty for years. It was here that many refugee families now stood careful guard over their caches.

Initially, Ken had been able to obtain a bit of food here and there from first one family and then the next. This success had encouraged the Fitzgeralds to take up temporary residence, along with three other families, in the little store beside the railroad tracks now emptied of its contents and abandoned by its storekeeper. However, as the days progressed, it appeared that just as with the Titus family, the generosity of the people around them diminished as foodstocks decreased, and it became apparent that conditions would not significantly improve for the foreseeable future.

Ken had done his best to provide for Fran and the children. He constantly searched and scrounged for his family's next meal. Without him she had no idea how they would have gotten by. The physical security that he offered was of equal importance. It seemed obvious that now, more than ever, it was truly a man's world.

"Mom, do you think we'll be going to Aunt Rosie's soon?" asked Cindy, the ten-year-old.

"I don't know, dear. It's such a long way, and we still don't know much about what it's like in Tennessee. It's over a hundred and forty miles, and that's an awfully long walk. You know how dangerous it's supposed to be out . . ."

Fran stopped abruptly as someone, lightly bearded and deeply suntanned, appeared in the doorway.

His forehead wrapped in a sweatband made from a blue bandana, the man stood before her silently, a sawed-off shotgun in his right hand. Though he did not point the weapon in a menacing manner, it still indicated a threat to her and her children—the kind one might sense when entering a yard and discovering the unanticipated presence of a large guard dog. As she stared at the man in the doorway, she noticed for the first time the light rain that was beginning to fall. The man took a step forward into the store and said, "Do you mind if I get in out of the weather?"

Despite the innocuous query, Fran still had serious concerns about the intruder's presence, but did not see any way to object. "No, of course not. Nobody here has anything more than squatter's rights anyway." She hastily and awkwardly added, "My husband and son should be back any time."

The man came forward and brushed the raindrops from his shoulders, arched his back, and removed the large pack he was carrying. He then sat down beside it on the floor and leaned back against the checkout counter. Seemingly oblivious to her presence, he reached into his pack and pulled out an oily rag wrapped in a piece of plastic, and then began to wipe the rain from the shotgun with long, almost loving strokes that people usually reserve for works of art, or objects of high sentimental value. Next, he pulled a long-barreled Smith and Wesson magnum revolver from the holster slung low on his hip and gave it, too, a wipe with the cloth before returning it to his side. He said nothing.

He pulled from his pack a can of Dinty Moore's Beef Stew, and reached into his pocket for a small GI can opener he then used to open it. He pulled a spoon from his pack and began to eat.

Melanie and Cindy sat with their mother, their attention riveted on this man who was devouring the sort of food they had only been able to dream about lately. After he had eaten about half the stew, it seemed that for the first time he became aware of their attention.

"How are you fixed for food?" he asked in a flat tone.

"Not well. We got a few pounds of dry corn from a man yesterday."

The man looked around the store at the other families who clearly had cans of vegetables and other staples in areas of the building they had staked out as their own. "What about them?"

"They don't have much that they can, or at least, will give us. They've got to look out for themselves, I suppose."

The man looked back at the others who seemed for the most part to be ignoring his presence. After a moment, he leaned forward and handed the can to Melanie. Fran took the can from her daughter and evenly divided the contents on a couple of plates.

The man sat silently as each of the girls quickly ate her portion. An almost imperceptible smile came to the corners of his mouth as he watched.

"What's your name?"

"Fran Fitzgerald. This is Cindy and this is Melanie."

There was no immediate response from the man, so Fran, summoning her courage, finally said, "And you. Do you have a name?"

The man looked her straight in the eye without immediately responding, and then looked back at the others across the store and said softly, "O'Hara."

"Do you have a first name, Mr. O'Hara, or is that it?" She smiled, trying to pursue the conversation, but he made no response. "Where are you from?" she asked, but again there was no reply.

Finally, O'Hara asked, "Where are *you* from?"

"Louisville—St. Matthews, actually. Like most everyone else in this place, we're all just trying to get by, but it has been awfully hard since most people seem to be just looking out for themselves."

"I noticed."

"You seem to be getting by all right though." She became aware as she spoke that he seemed to have his attention fixed upon Cindy and Melanie. "Do you have a family nearby?"

Turning his eyes away from the girls, he looked out the door of the store. "I had a wife."

His words told her enough, and she replied softly, "I'm sorry," and then added, "I guess we have to try to look at what's happened as God's will, as hard as that might be to accept. That's the only way to make any sense out of it."

O'Hara's eyes flashed at her with an intensity that made a cold chill run down her spine. "If that was God's will, lady, then maybe the guy needs more *willpower*! Or maybe the simple truth is just that God doesn't particularly give a damn about what happens on this miserable little planet and we had all better adjust to that!"

With that, he reached abruptly and untied the straps to the blanket on top of his pack. He stood up and spread it out on the floor before her. "And now, if you don't mind, I'm going to get a little sleep." He lay down and, almost as if on command, he was asleep in less than a minute.

Cindy and Melanie became occupied with other things, but Fran continued to study O'Hara who was asleep but not, it seemed, at rest. She wondered what inner torments, what images from the past plagued him. She contemplated him with the same strange mixture of warmth and distrust as she had that stray alley cat Cindy brought home a couple of years before.

A huge shorthaired manx whose ears were in ribbons and tatters from innumerable fights over the contents of countless garbage cans or the affections of countless females, the bobtailed cat had the stiff-muscled touch more typical of a bull-terrier. After she and Cindy had finally coaxed him into the house for a saucer of cream, she still felt it necessary to stand back from him in fear that he might at any moment turn on her.

The cat remained only a few days before he answered

some silent call of the wild that beckoned him elsewhere, but Fran had always felt that whatever this cat faced in the future, and no matter how great the odds, he would pull through. She had the same feeling now about O'Hara.

After an hour or so, Ken came abruptly through the door of the store. He was drenched from head to foot, though the rain had subsided by now. In his arms he was cradling ten or twelve potatoes and his pockets were filled with others. "I've hit the jackpot!" he exclaimed. "There's food in Bardstown!"

O'Hara, startled from his sleep by Fitzgerald's noisy entrance, spun in the blanket. His revolver flashed from its holster toward Fitzgerald, bringing the man to an immediate halt, and sending several of the potatoes bouncing across the floor in the process. Fran immediately screamed, "No!"

Finally, realizing this man must be the missing husband, O'Hara slowly lowered the revolver and placed it back in its holster. Without comment, he picked up his blanket and rolled it up. Fitzgerald hesitantly walked over to Fran, and then awkwardly began to pick up the scattered potatoes.

O'Hara took several cans of soup, tuna fish and evaporated milk from his pack, looked at the two girls, and handed the cans to Fran. When he saw Michael walk into the store, O'Hara reached into the pack and handed her two more.

Delighted at the gift, but concerned about the sacrifice he was making, she said, "Thank you, but are you sure?"

"Don't worry," he said without emotion. "I have ways of getting more. I'll always do whatever's necessary to get by." He slung the pack on his back, picked up his shotgun, jacked a round into the chamber, and strode out the door.

Fran walked to the doorway, watching him stride down the road toward Bardstown, and she thought what a very strange and different man he was. And she thought about that cat.

TUESDAY, JUNE 18TH:
The Thirty-Third Day

Hamilton sat in the Orderly Room at a gray desk that matched the other familiar gray metal government furniture around the room. Gray desk, gray filing cabinets, gray bookshelves, gray everything. All of it had no doubt been selected by bureaucrats with tastes and imaginations as banal, bland, and colorless as these furnishings.

Hamilton poured over a report to the county judge by an ad-hoc committee of engineers and others. They were attempting the difficult job of reactivating one of the local distilleries which had previously been modified to produce alcohol for automotive fuel. Though the facility had been dormant many years, there was the prospect of at least limited production within the next few weeks. If there was enough to fuel the police, Guard, and other emergency vehicles this would be a real breakthrough, he thought. He also thought about the fact that ten years at First Fidelity had done little to prepare him for the myriad problems that beset him each day in this job.

He'd spent most of the day supervising the food distribution system, which was steadily becoming more important as an increasing number of refugees ran out of the food they had brought from the city.

The battery had been occupied with two primary tasks, both of which it was woefully unprepared to accomplish. The first was providing security backup to the local police patrols, and the second was the transport of food from local farmers to the food distribution points. Shortages of personnel and equipment created a logistical and operational nightmare, and Hamilton took the opportunity to return to the farm for peace and solitude whenever the opportunity presented itself.

161

On the bright side, six refugee centers were functioning fairly well, the one at Nazareth College being the most successful. The physical limitations of the facilities meant that new refugees were not being accepted, however. Efforts to establish other centers around the county had not been very successful due to the lack of suitable buildings necessary to form a camp core. The bickering, jealousy, and failure to cooperate among the refugees hadn't helped the effort either. And many had refused to submit to the regimented camp lifestyle at all.

Satiating the ever increasing food demands of the refugee horde while trying to maintain law and order was taking a heavy toll on the Guardsmen, not to mention the local police. A siege mentality had developed among the local people in response to the flood of homeless. It had created an "us" and "them" attitude that made the possibility of finding suitable solutions more remote.

Hamilton glanced at a report from Spaulding's office on the refugee situation. He decided that there was nothing new to be learned from it that couldn't wait until morning. And getting home for the first time at a decent hour would help quiet Roseanna's complaints about the time he was spending at the armory. After coordinating with Ackerson and Jackson, he took off for a well-deserved evening away.

Spec. 4th Class Dennis Cochran drove Hamilton to the farm this afternoon. PFC Terry Robinson rode in the back, providing additional security. As Hamilton's jeep rolled down the highway, he noticed against the brilliant, fiery red sky of late afternoon—so common now since the war began—a heavy coil of smoke from the other side of the ridge ahead. When the jeep crossed the ridge he could see that the smoke was coming from the vicinity of a grove of trees a few hundred yards from the main road. A narrow gravel road led toward the area.

At Hamilton's signal, Cochran stopped when he pulled even with the road. "What's back there?" Hamilton asked.

"I hunted back there a couple of years ago, sir," Robinson replied. "If I remember correctly, there are two homes. You can see that two mailboxes are being used," he said, pointing.

"Well, it may be somebody just burning a brushpile, but it wouldn't hurt to investigate."

Cochran turned sharply and drove down the gravel road, leaving a cloud of dust rolling upward behind them. They entered a narrow neck of woods, and as they came out the other side, Hamilton stiffened. Less than a hundred yards away he saw a small house consumed by flames and a nearby mobile home spewing coils of black smoke. Bodies lay scattered about. An old, banged-up pickup truck and two motorcycles were parked on the narrow road running between the two dwellings.

A group of six men was loading the last of several items on the truck when one of them caught sight of the jeep. Hurriedly, two of them jumped on the cycles, two got into the cab, and two hopped in the back of the truck, grabbing at rifles. A burst of shots rang out and one whizzed past Hamilton's head. Another shattered the windshield. The truck then tore away, wheels whirling and gravel flying.

Cochran slid the jeep to a halt in front of the burning home and Hamilton vaulted from the vehicle, pistol in hand.

He ran quickly across the grass and found a middle-aged man lying frozen in death. Fifteen feet away was a woman in her forties, nearly nude, with two gunshot wounds in her chest. Seeing no one else about, and the heat and smoke from the house making it clear that no one could possibly be alive inside, he ran back to the other side of the road.

Robinson ran toward him, gesturing. "Forget it, Major. They're all dead!" Robinson's normally ruddy complexion was now pale and pasty.

Hamilton looked past him and saw the bare feet of the body of a young man clad in jeans lying in the doorway of the mobile home. The small, lifeless body of a young woman was lying in the grass at the end of the little sidewalk. Her only piece of clothing was the halter top gathered up around her armpits.

Hamilton clenched his teeth, spun, and then shouted, "Come on! Let's go get those bastards!" The two men jumped in the jeep and Cochran floored the accelerator. Hamilton jammed his .45 into his holster and grabbed for Cochran's M-16, disengaging the safety. His nostrils flared, he was seething in silent rage as the jeep sped down the gravel road that quickly transitioned to a dirt road across a pasture.

The jeep shot past the twisted remains of a steel farm-gate and just as the guardsmen topped a small rise, the pickup and motorcycles came into view. The truck had bottomed out and gotten hung up in the muddy depression at the bottom of the hill. The group had just finished pushing and frantically shoving it to solid ground.

Because the jeep's canvas top had been recently removed, Robinson was able to stand up and cut loose with three separate four-round bursts of automatic fire. Two of the men at the rear of the truck wrenched violently and slammed against the tailgate, ricocheting into the mud. Another dived into the back of the pickup and two more jumped on their motorcycles. The truck spun its wheels and fishtailed wildly in the soft earth before finally obtaining traction.

As the jeep approached the bog, Cochran swerved quickly and rolled over one of the prone figures still moving. Hamilton shot a glance at Cochran and saw him staring forward with a locked jaw. His eyes riveted ahead, he shifted gears and said, "That'll make damned sure."

A bullet fired from the man in the rear of the truck whizzed overhead, and Robinson cracked off several more in return. Due to the rough terrain and the jeep's rebounding suspension, most of the shots seemed to miss their mark widely. The two vehicles nevertheless continued as fast as the two drivers dared push them until, at last, the truck came out on the highway. Again, it crashed through a gate and then made a hard right turn on to the asphalt.

At that point Hamilton's jeep closed on the truck, and he fired a short burst of automatic fire from his M-16. The man in the back of the truck spun, then fell out of the vehicle, scarlet pennants of blood trailing behind him as he crashed into a mailbox at the side of the road and snapped in two the wooden post supporting it. The truck continued on, however, picking up speed rapidly and taking advantage of the straightaway to increase the gap between the jeep and itself. The two motorcycles ahead of the truck easily pulled away from it and disappeared down the road.

The chase continued for two miles. Hamilton had just emptied his magazine and had popped it free in order to ram another in its place when he felt the vehicle approaching a turn. He looked up just in time to see the curve ahead, but what he did not see until it was too late were the two motorcyclists who had dismounted—and who were now waiting for him.

Cochran snapped back violently, and then slumped forward after a bullet crashed through what was left of the windshield and slammed into his chest. The jeep left the road and shot down an embankment. It crashed into several small trees and rolled over twice before coming to rest.

Hamilton's initial horror at what was happening when he was suspended in air was abruptly replaced by excruciating pain when he slammed into one of the smaller trees and tumbled into the underbrush.

When he finally came to his senses, his brain still dully swirling, he concluded that he must still be alive. He hurt too much to be dead.

He saw green leaves floating above him, almost dancing against the gray-red background of the sky. He felt a warm, wet, oozing sensation from the top of his head and the trickle from the furrows left by briars across his cheek. His left shoulder felt as if it had been hit with a sledgehammer, and his legs felt no better.

It was as if somewhere within him a dam had burst and a wave of pain now rolled through his body. Except for the whirling front tire of the nearby jeep, there was silence. Dead silence.

After a few seconds, he finally remembered what had happened. As he lay motionless on the hillside among the weeds and the brush, Hamilton could hear the crackle of dry leaves and the sounds of voices from the area above him.

"Hoss! There they are!" exclaimed one, a young, plump man with long, frizzed hair and beard. He wore a black T-shirt emblazoned with a Harley-Davidson logo and bearing the slogan, If They Don't Have Harleys In Heaven, I'll Ride Mine Straight to Hell. He continued down the hillside and shouted, "I wanna make sure these bastards are dead!"

"Aw, c'mon, Butch, you jackass," Hoss said. "We should be laying rubber. Somebody's gonna be coming along. To hell with these mothers."

"*No way*, man. They got Moose and Bob, and they're gonna *pay*!"

"What about Cowboy?"

"To hell with Cowboy, I never liked him anyway," Butch chuckled, picking his way gingerly through the heavy briars. "I wouldn't have walked across the street to piss in his mouth if his teeth were on fire."

"Man, you must have an asshole under your nose, cause that's where so much shit comes out."

So this cretin was coming to kill him, Hamilton thought. Through his mind flashed an image of Roseanna widowed and the kids fatherless. Well, not yet—at least not so easily. If this was his time to go, and this son of a bitch was going to kill him, he decided that Jack Hamilton's little portion of the world would end with a bang.

Moving very slowly, he reached down and pulled his .45 from its holster. With salty sweat rolling down into his eyes, he quietly cocked the hammer and waited, perspiration slickening his grip, his heart pounding wildly.

"They're right down here, Hoss," the first man called out reassuringly to the other. "I gotta get these M-16s, too. Do you realize what a guy can do with one of these automatic motherfuckers? Man, there will be no stopping us!"

When Butch was about fifteen feet away, Hamilton summoned all of his strength and then quickly rolled over and fired one quick shot that struck the man squarely in the chest. Butch was instantly pounded backward against the trunk of a large oak tree, and for a moment, he looked like a large woolly bear scratching his back against the tree. His bulging incredulous eyes, and the protruding tendons of his neck, however, were proof that it gave him no pleasure or relief. Crimson stains spread across his T-shirt like a red rose budding in time-lapse photography. He slid to his knees, dropped the rifle, and with a look of total disbelief on his face, fell forward on his chest.

The man named Hoss, still much further uphill, found that the thick undergrowth made it impossible for him to draw down on Hamilton immediately. While Hoss struggled to get a clean shot, Hamilton judged where he thought the man's torso to be in the brush, then fired three shots in rapid succession. One of them smashed through the man's sternum, through his aorta, and beyond. The man collapsed with the grace of the instantly dead. He rolled limply several feet down the hillside through the heavy briars, a scream frozen forever in his throat.

Hamilton listened intently as a finger of gray-blue smoke curled from the barrel of his automatic. Silence. Dead silence, once again.

Slowly he worked himself to his feet and loaded a fresh magazine into the pistol. With considerable difficulty and excruciating pain, he made his way on rubbery legs to the two men and checked to see if they were actually dead. Satisfied, he made his way to Cochran, only to find him dead also. After searching for a couple of minutes— minutes that seemed more like hours—he found Robinson. He had not been wounded in the ambush, but he was dead from the impact. His brain throbbing, Hamilton slumped to the ground, trying to gather his strength.

Finally, he pulled himself to his feet again and made his way, one halting step after another, up to the highway. He stumbled to the pavement's edge and sat down on the grassy shoulder. His head was pounding and the blood continued to run down his temple from the cut in his scalp.

The world spun before his eyes, and he thought he was about to vomit. But then he heard the sound of an engine, and as it grew louder, Hamilton groped lamely for his pistol. In the blur he could see that it was a pickup approaching, and he pointed the gun toward the vehicle—ready for one last stand. Finally, he relaxed and gave out a sigh of relief as the truck slowed down and he was able to see that the occupants were a young couple with two small children.

The young man in a red International Harvester baseball cap got out of the cab and walked cautiously over to him.

"Jesus, mister! You look like you've been in all kinds of trouble," the man said.

"You could say that," Hamilton replied, just before he passed out.

WEDNESDAY, JUNE 19TH:
The Thirty-Fourth Day

When Hamilton awoke, the first thing he saw was Chris above him checking his dressings. She smiled when she saw that he was awake, "You know how to give your sister-in-law a good scare, fella," she said.

"Where am I?"

"In the principal's office of the high school. Since the hospital's just next door, we're keeping the less severely injured patients here. A family found you lying on the side of the road yesterday and brought you in."

"How bad am I banged up?" He awkwardly tried to pull himself up in the bed. His effort was cut short by the stabbing pain in his shoulder.

"All things considered, you came out of it very well. A nasty cut to your head, a dislocated shoulder, a slight concussion, and a badly bruised remainder-of-your-body, you might say. On the whole, nothing that you'll notice very much in a couple of weeks. Given the press of people here, only the possibility of a serious head injury got you this bed. Dr. Raymond wanted to get you out of here last night, but I got you put in here until the morning. That's what 'friends in high places' are for. Right?"

Hamilton looked at her and returned her warm smile. That Chris was something else, he thought. A heavenly body and a devilish disposition. He had not seen her very much since she'd left the farm that first day after they left the fallout shelter. According to the reports he had been getting from others, she had performed like a true professional in recent weeks. He could tell she was fatigued now.

Her performance would have pleased her mother, who had worried all her life about her daughter's tendency to party rather than seriously apply herself to anything. How

168

she had ever been able to handle her social life and get through nursing school was an amazement to her mother as well as Roseanna. Roseanna the student. Chris the party girl. Maybe now it was just that all the parties were over.

"We've been trying to figure out exactly what happened out there," Chris said. "Can you remember?"

Hamilton began recounting the discovery of the murders and the ensuing chase, and then finally asked, "Does Roseanna know about me?"

"Of course. She's been here all night and should be back any minute. Your lieutenant friend, Ted, was up here also. He asked me to let you know that he's taken care of the wrecked jeep and the arrangements for the two young men who were with you yesterday. I'm very sorry about the two boys. It must have been awful. All that killing."

"Yeah," Hamilton responded, without elaborating. Before that day, the only things that Hamilton had killed were two rabbits and that rattlesnake they found on the Boy Scout trip when he was a kid. One of the other scouts had found it just outside the tent one morning, and Hamilton's quick blow with a well-aimed hatchet had dispatched it to rattlesnake heaven. All that stuff he had been taught in the scouts about the environment and nature's balance aside, he felt good when he saw the snake lying lifeless, its fangs no longer of any danger to anyone in the camp.

Oddly, he had the same feelings about killing the three men yesterday as he had after killing that snake. A strong sense of satisfaction. He decided against expressing these feelings to Chris, however, because he didn't know how she might react to this new side of him. In the long run, he didn't know how *he* would react to this new side of him.

Roseanna walked into the room, came up to the bed and kissed him. Pressing her hand against his she said, "Sweetheart, you had me nearly worried to death again. How are you feeling?"

"Every inch of my body is sore."

"Listen, after we get you home, I'll give you a good rubdown with some liniment. The jeep is supposed to be here in a few minutes, so let's get you dressed while you tell me all about what happened."

"How did you know I would be up and about by now?" he asked as Roseanna started to help him sit up.

"We didn't," replied Chris as she started out the door. "It was simply that one way or another, you had to be out of that bed by ten o'clock. Your *friends* weren't in *that* high a place!"

The jeep arrived to pick up Hamilton just before ten. Hamilton related to Ackerson the gory details of the previous day's incident, and Ackerson reported other incidents that had occurred that night around the county. To Roseanna's consternation, Hamilton refused the wheelchair and walked haltingly to the jeep that awaited him. As he got in he said, "Before I go to the farm, Ted, I want to talk to Spaulding."

"Oh really, Jack! You're going to kill yourself for people who couldn't care less about you. Can't it wait?" Roseanna exclaimed.

"No, it can't," he replied firmly. "Before I go back to the farm to lick my wounds I've got to talk to him face to face."

Ackerson drove the jeep to Spaulding's office. After pulling up in front of the building, Ackerson sprang from his seat and jogged down the sidewalk and inside to find Spaulding. After a couple of minutes, both Ackerson and the judge came out the door and walked to the jeep.

"Judge Spaulding, I don't believe you've met my wife, Roseanna."

After an exchange of courtesies and the usual compliments, directed to Roseanna, that Hamilton expected from a politician, Hamilton continued, "Sorry to have to ask you to step out here, but I'm not in shape to tap dance my way up those steps right now."

"Certainly," replied Spaulding. "My boy, you had a close one from what we heard. You're just lucky to be alive. And I'm so sorry to hear about those two boys. I know their parents quite well."

"Which is part of the reason why I'm here. I think these random killings for a loaf of bread or a box of shotgun shells or whatever are going to increase. I don't think these incidents are being committed by the same people. They're too widespread. Just different groups who came to the same conclusion about how they should deal with the shortages and get what they want. The method they've chosen is likely to become more common in the weeks ahead, I suspect.

We've just been lucky that the lid has been kept on as well as it has so far."

Spaulding frowned at his words and stared into the distance for a few seconds as he contemplated their meaning. "What exactly are you proposing that we do about the problem?"

"Well, it's obvious that the arm-twisting efforts to encourage locals to take in the homeless were not well-received. Lots of the refugees were sent packing within the hour by their new landlords. And the efforts at organizing the refugee centers haven't been a great success, either, though we can't give up.

"But now, I'm proposing that we go out to the people on the farms and anyone else with a patch of land big enough to cultivate and tell them, preach to them, and if necessary, beg them to take in as many homeless people as they can handle and put them to work. First, it will eliminate the idleness and boredom which are causing so many of the problems in town. Second, it will permit the refugees to start answering for themselves the food shortage problem, and prevent many of them from turning to violence to obtain the food they need. Third, the farmers or other people who take in these people will have labor to work the land they won't be able to work with mechanized means in the long run because of fuel shortages. Fourth, the farmers who take in the new people will be more secure with the extra 'company' than they would be otherwise. Simply a case of strength in numbers, rather than waiting out there like fruit ripe for the picking. And last, it may end this 'us' and 'them' attitude which, if it persists, will be the damnation of us all."

Hamilton paused and studied the judge's impassive face.

Finally, Spaulding looked back to Hamilton and said, "Major, if you had come to me with this idea a week ago, I would have told you that you were crazier than hell if you thought that the farmers around here would allow themselves to be saddled with some of the ragtag elements that are overrunning the town. Not that they wouldn't do what they could to help out the less fortunate—to a point. But opening themselves up to what might be people who would pack off everything of value seems over the line. And then there would be all those extra mouths to feed. Besides, the whole idea sort of smacks of feudalism, doesn't it? I mean, almost like landowners and peasants, or at least sharecroppers."

"I don't care what you call it, Judge, and many of them may not go for it. But for every person we get out of town and on a piece of land, that's one less mouth to feed here, and one less problem for me and *you* as well. For the farmers, it's one more hand to have there to help in times of emergency or otherwise. Both sides are doing what's in their own self-interest, but everybody makes out."

"It's something to think about, Major," responded Spaulding. "Maybe we'll just have to figure out how to sell the idea to the local people. I'll think this over and maybe we can get together and talk about it further as soon as you're feeling a little better."

"Great, Judge. I just hope that we don't have a higher body count in the meantime. I'll see you in a few days." He turned to Ackerson and signaled him to proceed to the farm. As the jeep started forward, however, Hamilton noticed Johnson approaching them in another jeep. Johnson was obviously agitated, and Ackerson brought his vehicle to a quick halt and waited for him to pull alongside.

"What is it, Top?" Hamilton asked.

"It's bad, sir. Four of our boys on patrol near Holy Cross were ambushed. Goodman, Savage, and Simmons were killed, and Thomas was left for dead, though he looks like he'll make it. Their jeep was taken and so were their weapons. Just left all of 'em lying in a ditch along the road without a clue as to who did it. Another one of these goddam roadside ambushes!"

"Get me back to the armory!" Hamilton snapped angrily. As the jeep took off and sped through town, Hamilton wondered how he was going to hold the unit together with the steadily increasing casualties to both Guardsmen and citizens being inflicted by unseen, or at least, very elusive foes.

His initial burst of anger at the grim news gave way to a profound depression.

FRIDAY, JUNE 21ST:
The Thirty-Sixth Day

Jack and Roseanna stood next to each other among the crowd of two hundred who came to attend the funeral of the five slain Guardsmen. For the first time since they had left the fallout shelter, the weather was clear and sunny. Another of those weather fronts of cool air that were so common since the war began had pushed through the area the previous night. The sky was dotted with delicate puffs of small clouds, and if there ever was a nice day for a funeral, this was it.

As the procession approached the grave sites, the firing party positioned itself so that it could fire properly over the graves. As none of the civilian hearses in Bardstown had run since the day of the nuclear attack, a pair of two-and-a-half-ton trucks served as simple hearses for the five caskets. Ackerson, as the escort commander, cleared his throat and commanded, *"Present, Arms!"* in a firm and emotionless voice, trying hard to maintain a professional demeanor, though emotion tugged at him.

As the pallbearers began removing each flag-draped casket from the vehicles, the minister led the crowd in singing "Amazing Grace."

The caskets were slowly carried one by one to their graves. Families of the dead soldiers took their positions next to the graves, and Ackerson then gave the escort the command, "Parade rest."

The minister stepped forward and looked at the assemblage. "Dearly beloved," he said, "it is with heavy hearts that we come here today to pay our final respects to the brave young men who gave their lives in the service of their country: Lawrence Savage, Marshall Goodman, Terry Robinson, Dennis Cochran, and Kyle Simmons. They were fine young men who were loved by their families and friends, and who were respected in the community. They served their country well."

The minister, a tall, middle-aged man with an ascetic look, proceeded to mention each dead soldier by name and to extol his individual virtues. "It is ironic," he continued, "that after surviving the horrible calamity which has caused more loss of life than our country, or any other country, has ever known, that they should at this time die in the service of their state and nation. So ironic and so unfortunate. Yet, we are reminded of Him who also laid down His life for all of us so long ago.

"Perhaps on similar occasions this particular hymn might not be used, with perhaps others being deemed more appropriate. But now, considering the circumstances of the great task and the great hardship confronting us in the coming months and years, please join with me in singing a hymn which I believe expresses the hope of a Christian people, and their faith and trust in their God in seeing them through a time of great suffering and trouble."

The minister began the old religious standard, and the mourners followed, singing it perhaps with more emotion and fervor than ever before:

> *A mighty Fortress is our God,*
> *A bulwark never failing;*
> *Our Helper He amid the flood*
> *Of mortal ills prevailing. . . .*

As the final strains of the hymn echoed, the minister continued. "In searching for comfort at the loss of these five boys who gave their lives in war as surely as did any soldier on any foreign battlefield, let us turn to the Book of Isaiah, where it refers to a better time, and says, '. . . For out of Zion shall go forth the law, and the word of the Lord from Jerusalem. And he shall judge among the nations, and shall rebuke many people: and they shall beat their swords into plowshares, and their spears into pruning hooks: nation shall not lift up sword against nation, neither shall they learn war any more.'"

After the minister's concluding comments about the Resurrection and eternal life, Ackerson brought the escort to attention, and then to present arms. Three rapid volleys were fired. "Taps" was then sounded, and as the mournful notes of the trumpet carried across the cemetery, each soldier in the crowd came to attention and saluted. The only accompaniment to the sound of the trumpet was the weeping of relatives and friends.

Finally, the flags were presented to the next of kin, ending the ceremony.

Hamilton walked hesitantly toward the road, leaning on Roseanna for support because of the painful injuries to his leg. He stopped where some of the families of the dead Guardsmen were accepting the condolences of friends, and finally approached the mother of Dennis Cochran, his dead driver, trying to find a few words to comfort her.

"You know," she said to him, though her eyes were fixed in the distance, "what the pastor said is so true. My boy survived one of the world's greatest disasters, and then had to die like this. It really *is* ironic. But you know, after he said that, I started to think about what the situation really is now, with all of this killing going on and such. I guess what it comes down to is this: first, you survive the Russians, and then you have to survive your own people. I never thought about it that way until now, but this is really all part of the same war, like he said. That's just how it is."

"Yes, ma'm," Hamilton replied, searching for a better response, but unable to come up with one.

"Come along, Alice," said the woman's husband. He took her by the arm, and then shook Hamilton's hand in silence with only a slight nod.

As the couple walked away, Hamilton stood there looking at the shattered families of the slain Guardsmen. They now clutched at the folded flags in grief and bewilderment, almost as a small child clutches a favorite blanket in times of stress or insecurity. He watched the crowd slowly moving away from the gravesites and reflected upon how small the number of mourners had been. As he did so, a steadily increasing resentment arose in him.

Of the many thousands of people now in the county, only this token crowd of two hundred, half of them Guardsmen, had bothered to pay their respects to these five men who had made the ultimate sacrifice on their behalf. He felt betrayed. And it angered him.

He looked at the small knots of mourners moving away from him. There is no romance of a noble, heroic death here, he thought. Just children who will never see their fathers again, and wives who will never know their husbands' affectionate embraces.

After a few moments, he walked slowly back to the jeep with Roseanna. He then turned once more toward the gravesites and said in a voice Roseanna had to strain to hear, "First, you survive the Russians. *Then* you survive the Americans."

"I am sick of this shit!" the young man screamed at the couple across the campfire. He stood in front of a shelter recently constructed of scrap lumber, canvas, and cardboard.

Charlie Brighton might have backhanded his son for this sort of talk just a couple of years ago, but his aging process, and his son's growth process had irreversibly shifted the balance of physical power between Charles, Jr., and himself. At six feet three, Charles, Jr., was four inches taller than his father, and forty pounds heavier. He was the sort of hulk who had prompted college football coaches to spend many days and evenings with the Brighton family over the past year in hopes of signing Charlie's son. All that had changed now.

Charles, Jr., or Charlie Boy as the family still called him, was as physically imposing as he was emotionally immature. He had been accustomed to the deference reserved for a star athlete throughout his high school years, and his demands for getting things his own way had been fueled by an overindulgent mother who catered to his every whim, especially if she thought it might further the athletic career in whose reflected glory she hoped to bask.

Charlie blamed himself as much as his wife for the way she had pampered Charlie Boy, because he had not acted effectively to correct the situation. With his being transferred so often, and spending so much time away from home on one Marine Corps assignment or another, most of the child-rearing duties had been left to her by default.

On the other hand, it was Rick, the son a year younger, who seemed to have the good head on his shoulders. Unlike his brother, his prowess was at books and learning. Though he was slightly taller than average, Rick was proof that athletic ability was not always something that ran in the family.

"Don't talk to me and your mother like that," Charlie snapped after his son's outburst, "or I'll. . . ."

"Or you'll what?" shot back Charlie Boy contemptuously.

"Or *we'll* kick your ass," Rick interrupted.

"Fat chance!"

"Stop it! Stop it, all of you!" Eve Brighton shrieked. "We've got to keep this family together and this isn't going to help things at all!" This was the third time in as many days such an exchange had taken place, and she wasn't sure she could handle any more.

Lowering his voice somewhat, Charlie Boy gestured to the hundred or so other families scattered across the state park campground on the edge of Bardstown. A crazy quilt of makeshift shelters, the area was the site of an attempt to organize a formal refugee center operated and maintained by the refugees themselves. Petty rivalries as well as an unwillingness to work for group needs as opposed to individual needs, had doomed it from the start. Now it was a ramshackle shadow of the camp that had been originally envisioned.

"Look at this shit! People living like animals. Like goddam apes outta some goddam Tarzan jungle movie. Well, the world *may* be a jungle now, but I wasn't made to live like this! We're livin' in filth, and each night we get eaten up by mosquitoes. Swarms of flies, rats runnin' about everywhere, and people taking shits where ever they feel like it! Christ, is it any wonder that so many people are coming down sick?

"It's like we're welfare scum or somethin', waitin' for some goddam cheese giveaway. All day long we just squat in these shacks waiting for those soldier boys who think they're *God* to drive up with a few miserable sacks of grain, a few potatoes or what have you. Do you think those soldier boys are eatin' that shit? Hell, no! Goddam helicopters bring in *their* food! I've had my fill of eatin' gruel made from cracked corn, and if I *ever* see wheat sprouts again, I'm gonna vomit!"

"But they're full of vitamin C, son," his mother replied.

"*Screw* vitamin C, Mom!" he exploded. "Human beings

shouldn't have to live like this. It's just not right, and somebody ought to have to pay. God, what I'd give for some meat! Real meat! I'm not a goddam vegetarian!"

"You're acting like an eight-year-old!" his father shouted. "Maybe we shouldn't have to live like this, but you're just damned lucky we made it this far."

Unable to avoid overhearing the argument at the shanty adjacent to her own, Fran Fitzgerald, a new arrival, walked over to the Brighton campfire, and attempted to help her new friends end the squabble. "Excuse me for interrupting, but Ken was able to come across a few canned goods this morning, and I thought we might share some with you. Would you care for this can of pork and beans?"

Charlie Boy swung his hand and smacked the can from her grasp. "Screw your beans, and screw your charity, bitch!" he screamed. "I'm sick of always living on other people's charity!"

As if in response to a quarterback's signal, Charlie and Rick bolted across the small fire and hit Charlie Boy at the knees and mid-section as charging linebackers might a hapless quarterback. The three went sprawling and Charlie Boy found himself pinned to the ground beneath the two.

"Now you apologize to Mrs. Fitzgerald," said his father after the struggling stopped, "or I'll slap the crap out of you!"

At first Charlie Boy said nothing, and then finally he said, "Mrs. Fitzgerald . . ." Before he finished, however, he jerked rapidly and caught his two captors off guard, causing them to lose their holds, and allowing himself to fight his way to his feet. Once upright he stood hunched over breathlessly with both hands clenched, as if daring the two smaller men to continue the attack. After a few seconds it was obvious that there would be nothing further from his brother and father, and he said bluntly, "I'm leaving." He walked resolutely into the shelter and grabbed what few things he had, stuffing them into a gym bag while his mother repeatedly begged him to reconsider.

Ignoring her, he left the shelter and looked at his father, brother, and Fran Fitzgerald. "A man, a real man, doesn't have to get by like this. I've heard there are plenty who don't, and I mean to find them. I pity you if you're going to keep living like this!" He then turned abruptly and walked away.

With tears pouring down her cheeks, Eve Brighton called out to him. "If you decide to come back, son, we'll try to leave word where we are if we have to move!"

Rick took his mother gently by the arm. "I have a feeling he won't be coming back, Mom."

Charlie, his jaw clenched, watched silently as his son walked away. Part of him wanted to call out and beg the boy to stay, but another part said no, at least not on the boy's terms.

Fran Fitzgerald walked silently back toward the little shanty next door, somewhat embarrassed at having become involved in her neighbors' private matters.

Thank God, she thought, at least her family was still together.

SATURDAY, JUNE 22ND: The Thirty-Seventh Day

"Chris Whittington?" the young man asked.

"Yes," Chris said, brushing aside a wisp of hair that kept falling into her eyes.

"I'm Bill Lee, Deirdre's husband."

Chris's face lit up, and she forgot the fatigue that was tearing at her from too many hours without sleep. Deirdre and she had been the best of friends for three semesters in nursing school. Deirdre found it necessary to drop out of school for personal reasons, but she and Chris had maintained occasional contact ever since. "Deirdre's husband?" she exclaimed. "It's really good to finally meet you. I'm sorry that I wasn't able to get to your wedding. How is Deirdre?"

"Not well, and that's why I'm here," he replied.

From the expression on his face, Chris could see that the matter was serious. "She was helping me on the roof of the house with some loose shingles. She lost her balance and fell. I'm afraid to move her and the hospital in Lebanon is so swamped that they can't send anyone for her. We've done the best we can for her, but she's still lying where she fell this morning. We heard last week that you were over here, and so I thought you would be the only chance to get medical help anytime soon. She's hurt *really* bad. Can you come?"

"Certainly," she said. "Just give me a minute to let somebody know."

When she walked up to the nurses' station, she explained the situation to Charge Nurse Miller.

"Wait a minute!" shot back the nurse. "We need you here. There are all of these people here and only you and I in this ward. You can't leave now. You have professional responsibilities."

Chris flushed at the remark about professional responsibilities, a bugaboo term used to subdue nurses anytime their personal needs conflicted with someone else's, whether in salary negotiations, strike votes, or otherwise. As usual, it produced the desired effect. Chris responded defensively. "Listen. I don't have time for the mathematics of who's here and who's there! I've chained myself to this place for weeks without a day off. I've got six hours of overdue sack time coming right now, and if I choose to use it this way, that's my business! You can always get Jill in here." Taking off her white lab coat and slamming it down on the counter, she said, "Besides, these people are total strangers, and a good friend out there needs me. I'm not on your damned payroll, so to hell with you and your professional responsibilities!" Pausing only long enough to throw an emergency kit together, she stalked down the corridor, out of the hospital, and up to the waiting truck.

Lee and another man were standing by the truck when she exited the hospital door. "Ready?" Lee asked anxiously.

"Yes, except that I haven't had any sleep for so long I've stopped counting, and those bags of feed back there look like they might make a decent bed. Mind if I crawl up on that stuff and try to cat nap on the way?"

"No problem. Hop in. By the way, this is Todd."

Todd smiled and quickly moved toward her to take advantage of the opportunity of placing his hands around her waist to help her up. Before the truck had cleared town, she was soundly asleep.

She remained that way until her rest was abruptly interrupted by a series of loud noises and the violent maneuvering of the truck. Her bewilderment was absolute. The truck careened off the road and over a large log, catapulting her into the air. Though her effort to tuck and roll helped considerably, her body met the ground with a brutal impact.

She had no idea where she was or what was happening. Though her head was still spinning, Chris could see the truck lying on its side about fifty feet from her. Had there been an accident? The reports of two gunshots immediately caused her to flatten her body to the ground.

After several seconds, Chris heard footsteps approaching through the high grass. She could smell him before she could see him. Cautiously, she looked up at an obese man with a red beard, a redder face, and brown scum between his teeth.

The man held a shotgun pointed directly at her. The look on his face was clearly one of amusement. The feeling was not infectious.

"Well, little lady, you're the bonus prize, I expect. Almost missed you in this grass. Hey, Roy!" he yelled to his unseen partner. "Come over and see what we got ourselves here!"

Chris raised up and saw another man, who was leaning into the window of the pickup. In response to the first man's call, he looked at her with a sickly, almost toothless grin. She felt a chill as she realized the seriousness of the situation. "They're dead, Frank," said the gangly, razor-thin man standing by the truck. His voice held no hint of remorse.

"Aw, to hell with them, look at this!" Frank looked back at Chris with a twinkle in his eye.

Chris sat up and tried to keep control of herself. As Roy walked up, she saw that he, too, was carrying a shotgun. Roy was even seedier looking than Frank, and he looked as if his gray-speckled beard was working on its second week's growth. "Well, I'll be damned!" he said. "We didn't know you was in the truck, or else we'd've been more careful. Wouldn't've wanted to damage the merchandise." With that the two broke into laughter.

"You mean you just killed those two men like that?" she cried in disbelief. "For what?"

"Well, for whatever they had," said Roy. "They had this nice revolver and twenty rounds of ammo," he said, holding up the gun and pistol belt that she recognized as the one Bill Lee had been wearing. He strapped it on like a child who had received a new toy. Roy was definitely from the shallow end of the gene pool.

"You mean you murdered two men for a gun and a few rounds of ammunition?"

"Aw, hell, lady, you never know," said Frank, the fat one. "Sometimes we do better, in fact most times. Right, Roy?" The thin gunman nodded with a toothless grin that might almost have been described as bashful. "That feed on there is worth somethin'," he continued, "but for us it's too bulky to screw with. But this gun's worth the bother, and the gasoline's damned important with all the shortages. Hell, me and Roy can eat high on the hog for a month with just that ammo to trade, and we can even use it to make our next 'transaction' with somebody else!"

"Right, Frank. Our *transactions*. But this transaction ain't complete. So let's get on with it!" Roy said with a boyish glee as he laid down his shotgun and grabbed Chris roughly by the upper arms. Chris immediately started to struggle and scream. Frank quickly backhanded her.

"Little lady, now don't make this hard on yourself, cause I can get a lot rougher. Besides you just might enjoy yourself!" He stepped forward and grabbed both sides of her blouse, ripping it open down the front. She jerked and fought as he pulled at the zipper of her jeans, kicking at his crotch and barely missing.

Her struggle caused Roy to lose his balance, and together they fell to the ground. Roy howled with delight. "Frank, we got ourselves a real wildcat!" It was clear that he was enjoying the contest as a kid might a pillow fight.

Frank unbuckled his belt and unzipped his fly, saying, "Well, we'll just see how wild . . ."

Frank's head exploded like a melon hit with a ball bat, spraying Chris and Roy with a cloud of pink steam. The report of a rifle shot followed a split-second later. Roy immediately released Chris, gasping, "J-J-Jesus Christ!" He sat there paralyzed with horror, looking at Frank's nearly headless body sprawled on the ground. Finally, Roy was on his feet and running. In his haste he left his shotgun behind.

Chris wanted to scream, but couldn't. She rolled over to search for the source of the rifle fire, her terror complete. Within seconds she heard a motorcycle approaching through the woods. Out of the tree line running along a creek bed thundered a solitary helmeted rider, dressed in black and silver racing leathers.

The rider continued full-throttle across the field until he met the embankment leading up to the highway, taking it at an angle. Rider and cycle shot effortlessly over the wire fence separating the pasture from the road.

The rider came to a perfect landing on the gravel shoulder of the road, then raced toward Roy, who was now running toward an old car parked back in the bushes a couple of hundred feet down the road.

The rider reached down and pulled out a machete from a scabbard attached to the side of the bike, and then stood up on the footrests as he neared Roy. A few seconds too late, it dawned on Roy that the newly acquired pistol was on his side. As he pulled it from its holster, the machete came down swiftly with a well-placed blow that definitively terminated the chase.

The rider slowed to a halt thirty to forty yards down the road, replaced his machete in its scabbard, and then turned around. Stopping at the prone figure, he took the revolver and pistol belt, then continued back toward Chris.

Chris clutched at her blouse, trying to cover herself as well as she could without buttons, and then wiped at her eyes. The rider slowed as he came across the grass and stopped his cycle about ten feet from her.

He dismounted, knelt before her, and raised the dark visor to his helmet. Finally, sliding the helmet off his head, he looked her in the eyes saying gently, "My name is Kurt Rogers. Are you all right?"

"My God!" she cried, fighting back the tears as she clutched at her blouse. "I've never been through anything like this in my life!"

"Most people haven't. Unfortunately, it's becoming more common every day." Extending his hand, he helped her to her feet. She continued to struggle with the blouse. "Try a loose square knot at the bottom," he suggested.

"Thanks," she said, wiping at her cheek and then acting on the suggestion. "Just where did *you* come from, anyway?"

"Up on that ridge. I was trailing some dogs that tore up some of our livestock last night when I heard the gunfire. I rode up to the top of the hill to investigate. That's when I saw you and this scum," he said, motioning to the man lying in the grass.

"You mean you shot that man from up there? That must be a half mile!"

"Three hundred yards is more like it. That's an HK-91 rifle. German military," he said, pointing to the strange black weapon slung in a scabbard on his bike. "With a scope on it like that, and using Glaser Safety Slugs, it was a good shot, but not a great shot. I was actually aiming for his chest. It's a terrific gun when you *really* want to 'reach out and touch someone.' "

"Well, thank God for small miracles. But was that machete really necessary? You could have captured him, couldn't you? Even if the bastard had it coming, you could have turned him in to the authorities."

Rogers leaned forward as she talked and brushed the hair on her temple gently to the side as he checked the small cut on her head. "Maybe it was the challenge," he said simply, preoccupied with the wound to her scalp. "But turning him in to 'the authorities' as you put it is almost a laugh now. What are they going to do with him with no courts operating for who knows how long? Anyway what are you doing out here?"

"My girlfriend has been hurt, and her husband and a friend came after me. I'm a nurse and I was helping out at the hospital in Bardstown. We were ambushed as you can see. Jesus! I almost forgot! I'd better check on Bill and Todd."

Chris got up and, with Rogers' help, limped to the truck. She checked first one and then the other. "Both of them are dead," she said solemnly. "This'll really be hard on Deirdre."

"Deirdre?"

"My girlfriend. Do you think you can get me there? I've got a vague idea where she lives. It's not far from Raywick."

"Do you think you're in good enough condition to ride on the back of this thing?" he asked, motioning over his shoulder to his cycle. She nodded. "Then come on. We're just a stone's throw from Raywick. We'll go there and ask around. Somebody is bound to know."

He quickly gathered the firearms, carried them to the cycle, and tied them to the side. He swung his leg over the seat, and then held out his hand to help Chris take her place behind him. Two rapid kicks brought the motor to life again. Rogers revved the engine, engaged the clutch, and set off across the pasture to the road.

SUNDAY, JUNE 23RD:
The Thirty-Eighth Day

As Chris Whittington slowly retreated from sleep, she sensuously stretched her legs and arms. As sensuously, that is, as one whose entire body was one large bruise *could* stretch. She turned over to peer out the window at the late morning sky. It had been wonderful sleeping weather, as usual. After all, it hadn't even hit the mideighties this summer, a welcome departure from the norm.

After inquiring around Raywick the previous day, Rogers had been able to locate someone who knew where Deirdre lived. Upon arriving they found that Deirdre had died just after her husband left for help. Together with the day's earlier events, the news was more of a shock than Chris could tolerate. Rogers insisted that she come to The Aerie where she could get some badly needed rest in a safe environment.

With considerable trouble, Chris sat up in bed and examined her "night clothes," one of Rogers' sport shirts. At just that moment, the door to the other end of the trailer opened and Rogers entered. She peered around the partition and said "Hi."

Rogers placed the canned goods he was carrying on the counter and responded, "Good morning. How're you feeling?"

"Not well, not well at all. I've got bruises in places where I didn't even know I had places."

"How about some aspirin?" he suggested as he reached up to a shelf by the sink and picked up a container.

She rose from the bed, wincing from soreness, and walked toward him. "I appreciate all you've done for me. You've been terrific. A lot of people wouldn't have lifted a finger, not wanting to get involved and all that." She reached out and took the two aspirin and the glass of water he held out to her.

"Well, I would have killed those two Neanderthals for anyone, and I'd have helped anyone into town. But to tell you the truth, the fact that you're so warm and attractive had just a *little* influence on my bringing you back here." His handsome face broke into a broad, infectious grin.

"Attractive? I must look a horror right now."

"Not to me."

"Well, anyway, when do I get the tour?"

A puzzled expression came to his face. "The tour?"

"Of the farm. You said yesterday that you would show me around."

"Oh, yeah. Well, anytime you want. How about some Sunday brunch first? And as long as you're feeling okay, we'll do it after that."

"Fine," she responded. "But first can I get a bath or shower? I haven't had a chance to bathe at the hospital for three days now."

"Sure. Right in that door. Dana Jackson has some breakfast ready, so I'll just go over and tell her to set another plate on the table," he said, stepping out the door.

Chris turned around and disrobed. She examined herself in the full-length mirror on the bathroom door, letting her hands glide lightly across her body. What a mess, she thought as her fingers traced the outlines of the bruises whose rich shades of purple and blue painted her ribs and thighs. Still, with the upturned breasts, tight waist, and firm buttocks, anyone would have thought she had spent the last several weeks in an aerobicise class instead of at Flaget Hospital. Not bad for a girl rapidly closing in on the Big Three-O.

Carefully stepping into the shower, she let the warmth pour over her battered body. It comforted her bruised hip, ribs, and thighs immediately. The water's warmth helped to reduce some of the stiffness, and she lathered herself enthusiastically.

How wonderful it felt as the water poured down, rinsing waves of lather from her breasts and then down her abdomen and thighs. Only concern about using all of her host's hot water caused her to shorten the delightful experience. At the hospital, showers were few and brief due to restrictions on hot water use. This was a treat, indeed.

She stepped out, toweled dry, and then looked around for her clothes. She heard someone approaching, so she stepped back behind the partition when she heard Rogers enter.

"I almost forgot," he said closing the door behind him. "I'll bet you are looking for these." He held her neatly folded clothes in his hands.

Chris reached around the partition, and took the clothes. She examined them, noticing that the buttons had all been replaced, and then held them to her nose. The fresh clean smell of well-laundered clothes was unmistakable. "Why they've been machine washed and dried!" she cried in astonishment. "Do you people have everything here?"

"Not as much as we'd like to have, but we have enough. Simply a matter of preparation." He smiled and sat down on the sofa as he waited for her to change.

When she finished, she said, "My compliments to the seamstress. She did as much as possible with what's left of this blouse."

"That was George Anderson's wife. She can do anything with a needle and thread. It looks as if she'll be busy in the future patching and altering most of the kids' clothes. It's too bad we don't have a good shoemaker. It's damned hard to make a decent shoe or boot unless you really know what you're doing," Rogers said. "But come on. Let's get some breakfast."

They stepped outside and Chris looked across to a nearby trailer. She saw a table set up to the side complete with tablecloth and napkins. Large plates of sausage, bacon, scrambled eggs, and biscuits were spread over the table. Several people were gathered around the trailer, and as Chris and Kurt approached they moved toward the chairs. "My God!" she cried in disbelief. "I haven't seen a meal like this in the past two months. Do you always eat like this?"

"Well, not quite this well. A lot of this stuff," Anderson said "is from our stored food, freeze-dried and the like. We're trying to hang on to our livestock for breeding or bartering. Fortunately, we have enough food put aside for quite a while—long enough I expect. By the way, I didn't get a chance to meet you yesterday. I'm George Anderson," he said, thrusting out his hand.

Rogers made the rest of the introductions, and together they sat down to the table and commenced the meal. After a while, Chris said, "You're really so fortunate. Lots of people in Bardstown haven't eaten anything much more than wheat bread or cornbread in the last few weeks. It's bad, really bad."

"They'd be a lot better off if they'd just take some of the soybeans from the farmers and process them into tofu. It's not very difficult," Dana Jackson said.

"Tofu?" I've heard of it but really don't know much about it."

"It's a Chinese word for bean curd. Sounds a lot better, doesn't it?" she said, giggling a bit. "They've used it for two thousand years or more. It's super high in protein, and it's practically tasteless, which is its beauty. It takes on the taste of whatever you mix it with. Why, many children used to be raised on soy milk as a substitute for mother's milk or cow's milk. I'm sure you're familiar with Isomil formula."

"Of course. A soy formula is what we've been recommending to a lot of the mothers. A lot of the babies would have died without using it as a regular formula substitute." After drinking the last of the milk in her glass, she said, "Lots of people have balked at the idea of eating soybeans. They still think of it as horrid-tasting animal food."

"Well, to hell with those who won't help themselves," piped in Larry Jackson in a very chilly tone. Jackson had been miffed at Kurt for bringing the outsider to the farm, and it was clear that he was using the occasion to express his hostility. Rogers had violated Rule One.

Rogers immediately recognized the true source of Larry's

pique. With a condescension sometimes reserved by older brothers for younger *enfants terribles*, he attempted to redirect the conversation. "Why don't you tell everyone about how you happened to be out here when the war started?"

Chris related her fortunate decision to accompany Roseanna to the farm. She tried to avoid the unpleasant details of the hospital cases, and instead spoke only in generalities about the injured. The realities at the hospital and the idyllic conditions on this farm were so far apart, that to rub her hosts' noses in the situation elsewhere seemed much like babbling about the skyrocketing divorce rate at a wedding reception.

"You seem to keep armed guards around all the time. I noticed them when we came in, and I see those people over there now," she said. "Didn't you consider me a 'security risk'? There surely are a lot of people out here who would take away everything you have here in a heartbeat if they had the chance."

Rogers looked at Jackson, who seemed to be trying his diplomatic best to hold his tongue. "It was a judgment call," Rogers said. "I size up people pretty quickly. I had enough contact with you yesterday to feel that you could be trusted. I also thought that a trained nurse would be a valuable addition should you decide to stay. Besides, we aren't totally unprepared to deal with anyone who decides that he wants what we have. Forewarned is forearmed," he said as he patted the Sig-Sauer 9 mm pistol at his side.

Chris smiled weakly and ate the last few bites of her meal. After everyone finished, she walked away from the table with Rogers.

"How's your brother-in-law handling the loonies around Bardstown? I bet he's got more than a handful."

She related the details of Hamilton's own ambush a few days earlier. "He's doing as well as he can, I suppose. Everybody wants food, food, and more food. He says dealing with the refugees is sort of like dealing with a nine-hundred-pound gorilla in the old joke. You know— 'anywhere he wants.' If those people decide to make trouble on a large scale, God only knows what will happen. So far there have been no riots, but who knows how long that will last? Several guardsmen have gone AWOL so far. Most of them are torn between their duty as soldiers and their duties as fathers and husbands. And they've been taking a lot of heat from the refugees who blame them for the lack of food. Seems they have no one else around to blame. The casualties from shoot-outs with thugs and the hostility from the people they're trying to help seems to be killing the troops' morale."

"I don't envy them at all," Rogers said. Spotting Josh coming around the corner of the barn, he called out. "Josh! Josh! Come over here." As the boy approached, Rogers said, "Chris, this is my son, Josh, who you didn't get a chance to meet last night. He's thirteen, though he thinks he's a lot older from time to time." He ruffled his son's hair, and said, "Say hello to Miss Whittington, son."

"Hello," the boy replied cautiously. He was very curious about the first outsider he had seen since Black Friday, and he was even more curious about his father's interest in this woman. Curious and suspicious.

"Hello, Josh," Chris said. "You certainly are everything your father described to me. I can see you have your father's good looks. Did you know," she added, "that your father probably saved my life yesterday?"

"*Really*?" The boy was surprised at the revelation. His reaction caused Chris to look to Rogers.

"I hadn't really gone into the details," Rogers said. "I'll tell you about it later, son. I expect that they can use your help in the garden."

The two continued walking down to the barn. Chris looked out at the people working in the large garden that by now was well on its way to a reasonably good harvest. "It's so quiet and peaceful here, so much unlike the situation in Bardstown. Your people seem to be doing quite well for themselves."

"Like I said, it's simply a matter of prior preparation. Maybe like the fable of the ant and the grasshopper. But if you consider everything involved, I suppose it was more. You see, Larry, George, and I were all typical products of the Baby Boom era. But even though, or perhaps I should say because we shared such a comparatively high standard of living, we felt more insecure than we might have otherwise have felt.

"The very lifestyle which gave us so many benefits had its

negative side. Our generation seemed to have lost its comprehension of the principles which made things work. If you will excuse the paraphrasing of Thoreau, the mass of men lead lives of quiet dependence on a system they do not comprehend. As a society we had become addicted to a supremely complex technology without understanding the science behind it. Maybe like being able to punch the right buttons on a calculator or computer but not being able otherwise to add, subtract, multiply, or divide. George, Larry, my brother Travis, and I didn't feel very comfortable being at the mercy of a system which was obviously so easily disrupted. So, we decided to do something about it. By not being so dependent on the technology, we actually started to feel in *control* of our world.

"Anyway, we got the chance to buy this place. We paid a pretty good price for it, but the previous owner had made a good start on some of the self-sufficiency projects. It was nearly perfect for our purposes.

"Since then we've tried to develop this farm to the point that when the rest of the world went crazy we could make it on our own. Of course, we remembered the Cuban Missile Crisis. More recently we saw the serious monetary problems developing as Third World countries borrowed more and more money that was unlikely ever to be repaid. And then there were the domestic recessions. We felt it was only a matter of time before something snapped and things really came to a head. Instead of being in a postwar era, we felt more like we were in a *prewar* era.

"Larry got a little short with you back there at the table. You'll have to forgive him and not take it too personally. For years he's been trying to convince people that not preparing for possible disaster was, if you will excuse the expression, like playing Russian roulette."

"That's an interesting way to put it, given what's happened."

"Yeah. He used to talk to his friends continuously and do his best to show them that they needed to do what he's been doing here. He didn't succeed very well. He'd argue till he was blue in the face that everyone was living under a nuclear sword of Damocles, but he got nowhere. People would always want to talk about more pleasant things. Now he's cynical and bitter about the results, that's all. A victory without satisfaction. So don't take his attitude personally. He's really a very decent guy."

"I suppose that after coming this far, now the question is whether you can hang on to all of this."

"Obviously, there are plenty of people out there who would slit our throats in our sleep for a bushel of vegetables. But we're on guard at all times. Laura named this place The Aerie after what she imagined to be the eagles' nesting places in the limestone cliffs long ago. But *we're* the eagles now. Like the one on the U.S. Seal, an olive branch in one hand and arrows of war in the other. If necessary, we'll use our guns in self-defense. I'm not the only one here who can use a gun."

"And yesterday, when you used your gun, I'm curious. When you pulled the trigger on that fellow, what did you feel?"

"The *recoil*."

She paused and studied his face. "But did you really imagine a year ago that you might be down here killing people under these circumstances? After all, isn't all of this a bit unreal?"

"Did I imagine? Surely. And that's why we're here and so well prepared today—because we *could* foresee the possibility of the situation arising, and we took steps to prepare for it. It's just unfortunate that few others did the same."

He paused and took his sheath knife from its scabbard, and he began shaving the edge of a board in the fence before him. "My brother, Travis, used to say that everybody needs a sanctuary to flee to in times of trouble—some place to go when the rest of the world becomes too dangerous. For us, this is the place."

She shook her head. "But people didn't behave like this. I mean, not civilized people. I never expected three thousand years of civilization to be wiped out like *that*."

"Didn't behave like this? Are you serious? My God, Chris, one day you'd read in the paper of a mob killing thirty over some stupid soccer game. The next day you'd read about strikers sniping at others in a labor dispute. Christ, on *any* given day you'd read of somebody getting their throat sliced over five dollars in the ghettos. The strong have always tended to prey on the weak. Was there any question of what would happen when *all* the rules were gone?"

Chris studied him for a few seconds and said, "It sounds almost as if you believe the world is divided into two groups, predator and prey."

"Something like that. Civilization, at least as I see it, is a veneer or facade on the soul of mankind. As long as things proceed smoothly enough and there's no great stress, civilized man prevails well enough—within his limits. At least that's the situation for the majority of people. But given a situation where he must endure sacrifice and deprivation, where the comforting assurance of three meals a day and a warm place to sleep suddenly disappears for an extended period, the veneer quickly falls away. Some people have different breaking points than others, that's the only difference."

Chris looked at him and shook her head. "I can't accept that. Even if it's true. I refuse to believe that we are all like that, and that the majority of us won't face whatever happens with dignity and compassion for others. I don't want to base my life on such a pessimistic and depressing philosophy."

"Depressing? Perhaps. But it's kept us ahead of the game here. Some friends back home used to say I was always so pessimistic. Me? I'd say. *I* was the optimist because I was the one who expected to make it, regardless of what happened. I was preparing for the day *after* Doomsday. Believe me, with the way things turned out, just like with Larry, it gives me no great pleasure to say that I was right and they were wrong.

"But maybe I did overstate my case," Kurt continued. "I suppose that most of us, at least, will *try* to do the right thing regardless of what the problem might be confronting us. It's just that so damned many won't."

"That may be hard for me to argue with, considering how things have been going lately," she replied. "But listen, I really hate to cut this short, but you know that they really need me back at the hospital. Do you think you could get me back there today? I'm feeling well enough to ride your bike if you'll take me."

"But the tour's not over yet," he protested. "You haven't seen the generators, the solar collectors, the machine shop, and God knows what else! How am I supposed to lure you into joining the group if you haven't let me show you half of the bait?"

"I appreciate the effort, but for now I'm afraid it's no deal. I'm needed too badly at the hospital, and I left there yesterday telling them I'd be back in a few hours. I must get back as soon as I can."

"Well, if you're absolutely sure that there's no chance that I can talk you into staying, I'll take you back as soon as you're ready. I've just put several gallons of ethanol in the Bronco, and with the top down, it'll be a much more comfortable ride than the cycle. But I really do wish you would stay."

As they started walking toward the trailer, she replied, "It's awfully tempting. Maybe after everything settles down to a normal level at the hospital, we can get together if you like." She looked to him hoping for some reaction.

"Waiting for things to get to a 'normal level' may be quite a long time, but I'd like that." He opened the door to the trailer for her, and when she stepped inside she turned around to meet him as he followed. Without warning she placed a long lingering kiss on his lips, and then pulled back to judge the effect.

Rogers looked at her silently, and then pulled her close and pecked her on the forehead, gently brushing the blond tresses past her temple and down the side of her ear.

"What is it?" she asked, hardly expecting this response to such a direct pass. "You don't find me appealing?"

"That's hardly the case. It's just that you're the first woman I've even tried to be this close to since Laura died. It's still difficult. Maybe things will change. I really do want to see you again." He opened the door and repeated, "I really *do* want to see you again."

Well, I'll be damned, she thought. This must be the first guy she had ever been attracted to who wasn't doing his damnedest to get into her pants. A very strange man, this Kurt Rogers. Very strange.

Chris grabbed her emergency kit from the counter and followed him quickly, arriving at the Bronco where Rogers was folding down the convertible top. He then picked up a short, strange-looking gun from the front seat, cleared it and checked it for proper functioning.

"What's that?" she asked.

"An Uzi submachine gun."

"What happened to the one from yesterday?"

"That was yesterday. Today I feel like an Uzi," he said with a grin, much as if he were talking about an item of wardrobe. "Tomorrow, who knows? Besides, I can handle it better from behind the wheel. Come on."

"Isn't that an automatic weapon, for crying out loud? That's illegal, isn't it?"

Rogers couldn't contain his amusement, and chuckled. "Illegal! Now? I was beginning to believe that nothing was illegal now. But if it makes you feel any better, it was registered and perfectly legal before things went crazy."

Bob Rose walked up to the Bronco and got in the back seat, carrying an AR-15 assault rifle. "I'll be riding shot-gun," he explained.

Rogers backed the Bronco around, and then started forward down the narrow road past the two young men at the security point, and then on to the asphalt road. With few vehicles on the road because of EMP damage and gasoline shortages, Rogers sped along with little concern for traffic. Speed, he knew, also made effective ambushes less likely.

The three continued into Raywick. The little town was awash with four or five hundred refugees. They were scattered in tents, automobiles, and whatever else was available around the picturesque little country church by the elementary school.

Guards were posted at each road leading into the cross-roads town, and they waved Rogers through. Picking up speed, Rogers raced onward to Bardstown, and within a half hour, Chris was back at the hospital and on duty.

The sun bathed the courthouse in an early morning glow as Hamilton walked into Judge Spaulding's office. Spaulding was adjusting the blinds in order to reduce the sunlight pouring across his desk. He turned and smiled when Hamilton crossed the threshhold. "Good morning, Major. You're looking far better than you were when I last saw you."

"I feel a lot better, too, Judge," responded Hamilton. "Are you ready to get on with it? We'll have to be there in ten minutes or we'll miss the opportunity."

Spaulding looked at his watch. "Very well, let's go. I'll warn you right now, though. I'll do my very best, but I'm not that confident that you'll get very far. I agree now that it is worth a try, though."

"Then let's do it." Without further delay the two men walked out to the front of the courthouse where Ackerson, Nugent, and another driver waited with a couple of jeeps.

As the party came to a halt in front of St. Joseph's Proto-Cathedral, a church built in 1816 by early settlers, Hamilton, Ackerson, and Spaulding walked up the sidewalk through the assortment of tents and impromptu shelters which festooned the large lawn that surrounded the building. As one of the distribution points for the county food distribution program and the focal point for the church's private charitable efforts, the area around the former cathedral served as a natural gathering spot for refugees. Hamilton led the way through the throng and up the church steps. Making his way through the overflow crowd in the vestibule, he entered into the church proper just as the priest was ending the Mass.

The interior was packed to its limit with people. Refugees and local people stood side by side. War, Hamilton thought, and the suffering and pestilence that inevitably accompany it, always have a peculiar way of bringing out the religious side of many people, or as Nugent put it, "H-bombs tend to give a man religion."

The crowd here was attending one of many services scheduled. Hamilton was prepared to repeat what he was about to say several times here and at other churches around town.

The priest at the altar saw Hamilton signal to him, and then said, "Before we end with a hymn, Major Hamilton of our National Guard unit and Judge Spaulding would like to say a few words to all of us."

Hamilton and Spaulding worked their way to the sanctuary and turned to face the congregation. It was still early, but the heat was already starting to rise in the building, jammed with seven hundred people.

Spaulding mopped at his forehead with the large red bandana-style handkerchief he always carried, then stepped forward. "Thank you, Father Rutledge. For you good Nelson County people, I don't have to tell you who I am. For everyone else, I'm Leon Spaulding, the county judge here. Major Jack Hamilton is in charge of the National Guard unit, and I'm going to step back and just let him talk. He and I are of one mind, however, and I reckon what he's about to say makes good sense as far as I'm concerned. Major?"

Hamilton stepped forward and took a deep breath. "Thank you, Judge Spaulding, and thank you, Father Rutledge for letting us take this opportunity to address everyone."

Someone in the back of the church sang out, "Can't hear you."

Distracted, Hamilton paused to clear his throat and stared at the blur of impassive faces that appeared to be studying him.

He took another deep breath and continued. "I don't have to tell you people that even though we've survived the most dangerous event in American history, we're hardly out of the woods yet. We have thousands homeless right here, and God only knows how many elsewhere. People are on the road, traveling continuously in search of food and shelter. I think the situation is going to get worse before it gets better for these road people.

"Even though it was an excellent idea, due to the independent nature of many people, the county's efforts with the refugee centers have not turned out as well as we'd have liked. That's not to say, however, that the idea isn't worth pursuing again, and we will.

"For now though, food is in short supply. Some people have been generous to a fault, while others have not contributed the first thing. Supplies are running low here in town. But it's obvious that there is still a large quantity of food on the surrounding farms, even if it's the kind of food that causes many people to turn up their noses. Although it's been touch and go, we've been able to get by with voluntary contributions from farmers and others—so far." He paused briefly so that his audience might be able to appreciate the implication.

"It'll come as no great surprise to you that the acts of violence have been becoming uglier and more common lately. I don't need to repeat the gory details to you here. Sheriff Osborne and the other law enforcement people are doing their best, and I can assure you that the Guardsmen are doing their best, but it's simply not enough. With the limited personnel and limited communications we have, we usually get to the trouble spot too late to do anything but file a report and, in all too many instances, to bury the dead.

"What is becoming increasingly clear is that if you people—and I'm speaking directly to the local people now—if you people want to remain secure in your homes, you will find it necessary to call on the refugees for help."

Hamilton paused briefly and looked at some of the faces in the crowd. It seemed clear that he had them hanging on every word and, encouraged, he continued. "What I am proposing is this. Every landowner who has tillable land should take in as many refugees as possible and allow these people to go to work raising their own food. It's still not too late to plant many things. Every one of you farmers must realize that the fuel you have stored out there won't last forever, and when it's gone, you'll have to resort to physical rather than mechanical means to farm your land. How many of you expect to farm two hundred or three hundred acres by yourself?

"So, by acting now you merely accelerate the inevitable. Oh sure, we'll be working on making more alcohol fuel available, but production on the county project is going to be very limited for the near future, and it will come nowhere near meeting the demand for a long time. And maybe if this country ever gets its feet back on the ground again, the gasoline and diesel fuel will be available in increasing quantities. But who knows how long that will take? I certainly don't, and I don't think anyone else here does. There's been nothing to indicate that there's any permanent truce in the wings, so we may be in a state of uncertainty for longer than we'd like.

"And what do you get in the meantime as an exchange for opening up your farms and homes? You get a share of the refugees' produce, and perhaps more importantly, you get increased security. A farm with forty people protecting it is a less inviting target than a farm with five. And I'm not just talking farms for that matter. People with five and ten acres should be considering all of this, and maybe even people with less land, if they're physically unable to work it.

"For every additional refugee on your land, you have less chance of being a victim of these roving bands of crazies, and a headstart on building a viable system of labor for the future. It's 'enlightened self-interest' on everyone's part. Besides," Hamilton added as he looked toward Father Rutledge, "it would be the Christian thing to do.

"I'm not asking anyone to like the idea. I'm only asking that you accept it. We can't go into the winter with all these refugees packing the open spaces here in Bardstown. Hunger and the elements will take a staggering toll. If that starts to happen, what will result will be a contest between the 'haves' and the 'have nots.' I don't think anyone is prepared for such a confrontation. But the choice is up to each of you, and I hope you make it wisely," Hamilton said.

"And before ending here, let me add one thing. I received a report from the Guard commander over in Springfield that there have been incidents in the past week where as many as twenty to thirty armed men have attacked homes and farms on four separate occasions. Ask yourselves as you sit at home tonight whether you think you and your families could hold off such an attack by yourselves. That's all I have to say. Father?"

Hamilton backed away from the center of the sanctuary and the priest stepped forward once again. "As far as I'm concerned, Major, what you've just said makes all the sense in the world. I just hope and pray that everyone here takes heed and acts accordingly. I certainly echo the sentiments about Christian charity."

Spaulding leaned over and whispered in Hamilton's ear, "That certainly *was* a nice touch, Major. Have you ever considered politics?"

"Thank you, you old rascal," he replied with an almost imperceptible smile, but his eyes were fixed on the sea of faces, trying without success to determine the crowd's reaction.

"You didn't mention anything about taking in families yourself, I noticed."

"I've already got one family out there. Been there since the first day. But I have some ideas in mind about using the place that I don't want to go into right now."

Father Rutledge continued speaking, "And now, if everyone will turn to No. 31 in the hymnal." The antique pump organ that had recently been pressed into service to replace its electric predecessor intoned the hymn's introduction, and the congregation stood and joined in.

Throughout the verses, Hamilton stood beside Spaulding hoping, and finally praying, that his words had not fallen on deaf ears.

Four couples, including Reuben and Clara Cissel, had assembled near the steps of the church after services were completed. This was a customary time to exchange news of the community, whether it was news of a daughter who had given birth, or a son who had become engaged. On this particular day, the subject dominating conversation was Hamilton's appeal to the congregation.

"Reuben, what do you make of what that fellow had to say?" asked the tall, square-shouldered man with the beaked nose and prominent chin.

"Well, George, I'm prejudiced, of course. I've known him since he was knee-high. He's half-owner of the farm across from mine, though you didn't use to see him out here that often. But he's a straight shooter. Always has been."

"I'm not sure. You've gotta remember he's from Louisville. Know what I mean? He may just be trying to take care of his own, and that don't sit right with me. I suspect his motives."

"Still, what he said makes sense, now," said one of the women. Turning to the others she said, "We were worried about even coming today, to tell you the truth. All those reports of killing and robbery and such. We left our boy and his wife at home to watch over things but I still feel uneasy, and I don't mind telling you so."

"But are we gonna be any better off with these people on our places?" George, the first man, responded. "I'd be worried to death that they'd pack off everything I had if I didn't place a twenty-four hour guard on them. What kind of security is that? Know what I mean?"

"Well, like Jack Hamilton said in there, it'll be in their best interest to work," Clara Cissell replied. "If they run off with stuff, where do they have to go? At least this way they have a reasonable chance to make it. Besides, how is anyone here going to work four hundred acres of land without any fuel next spring? At least you can sharecrop it and get a portion of the crop, which is a lot better than nothing. And for crying out loud, here we are standing practically in the shadow of the church and not even considering the morality of not doing something to help these people!"

"I don't know. I just don't know," responded another man in the group. "Me and Gloria will just have to think about it."

Reuben added, "Clara and me got some talking to do about this, too before we go off and bring a bunch of strangers out to the farm. This is an awful big decision."

It was about three o'clock that afternoon when Reuben Cissell returned to Bardstown in his flatbed truck. He had given up arguing with Clara about his reservations. He had decided that whatever problems the refugees might cause would pale in comparison with the problems Clara was causing him now about postponing the decision. Wives sometimes had a way of doing that.

He pulled up to what had previously been a large grassy area at My Old Kentucky Home State Park and parked his truck. Before him, spread out in all directions, was one of the larger focal points for late arriving refugees who had been denied entry to the organized centers. It had been quickly transformed into a latter-day equivalent of a medieval county fair or flea market. "Merchants" of all sorts hawked their wares, most of which were used items, bartered or stolen from their previous owners.

A major source of the merchandise was the Louisville area, where the more venturous or desperate individuals returned to loot the abandoned homes and stores. The risks of being caught there during a new attack, as well as the fear of unknown radiation hazards, kept most people away.

National Guardsmen checked the larger commercial markets and monitored the items being sold or bartered for the radioactive contamination that occasionally showed up. Any items determined to be "hot" were seized. Most of the merchants had become skillful in decontamination procedures, though in the procurement and decontamination, they undoubtedly exposed themselves to greater health risks. This was the price of commercial success in a nuclear economy.

From the law enforcement perspective, it was obvious that the goods were frequently the product of looting and theft. Actually proving it was all but impossible. Regardless, due to the intense needs for the goods, and the unavailability of items from any other source, the situation required the police and Guardsmen to be somewhat less than aggressive in insuring that the sellers possessed full legal title to all their wares. There was, however, no official admission of this.

Cissell walked down along a row of tents, hootches, and shanties that opened to the front in the tradition of Old World bazaars. Smells of every sort assaulted his nostrils. Open fires from nearby shelters warmed pots of stew and soup for those lucky enough to locate the ingredients. The smell of outdoor privies, which many of the homeless only occasionally bothered to use, mixed with dozens of odors to form an odor that was at once sweet, sour, and rancid. It permeated the entire area and well beyond. God, he thought, is it any wonder that cases of dysentery, typhus, and typhoid fever are increasing?

"Hey, mister!" a teenager cried. "Wanna buy a new pair of insulated boots? They'll be awfully nice next winter, and you ain't gonna find many like these around. A few rounds of that ammo," he said as he pointed to the pistol belt Cissell was wearing, "and they're yours! Or maybe you got some medicine? How about gasoline? Maybe cigarettes? A pack of cigarettes, man, and you're a king!"

Cissell walked over to the young man, who reminded him of the carnies on the midway at the state fair. He picked up the boots the boy was offering and examined them closely. Despite the assertion that they were new, it was obvious that they had seen better days.

Reuben looked around at goods that packed the little shanty store. "These are 12-D's," Cissell responded. "I need 12-E's. Got any?"

The smile faded from the young man's face. "Nope. Not in boots. Awfully hard to find." His face brightening again, he reached under the counter and pulled out a pair of dress loafers. "But you're in luck, cause I got these."

Cissell took the shoes and examined them for a second before turning up his nose. "Naw, I need working boots, not thin-soled Sunday shoes."

"Ya sure? Before too long people will be happy to get any kind a store-bought shoe at all." His remark produced no reaction from Cissell, so he continued. "Well, then how about some T-shirts? Brand new ones even." Pointing to the boxes to his side where new cotton shirts were carefully displayed, he grabbed one of them and said, "We got yer smalls. We got yer mediums. We got yer larges. And we even got yer extra-larges. So how about it?"

Cissell turned and started to walk away. In frustration the young man called out to him, "You don't know a deal when you see it, old man!"

Cissell waved his hand, abruptly dismissing the obnoxious young vendor, and walked on down the row. Before walking more than a few yards he was approached by a shapely young woman in her late teens who entwined her arm around his. "Gramps, I can be real nice to you for five of those bullets. Why don't you come over here to my tent and we'll talk about it?" she said, smiling sweetly and reeking of cheap perfume and recent sex.

Cissell looked down at the thin tank top stretched tautly across her large breasts. She rubbed his upper arm and gently tugged at him, but Cissell pulled away saying, "Sorry, honey, but I'm not interested. I'm here on business, and I'm too old for that kind of stuff anyway."

As he walked on, he met a large group of people milling about in one of the more open areas. He looked at the collection of adults and children, who in more normal times might have represented a cross section of any community. At present, given their unkempt and ragged appearance, due to the lack of proper hygiene facilities, they could only be said to be a cross section of the refugee community.

Cissell looked around for a few seconds, then cleared his throat and said loudly, "My name is Reuben Cissell." Although this pronouncement did not seem particularly significant to the crowd, the tone in which he said it seemed to indicate that there was information of a more important nature to follow. He continued in a booming voice. "I have five hundred acres, three hundred and fifty of which is good tillable land. I've got two old tenant houses on them that aren't much, but they're decent enough shelter, especially considering what I see around here. I also have a tobacco barn with a large stripping room which can be used for shelter, if necessary. I'm looking for a few families to help me work the farm. I haven't exactly figured out what the arrangements will be yet. Maybe I'll pay people in kind at a set rate, or maybe we'll work out a percentage arrangement. Regardless, I'm a fair man, and it's probably a helluva lot better 'n what you've got here. I'm willing to talk to anybody who's interested."

Many of the people in the crowd immediately started to press forward to him, talking all at once. "Quiet!" Cissell boomed. "I'll talk to all of you, but one at a time. I can't even hear myself think!" He looked at the man nearest him and said, "What did you do before the war?"

The man before him was dressed in a dirty sleeveless denim jacket and even dirtier pair of Levi's straight-legged jeans. "I was a trucker." Though it was not reflected in his voice, desperation was plainly evident in his face. He wanted very badly to say the right thing.

"Any special skills?"

The man looked puzzled, and his blank expression caused Cissell to quickly turn his attention to the next man. "You," he said, pointing to a man in his early forties with traces of burns on his neck and arms. "Do you have any special skills?"

"I ran a gas station in St. Matthews before the war. I can fix almost anything that runs on gasoline, diesel fuel, or electricity—at least anything you're likely to have. My wife, Fran here, is an expert gardener. If you've got the seed, she can make it grow." He placed his arm around his wife and waited for Cissell to respond.

"What's your name?"

"Ken Fitzgerald."

"Well, Mr. Fitzgerald, there's a green Ford flatbed truck out there by the entrance. I'm leaving in a half hour or so. Can you have you belongings on it by then?"

"Sure can," responded Fitzgerald enthusiastically. In obvious relief, he and Fran turned quickly in order to attend to necessary matters. "And thanks," he added.

Cissell continued on. "You, what's your background?" he said to the next man. The man was in his late fifties or early sixties and had silver, wavy hair, and glasses. His clothes hung around him in an ill-fitting manner, something now very common among the refugees.

"Retired air force. I was a pilot. I've been working for an insurance company for the past few years," said the man, tapping the bowl of his pipe in the palm of his hand.

"Don't need no pilot or insurance now. Got any other skills?"

"Not really. At least not any of a great deal of use to you."

Cissell turned to look at the next couple in front of him, when the man suddenly added, "But I do have three M-1 carbines and two .45 automatics with about three thousand rounds of ammunition in all."

Cissell's head snapped back immediately. "You're hired. Go ahead and get your things to the truck."

Cissell continued through the crowd, and after fifteen minutes of questioning, he had selected five families. He decided that this would be a start for now, and he returned to the truck. When he arrived he found Fitzgerald and the pilot waiting with their families.

As the group began loading their belongings on the truck, the other families arrived and everyone clambered aboard. After insuring that everyone was safely in place and that their possessions were securely fastened down, Cissell got into the cab of his now overloaded truck and started the engine. He then drove slowly out of town toward his farm with the strange cargo.

Charlie Boy's stomach was drawing into what felt like a small baseball. The hunger pains were getting worse and worse as he neared Lebanon, a town southeast of Bardstown, and the county seat of Marion County. On the road for three days, he had meandered aimlessly, looking first one place and then the next for food and shelter. The crude bandage that graced his left bicep was evidence that he had looked in the wrong orchard for green apples. The grazing sting of a .22 caliber bullet, and the string of profanity which ended with "goddam city people! I knew we shoulda blowed the bridges!" had sent him scurrying. He now had a much better appreciation of the importance of obeying the strings of No Trespassing signs popping up along the roads.

Charlie Boy's hair hung down the back of his neck like black licorice. His clothes smelled like a pile of unwashed jockstraps in the bottom of a gym locker. He couldn't believe how bad the human body could smell after a few days without a shower or deodorant.

Since the first day of the war, Charlie Boy had lost fifteen pounds. For a young man who had always taken the greatest care of and pride in his physical appearance, this was extremely irritating. His jeans were now gathered by the much tighter belt around his waist, and his T-shirt had begun to take on a baggy appearance. Not that he still didn't present a remarkably imposing physical appearance at six feet three, and now two hundred and ten pounds, but he certainly was looking a little ragged around the edges, and he knew it.

The hunger and hardship of the past few weeks had been trying. However, the even greater gnawing within him which dogged his every waking moment was the frustration and anger at the reality of this new world. Now he would be cheated forever out of the glory days on the backfield of the University of Kentucky football team. No Autumn Madness, no hero worship from an entire student body and half the state's population, no helpful "contacts" with the alumni association, and no adulation from throngs of coeds just creamin' in their jeans to be Charlie's girl. All of that was gone now. Only bitterness remained.

As Charlie Boy neared town, the activity along the road increased, and finally he came to a large area enclosed by a six-strand barbed-wire fence. At various points, men stood with shotguns or an occasional rifle to inspect those attempting to enter the compound. Charlie Boy looked at the amateurishly painted sign atop one of the entrances which read:

MARION COUNTY REFUGEE CAMP
K. C. ROBERTS, CAMP MANAGER
"TOGETHER, UP FROM THE ASHES!"

Charlie Boy walked up to the young man in a yellow

T-shirt holding a shotgun. He had a self-important air about him, and he stopped each of those who entered. He had a wad of chewing tobacco tucked firmly in one of his chipmunk-like cheeks, and a brown stain appeared at the corners of his mouth. As Charlie Boy approached, the young man let loose to his side with a long streak of brown juice, and then wiped at his lips with the back of his hand.

"Lemme see your pass."

Charlie Boy stopped short. "My what?"

"Your pass," he said irritably in a way which seemed to imply an unspoken "shithead" at the end. "Nobody comes in without no pass." The camp was obviously this bantam rooster's barnyard.

"Where do I get a pass?"

"Down at the next gate at the Reception Center." It was apparent that the young guard had been through this routine many times. His brusque attitude briefly caused Charlie Boy to consider snatching that gun from his hands in order to improve his manners, but he reluctantly decided against it and walked silently to the Reception Center entrance.

The main camp was composed of a former garment factory and its surrounding grounds. A couple of hundred people could be seen about the grounds in all manner of activity. The entrance led into a narrow fenced corridor that then led into the building.

Charlie walked up to the frail, elderly man at the folding table just inside the door of the large room. Across the room, twenty or so men, women, and children sat eating a lunch of milk, thickly sliced bread, and my God, he thought, fried chicken! It wasn't *beef*, but each person did have a large piece of fried chicken. The prospect of meat, real meat for the first time in weeks, made his mouth water.

"Can I help you young man?" the elderly man said with such authority in his voice that it made his question sound more like a command than an inquiry.

"I was hoping to get something to eat," Charlie Boy said as his eyes drifted over to the table where the food was being served.

"If you want to eat you have to become a camp member. Just sit yourself down over there and fill these out."

With a puzzled look on his face, Charlie Boy obediently took the papers from the man and walked slowly to the table, thumbing through the crudely mimeographed sheets as he went.

The first sheet contained a request for biographical information: name, former address, age, sex, etc. The second asked for a medical history: childhood diseases, special medical needs and conditions, including estimated level of radiation exposure (Check One: High, Medium, or Low).

The third asked for the respondent's itinerary week by week since the first day of the war. Included were specific requests for estimates of conditions of domestic animals and wildlife in each location.

The fourth page asked for all skills and special interests of the respondent that might be useful to the camp.

The fifth asked the respondent to pick in his order of preference three of the following categories for temporary daily assignment by the Camp Advisory Council: cooking and food services, water services, trash and garbage collection, construction services, horticultural services, and random day-labor.

Security patrol was the final listing, but it appeared that an unsteady hand had lined through it, placing a notation beside it which said, "Filled."

The last page was one labeled "Agreement". In several paragraphs it informed the respondent that if he were selected to become a camp member, then and in that event, he would agree to abide by the rules and regulations of the camp and to submit to the directives of the Camp Advisory Council or face disciplinary action as deemed appropriate by the council.

Charlie Boy dropped the papers to the table. Even now, a goddam bureaucracy! he thought. Filling out all of this was going to take forever. He looked across the room to the milk, bread, and that wonderful fried chicken of which only a few pieces remained. He gritted his teeth, sat down, groped for one of the pencil nubs on the table, and began to write clumsily for the first time since the first day of the war. It was almost as if his fingers had forgotten how to write, and this frustrated him even further.

He had only filled in a few of the blocks when the point of the pencil snapped. "Bullshit!" he cried. Charlie sprang to his feet and threw the papers to the floor, and then stalked back to the man at the entrance.

"Screw your damned forms, old man! I just want something to eat, and if I don't get it pretty soon it's gonna be all gone!"

The old man looked at him patiently. "Those 'damned forms' as you call them give us enough information to place the round and square pegs in the right holes. We run a clean camp. No dysentery, typhus or flu, and everyone's getting enough to eat. Families are safe here, but only because we all pull together, and each works for the benefit of all. You're welcome to go elsewhere if you don't like it. You'll find plenty who don't. Frankly, I don't think you'd fit in here, anyway."

Charlie Boy glowered at the man, and then at the table of food. Now there were only two drumsticks left. Suddenly, he spun and walked over to the table and began stuffing his pockets with bread while he thrust a drumstick to his mouth taking most of the meat from the bone in one bite.

"You can't do that!" shrieked the old man who sprang to his feet and rushed toward him, trying to prevent Charlie Boy from seizing the second drumstick.

Charlie Boy walked back toward the door and brusquely shoved the old man to the side. The man spun with arms and legs flailing wildly on to the table where a family of refugees sat eating their meal.

When the old man continued to shriek at him, Charlie Boy began to run out the door and down the sidewalk to the entrance. The cocky young guard who had stopped him earlier was now standing in his path at this entrance talking with a young woman, and was doubtless impressing her with the importance of his duties.

As Charlie Boy approached, the young man turned in response to the cries from within the building. He saw Charlie Boy bearing down upon him like a runaway locomotive. He hastily tried to bring his shotgun to bear—a half second too late. Charlie Boy crashed into him with the experience born of a thousand ground attacks as a fullback, hitting the young man's midsection, separating the guard from his shotgun, and causing him to swallow whole a mouthful of chew.

Charlie Boy sprinted hard down the road. He broke into a wide grin when he shot a glance over his shoulder and saw the guard heaving the contents of his stomach on to the pavement in front of the horrified young girl.

Ol' Coach Clemson would've been proud!

Nightfall found Charlie Boy at one of the scattered refugee shanty camps on the outskirts of Lebanon, this one near the intersection of Miller Pike and the road to Campbellsville. The few slices of bread and the chicken he had stolen earlier in the day had begun to fade into memory, and his stomach was beginning once again to demand more attention.

As he followed a meandering course through the shanties, he saw a dozen men gathered around a campfire. Hesitantly, he walked up to the group and sat down slightly to the rear of the inner circle around the fire.

A bottle of bourbon was produced from a pack by one of the men who proceeded to open it, take a heavy swig from it, and then pass it around the circle. Two empty bottles already sat on the edge of the fire. No one bothered to pass the bottle back in Charlie Boy's direction, however, and he didn't ask.

One of the men, a chunky, unshaven man with watery gray eyes said to another across from him, "Where ya from?"

"Indiana."

The first man's eyes lit up. "A Hoosier? How in the hell did you wind up down here?"

"I was making deliveries south of Louisville when the bomb hit. Couldn't get back across the river, so I lit out south."

The first man looked at the fellow to his side and said with a wink, "Hey, Buck. You know why most Hoosiers have moss growing on the back of their necks?"

"No, why?"

"From standing so long on the northern bank of the Ohio River, staring at the Promised Land!" The two of them broke into sidesplitting laughter that seemed a little bit forced to Charlie Boy. Charlie Boy chuckled a bit, too, but since he hadn't had anything to drink, the joke didn't seem nearly as funny to him.

That the Hoosier failed to appreciate the humor was very evident. His face became very drawn and his nostrils flared, but he said nothing. The man's friend to his left said something which Charlie Boy couldn't quite catch.

Fresh on the success of his first effort, the campfire comedian continued, "Hey, Buck. You know what girls from Indiana put behind their ears to attract men?"

The second man feigned ignorance, and after pausing for a few seconds, replied, "No. What?"

"Their *legs!*"

The two men broke into unrestrained laughter again, and they were followed by most of the people around the campfire. The man from Indiana decided, however, that this was clearly enough of this brand of humor. He leaped to his feet and dove across the circle into the comedian, and together the two went sprawling. They traded quick blows until it was obvious that the man from Indiana was getting the upper hand.

At that point, the comedian's friend jumped into the melee and set upon the Hoosier. This in turn brought the Hoosier's friend into the fray.

After much struggling, the comedian finally made it to his feet and to the fire. He reached down and grabbed two small logs about two feet long. He tossed one of them to his friend and then he swung at the Hoosier, bashing him in the back of the head. The comedian's friend connected with a sickening crunch to the collarbone of the Hoosier's companion.

The comedian reeled when a small, teary-eyed boy ran up to him with arms flailing, screaming, "Leave my daddy alone!"

A scowl quickly came to the man's face. He grabbed the child by the arm and heaved him upward and backward into the crowd. Before the child hit the ground, a loud and unexpected explosion of a gunshot from behind Charlie Boy sent the comedian hurtling into the darkness. In no more time than it took to pull the trigger, another shot rang out, doing the same to the comedian's friend.

Charlie Boy spun around to see in the pale light a bearded man with a large magnum revolver in his hand. Slowly the man replaced the gun to his holster, and then faded into the night, seeming to pull together a curtain of darkness behind him.

MONDAY, JUNE 24th:
The Thirty-Ninth Day

Charlie Boy crawled out from his blanket and wiped the sleep from his eyes. A heavy dew lay on the ground. Fifty feet from him, across several empty bottles and assorted pieces of trash and litter, were the twisted bodies of the dead men, lying where they had fallen the night before. There were apparently no friends or relatives to take the bodies away, but someone had placed a couple of pieces of plastic over their upper torsos.

A sheriff's deputy was walking slowly through the camp, cautiously checking out those he passed. Charlie Boy knew there would be questions, lots of them. Even though he was sure no one could implicate him, prudence still dictated a rapid exit.

Charlie Boy was on his feet and was scrambling to get his belongings together. The haste of his efforts apparently had an effect to the reverse of what Charlie Boy had intended.

"What's the hurry, son?"

Charlie Boy looked up and saw the sheriff's deputy standing over him. Charlie Boy squinted into the blazing bright sunlight pouring from behind the man. He stammered, "N-No hurry. Just time to move on."

"You don't happen to know anything about what happened to those guys over there, do you?"

"Don't know nothin' about it, Sheriff. Got here after it was all over."

"Funny how *everybody* in this place must have come in

here late last night. Nobody seems to have been around when it happened."

Charlie Boy finally had everything in order and stood up. "Well, there *were* a lot of people moving into this place last night. Damnedest thing."

"Yeah. Damnedest thing," the deputy said in disgust, and then he turned and walked slowly away.

Charlie Boy seized the opportunity and made away from the camp, deciding to head toward Springfield.

After walking most of the day, he was there. He found himself once again at a campfire among strangers that night.

Charlie Boy sat on a log surrounded by a rough crowd of men and women. Certain shanty camps had rougher reputations than others. This one was as rough as any.

An extended "bitch session" was in progress, and Charlie Boy listened in on the conversation.

"I'd like to get my hands on the son of a bitch who started all this!" The speaker was a young man in cast-off army fatigues and a beat up cowboy hat.

"Damned right!" joined in a couple of the others.

"I had a decent job on the line at G.E., a nice home, a Firebird, a great bass boat—and now this! I'm sick of livin' like somethin' lower n' a snake belly." He paused, and then half to himself said, "Frankly, I don't exactly give a shit how I improve things, just as long as they improve."

Another man joined in. "Yeah. Lousy food, stinkin' shithead farmers who'd as soon shoot you as look at you for eyein' a goddam chicken, and living like pigs in this sty of a camp. Christ, I even got lice! *Lice*! Can you believe it?" The men on his right and left could. They moved a little to the side at this announcement.

"Well," came a voice out of the darkness, "maybe people *don't* have to live this way."

The group turned to see a man walk up slowly into the circle and take a position in the inner ring around the fire. Following him was a small man who stood a little to the rear, arms folded, saying nothing. Slowly, Charlie Boy came to recognize the man before the fire as the man who had dramatically ended the fight the night before in Lebanon.

"Consider the problems before us," Tom O'Hara began. "We've *all* got our needs, and our needs *have* to be met.

Think about them for a minute. Take shelter, for instance. It's hard to come by now, decent shelter that is. And then there's water. It's not that much of a problem—as long as you have a well. The problem is that a lot of the people with wells are not that excited about just anybody drinking from them."

O'Hara paused for a few seconds and surveyed his listeners. Their eyes were fixed on him.

"Heat is no problem now. But it will be soon, too damned soon. Spending the winter in miserable huts like these will be brutal. And finally, there's food. I don't have to tell any of you about that. What you've been getting is probably no better than pig swill. It doesn't take any mental heavyweight to figure out that, with such lousy food, one helluva lot of you aren't going to be in shape to make it through the winter in places like this," he said, sweeping his hand broadly to the camp around him.

Finally, one of the men asked, "Well, what can we do about it?"

"Not very much by yourselves. *Together*—that's a different situation. You might say that right now *I'm looking for a few good men.*"

Several of the listeners looked warily back and forth at one another. Charlie Boy looked at O'Hara and, summoning his courage, asked, "What are these 'few good men' as you call them going to do about the problems?"

"Whatever's *necessary*," replied O'Hara, looking straight into Charlie Boy's eyes, seemingly to the very back of his skull. Though physically he could tower over this man, Charlie Boy felt almost intimidated by his presence, one which radiated control and supreme self-confidence. Suddenly a chill raced through him. Charlie Boy felt almost naked.

There was a long pause after O'Hara's words, and then one of the young men said, "Count me in. I got nothin' to lose." Three others, all of whom appeared to be in their late teens or early twenties, quickly agreed.

"Me, too," Charlie Boy said finally.

"Good." O'Hara stood up and then looked more closely at Charlie Boy. "Didn't I see you last night in Lebanon?"

"Yeah," he replied hesitantly. "I think so."

"Anybody asking any questions?"

"A deputy came by this morning."

O'Hara regarded him intently. "Did he get any answers?"

"Not from me."

"Good. I like a man who knows how to stay out of matters that don't concern him."

Charlie Boy's chest swelled a little as O'Hara called him a "man," just as it had a dozen times last year after similar remarks from Coach Clemson.

"What's your name?"

"Charlie B—uh, Charlie Smith."

"Good to have you on the team, Charlie." O'Hara knew he was lying. Lots of men used phony names now—with good reason—and a smart man didn't press the matter further. O'Hara himself used only his last name.

O'Hara turned to the uncommitted members of the group still sitting around the fire and gestured to the little man beside him. "Any of the rest of you change your mind and decide to throw in with us, then see Huey here, or see me before we move out in the morning. And you others," he said to the young men who had joined with him, "if you have friends around here who might want to throw in with us, go talk to them. We're only *starting* with a few good men."

TUESDAY, JULY 2nd:
The Forty-Seventh Day

Jack Hamilton finished reading the packet of information dropped off during the latest helicopter visit. It gave him an update on the world and national situation.

Reliable information was still sparse in Frankfort, and much of what was sent to him was speculation based on the bits and pieces of news that had come in. Though nothing in the packet specifically said that the U.S. had gotten the worst of the fray, the fact that the Russians were said to be in Paris and soaking their feet in the Seine River said something about the relative strength of the Soviet war machine in the postnuclear exchange period. Britain, or what was left of it, was again an embattled island, but this time it would not be able to count on American help. Nothing in the packet even mentioned the situation in Iran, the start of it all.

A brief note also indicated that fifty-five Chinese divisions were poised along the Sino-Soviet border. Hamilton wondered whether this was connected to the lull in the fighting.

On the home front, the president had ordered the evacuation of much of the Northeast, and now a wave of homeless people was reported to be moving west and southwest.

Another report indicated that violence, as well as crime in general, was occuring on a grand scale in most places. For the past week, police, National Guard, and Army personnel had fought a no-holds-barred battle with looters in what was left of Detroit. The governor had ultimately issued shoot-to-kill-orders in a final effort to quell the disorders. And in Chicago's South Side, several square miles had been isolated by Guard and police units who now merely attempted to prevent the spread of riots and looting to other portions of the city. Problems were so severe along the heavily populated areas around the Great Lakes that federal efforts to move food and critical equipment now required the use of convoys because of repeated hijackings.

Compared to other places, Bardstown seemed an island of peace and order.

He placed the papers aside and picked up a notepad on which he had started figuring how to divide the most recent load of grain among the refugees who were demanding, as usual, more food than he had been able to find in recent days. The local farmers' charity had long since worn thin. Shortages were causing more than a few problems among the refugees who had not been able to find a farm on which to relocate, or who were unwilling to try.

As Hamilton poured over some of the figures, making mental calculations of the quantities to be distributed at various distribution points, a jeep came roaring up to the armory and young guardsman jumped out and ran toward the door. Sensing trouble immediately, Hamilton bounded to his feet and met the soldier at the entrance.

"Sir!" the young soldier exclaimed. "There's trouble down at the courthouse. Not enough enough wheat, too few tomatoes, and too many people! It's getting out of hand. Sergeant Mattingly sent me to get help fast!"

Those damned tomatoes! He should have anticipated that the first few samples of the summer crop would cause trouble. After weeks of food hardly better than gruel, the prospect of fresh juicy tomatoes was bound to have been too much for many of the refugees.

"First Sergeant!" Hamilton yelled to Johnson, who was standing in the large drill hall. "Get those men and their weapons and come on!"

Hamilton ran to the jeep and got in the front seat. Four soldiers piled into the back of his jeep, which was minus its canvas top. Johnson and four others did likewise with another jeep. The two vehicles roared off toward the courthouse. As they left, Ackerson was getting a truck ready to bring reinforcements.

When the two jeeps pulled within a couple of hundred feet from the courthouse, Hamilton could see a large crowd gathered around and hemming in the National Guard truck parked in front. Mattingly and four soldiers were standing in the back of the truck, looking like treed bobcats as they attempted to fend off the angry crowd.

Hamilton quickly formed the men in a line and ordered them to fix bayonets. Cursing himself for not having more men ready to respond, he ordered the men to chamber the first round in their weapons as it became obvious that the mood of the crowd was becoming steadily more violent. He then moved the detail to the rear of the mob, just as the crowd started to rock the truck from side to side. Only a few people had even noticed his presence, so intent were they on getting to the truck's contents. Hamilton drew his pistol and quickly fired two warning shots. This immediately turned the attention of the crowd in his direction, just as the truck started to tilt to a precipitous angle.

"Now that I have your attention, would someone mind telling me just what the hell is going on here?" Hamilton said, his pistol still pointed in the air.

A man wearing a dirty business suit and grimy silk tie started working his way through the crowd from his position near the truck to a point within a few feet of Hamilton.

"*I'll* tell you what's wrong. We're sick and tired of not getting our fair share of food. What you're giving us is hardly food anyway. It's not enough to keep a bird alive. Other places are getting more, and particularly more of the good stuff. That's not fair. It's discrimination!"

"Discrimination!" Hamilton exploded. "Just what the hell do you know about discrimination?" he said clenching his teeth.

"I'm a lawyer, soldier. It's my business to know about such matters. And this is how we're making our statement."

"Well, I'll tell you what *my* business is, counselor. My business is to distribute what little food there is and to try to keep the peace while doing it. In seeing that this food is distributed, it's damned hard to make sure that everyone in this town has precisely the same amount every day. We never know how many will show up at any point, or how much we'll have to distribute from one day to the next. But I will tell you this," Hamilton said, pointing his .45 directly at the man's nose. "Anyone who thinks that he can take the food off this truck by force had better think again. Do we understand each other?"

The man did not offer a quick response. As Hamilton lowered his pistol, the man said. "Well, what are we supposed to do? Slowly starve to death?"

"It's all been said before. You can go out to these farmers and other landowners around here and find someone to take you in so that you can raise your own food."

The man before him sneered. "I tried that a couple of times and got nowhere. Besides, raise my own food? What in the hell do I know, or what do most of these people know about raising vegetables and livestock?" Turning back to the crowd he said loudly, "But we all know we're being shortchanged here, though, and that's enough!"

The crowd reacted strongly to the lawyer's words and started to press forward toward Hamilton. He quickly raised his pistol to the lawyer's face. "Well, counselor, I suppose that instead of inciting a riot that you had better learn about vegetables and livestock real fast or be prepared to learn about M-16s and automatic rifle fire!"

As he was speaking, Ackerson and fifteen men rolled up in a two-and-one-half-ton truck. Ralph Osborne and two deputies were close behind. The men quickly dismounted and moved to the line behind Hamilton, making it clear that the tide, psychologically and otherwise, had turned. The crowd slowly started to disperse.

Sensing that his constituency was deserting him, the lawyer slowly turned and walked away, but not before casting a scornful glance at Hamilton. Standing his ground until he was absolutely certain the crisis was over, Hamilton looked at Ackerson, patted him on the shoulder, and said, "That was a close one, but we got by."

As the two walked back to the truck, Ackerson said softly, "For now."

"Are you out of your mind?"

Roseanna stared at Hamilton with her arms folded across her chest with a breast at each elbow, the time-honored body language used by irate wives and mothers since the family unit began.

"What do you mean?" he replied defensively, feeling uncomfortably like an adolescent schoolboy being called on the carpet as he walked into the kitchen.

"You know *exactly* what I mean, Dudley Do-Right! I talked with a couple of the men who were at the courthouse today. There you were like Gary Cooper in *High Noon*. Just how many people in that crowd do you think were carrying guns?" she demanded.

"Quite a few, I suppose."

"Exactly. And just how long do you think you would have lasted if shooting had started?"

"The point had to be made," he replied as he commenced washing his hands at the kitchen sink. "We couldn't just let those people have their way on the matter. Let them have their way today and there will be no controlling them tomorrow, once they figure out that we don't have the will to meet them head-on."

She shot back. "And once you've met them 'head-on,' as you call it, what do the kids and I do without a husband and father? That's exactly what would have happened if just one of them had pulled a gun!" Having said this, she walked over to the kitchen table and dropped into the nearest chair, satisfied that she had made her point.

Hamilton rinsed the soap from his hands and turned to her as he dried them. It was clear to him that her emotions were deep and genuine on this matter, so he tried a placating approach. "Listen, sweetheart, I have responsibilities, like it or not. I'm not trained to run an operation like this, so I may not necessarily choose the right solution to every problem that pops up. That certainly has become painfully clear to me at this point. I didn't ask for this job, but I've got it now. I have an obligation to those people out there, so I'm just going to have to meet it."

Tears welled up in her eyes as she listened to his words. It was obvious that she had met a brick wall, and she had been through situations like this a hundred times with him. Irresistible force had once again met immovable object. Nevertheless, as usual, it did not keep her from pursuing the matter. "Obligation? Responsibility? To *whom* or to *what*? You've got to get out of your Boy Scout mentality, Jack! Those people in town don't give a damn about you or your men. You're just someone to blame, or someone to serve their purpose temporarily. Just someone to *use*. You go out there every day and get *nothing* for it. No one even says thank you. How many of the 'good citizens' out there will back up you and your men if there's really serious trouble? And speaking of *High Noon*, you'll be just like Gary Cooper when the outlaws come to town and the 'good citizens' suddenly decide that they don't have much stomach for real trouble!"

She pounded the table lightly for emphasis and continued. "Your first obligation is to your family, now more than ever. All of those enlisted men out there know that, and I'm not blaming for a second those who have slipped away. God knows I wish you could. But if you *have* to do your damned soldierly duty in the future, will you just promise me that you won't take such big risks?"

Hamilton walked over to the table, pulled her to her feet, and looked into her moist eyes. "I promise I'll try to use a little more discretion next time. But remember, in *High Noon*, Grace Kelly stood by her man."

She smiled weakly and hugged him tightly. "That's the problem. You know that I will, too."

The sporadic motion of the dark form beside her summoned Kiki Callahan from a sound sleep. "Kiki" wasn't her real name, of course. But since the war had ended her former life and lifestyle, she had decided that Kiki had a better ring to it than Mary Bernardette. This was a new world. She was no longer living at home with her parents, going to the University of Louisville, and working part-time at the cosmetics counter at Snyder's Department Store. So why should she be saddled any longer with a name that had served only to provide her mother with a remembrance of a dead aunt? Kiki was damned sure that she herself had never felt this obligation.

The increasingly jerky movement roused her further, and she raised herself on one elbow, as much to remove her bare chest from the hot, sweaty contact as to find out what was really happening. She looked down in the darkness, and saw O'Hara in the throes of another of his bad dreams, muttering fitful, incoherent syllables.

Kiki threw back the sheet and shook O'Hara when he began to talk louder. Finally, O'Hara bolted upright like a jack-in-the-box and gave out a guttural scream. He continued to stare blankly into the darkness, and slowly he came to realize that what had beset him was only a dream.

Kiki sat up beside him and said assuringly, "Come on, baby. It's just another nightmare."

Though O'Hara hated it when she called him "baby", he hesitantly returned back to the mattress. He kicked fitfully at the bedsheets now gathered around his knees, forcing them into a knot at the foot of the bed, and then pulled her to him. They lay there naked in the darkness, Kiki soothingly stroking O'Hara's hair and telling him that everything would be alright.

Without warning, Charlie Boy burst in on them with a pistol in one hand and a dry-cell lantern in the other. "You alright, O'Hara?" he asked, shining the blinding light directly in their eyes. Huey stood right behind him.

Kiki bolted from the mattress like a she-dog protecting her litter and rushed naked toward the door. "Go on, get out! He's okay!" Pushing at Charlie Boy's massive chest, she backed him into the hallway. She then returned to the bed and rolled a long slender leg over O'Hara's thigh, commencing to stroke his hair once again.

"Who is Brighton?" she asked.

"Where did you come up with that?"

"You. It was one of the names you said. Said it last night, too. Most of the rest of it was too jumbled up to understand, except for something about fallout."

Kiki had known O'Hara three days, and he had not confided in her, or anyone else for that matter, about his past life. She had blatantly pursued him at a chance meeting because he was an attractive male with a compelling, powerful presence. It was certain that he and his men would be able to provide her with almost anything she wanted as long as she was *his* woman. She felt certain that in O'Hara's world there would always be more—more of everything. More food, more clothes, more things. Nice things.

She wasn't altogether sure that she approved of his group's methods, but so far at least, nobody had gotten killed. The bottom line, however, was that a girl couldn't be that choosy in these times.

She modestly regarded herself as a knockout—weren't the girls at the cosmetics counters always the prettiest in the store?—but even so, she knew that keeping O'Hara for long, and especially all to herself, would be difficult. It looked as if it might be good while it lasted, though, and Kiki Callahan was definitely along for the ride.

O'Hara slid out of bed. He walked to the window and placed his arms above his head against the frame. He stood there in the darkness, staring into the blackness of night, feeling the cool night breeze blowing gently against his hot, damp skin. He listened to the steady rhythm of the insect chorus. He remembered how his grandmother had told him as a child that the insects argued "Katy did, Katy didn't" back and forth through the night.

All else was silent. But this stillness was only an illusion. The stillness belied the turmoil, pain, and violence filling the countryside. How much of it had he himself caused? How much more would he cause?

A garden spider's gossamer web stretched as a net between the outside edge of the sash to the shrub beyond. The huge, grotesquely bulbous body of the black, tan, and brilliant yellow arachnid hung motionless among the dried exoskeleton hulls of hapless prey that had found their way to the spider's silken world.

The arachnid's patience was rewarded. As O'Hara watched in the moonlight, a small moth flitted by and became ensnared. Its gray-brown, velvety wings thrashed wildly in its futile effort to escape.

The spider moved. Within three seconds, it was across the web, its mandibles buried in its victim. The moon passed behind a passing cloud and the darkness was complete. In the insect world, there are no screams.

O'Hara turned to the nightstand where a bottle of Very Old Barton and two glasses rested. He poured two fingers of bourbon. Half of it disappeared in one gulp. He had become quite good at that lately.

"So?" she asked.

"So what?"

"So who is or was this Brighton fellow?"

"A man I knew a thousand years ago."

"Is he dead now?"

The other half of the bourbon in the glass disappeared. "Yeah," he said softly. "I suppose he is."

"Is that good or bad?" she asked, pressing him further, trying to get inside and past his barriers.

"Good," he whispered.

"Then I'm *glad*."

She intuitively knew that it was probably better that she not ask him about the other name he had mentioned, Cathy, regardless of how curious she might be about this woman.

O'Hara turned around and looked at her when a passing cloud once again spilled a roomful of moonlight through the window. Her reclining figure lay in front of him naked, tempting. Her long, graceful legs stretched without a dimple or rimple down the bed, and her broad patch of dark pubic hair looked even darker in this light. Its glistening seemed to beckon him with a silent biological invitation.

His eyes savored her waist-length, raven-black hair. It wrapped sensuously in a serpentine fashion down her shoulders across her full breast and then down to the sheets.

He felt something powerful, something primal stirring within him. Something verified, fortified, and finally magnified by the biological imperative of a million years of evolution propelled him toward the bed.

Kiki smiled as he placed himself on his hands and knees

over her and then brought his lips to hers. She reached down to the warmth between his legs and said, "I think I know what you need."

"Then go for it," he whispered hoarsely.

WEDNESDAY, JULY 3rd:
The Forty-Eighth Day

The sharp report of an explosion echoed along the river bottom. Rogers dropped the fencing pliers and the roll of barbed wire from his hands and bounded toward the barn. The green army field-phone to one of the security posts was ringing in rapid, staccato bursts.

George Anderson beat Rogers to the phone and grabbed the receiver from its cradle. "What is it?"

"Dunno. Came from just up the river and sounded like someone hit a trip wire," Bob Rose replied. As usual, there wasn't the first hint of emotion or excitement in Rose's voice. There never was.

"You stay put. We'll have some people out there to check it out."

"Wait a minute. I can see them now. It looks like a family with kids."

"Well, keep low and maybe they'll pass by."

"Can't. Looks like they've spotted us. They're heading this way."

Anderson shot Rogers a look of disgust. "Just keep cool, and we'll be out there."

"Roger that."

Anderson placed the phone back in the cradle. "Dammit. Looks like some wandering road people. I'll stay in charge here if you want to check it out. You're better at that sort of thing."

Rogers nodded and pulled his automatic from his shoulder holster, checking to make sure a round was chambered.

When Larry Jackson rounded the corner he said, "C'mon, Larry. We're going to see who our company is."

"Should I get my Mini-14? Might need more fire-power."

Kurt smiled. "No, Larry. I don't think it's likely to be that serious."

The two men quickly trotted out to the security post. When they arrived they found a refugee family standing with Bob Rose and the O'Connell boy.

"Okay," Rogers said. "What's going on?"

"They apparently hit one of the signal booby traps," Rose whispered. "Now they're looking for a handout."

Rogers examined the people before him. They carried a few ratty possessions in the improvised packs on their backs and on the golf cart the man pulled behind him. They looked as if they had not bathed in a couple of weeks, and their clothes looked as if they had not been laundered long before that. The three children stared blankly at Rogers. The little girl firmly clasped a blond, dirty, Cabbage Patch doll to her chest.

"What do you people want?" Rogers asked in a business-like tone.

"Same as everybody else. Food and shelter," the man softly replied.

Rogers studied the man before him. Hair crept down his ears and the back of his neck like crabgrass across a sidewalk. A week's growth of stubble appeared on his cheeks, and his fingernails showed crescents of black at the tips. He was of medium stature, with nothing particularly striking about his features. Probably the sort of man Rogers would have stood behind in a supermarket line before the war and taken little notice of. A computer salesman? An accountant? A drugstore manager? Obviously he had gone through a period of severe weight loss judging by the baggy appearance of his clothes. Rogers inhaled deeply, and said, "I'm sorry, but we can't help you here."

"Can't or *won't*? You're obviously doing well from the looks of you. I expect you could give us a lot of help if you really wanted to."

"Why don't you try the camps?"

"We've *been* there. There's little food, poor shelter, filth and disease everywhere." He grabbed the hand of his younger boy and thrust it toward Rogers. "See that, mister? Know what that is? That's a rat bite. You stay in camps like that long enough and you'll end up six feet under."

Rogers looked at Rose and Jackson. He jerked his head slightly, signaling them to follow him away for a few steps. "Look," he whispered, "These people need help badly. We ought to do something for them."

Jackson quickly shook his head. "No way, Kurt. You let it begin here, and then where does it stop? One, then another, and then another family will be here, and soon we're as bad off as they are. They could have done something to prepare and they didn't. So piss on 'em!"

Rose looked straight into Rogers eyes. "I won't put it quite that way, Kurt, but he's right. Even if you just give them a small handout today, it's likely to mean that we have twenty people here tomorrow morning looking for the same thing, and forty the day after that. We all agreed in the beginning as to how it was to be. There's no reason to change now."

"You already broke the rules once," Jackson added, "so don't make it any worse."

The obvious reference to Chris wasn't lost upon Rogers. Larry hit home with that one. Slowly he walked back toward the family, paused, and then cleared his throat. "I'm sorry, but you'll have to turn back."

A flash of defiance appeared in the man's eyes. "And if we don't, what are you going to do? Shoot two people with a bunch of kids?"

"No," replied Rogers firmly, "but you've already hit a harmless signal device. A little further on, it turns nasty, and there are things out there that can get very hazardous to your health if you don't know the way. I don't think you want that to happen to any of your kids."

The man's defiance flickered, then faded to despair. Finally, he turned and gestured at his children. "I hope you can live with yourself."

As he walked away, his wife and children following him, Rogers called out lamely, "Try the camp at Lebanon. I hear things are better there."

Rogers and Jackson didn't speak a word on their walk back to the retreat. Several members waited for them, looking expectantly at the two as they crossed the barnyard.

Josh ran up to his father and asked, "What was it, Dad?"

Rogers' expression was grim. "Nothing." He walked straight to his trailer and headed for the bathroom.

He had seen hundreds of refugees since it began, so the sight of this family had been nothing new. However, he had always been able to maintain a comfortable psychological distance when he came into contact with the refugees in town. After all, hadn't it always been easier to pass blithely by a beggar on a downtown street corner than to ignore one who knocked on the front door of the house asking for help?

He thought about Chris and how he had justified bringing her to the retreat because she was a nurse and had important skills. To be honest about it, had she been twenty years older and much less attractive, he doubted that he would have done as he did. Yes sir, a real humanitarian he had been all right.

He brusquely grabbed at the bar of soap and began to lather his hands with a pronounced intensity. He kept his eyes fixed on his hands in the sink. He didn't care to confront his image in the mirror right now.

THURSDAY, JULY 4TH: THE Forty-Ninth Day

"Well, Happy goddam Fourth of July, sir, but we've gotta do something, and the sooner the better."

Hamilton sat at his desk in the Charlie Battery Orderly Room and brooded over the morning report that Ackerson handed him. The handwritten figures showed more AWOLs since the previous day. It seemed that the trickle of AWOLs was continuing at an alarming rate, though a few of them did report back from time to time. Given the lack of support from the community, the confrontations with the refugee population, and the increasing violence, it was no wonder that the last few weeks had seen a serious decrease in the battery's strength.

Finally, Hamilton laid down the slip of paper and said, "Ted, sit down. Top, will you go get Sergeant Reichert? I want him in on this, too."

In a minute or so, Johnson returned with Sgt. 1st Class Kenny Reichert, the so-called "Chief of Smoke," the actual ramrod of Charlie Battery's howitzer crews.

"Sit down everybody, and let's get on with this," Hamilton said. "We need to talk about the condition of this unit while we still *have* a unit." Turning to Johnson he said, "Who were those two AWOLs again?"

"Nix and Combs, sir."

"Okay, so counting the four who disappeared last week, we've got an AWOL rate of almost 35 percent since this whole mess began. We're going to have to do something fast."

"It's bad and gettin' a helluva lot worse, that's for sure," replied Johnson.

"Major, one answer to your problem will come when you figure out how to help these guys take care of their families," said Reichert, a rotund, rubber-faced, red-headed NCO who even in this period of dire shortages was still able to find cigars that stunk up the Orderly Room. Sitting there enveloped in a blue-gray cloud of dense smoke, he continued. "I'm speaking for myself on this as well, Major."

Ackerson joined in, "He's right, sir. We gotta find a way to let these guys do right by their families while they're doing their duty here. If we don't, it's gonna be a real disaster soon. Since they know we'll come knocking at their door as soon as they disappear, most of them are sneaking off to relatives and friends where we'll never find them." The tone of his voice shifted subtly as he added, "Given the way things have been going, I'm not so sure that I can blame them."

Hamilton stood up, walked over to the window, and then turned back to the group, "If we could figure out how to pay them in anything other than worthless paper money, maybe they would have a way of providing for their families while they're here. With the banking system in a shambles everywhere, the paper money isn't worth a damn. By keeping these guys tied up on security patrols and the like, they can't take care of their families at all. Only a goddamn fool would expect to have an effective unit under these conditions."

"Of course, the county sheriff's people and the other police are in the same boat, which explains why so many of 'em have walked off the job," added Johnson. "No taxes, no salaries. No salaries, no deputies. If you can't pay in something other than paper money, you might as well not pay at all. And a man's sense of duty can only be strained so far."

"At this point," replied Hamilton, "I'm not nearly as concerned about these other people as I am about our boys. I'd like to have you guys consider an idea I've been knocking around in my head for the past couple of weeks. My brother and I own that big farm out there. It may not have all the comforts of home, but it will be secure enough for any soldier's family that decides to move out there. That's damned important to these men. When a Guardsman is not on duty, he can quickly go out there to his family. He and his family can also work a piece of ground. We still have plenty of time for a fall garden. I don't know how many of them will go for this, but it's worth a try until we can find a permanent solution to the problem. What do you think?"

"Frankly, sir," Reichert replied, "I don't think it will work. I don't expect many of 'em will voluntarily leave their own homes in order to go out there, and for those that don't, I expect to lose them with further signs that law and order are becoming things of the past. And that point may not be that far away. These boys will put their families first. That's just common sense."

"But we've nothing to lose by trying it, Major," Ackerson interrupted, trying to sound an optimistic note. "It might extend the effectiveness of this unit for a crucial period. If we can offer most of the men a secure place for their families, it'll be awfully good for morale." Johnson nodded in agreement.

"Then it's settled. Chief Reichert, I'd like you to come with me to look over the farm and figure out how we can secure the place a little better." Hamilton picked up his cap and started for the door. "After we figure out the preliminaries, we'll announce this to the battery and make our sales pitch. Until then, let's keep it to ourselves."

Hamilton, Reichert, Ackerson, and Nugent rolled up to

the farm at noon and began to inspect the area. Cliff came out from one of the barns when he heard the jeep drive up. Together the five men walked around the buildings that were clustered atop the hill.

"This hilltop strikes me as an excellent place to defend. You can see that there are at least three hundred yards cleared in that direction," he said as he pointed across a field of corn to the creek, "and four hundred yards in nearly every other place, except toward the Cissell farm. And except for that ground toward Reuben's, we're elevated above the rest of the area. Why, we can look down on most everything that moves out there. What do you think?"

Reichert didn't respond right away to Hamilton's enthusiasm. Diplomacy was definitely one consideration. As one of the few Guardsmen still around who had actually seen combat, he was experienced in occupying and defending fire-base positions. He looked at the ground with a keener, more practiced eye than Hamilton.

He walked a few steps in order to peer around one of the smaller outbuildings, and then returned to the group. "Well, sir," he said finally, "as a defensive position I've seen better, but I've seen a helluva lot worse. There's a lot more cover on that slope down there than I'd like, and more between us and that farm over there than ideal. But given the fact there are buildings here that can be adapted fairly well for shelter, it seems like a reasonable choice when everything's considered. Still, we'll need an awful lot of men to defend this entire hill. What am I saying? I'm beginning to sound like I'm back in Vietnam!"

"Well, this isn't Vietnam, but I want to make sure that we don't downplay security here. There's no reason not to keep people busy. Hell, I'm talking revetted trenches, breastworks, foxholes, the works. We've got that bulldozer over there, and with that kind of help, there's no reason we couldn't knock out the job in a week," Hamilton said.

"We've got several rolls of concertina barbed tape back at the armory, and I know where I can get a lot more barbed wire," Johnson said.

"I think I can get several bags of ammonium nitrate if you think we might ever have to use it, Major," Reichert added.

"You guys want fertilizer?" asked Cliff who had been listening silently to the discussion up to this point.

"Not just fertilizer. This stuff makes a dandy low-grade explosive if used properly. If necessary, I can do some nasty things with it," Reichert said.

"Well, maybe we shouldn't get too carried away, but if you can get it, bring it out here and we'll hang on to it," Hamilton said. "Let's walk on back to the house and sit down and plan this thing out."

The group gathered around the kitchen table. Over coffee, Hamilton and Reichert sketched the area, and worked out the details of the defensive perimeter Reichert would prepare. The main feature was the earthen berm to be built with the bulldozer. It would circle the Hamilton side of the saddle around the main buildings. Roseanna and Marge came in and watched attentively as the men traced, erased, and retraced the drawing of the defense plans.

"Okay, I'm satisfied," Hamilton said finally. "Now let's go back and see how many we can persuade to buy it. I have no problem ordering the single, unattached men to come out here and start using this place as a 'barracks.' The married men are another problem. I can only stretch my authority so far. After that I have to persuade them instead of trying to order them to comply. But if I can convince them that it is in their families' best interest to come out here, we'll be okay. If I can't do that, then there's no reason to bring the single men out here."

"I agree, Major," Reichert said.

"But how about you, Kenny? Ackerson's single, and Johnson is divorced without any kids. But you, you've got a wife and three kids. Your coming out here with them would be a great example to the others."

Reichert tightened his lips for a few seconds and turned his head aside. Finally looking at Hamilton, he said, "No, sir. At least not yet. Not until I get more worried about the situation. Until then I want to keep my family where they are, at home. I'm not saying that I might not change my mind later, but for now, no."

Hamilton's face registered his disappointment. Reichert responded, "But listen, Major, that's only because of my family's particular situation. I'm sure a lot of our boys will not have it as good, and it'll be a lot easier for them to decide to come. I'll do as much as I can to convince them."

"Okay," Hamilton said reluctantly. "Let's get on back."

As the group got up to walk out, Kip ran into the kitchen.

"Dad! Uncle Cliff! One of the cows is dead out in the south pasture! It looks like it's been eaten on by something!" he said, making a strange face.

"Goddam it!" exclaimed Cliff. "I bet it's those goddam wild dogs. I heard a pack of them last night. Killing cattle. Shit! Come on, Kip. Show me where it is."

At the afternoon formation, Hamilton made his pitch to the battery. His efforts were somewhat bolstered by the latest news of crimes that day and the previous night. Four murders and twenty-five separate cases of armed robbery had been reported, as well as a host of thefts and a few rapes. The violence was escalating, he told them, and there was no end in sight.

By afternoon of the following day, ten families of the twenty Hamilton was hoping for had decided to move to the farm. "It's a start," he said when Ackerson gave him the report. "We'll just have to wait and see how things develop."

"Sir, if you don't mind me saying so," Ackerson said, "our success in attracting families to the farm may be, in a manner of speaking, inversely related to our success in keeping things under control around the county. In other words, the faster the situation goes to hell here, the faster families will come to the farm."

Hamilton did not bother to reply. Ackerson was obviously right.

FRIDAY, JULY 19TH:
The Sixty-Fourth Day

Fran Fitzgerald stood before the ancient porcelain sink of the old farmhouse. She mopped at the beads of perspiration on her brow as Ellen Randall handed her a heavy iron skillet. The skillet had been used to prepare the evening meal for the two families now sharing the tired old home. Formerly the main farmhouse, the place had always been a modest structure, though it had been attractive enough in its day.

Now, however, the battered walls of the kitchen were a pale and faded turquoise. They had probably seen their last coat of paint about the time Fran had graduated from high school. The kitchen floor, now tidy after much effort, bore the insults of three generations of use and abuse. It creaked and groaned in protest as Ellen crossed it with a handful of dirty dishes. An attractive thirty-two-year-old woman, Ellen had finally wound up in Bardstown with her family after an intense ordeal. Like the house in which she lived, Ellen seemed to be merely a shadow of her former self.

Fran vigorously scrubbed grease from several utensils. She watched out the window as Ken and Marvin, Ellen's husband, worked in the garden, hoeing between the rows of precious tomatoes, squash, beans, and other vegetables they hoped to harvest in the late fall. Ellen's three children, as well as Melanie, Michael, and Cindy knelt between the plants pulling the weeds that sprouted daily to compete with the vegetables for sun, water and nutrients. The chatter from the children made it clear that their efforts came in fits and starts.

Fran dipped the skillet in the rinse water and reflected on how thankful she was that Reuben had the vegetable seeds on hand when they had been needed. Clara, it seemed, had taken advantage of an end of season clearance the preceding September, and had more than enough seeds on hand. "Only seventeen cents a package!" Clara had boasted. Many people on the farms in the area hadn't been as fortunate.

Fran had been designated by Reuben as the farm's chief gardener, and she had expertly laid out the plots and supervised the planting with the experience accumulated from annual backyard efforts in the city. Her labor had always produced a bounteous supply for her family and relatives. The harvest here looked to be equally promising should nothing unexpected happen.

It was a much thinner Fran Fitzgerald who stood there, just as she had planned prior to Black Friday. Given the tremendous physical efforts around the farm, and the period of hand-to-mouth existence before, she had lost twenty pounds, most of it in the right places. Her figure hadn't been this slim since she married Ken. It was not, however, a diet she would recommend to anyone else.

As she finished with the last of the knives and forks in the sink, she watched Clara Cissell coming down the hill toward the house. Clara knocked at the rickety screen door and poked her head in, cheerfully chiming, "Anybody home?" She stepped inside without waiting for a reply. It was obvious who was landlord and who was tenant here.

Fran greeted her warmly and Clara sat down at the kitchen table, which by now had been cleared of any evidence of the last meal. "Goshawful weather, isn't it? Lordy, gettin' back to normal for this time of year, I guess."

Fran and Ellen agreed, and Fran continued, "How do you like the looks of those beans out there?" she asked proudly. "Not many people around here have green beans looking that good."

Clara and Ellen readily agreed. "For a crop that young it looks wonderful. You've been a real godsend, that's for sure, you and your gardening know-how and all!" Clara exclaimed.

"I'm just glad to have the opportunity to use it," Fran replied sweetly. She was always careful to express her gratitude to Clara as often as possible in order to cement her place and her role here on the farm.

Every couple of nights she would have the recurring dream that she and her family were homeless again, running in the darkness, and that they were being followed by faceless pursuers. She would find herself staring into the milky-gray eyes of a dead man, and then awake in terror and panic until Ken calmed her and convinced her it was merely a bad dream and nothing more. With the family's ordeal over the past couple of months, wasn't a little insecurity to be expected of anyone?

The dread she felt from time to time was nothing compared to that felt by her children. Why one day Michael had run into the house and flung himself into the chair, breathless and shaking. Upon prodding him for a minute or so, she learned that he had seen the contrails of an aircraft at high altitude, now a very rare occurrence. He had become immediately convinced that it was about to drop another nuclear bomb. He had seen that mushroom cloud once, and was terrified at the prospect of seeing another.

And Melanie. Fran had even overheard Melanie talking to Cindy one time a couple of weeks ago when she thought no one else was around, saying to her, "If I get old enough, I'm gonna . . ." She had said "if." *If* with all its heavy, terrible implications.

Clara, in responding to Fran's comments, said "Well, I guess we're all fortunate to be here. I can just imagine what all of you went through to get here . . ."

"No you *can't*," Ellen interjected, with more than a slight edge to her tone. "*No one* can imagine unless they were *there*. Not even you, Fran. You saw part of it, but only from a distance. My family and I came through the *whole* thing, right there in the city. God only knows how we all made it. Marvin at work, the kids at practice. I ran most of the way to school. Homes burning, trees flattened, gas mains exploding. Think of my relief at finding my children, but the horror at finding them so bloody and battered that at first I didn't even recognize them. And even this was only because they had been fortunate enough to go inside the school to get a drink of water just before the explosion. Or how about seeing Marvin staggering half dead through the door hours later with a shattered arm and face? And even now, I worry about the leukemia or cancer that might be waiting for all of us in a few years. A time bomb just ticking away. You can empathize and sympathize, but *you'll* never really imagine how it was because you weren't *there*!"

The intensity with which Ellen had spoken brought an embarassing silence that hung awkwardly about them after she finished. Finally, Fran placed the dishcloth in her hand to the side of the sink, and she wiped her hands on her apron. She cleared her throat and, in as cheerful a tone as she could muster, said, "Well now, why don't we all go out and see just how our garden's coming along? It's been growing so fast you can almost see the plants growing larger by the minute."

Clara seized the opportunity to occupy herself with more pleasant matters, and she started for the door behind Fran.

"Excited?"

"I suppose I'd have to admit that I am," Chris replied.

She was finishing up a few charts and readying herself for some time away from the hospital. "I guess I sound like a schoolgirl, don't I?"

"Listen, honey," the other nurse replied, "if Kurt is only half as good as you describe him, I'd be doing the Dance of the Seven Veils to lock on to him!"

"Right!" Chris tossed back her head and laughed heartily. It felt good. Relief from the tension had been too scarce lately.

"What's this now? Three times you've seen him in the past month?"

"Something like that I guess." She stood up, picked up some medical supplies, and said, "I'll take care of these things for you, and then I'm going to get out of this place." She walked directly to the floor's Med Room carrying the items.

A pair of hands suddenly came across Chris Whittington's eyes, and there quickly followed, "Guess who? Remember me?"

Chris turned around after placing three syringes on the crash cart and came face to face with Bernie Weintraub. "I don't believe it!" she exclaimed. There was as much irritation as surprise in her voice. "How in the world did *you* get here?"

"Aw, I've been sitting out the storm at a friend's place. Got so bored I couldn't stand it any more. Thought I'd come in here for some professional challenges to keep the old gray matter working."

"We could have used your ass around here for the past few weeks, Bernie. And you only came in because you were *bored*?"

It was just like him, she thought. She could hardly believe that she had been almost fond of him at one time. But that was when she had been a naive young nurse fresh out of school.

He had been a young intern. Tall, with dark hair and Mediterranean good looks that gave him a deep, rich tan. Even in winter, he always looked as if he had just returned from someplace expensive. Back then he had been less convinced he was God's gift to the female of the species, and more interested in the welfare of his patients, or so it seemed.

He had fallen all over himself to impress her. Almost a boyish awkwardness about him, even at the ripe old age of twenty-six. They had a brief fling over three months. A skiing trip to Snowshoe one January, and a weekend trip later to Chicago.

The more she got to know Bernie, however, the less she liked him. Too much of his conversation was spent on future investments he intended to make, stocks he wanted to get into as soon as possible, *ad nauseam*.

"Real estate is really where it's at, though," he would repeat, over and over. "Three things affect the value of real estate, you know: location, location, and location."

It got to the point that she wondered why he had spent so much effort obtaining a medical license when what he really seemed to need was a real estate broker's license.

Finally, she came to recognize that he was like some of the other doctors she had met from time to time at the hospital. Medicine was only a means to financial success for them, and not very much more. To the question of why so much elective surgery was always scheduled in November and December, Chris came to appreciate why many of the nurses would often mutter under their breaths, "Doctors like to have good Christmases, too."

Another thing she had disliked about her relationship with Bernie was the feeling near the end that she was just another notch in his bedpost, representing a blue-eyed blond he had laid. Why was it with doctors that the darker the complexion the more desirable a blue-eyed blond nurse? Later she decided that she had been unfair in limiting this question to doctors, or nurses, but she still wound up resenting Bernie for it anyway. Regardless, Bernie was a jerk anyway you cut it.

"Aw, c'mon, now. Don't give me a bunch of grief. I'll be doing my part now," Bernie pleaded. "But that doesn't mean that we won't have time to *rekindle* something from the past." His eyes danced a little at the word "rekindle."

"Forget it, Bernie. I'm more than occupied with things around here and I don't have time for *you*."

His tone turned supplicant, with a little-boy pout to his lips. "But Chris, now more than ever we need each other. Most of our attachments to the past are gone and we need to grasp and hang on to as many of them as we can."

Her glance grew glacial, and she turned away from him and walked toward the door. "Screw the past, Bernie. It's gone for me, just like it is for everyone of those people out there. I don't even care. So much has happened in the past few weeks that I'm not the same person I was then. You're probably not, either, I *hope*."

"Well, maybe we can try it again and just see how it goes," he said as he started to follow after her.

"Forget it, Bernie. The little time I have I'm spending with someone who seems to be more made to order for this new world of ours, and there's no place in my life for *you*. I'm off-duty in two minutes, and he's probably out in the parking lot waiting to take me back to his place until Sunday."

A sudden look of recognition came to his face. "Oh, don't tell me! Is it 'Clint Eastwood' out there in that Bronco?"

Chris didn't bother with a response. She continued walking down the corridor and heard him mutter, "Bitch!"

She was wrong about him having changed. Bernie was, and always would be a jerk—anyway you cut it.

PART FIVE

Swept with confused alarms of struggle and flight,
Where ignorant armies clash by night.

—Matthew Arnold,
"Dover Beach"

FRIDAY, AUGUST 1st:
The Seventy-Seventh Day

"Will you two just shut up!" Larry Howard snapped.

Specialist Fourth Class Arnie Ewing, the jeep's driver, looked at him and asked, "Man, who dropped the turd in your punch bowl?"

"One more remark like that and I'll have an Article 15 on your ass so quick it'll make your head swim."

Ewing was silent, but he did glance at PFC Steven Forrest who rode in the back with PFC Bobby Bickett. Forrest looked toward Howard, rolled his eyes upward, and silently mouthed, "Asshole." Bickett just grinned.

The security patrol continued a mile or so, when Ewing finally asked, "Somethin' eatin' on you today, Sarge?"

"Yeah," Howard admitted. "My ol' lady's been getting worse and worse about me leaving her and the kids alone all the time. She's getting more worried everyday. I tell her, 'So why not go out to the major's place.' She says, 'Cause I want to stay near Mom.' I give up. I can't win for losin', and I've just about had it up to here with the goddam Guard, her, and the rest of the world."

Ahead, Ewing spotted a man at the side of the road, alternately waving his hand and pointing up the hill.

"Now what the hell does this guy want?" Ewing asked.

"Dammit," Spaulding said, "somebody give me some answers." Hamilton, Mattingly, and Ackerson stood among a group of six others near a barbed wire fence ten feet high. Inside the fence was a prisoner compound packed with over three hundred male prisoners. Close by was a smaller compound for the female prisoners. Tarps served as the only shelter from the elements, and the sanitary facilities were primitive at best. A large number of inmates lined the fence jeering at Spaulding's group. Several prisoners made remarks suggesting that Spaulding had an unnatural relationship with his mother. A couple began heaving small rocks in his direction, causing the group to withdraw a few steps out of range.

"This situation is getting totally out of hand. We've got so many right now, we can barely squeeze them in!" Spaulding's broad face grew steadily more flushed. "And shelter? I'll be damned if I'm going to take the decent, law-abiding citizens out of any public buildings here in Nelson County this winter in order to house this scum. Here it is August already, and with cold weather not that far away, we've got to come up with something. Pretty soon every deputy we've got left will be needed just to guard the prisoners."

One of the county magistrates spoke up. "Well, Leon, I expect that by next week we should have some temporary shelters constructed to house them in, though I can't really say the shelters will be all that much. And maybe we can get Judge Robbins over here from Bloomfield to hear some cases soon—if anyone can convince him to leave his home long enough. I hear he's as scared to leave his place unattended as everyone else is."

"The trouble with the trials," Ralph Osborne said, "is that even if these people are tried and sentenced, where the hell do we send them? The state sure as hell isn't going to be accepting any more prisoners for a long time, especially since that big prison break at LaGrange last month shows that they can't hang on to what they already have. Not enough guards left."

"I wish I had authority to try them," Spaulding responded, "but I don't. I'd handle each one of these low-lifes in about five minutes."

"Leon, remember that they're innocent until proven guilty," said J. C. Sims, the first magistrate. "All of them still deserve justice."

"Justice?" Spaulding exploded. "Let me let you in on a little secret, J.C., one that you may not have heard while you've been teaching those civics lessons to your high school classes. Justice in its true sense is seldom meted out by the courts, or at least when it is, it's as much by accident as by design! What we have is Justice as opposed to *justice*. We set up elaborate rules and case precedents that as often as not hamper the process as much as help it. And we develop intricate rules of evidence that so often prevent important information from being admitted for a multitude of reasons. What we have is not a search for absolute truth, guilt, or innocence which results in *justice*, but merely a procedure that involves a highly contrived legal process which instead produces a *result!* And this we have grandly and self-servingly named the Justice System!"

Sims was undaunted by Spaulding's diatribe. "Leon, you still have to remember that, like it or not, they're innocent until proven guilty."

"Innocent, hell!" Spaulding cried. "Ninety percent of them were caught in the act! We're stretched too thin to investigate the tough cases. With so many transient refugees around, they can come in, clean out a family, kill all the witnesses, and then fade out into that mass of humanity out there. And there's not a thing I, Ralph Osborne and his people, or Jack Hamilton and his people can do about it! If I could legally try them, I'd give them one chance in court, and then if I found them guilty, they'd get about a day to make their peace with their Maker! As it is, if I were to try them by setting up some sort of temporary court myself, I'd be constantly wondering what sonofabitch out there would be watching just so he could accuse me of being some sort of *war criminal* two years from now!"

Hamilton listened to Spaulding's tirade, and after giving him enough time to vent his spleen, said, "This will probably be fuel for the fire, Judge, but some refugees coming through a checkpoint last night indicated that two more of those bands of 'crazies' numbering over twenty people hit several farms about halfway between here and Springfield in the last week. That's a lot closer and more serious than in the past. We had another delivery by helicopter this morning, and the pilot, Terry Rockwell, said that this isn't just an isolated situation. Even larger 'wolf packs,' as they are calling them, are operating around the state. They're running scared in Frankfort about all of this. Some places are trying to organize militias of a sort in order to provide some measure of security.

"As for around here, we haven't exactly been overrun with people volunteering to go out there without pay and get their tails shot off. We had two men join up last week, but they walked off with two M-16s at the first opportunity."

The news of the wolf packs pumped up Spaulding even further, and the next five minutes consisted of another tirade against the murderers, the crazies, and the thieves who increasingly threatened his community. The group listened patiently and offered comments, but few solutions.

"I want to think about this militia idea, though," said Spaulding as the group left the prisoner compound. "There are enough guns in the right people's hands to make a difference, at least if the people were properly organized. Maybe Ralph can get together with you, Major, and the two of you can give some more thought to the matter."

When Hamilton arrived back at the armory an hour later, Rockwell was standing beside his helicopter. "Got time to take me up for a look-see, Terry?"

Rockwell looked at his wristwatch and said, "A short one, Major. We still have more stops to make today."

Hamilton turned and spotted Johnson coming out the side door of the building into the motor pool and he called out to him. Johnson came over to the chopper and said, "What's up, Major?"

"Come on with me. Rockwell's going to give us an aerial recon. We might learn something about the current situation from up there."

"Now, Major, you know I don't have any use for these damned things," he pleaded as he gestured toward Rockwell's helicopter.

"Aw, c'mon," Hamilton said with a smile. "It won't hurt a bit."

"Just one thing," Rockwell piped in. "First Sergeant, would you look out periodically and keep an eye on that large nut up there?" As he spoke, Rockwell pointed up to the rotor-blade assembly and shaft. "That's the Jesus Nut."

"Okay," replied Johnson naively. "But why do they call it a Jesus Nut?"

With a gleam in his eye, Rockwell came back, "Because if it comes off, everybody on the chopper screams 'JEEE-ZUSSS!'"

As Hamilton broke into laughter, Johnson cried, "Oh, bullshit!" and reluctantly strapped himself into his seat. Within a few minutes the helicopter was airborne.

A few miles away, Ewing and Forrest held at gunpoint two prisoners who lay spread-eagled on the ground in front of a farmhouse. Sgt. Larry Howard wrapped the gauze of an army field dressing around a teenage boy's head. Beside the nearby jeep lay the body of PFC Bobby Bickett, who had been killed by one of the two prisoners when the jeep pulled up to the house.

The evidence of the previous night's raid by a band of armed men was strewn about the lawn and asphalt driveway.

Inside, near the window, lay the boy's father, lifeless. Around him were several expended shotgun shells from a desperate but unsuccessful defense of the home. His mother also lay dead at the kitchen door, and outside, a black-and-tan German shepherd lay dead a few feet from the same door.

The young man's head had been grazed by a bullet. He had been left for dead by the intruders until the guardsmen, acting on a report of gunfire, had found him.

"They came in before Dad had a chance to stop them," the boy said between sobs. "First, Duke was going crazy, so Mom let him out to check on things. We thought maybe it was just a fox or some wild dogs or something. Duke was no more than out the door when they cut loose with I don't know how many guns, killin' Duke and Mom. Dad tried to stop 'em, but they came in too fast," he said with tears rolling down his cheeks.

"How many of 'em were there?"

"I saw lots of 'em after I came to, but not all at one time. I just kept real still. I expect there was somewhere between fifteen and twenty, but I can't be sure, since I tried to keep my eyes shut pretty good. I could tell they had women with them, though."

He pointed to the two prisoners. "Those two must have found the whiskey that Dad had been keeping to barter with. They really got crocked, and didn't want to leave with the others."

"What about the guy inside?"

"Yeah, that was somethin'. The guy who must have been the leader showed up a few minutes after I came to. He got all mad at the guy 'cause he said he screwed things up. Said they were sent for guns, ammo, and food only, and if he'd used any sense he could've done things without no killin'. He said he did a lot more than was necessary to accomplish the job. Anyway, one thing led to another and a big argument broke out, and the leader drew on him and shot him dead. Then he said leave the two drunks and told everyone to get on away from here."

"Do you think you could recognize any of them again?" Howard asked.

"I really dunno. It was dark and the only light after the shooting started was from their flashlights. I caught a few names though. One really big guy was named Charlie, and a little guy was named Huey. Another guy was named Smitty, I think. The leader was some guy named O'Hara. They never called him by a first name. Just O'Hara."

Howard helped the boy inside and had him lie down on the sofa. He then walked out to where Ewing and Forrest were holding the two prisoners who were still very much under the influence of the two bottles of Scotch that now lay empty on the living room floor.

"Get up, you human scum!" Howard said with clenched teeth. The two men began to wobble to their feet. They turned and stood before him, weaving slightly from side to side. He had contained his rage in front of the boy, but now as he watched the drunken men in front of him, he vented his feelings. "You're trash! Not even worth a bullet in the head, although I've half a mind to take care of this matter right here rather than drag you back to Bardstown!" Every vein in Howard's neck was protruding.

"You got no right to talk to me that way," said one of the men. His eyes were badly bloodshot, and his breath reeked of stale alcohol. "I got rights, I wanna lawyer. I wanna see my lawyer! I know my rights and you're violatin' them, asshole!" Just as he finished speaking, he let loose with a mouthful of spittle on Howard's boots and legs, an ill-considered act.

Howard reacted as if he had been hit with a cattle prod. He turned quickly and, in one rapid and continuous movement, grabbed Forrest's rifle and fired a burst of automatic fire across the chest of each prisoner. Both men were carried several feet backward before dropping in ragged, bloody heaps that twitched grotesquely for several seconds.

"J-J-Jesus," Forrest stammered. "Are you fuckin' out of your goddam mind?"

"Aw, Christ," Howard said as he moved over to check the prone figures and confirmed what he already knew. "Something inside me just snapped. I've been to four scenes like this in the past two weeks. We always seem to get there too late. These animals always get away. When that guy did that, I guess I was just trying to get back at . . ."

Howard stopped and looked up as he heard the steadily increasing "whop-whop" of an approaching helicopter. He kicked at a loose dirt clod and cried, "Aw shit! This is *all* I need."

The three Guardsmen froze and watched the helicopter approaching, hoping that their presence would not be noticed. Such was not the case, however, and the Huey which had been following the highway suddenly veered in the direction of the Guardsmen, perhaps after the pilot had spotted the jeep.

The chopper circled the house as the pilot looked carefully for wire or other obstacles that might prevent the helicopter from landing safely. The bird then came to a gentle rest a hundred or so feet from the dwelling.

"Just remember," Forrest said, "I had nothin' to do with this."

The details of his upcoming court-martial flashed through Howard's mind, and he began to rehearse possible arguments he might make for lenient treatment based on his record of service. Oh, sweet Jesus! he thought, please help me now.

As the first figure exited the aircraft, Howard felt as if he were losing control of his sphincter. It was Hamilton.

Hamilton walked up slowly to the three, followed in short order by Johnson and Rockwell. The copilot, Glen Childs, and the crew chief, Skeeter Mulrooney, remained with the chopper. Hamilton looked to where Bickett's body lay, partially covered with a blanket. "What happened here, Sergeant Howard?" Before waiting for a reply, Hamilton walked over to Bickett's body and lifted the blanket.

Ewing and Forrest looked nervously at Howard. As Hamilton walked back to the three, Howard began relating the young man's story.

"Can the boy identify any of them?" Hamilton replied.

"Just that there was a guy named Charlie, one named Huey, and another named Smitty. The leader was some guy named O'Hara," Howard replied.

Hamilton walked up to the two dead men and rolled over first one, and then the other. Near the center of each man's chest were several small holes surrounded by dark powder burns. In the middle of their backs were large and very obvious exit wounds. "What happened to them?"

"They tried to escape, sir!" Howard replied, a little too quickly.

Hamilton paused for a second to examine further the two prisoners' wounds and then stood up. Casting a glance to Rockwell, he walked back to the group and said, "Well, if that's the way it happened, then so be it. Let's get that boy and Bickett's body aboard the helo. And see to it these two and the guy inside are taken back into town for burial. Fill out a report later."

"Yes, sir." Howard turned hastily and started walking away.

"And Sergeant Howard?"

"Yes, sir?"

"Make sure that your jeep drives through the center of town with them on the way back. And don't drive too fast."

"Yes, sir!"

Rockwell said nothing in response to all of this. He slowly turned and walked back to the helicopter, pausing only to cast one more glance at the escapees lying on the ground when he opened the door to the Huey.

Within a few minutes the boy and the body of the dead Guardsmen were aboard the helicopter, and Hamilton was in the air, leaving the three Guardsmen to their detail.

His inquiry into the incident was completed.

SATURDAY, AUGUST 2nd:
The Seventy-Eighth Day

The sun had just sunk behind a bank of gray clouds. The air smelled of approaching summer rain. Fran Fitzgerald walked up the hill from her house to the cluster of buildings around the Cissell farmhouse. Ken had a small generator in pieces on a workbench beside the main barn. His face turned crimson as he blew hard into a fuel line, trying to clear an obstruction.

Ken had come into his own in the past few weeks. Reuben depended upon him for most of the help on mechanical and electrical problems around the farm. There seemed to be almost a father-son relationship developing between the two.

From bits and pieces Fran had picked up from people who'd known Reuben in earlier days, she felt that perhaps he was trying to do things with Ken that he had been unable or unwilling to do right with his own three sons. Reuben's sometimes too firm discipline and his unrelenting work ethic had driven his three sons away from the farm and the family. Maybe Ken was Reuben's second chance.

When Fran walked around the corner of the barn, she came upon Helen and Dennis Waters and Sue Lyons in the middle of an animated discussion, which they abruptly halted. From the expression on the face of Helen Waters, a plump, fortyish woman whose gray roots in her black tinted hair became more obvious daily, Fran could tell that the discussion · involved her. She approached the three as Dennis Waters whispered something inaudible to Helen.

The woman shook her arm free of his grasp and declared, "I will not! I've said it before, and I'll say it again to Miss High-and-Mighty's face!"

Dick Carlisle, the retired pilot, poked his head out of the barn when he heard Helen's voice rising. He knew in an instant that it had to involve her endless bitching—which had lately become all too common. Carlisle walked outside, followed by his wife and a few of the farm children who wanted to watch the latest squabble.

"It's just not fair!" Helen continued. "Here Dennis and I and the four kids are stuck in that shabby tobacco-stripping room and two families are squeezed into that pitiful excuse for a house over there, while Fran and Ellen and their families have the biggest and nicest house for their small bunch! Maybe it's not the Ritz, but then it sure looks a lot better'n what we got! And *now* I hear talk there might be more families coming here. I just *cain't* go on living like this, and I want something done about it!"

"Like what?"

It was Reuben. . . .

The blood drained from Helen's face, and she began

stammering, Reuben's unannounced arrival obviously taking her by surprise. "Well, Mr. Cissell, uh, like, uh, maybe rotating and taking turns in the houses. Yeah. Or maybe like at least building on to this thing or something," she said, as she pointed to the large room to the side of the barn. She looked to Sue Lyons for support and continued, "Mr. Cissell," she said plaintively, "we're all on top of one another in there. We don't even have any privacy at night from the children."

"Listen, if it would help," Fran began, "I could talk to Ken and maybe we could see about this rotation idea. We're all in this together and we need to work this out to keep everyone satisfied. And—"

"No we don't," Reuben interrupted. "We have to do as I say. I put people where I wanted 'em. The Fitzgerald and the Randall families are the two most valuable to me on the farm, and so they get the best quarters. I'll try to see if we can improve things in there," he said as he pointed to the barn, "but until then, *that's* how it's gonna be. Got it? Now everybody go on about your business, and let's get inside before this rain starts."

Helen Waters and Sue Lyons stood staring at Fran. Then, slowly and sullenly they walked away, leaving Fran with the distinct impression that though the conversation was over, nothing had been settled.

THURSDAY, AUGUST 15th: The Ninety-First Day

Kurt Rogers and Jerry Mazurkis drove into Raywick around 5:00 P.M. They parked the Bronco near several tethered horses on the little town's main drag. The refugees' tent-and-shanty city spread in all directions. The several hundred people had gathered in the crossroads town in much the same fashion as birds flock together for security.

The collections of humanity across the rural countryside were much the same. Only the preexisting landmarks and the size served to distinguish the one in Raywick from the dozens like it in surrounding countries. Merchants displayed their goods, farmers offered their produce, and tavern owners provided bootleg alcohol to dull the pain. From Springfield to Lebanon to Hodgensville and every point in between, the picture was painted from the same palette.

When Rogers and Mazurkis got out of the Bronco, they were immediately approached by a man with a cardboard box that contained razor cartridges and shaving foam. He asked if they had anything of interest to trade. His competition was a novice "barber" at a nearby open-air booth who offered haircuts and shaves for whatever of value the prospective customer might have. Regardless of the lack of experience the barber might have had prior to the war, the straight razor, strop, and scissors provided him with a successful livelihood now. Rogers and Mazurkis brushed past both men and entered the tavern on the corner.

Inside they found a packed house where the monotony and boredom of the inactivity was temporarily relieved for well-heeled refugees and for more than a few of the local people. Beer had run short long ago, but local bourbon from the local distillery stocks was still readily available—for the proper price. Locally produced moonshine, of varying quality, could be had at a more modest price as local people drew on an almost forgotten art to meet the heavy demand for alcohol.

The lone pool table was the focal point for much of the activity. On the nearby wall, from a faded and torn movie poster, the image of Brigitte Bardot hung in silent vigil. Near the bar, a trio consisting of a guitar player, a banjo player, and a fiddler—no one there would have thought to call him a violinist—provided the only, albeit very adequate, entertainment. From the atmosphere and the attitude of those present, it would have been difficult to tell that there had ever been a war. When the trio began a spirited version of "Rocky Top," the crowd came alive, clapping hands and stamping feet until they seemed to shake the tavern's very foundations.

"Goddam, Kurt! This place is buzzing! Why in the hell didn't we come here before now?" asked Mazurkis, as he handed Rogers a drink from the bar. Kurt just grinned and shrugged his shoulders.

An attractive brunette walked up to Rogers as he turned back toward the trio. She was obviously not a local woman. Her clothes were a little too soiled and wrinkled, and she was not particularly well groomed. Most of the refugees were the same, camp life being what it was.

"Where ya from?"

"Louisville," he responded, yelling down into her ear so as to be heard above the din.

"What's that gun you've got there?" As she spoke she pointed to the automatic in his shoulder holster.

"A Sig-Sauer P-226."

"It's nice." She began to run her finger slowly up and down the holster while looking him directly in the eyes. "Are you good with your gun?"

"Good enough," he replied, smiling and casting a glance at Mazurkis, who was watching with great amusement.

"I haven't seen you guys in here before. Where're ya' livin'?" She yelled at them, as the crowd's roar increased.

"Got a farm two miles south of here," Mazurkis replied.

She frowned and asked again, "Where?"

"Two miles south of here," he cried just as music ended. His voice carried across the tavern and several people looked in his direction. Somewhat embarrassed, he said in a much lower tone, "Our place is two miles south of here."

"My name is Karen," she said turning again to Rogers. "Well?"

"Well, what?"

"Well, is a big handsome guy like you gonna get me a drink or not?" She smiled her sweetest.

Rogers looked at Mazurkis, who stood grinning like a Cheshire cat. "I think this girl wants my body," he whispered. Turning back to her he said, "Listen, Karen. You're sweet and you're pretty, but I'm not interested in getting together. No hard feelings, I hope."

The girl immediately frowned and then spun and walked away.

"Heartbreaker!" mocked Mazurkis.

"What *is* it about me that drives women crazy?" Rogers asked. Mazurkis punched him lightly on the shoulder, causing Rogers to spill some of his drink. Rogers laughed and ordered another round.

About two hours later the two left the tavern and started walking toward the Bronco as well as their unsteady condition would permit. Rogers saw a dirty and disheveled man leaning into the vehicle, pulling out foil wrappers which he was examining and then dropping to the ground. Mazurkis yelled, "What the hell do you think you're doing?" The startled man turned and ran.

Rogers and Mazurkis quickly walked up to the Bronco and looked at what the man had dropped. The labels indicated the contents of the various containers—dehydrated bananas, apples, apricots, and so forth.

"Damn!" Rogers said. "I told Josh not to leave that trash in there! Rule One is shot to hell, I guess."

"Yeah," Mazurkis replied. "But we should have checked a little better before we left the farm. It's not such a great idea to advertise that we're not exactly subsisting on cornbread and water. But he won't know where we live. I'll make sure that no one is tailing us on the way back."

The two men got into the Bronco and slowly drove out of town. The dirty man beside the tavern watched, unseen, as the vehicle turned and disappeared down the road. Beside him stood the attractive young woman.

Had he been nearer, Rogers might have heard her say to her companion, "Two miles south."

SATURDAY, AUGUST 17th:
The Ninety-Third Day

"I have to have a break, Kelly," Chris said as she sat down at the nurses' station and began to massage her foot. "I feel as if I've been on a forced march for thirty miles, and I still have two hours to go before I get off duty."

"You're not alone," the nurse beside her replied. "I'm functioning on willpower alone. But listen, do you think you can check on the IV in room 426, bed 2? I have to take care of this stuff."

"Thanks a million." Chris slowly made it to her feet. "I really needed this."

"You're a real trooper, kid."

Chris walked down the hallway and into the room. A quick check of the patient's intravenous drip rate indicated that everything was in order. Out of the corner of her eye, however, she saw something that caught her attention. She looked again and she saw that parked at the emergency entrance of the hospital was a familiar Bronco. That's just got to be him, she thought, and if he's here at this time of day, something's very wrong.

Quickly, she walked out of the room and down the hallway. As she rounded the corner she heard a familiar male voice say, "I'm looking for Chris Whittington."

"Kurt, what are you doing here?" she exclaimed, sensing the urgency in his voice. "Is Josh okay?"

"It's Larry, Chris. He got shot early this morning. We had some visitors who thought they would catch us asleep, I suppose. Anyway, they hit us around five-thirty and tried to overrun us. Must have been twenty or more. They didn't get very far, but it was bad. Dana was killed by a ricochet bullet, and Larry went berserk. He was John Wayne-ing it when he caught one in the abdomen.

"We got four of them, though. I brought Larry here because I thought maybe you could make sure that he got the best treatment available. They have him down at emergency."

"My God. Dana's dead? Let's go down there. Kelly, hold the fort for a few minutes."

When they arrived at the door to the ER, Bob Rose and George Anderson were standing by the door anxiously watching Jackson and the people treating him. George looked five years older than he had when she'd seen him last.

Chris squeezed George's arm assuringly when she walked past him into the emergency room. She saw Jackson stretched out on the table. An IV solution of Ringer's lactate was in place and being infused into his arm. Jackson's clothes had been removed and the parts of his body not covered by sheets had an ashen appearance. A nurse worked quickly at prepping his stomach and lower abdomen.

"Let's get him on into the OR," Bernie Weintraub said abruptly.

Chris turned to Kurt, George, and Bob. "Come on. You can wait up here." They walked together toward the small waiting area. Rose left for the parking lot to watch over his pickup and Kurt's Bronco. "I have to go back to my floor right away," Chris said, "but I'll be back down to check on the situation."

"Sure," Rogers replied. "We won't be going anywhere." He sat down with Anderson as Chris walked down the hall, and together the two friends began the wait.

Sometime later, Weintraub, still in his surgical scrubs, came down the hall.

"You're friend is going to be all right," he said. "We stopped the internal bleeding, and fortunately, no vital organs were hit. We'll want him to remain where he is for a while, but there's no reason he shouldn't be on his feet in a couple of days, and increasing his movement after that. For now, though, he's out of danger."

"Thank God," Anderson sighed.

Chris walked up just in time to hear the last of Bernie's remarks and said, "And thank Dr. Weintraub, too."

"Sure," Rogers said. "We appreciate what you've done, Doctor. That guy in there and the two of us go way back. We sure appreciate your help."

Bernie smiled and gave a slight wave of his hand as if to say, "No matter," and turned back toward the operating room. As he left he winked at Chris, but said nothing more.

"Listen, Kurt, I was feeling as if I were dead on my feet awhile ago, but seeing you has put a spring in my step. I'm off duty now, and there's nothing you can do for Larry. So why not come out to the farm with me? I'd sure enjoy your company."

"Go ahead, Kurt," Anderson said. "I'll stay. No need for both of us to sit here."

Rogers hesitated. "Oh, I don't know, Chris. Maybe I ought to . . ."

"C'mon, Kurt. Larry won't be coming to for a long time, and I'd like to show you off to my sister. I told her all about you," she said. "You really won't be able to do a thing here."

"Well, all right, I suppose I will. But George, you get word to us if anything unexpected happens, okay? I'll ask Bob to go on back with the pickup to let everybody know that

Larry'll be okay."

"Fine. Now you guys go ahead."

Rogers and Chris walked out to the Bronco after Chris picked up a few of her things from the nurses' station, and together they drove to the farm. When they reached the gravel road, Rogers stopped dead. "Jesus H. Christ! This place looks like the Maginot Line!"

"My brother-in-law's idea. There are about fourteen National Guard families out here at last count, and the battery is using it as a place to sleep and unwind when they're not on duty. Jack had the men put up all that wire and those earthen banks. They've really spent a lot of time on it."

"Whose is that on the other side?" Kurt pointed to the other side of the hill.

"That's Reuben Cissell's farm. He has several refugee families there, maybe eight or more now. Anyway, he and Clara have given them tracts of land to work and a place to live, and I suppose that they're doing reasonably well, all things considered. Reuben's been doing a little of that digging around his place as well. Sergeant Reichert's helped him out quite a bit with the planning. Jack has pretty much put Reichert in charge of the 'fort,' and he's been busy making improvements ever since. By the way, some of the men have been calling the place here 'Fort Hamilton,' but Jack doesn't appreciate the humor," she said as she chuckled a little.

He grinned, saying, "The American flag on top the silo *is* a nice touch," before continuing. Chris greeted the sentry, who opened a heavy gate and waved them through. Jennifer and a group of children playing hopscotch in front of the house stopped momentarily to look at the stranger. Roseanna was at the side door of the house, cleaning fresh ears of corn, when she saw Chris. She waved and then put the corn into the pan before her.

"Hi there, Sis! Who's that you have with you?" she asked, though she already knew.

"Roseanna, this is Kurt Rogers, the knight in shining armor who rescued me."

With this introduction, Roseanna walked directly to Rogers and planted a kiss on his cheek. "That's for saving the only baby sister I have!"

Rogers grinned broadly and said, "I can assure you that

the pleasure was all mine."

"Come on in, and let's all have a cup of coffee." Roseanna put one arm about Rogers, the other around Chris, and together they walked into the kitchen. Roseanna put a teakettle on the propane stove. Chris sat down at the table with Rogers, saying, "Kurt's place was hit last night. Dana Jackson was killed and Larry Jackson was wounded."

"My God, how awful!"

"Larry is at the hospital now. One of those wolf packs we've been hearing about tried to overrun their place, but they were driven off."

Roseanna's cheer faded now, and concern was evident in her voice. Turning to Rogers she asked, "Was anyone else hurt?"

"Only two minor wounds. They'll be okay. We killed four on the other side, and probably wounded others," he replied soberly.

"Aren't you worried about them coming back?"

"No. I think that this particular group will be taking a long time to lick its wounds. They didn't expect the reception they got. I expect they'll be looking for easier targets."

"Good grief. This whole situation has all of us worried here. Why, every day you hear about this family or that family that was robbed, or worse. Most of it seems to happen in the dark of night. Almost as if these packs of animals don't have enough courage to do their savagery in the light of day."

"Simply reducing the odds is all. They stand a better chance of surprise at night, and a lesser chance of receiving casualties or being identified," Rogers replied.

Roseanna poured a packet of instant coffee from an army field ration into each of the cups of hot water before her and handed one to Rogers. Rogers thanked her, knowing how scarce coffee had become, even for these Guard families who occasionally got supplies from Frankfort.

"Whatever the reason," Roseanna continued, "it sure has a lot of people scared to death. We've had two more families of Guardsmen come out here this week alone. Nobody feels safe any more, and there seem to be more incidents as time goes by."

"Of course we feel fairly safe here," Chris added. "Jack has really seen to it that this place is prepared. These families feel sheltered from most of the danger out there. Still, you might say that a siege mentality prevails, and that certainly isn't very healthy."

The three continued talking for a few minutes comparing problems the two groups faced. Finally, Chris said, "Well, I think I owe you a tour of this place, since you've never been here before. I'm afraid you won't find a library of 'How to Fix This' and 'How to Fix That' books, or all of the spare parts or medical supplies, but you might see some ideas you can use."

"Great!" Rogers replied, emptying his coffee cup. "And thanks for that coffee, Roseanna. I know that it's hard to come by now."

"Not to worry. We're expecting a helicopter delivery within a few days or so. Maybe they'll bring some more with them. Otherwise, we'll make do fine with concoctions from grain that a couple of the wives have come up with."

Chris and Rogers walked out to the yard and then to the barns and along the breastworks surrounding the hilltop. She introduced Rogers to a couple of the women with whom she had become friends, and pointed out the living quarters that had been fashioned reasonably well in the large barn. "This may not be the Taj Mahal, or anywhere nearly as comfortable as where they were living in before they came here. But this is a safe place, and that is the most important thing. Like that sanctuary idea you talked about at your farm."

"Yeah, I know what you mean." He looked around the enclave and said, "Considering that you started from scratch not very long ago, you've done extremely well for yourselves."

"It seems so to me, but then I don't know very much about defensive planning. That kind of stuff I leave to Jack and Sergeant Reichert. But come on. I want to show you my favorite place on the farm."

Together they walked out the gate, down the hillside, and across a large cornfield to the creek meandering along its edge. Huge brown-and-white-barked sycamore trees rose on each side of the banks, shading the water from the midday sun.

"Isn't this nice?" she said. "Sometimes, just to get away from it all, I bring a book and come down here to read and to find a little solitude. The bottom here is solid limestone," she said as she pointed out into the creek, "so it's perfect for wading."

Chris sat down, then lay back on the embankment. Following her lead, Rogers did likewise. "This is nice," he said. "It's like a world apart."

The rays of the sun, working through the leaves, bounced off the water and cast dancing reflections of light across Chris's golden hair. "The leaves will start changing soon, Kurt. I really love autumn. I sometimes think it's nature's way of rewarding us for the blistering heat of July and August, before it hits us with the awful winter. Sort of a respite. Except that this year it hasn't been so bad, I guess."

She reached up and released her blond hair from the barrettes holding it, permitting it to fall about her shoulders. "Sitting here, you'd never know that the rest of the world has gone crazy. It's as if you pull a curtain across the threshold after you enter." She paused and then said, "Do you think we'll have to live like this for the rest of our lives? I mean, in fear and without so many essentials?"

"I really don't know," replied Rogers. "We caught a shortwave radio broadcast from Radio Australia the other night. It said that there's still no formal peace between us and the Russians, just a tense stalemate. I know that's what we've been hearing from our 'official' sources, but the fact that somebody else is saying it makes it seem more reliable."

"Who do you think was hurt the most?"

"Just my opinion, mind you, but I can't help but believe that the Russians are in a lot better shape than we are—relatively speaking of course. With their massive civil defense system, compared to none for us, they were prepared to absorb much more than we ever could. And besides that, their industry and population were much more dispersed in the first place. But who really knows what the real situation is?"

"Well, even if peace is established, do you think we can get things going again?" she asked. "Everything is in such shambles."

Rogers stood up, picked up some pebbles and began skipping them across the water. "I expect that it'll be a long while. Our 'battery' may need a 'jump start' from countries that haven't been hit. Places like Australia and Brazil. And don't forget Japan or South Africa. Foreign help will come in time though, once peace is established. I'm sure of that. It'll simply be the pursuit of the almighty dollar, or peso, or yen, or what have you. Those countries and others will be looking at us as a very lucrative market for their goods, and it'll probably be the Marshall Plan in reverse."

"The what?"

"Never mind, not important," he said. "Made it!"

"Made what?"

"Four skips with the rock!" he said with a smile.

Chris returned his smile. "You know, Kurt, for all your guns and macho attitudes about so many things, there is still something very boyish and gentle about you."

Rogers sat down next to her. "You think so?"

"M-mmm, whether you'll admit it or not," she said as she placed her hand on his.

"There are some guys I tangled with last night who might respectfully disagree with you on that. That whole thing was a very bad scene." He watched the ripples fading in the water. "Poor Dana. I feel so awful about her. Larry's going to take this very hard."

Chris ran her hand slowly up his arm as he spoke. When he finished, he turned and gently pushed her against the embankment. He paused and looked straight into her eyes. Encouraged, he wrapped his muscular arms around her, and she her arms around him, in a fiery moment of rising desire. She felt his hands sliding up and down her sides and then to her blouse, unbuttoning and then pulling aside the thin fabric in his way.

She felt his powerful hands, followed quickly by his lips, move across her breasts. It was as if her entire chest became suddenly inflamed. Chris whispered, "Oh God, Kurt!" as his hands teasingly explored the rest of her body. She felt she had never known in her entire life a man with such a gentle, yet passionate, touch.

When the union came, it was effortless, and at the same time, magical—an unrestrained exuberance until the final wrenching explosion.

Finally, he broke away from Chris, rolling to the side of the first woman with whom he had been intimate since Laura died. He kissed Chris once again, and said, "It's been so long."

"Then let's not let that happen again," she whispered, then pulled herself closer to him.

A jeep rolled up to the armory and came to a grinding halt. Its tires screeched loudly enough to cause Hamilton to jump to his feet. "What the hell?" he said as he looked out the window. "Another riot?" Suddenly he realized that the jeep and two occupants were not from Charlie Battery. He walked quickly to the door and met the two young soldiers who were running into the armory.

"Sir!" cried the first young man, who appeared not a day older than eighteen. "I've got a message here from Captain Hart at Service Battery!" He thrust toward Hamilton a folded and crumpled piece of paper without waiting for a response.

Hamilton opened the piece of typing paper on which Hart, the Springfield unit commander, had scribbled a message in an unsteady hand:

Maj. Hamilton:

We were hit last night. They overpowered the sentries, and then they overran the armory.

We lost twenty killed and seventeen wounded. I estimate that we also lost forty-five M-16s and at least ten thousand rounds of ammo, two M-60s and five thousand rounds, and a .50 cal. machine gun with three thousand rounds.

Things are still a mess here, so this is only a rough estimate. There are probably some riot guns, sniper rifles, and .45s missing also.

When they left here, they hit the county prisoner compound. Their strength is unknown. We're holding on with what we have left.

Be on the lookout. Sorry.

> Good luck,
>
> Hart

As Hamilton read the message, the color drained from his face. "Damnation!" he cried when he finished. Ackerson had been in the drill hall. Sensing trouble, he walked out to the entrance, pencil and clipboard in hand. Hamilton thrust the paper toward him. Turning to the young trooper, Hamilton asked, "How bad was it?"

"Bad, sir," the first young soldier said. "I was at the armory when they hit. They came in hard and fast. We hardly knew what hit us. They were well organized and we were ripe for the pickin'. Captain Hart gave them a hell of a fight, though. Did he mention that he got hit twice? They was after them guns, sure enough. Guns and ammo. They didn't give a damn about nothin' else. Once they emptied the arms room, they got out of there real fast. Captain Hart expects that they might be trying to get some more."

Hamilton looked at Ackerson. "Ted, it looks like we're up to our asses in alligators. It took guts to attack that armory. Organization and guts. Now they apparently have enough weapons to arm maybe a hundred men or more, depending on what they had before. If they stay together and stay organized, it'll be hard to stop them. If they attract recruits from the prisoners they freed, God help us all."

"This is a piss-poor development, no doubt about it," Ackerson said. "What're we going to do now, sir?"

"First, you double the sentries here and double the ammunition each man on duty carries. Get word out to the farm and to each checkpoint about the situation. I don't want any heroes out there on those checkpoints around town trying to stand off the Mongol horde. Tell them to fall back to the armory or the farm if they make contact with these thugs. And next, get some of the barbed wire at the farm, if any is left, and try to set up some wire barricades around this place."

"Yes, sir. I'll get right on it."

"And get word to the sheriff and county judge about the situation. Tell them the details and tell them to plan accordingly. And let's not leave all of the extra guns and ammunition in the arms room. I don't want a repetition of the Springfield situation here. If we should get hit, they won't get as much as they expect. Oh, yeah, and when that stuff is taken to the farm, make sure that the weapons are covered when they leave here. No need to advertise to a thousand pairs of eyes what we're doing.

"If these guys decide to hit us, they'll probably need time to regroup. If so, maybe we'll have time to organize some of the civilians. Maybe like calling out a volunteer fire department, or calling out the minutemen to help us defend the town. But for now, you get moving on the other matters."

"Roger, sir!" Ackerson spun quickly and walked toward the motor pool.

"And pray!" Hamilton called out to him.

About a half hour later, Hamilton, having decided to handle matters at the farm himself, drove up to the compound. The guard quickly opened the gate, and he drove rapidly across the enclave, swinging widely around the adults and children gathered in a couple of places. Reichert was hammering the last nail into a stud that was part of an addition to one of the living quarters carved from the interior of the barn. He dropped his hammer and ran over to Hamilton. "What's up, Major?"

"Bad news. Really bad," Hamilton replied. Cliff and Rick Sheridan walked up to them, and Hamilton related to the three men what had happened the previous night in Springfield. "I want the number of people on guard here doubled, and when the weapons and ammunition get out here, I want you to start holding classes on the M-16 for the women who are even slightly familiar with firearms. Forget the total novices for now. It'll take too long to teach them. And get in touch with Reuben's people and let them know of the situation. It'll be important to hold that end of the hilltop should any group try to attack this place. We'll need the extra help."

"Will do, sir." Reichert turned quickly and walked away, yelling as he went for several of the men who were in the barn.

Hamilton looked over his shoulder and saw Chris approaching with a stranger. "Jack," she said, "this is Kurt Rogers, the fellow I've told you about." She then told him of the raid on the Rogers farm the previous night.

"I'm afraid the situation you faced last night isn't nearly as bad as it is going to be for many people," Hamilton said. He then repeated the news of the recent developments while studying the reaction and attitude of Rogers, a man about whom he had been curious since Chris had returned from Raywick.

"It sounds to me as if you have your hands full," Rogers replied. "But I really think these people will take the path of least resistance now that they have their guns and ammunition. They'll probably not be dumb enough to attack a place like this or try to take on another National Guard armory. With a force that large they can go for the small farms and homes. Simply give a family a choice. Surrender what you have or die. Of course, they'd probably love to have your weapons and ammunition, but the cost would be too great. Attacking here would be insane."

"I hope you're right for the sake of us all, though God help the others out there."

"Chris, I've got to get back to check on Larry. I'll see you tomorrow morning back at the hospital?"

"Sure."

He kissed her quickly and walked toward his Bronco.

Hamilton watched Rogers leaving, and then turned to Chris. "He seems like a really decent fellow."

"He is, Jack. He's really quite a guy," she said, following him with her eyes. "Quite a guy."

TUESDAY, AUGUST 20th: The Ninety-Sixth Day

Three nights later, Hamilton lay asleep on the small camp cot that he hauled into the Orderly Room each night he stayed in the armory. He felt now more than ever that his presence was required at Charlie Battery.

Suddenly, a shattering explosion brought him upright. In the confusion that often accompanies an abrupt return to consciousness, one thought raced through his mind: My God! Another nuke! He leaped to his feet. He could hear Ackerson already screaming orders to the men in the armory's drill hall.

When he left the Orderly Room, the scene that confronted him was one of supreme confusion. Excited soldiers scrambled for their equipment and weapons. He turned and ran out the armory door and saw a large yellow glow from Bardstown, apparently the explosion's origin.

"Get aboard that deuce-and-a-half!" Ackerson roared, and a dozen men, with much cursing and shouting, began jumping into the back of an open cargo truck. Ackerson ran up to Hamilton and cried, "Major, I'll take the reaction squad down there, and try to find out what the hell happened! Could have been an accident at the county fuel storage area, but it might have been sabotage. I'll let you know if we need help."

Hamilton nodded quickly. Ackerson pivoted and ran for the jeep that pulled up beside the truck. The two vehicles quickly moved out and drove rapidly toward Bardstown. Hamilton turned and ran back inside, barking orders to the remaining men to stand by to reinforce the reaction team, and to reinforce the positions at the side and, as a precautionary measure, on top of the armory. With only twenty men left in the armory, Hamilton did not have many others to worry about.

When he reached the Orderly Room, he grabbed for his pistol belt and checked his .45 automatic. He turned and started back toward the door, calling out for First Sergeant Johnson. Suddenly he heard the report and felt the rumble from a second large explosion.

Hamilton ran outside. Johnson was standing there, looking toward town. He heard the pop-pop-pop of rifle fire in the distance. "Oh, shit!" he muttered, and then he turned to Johnson.

Suddenly, the nightmare began. A deadly burst of gunfire ripped past the two. Johnson reeled into Hamilton, and both of them went sprawling to the ground.

Goddam! he thought, *I've been had! Took the goddam bait!*

Bullets ripped into the ground all around them, sending up little geysers of dust and gravel. "Come on, Johnson! We gotta get to cover!" he cried.

Johnson didn't move. Hamilton grabbed Johnson's collar with both hands and moved blindly as fast as he could toward the armory door.

A young soldier ran out firing his weapon in automatic bursts to cover their withdrawal. Gunfire slammed him back through the door.

Hamilton rushed through the entryway and fell with

Johnson to the floor just as the glass entrance shattered around him like a house of crystal. He pulled Johnson to a less vulnerable location and checked him for wounds. A gaping hole in the neck was obvious. Several heartbeats of blood shot through the air before Johnson's grip went slack and his eyes fixed in death.

Hamilton's shock passed quickly as bullets ricocheted wildly around the entryway. To the two soldiers firing nearby from exposed positions, he screamed, "Get back! Get back, goddamm it!"

In the darkness he could see shadowy figures moving. Moving toward him.

The first young soldier lay contorted before him. Hamilton reached out and snatched his M-16 and the magazine pouch on his cartridge belt. He yanked the cord from the generator. The front of the armory went black.

The intensity of the barrage increased. Bullets gouged jagged holes in the armory's concrete-block walls. Lying surrounded by the shards of glass from the entrance, Hamilton returned fire as well as he could, showered continuously with pieces of masonry and bullet fragments.

Breaking free, he ran out to the drill hall and saw a group of Guardsmen positioned around the doorways firing out into the darkness. Machine-gun fire slammed through one doorway, sending two soldiers sprawling.

The staccato gunfire reverberated off the concrete walls to a phenomenal level. With only one small light in the building still working, the flashes of the rifles perforated the near-darkness of the armory as if several cameras were trying to flash-blind the combatants.

Hamilton called out for Mattingly, who he knew had to be somewhere in the darkness. Suddenly, there was a horrendous explosion. The shock wave rolled through the building from the entrance, flinging Hamilton across the floor. His ears ringing, vision blurred, he tried to gather his senses. A smaller explosion on the roof sent debris crashing to the floor beside him. In the dust and darkness, he groped for his M-16. He heard someone scream, "They're on the roof!"

Mattingly came low-crawling toward Hamilton. "This is suicide, Major! We can't possibly hold them off with this few men! Let's get the hell outta here!"

A heavy burst of gunfire again came from the entrance. Hamilton looked about him trying to get a handle on the situation finally, he cried, "Head for the farm and regroup!"

Mattingly raced straightaway across the floor and started yelling orders to withdraw. Needing no encouragement, the men moved rapidly through the side door to the motor pool, covering each other as they withdrew. Outside, they began crawling through the crates, metal barrels, and storage materials in the compound.

Several attackers were through the front door of the armory before the guardsmen had completely withdrawn. Hamilton, his stomach and intestines feeling as if they were in one large knot, kept the intruders at bay by firing his rifle repeatedly at the entrance.

"Move it!" Hamilton roared to the last two men. After they were through the door, he turned and emptied his rifle at the front doorway, and then darted out, slamming the door behind him and knocking down a stack of crates in front of it.

A two-and-a-half-ton truck driven by a wild-eyed soldier lumbered straight toward him. Hamilton jumped out of the way at the last second. The truck's bumper caught the side of the compound's gate, sending it flying into the air. Several bullets whizzed past Hamilton's head just as Nugent roared up in a jeep, seemingly from nowhere.

Hamilton shot a glance over his shoulder at the doorway and saw the crates beginning to give way to the battering from inside. He leaped into the jeep, tossing his M-16 in the back seat. He grabbed Nugent's twelve-gauge riot gun just as the door burst open and the dark figures of two large men filled the doorway.

Hamilton stood to raise himself above Nugent. He fired two rapid shotgun blasts at the doorway. The two figures sprawled backward into the building.

Nugent abruptly floored the accelerator, nearly causing Hamilton to lose his balance and fall out of the jeep. With Hamilton hanging on for dear life, they sped through the gate, and then turned hard right across the grass into an adjacent field and the relative safety of darkness.

"Where to, Major?" Nugent yelled, turning on his lights after he judged himself a safe distance away from the armory.

"Into town to find Ackerson!"

Racing onward, the jeep finally came back onto the asphalt road.

The two were halfway to the center of town when they saw a burning wreck in front of them. The twisted remains of a small foreign car burned fiercely. Just beyond it were a severely damaged two-and-one-half-ton truck and an overturned jeep. The bodies of Guardsmen were strewn over the road nearby. A crowd had gathered nearby.

"Holy shit!" Nugent exclaimed, stopping about twenty-five yards short of the first wreck. Hamilton jumped out and ran up to the bodies of the nearest Guardsmen. "What happened?" he cried to the onlookers. Numbly, he began checking the bodies, not waiting for a response.

"Forget it, soldier. They're all dead," came a solemn voice from the crowd. "It was a car bomb in that Toyota over there. As the truck came by, somebody detonated the bomb. The men on that truck never had a chance." The speaker was Charlie Brighton.

"Good God!" Hamilton whispered.

Another voice came from the crowd, and though the face was not visible, the sneer was obvious. "Looks like you soldier boys done fucked up big."

Hamilton tensed and turned toward the speaker, fully intent on ripping the man's head from his body. The first man intervened, however, and pulled him aside, pointing in the darkness. "I have one of your men lying over here, but I'll tell you now that he's in pretty bad shape."

Nausea, numbness, and confusion arose in Hamilton as he walked blindly with the man. He found Ackerson lying nearby, both legs in splints, and an improvised bandage around his chest and stomach. Hamilton knelt down and said softly, "How are you doing, Ted?"

"I've been a lot better, sir," whispered Ackerson, who now lay bathed in sweat. "My jeep had just passed that car back there . . . and the truck was pulling up when the bomb went off. Goff lost control . . . rolled us . . . rifle fire after that . . . If this fellow hadn't pulled me to cover . . ." Ackerson gasped with pain, and was silent.

The man beside him nodded and said, "Charlie Brighton." As he spoke, the sounds of heavy gunfire came from the center of town.

Hamilton shook Brighton's hand quickly and, turning back to Ackerson, said, "Don't talk any more. Just save your strength. We're going to get you back to the farm right away. It'll be safer there than it is in town right now. Chris is out there tonight, so we can get you taken care of." He looked back to Brighton. "Can you help me get him to my jeep?"

With the help of a couple of onlookers, they carried Ackerson to the jeep and placed him in the back. Hamilton worked to make Ackerson as comfortable as possible and said to Brighton, "Charlie Brighton, huh? Don't I know that name from somewhere?"

"Maybe. I used to be the civil defense director in Louisville."

"Oh yeah. Got fired over those fallout shelter plans, right? Well, if you hadn't done that, I'd be dead and so would my family, with the way things worked out. Now it looks like I owe you for him as well."

"If you're really that grateful, you could take me and my family out to that farm of yours I've heard about."

As Brighton spoke, an explosion sounded from the downtown area. Hamilton and Brighton snapped their heads in the direction of the noise and saw an angry fireball rise above several buildings, and then, after a few seconds, fade.

Hamilton turned to some of the men standing in the darkness. "Would you fellows mind helping get the bodies of these men off the road until we can get some people back here for them?" Turning back to Brighton, he said, "Where exactly is your family?"

"Right here." Brighton looked to a group of people standing nearby and beckoned. Eve and Rick Brighton walked quickly to the jeep.

"Well, it's okay with me if you come, but are you sure that my farm is the place you want to be after what's happened tonight? You might be running toward a tall tree in a thunderstorm."

Brighton helped his wife up on the back of the jeep beside Ackerson, and then he and Rick climbed in and hung their feet over the side.

"Maybe, Major. But I expect with these guys running around here it's going to be a lot more unpleasant in town.

We'll come back for what few belongings we have when things have cooled down a bit."

"Then let's get out of here."

As the group in the jeep raced to the farm, Hamilton remembered the words of the heckler in the crowd. Had he "fucked up big"? He'd been sucked in by the diversion all right. Left himself and the armory just like sitting ducks, and let a truckload of men ride straight to their deaths. But what should he have done under the circumstances? Perhaps a man with more experience might have. . . .

As the jeep sped along in the darkness, self-doubt ate at him. Good God, he thought, I've surely made a mess of things tonight.

TUESDAY, AUGUST 20th: The Ninety-Sixth Day

The explosions and the gunfire in the early morning hours had not escaped the attention of Kurt Rogers. He had been sleeping at Jackson's bedside in one of the converted rooms in Bethlehem High School. George Anderson had already returned to the Aerie in order to deal with any new "visitors" who might try helping themselves to the group's food and supplies. Jackson was recovering well. He was, however, in a profound depression over the loss of Dana.

Kurt looked out Jackson's window toward the old cathedral for signs of activity from the wolf pack that had been reported moving through town. That Chris had spent the night at the farm and was, as far as he knew, out of danger, provided him some comfort.

Suddenly, an old red pickup came speeding from the center of town, swerving from side to side. Even from this distance Kurt could see that the men in the back of the truck were drunk. One of them turned and, for no apparent reason, fired a shot in the direction of the high school, shattering the window of a nearby room and causing a woman to run screaming into the corridor.

Kurt heard a burst of gunshots around the courthouse, then a muffled explosion. Black smoke billowed and slowly engulfed the entire area near the center of town.

Jackson watched out the window as he sat in his bed. "Jesus, Kurt. Things are going crazy out there! I hope Chris had enough sense not to try to come in from the farm this morning."

Charge Nurse Sylvia Miller poked her head through the door, crying, "A young boy just came in and said that all of the prisoners over at the compound have broken out. Your friend is well enough to travel, more or less. If I were you, I'd be getting away from here fast."

"What are you going to do?" asked Rogers.

"I'll stay here and take my chances. These people need me." She continued down the hallway.

Rogers went to the door after her and said, "But wait . . ." The woman was through the door to the stairway before he could say anything. "Well, shit! Come on, Larry. Let's haul ass out of here. I sure as hell don't want to get boxed in here! This isn't our fight!"

Jackson put his feet on the floor and slowly stood up, biting his lower lip as the mending tissue in his abdomen protested. "Haul ass? Easy for you to say," he muttered as he reached for his clothes.

"Hurry up," replied Rogers, grabbing the clothes out of Jackson's hand and stuffing them back into the small travel bag, "you can get out of those pajamas later."

He helped Jackson into a bathrobe and led him out of the building to the Bronco. Rogers ran around and got in the driver's side, starting to move out of the parking lot just as a bullet slammed into the side of the vehicle. Rogers looked around and saw the same red pickup he had seen earlier. It was now speeding toward him. He floored the accelerator and took off across the lawn.

Rogers sped through several side streets, cutting through driveways and backyards when they met a vehicle that looked unfriendly. A burst of gunfire sent bullets flying past Rogers and Jackson at one intersection. Rogers swerved and took the Bronco through a backyard picket fence to a safer street. "Jesus Christ, Kurt! Are you trying to kill me?" Jackson howled. He bent his head close to his knees and held his stomach, which now felt as if it were being ripped apart at the seams.

"No," Rogers replied grimly, jamming the transmission into high gear upon once again returning to the pavement, "but they are!"

As the V-8 under the hood blasted them effortlessly down the streets, to Rogers' dismay, he noticed in the rearview mirror another car following them. He looked ahead and saw the red pickup pull across the intersection. The three men in the back were firing at the Bronco.

"Why me, Lord?" Rogers looked desperately for a hole between the abandoned and parked cars lining the sides of the street but found none. "Get down!" he cried as Jackson poked his head up looking for the source of the gunfire.

Rogers grabbed his Uzi from the seat, and propped it on the rearview mirror outside the door of the Bronco. As the vehicle screamed onward toward the waiting truck, Rogers squeezed the trigger and the submachine gun barked angrily. As its magazine emptied, a deadly burst of copper and hot lead ripped through the truck and its occupants.

One of the bullets struck the gas tank, and suddenly the truck erupted in an enormous fireball. The concussion from the explosion nearly brought an end to Rogers and Jackson as they veered around it. The car pursuing them swerved to avoid the spreading flame. It struck the edge of the curb, flipped, and rolled twice before coming to a violent halt on its side against a magnolia tree. "All *right*, you sonsabitches!" Kurt whooped.

Onward Rogers raced, putting the whining transmission through its paces. Finally, at the edge of town, he turned to take the road to Raywick—and then stopped short. He saw two vehicles down the road, parked on either side of the pavement. The drivers and others standing nearby appeared to be less than friendly.

"Damn!" he exclaimed, smashing his fist on the dashboard. "I sure as hell don't feel like another banzai charge. If we go this way," he indicated with a jerking motion with his head, "maybe we can make it out to Chris's place."

"Then do it, for Chrissake!"

The men ahead of them fired a couple of shots at the

Bronco, one of which ripped a furrow along the left front fender. Rogers slammed the gearshift into reverse. The vehicle lurched, tires screaming, to the rear. As it entered the center of the intersection, Rogers violently spun the wheel around, threw the transmission into low gear, and mashed the accelerator to the floor.

Racing forward, the Bronco arrived at the farm in short order. As it pulled onto the gravel road leading up the hill, Rogers cried, "We made it Larry, old boy!" Up the road the Bronco sped until a burst of machine-gun fire danced down the middle of the gravel. Rogers jammed on the brakes and the vehicle came to a bone-jarring halt sideways in the road.

"What the hell?" Rogers screamed. Just then he saw the gate open and a middle-aged man pop into view. The man hurriedly signaled him to advance.

Rogers hit the accelerator again, and raced up the hill, but not before he heard more gunfire directed at him, this time from the creek bed.

The Bronco flew through the gate and into the compound. Chris, Roseanna, and several others were up to the vehicle before Rogers could get out.

"What kind of reception was that?" he exclaimed to Roseanna as he opened the door of the Bronco.

"That was a trigger-happy soldier who didn't recognize you and probably thought you were one of those guys out there," she said, pointing down the hill. "Fortunately, Jack got Charlie Brighton to stop him and wave you through."

Chris didn't wait for Roseanna to finish her explanation. Instead, she threw her arms around Rogers' neck and pressed her lips violently against his. "I'm so glad you're safe!" she cried. "What's happening back there?" Hamilton walked up as she spoke.

"Nothing very pleasant, as you can tell from the looks of this thing." Rogers pointed to the damage to the Bronco. He told them of the chaos in town while Chris helped Jackson out of the vehicle and led him into the house. Rogers then turned to Hamilton. "How many men are out there along the creek?"

"It's hard to say," Hamilton replied, "and we're in no condition to go out there and find out. We lost sixteen men killed and seven wounded last night at the armory."

Hamilton's tone made the news sound more like an apology.

"Jesus," Rogers replied. Hamilton's expression made it clear that Rogers should not inquire into the details.

"Our friends out along the creek have been there a couple of hours now. Probably just scouting and probing for our weak points. I suppose that they thought you were some of their own until Charlie waved you in. Anyway, I expect we're all going to be here awhile, so you might as well unwind. It'll be worse tonight. Darkness will be another enemy then."

"I understand that too well." Rogers then turned and walked off toward the house looking for Chris and Larry Jackson.

Below the farm, along the creek bank and out of sight of the hilltop's defenders was Tom O'Hara with a newly acquired M-16 slung across his back and a pair of ten-powered binoculars to his eyes. The shoulder holster that held the .45 automatic was prominently stamped "U.S." As the Bronco had sped up the hill, and after the burst of machine-gun fire had brought it to a halt, O'Hara had watched the figure jump from his protected position behind the earthworks along the crest and signal the Bronco forward.

O'Hara had focused on the exposed, beckoning figure. Squinting his eyes in disbelief, he closed them, and then looked again as the man jumped back to his covered position and the Bronco lurched forward.

Charlie Brighton. No mistake. Brighton all right.

O'Hara rolled over and stared at the sky, his emotions swelling within him as the men nearby fired at the Bronco.

Through his mind passed myriad images of times past, a millenium ago, of people gone. He saw himself as a child with his family. He saw his wife, Cathy. The day they first met, the day they married, the day she told him she was carrying twins, and the day he first pressed his hand to her abdomen and felt the first movements of life within her. He saw fleeting images of all the good times they had shared, and he saw how he imagined his children would have looked.

He also saw image after image of the night after the attack, how he had pulled Cathy from the rubble. He saw the scenes from the incredible march as he pulled her on the improvised litter through streets of a shattered city run amok. Images of the dead, the dying, and the mutilated assaulted and reverberated through the corridors of his mind.

O'Hara also saw Don Burns, his political mentor, and he saw the close relationship they had maintained throughout the rocky political campaign. He also saw himself as he *would* have been: mayor, governor of the state, U.S. congressman. And he saw what he had actually become.

Then he saw Brighton. *Brighton!* The one who had gone public with that stuff in the paper, who had ultimately given him, as it turned out, the opportunity to act, to do the same as many others: flee, in advance, the bomb's destruction.

Had he merely followed their example, things would have turned out very differently. For him, and for Cathy.

But in the confusion that accompanied his grief and pain, O'Hara was unable to accept any personal responsibility for results so disastrous, and instead transferred blame to another.

Brighton. Brighton's to blame. For all of this! Goddam him, he's alive! The rotten bastard should be dead! All of 'em up there, all the rotten bastards should be dead! They're alive and Cathy is. . . .

He squeezed shut his eyes so tightly that he saw sunbursts on the blackness inside his eyelids. *Gonna pay—gonna die. They're gonna die—Brighton's gonna die!*

"What's the matter, Boss?" the small man beside O'Hara asked.

"Ghosts," O'Hara said simply, opening his eyes to stare again at the sky.

"Ghosts?"

"I knew that man on the road before it all happened, Huey," O'Hara said softly.

"You mean the war?" Huey was puzzled. He had never seen his leader falter like this before. O'Hara had always been sure of himself. As tense as a cocked pistol, maybe, but always in control.

O'Hara rolled over onto his stomach and again placed the binoculars to his eyes. "Huey," he said to the little man who, next to Charlie Boy, was his most trusted subordinate, "we're definitely going to take this place." He paused for a moment as he strained for another glimpse of Brighton. "I want you to go round up the boys in Bardstown, and bring anyone else along who wants a chance at getting an M-16, ammunition, and all the gas he wants. Tell them all we're going to take this place, by God, and after that we'll *own* this county!"

Huey's eyes scanned the hilltop's fortifications. While Charlie Boy served O'Hara with brute physical strength, Huey provided a reasonably intelligent mind to rely on in the execution of any task assigned.

"Boss, do you really want to *own* this county," Huey asked hesitantly, "or is that just to get these men out here? Do they really have all that ammo, gasoline, and stuff up there?"

"It doesn't matter, just tell them."

"Boss, are you sure about this? I mean, they're as well armed as we are, and they're sitting behind all that dirt. Maybe we should try something easier if this ain't, like you say, *necessary* and all . . ."

O'Hara spun and grabbed the little man by the collar of his shirt, very nearly choking him, and with every vein in his face and throat bulging, O'Hara hissed, "Do as I say, you little shit! I don't give a damn whether they're dug in all the way to China. Tell those people in town whatever's necessary to get them out here, but just get them out here!" He shoved Huey aside and then rolled over and placed the binoculars back to his eyes.

Huey stood up slowly, brushed himself off, and walked away rubbing his throat. As he passed Charlie Boy, who was lying further down the bank of the creek, Huey looked at him and said, "Man, his lights are on, but nobody's home right now."

Puzzled, Charlie Boy turned toward O'Hara and yelled, "Hey, O'Hara! What're we gonna do?"

"Huey will tell you," O'Hara replied tersely, binoculars still to his eyes. "And tell Huey that I want the Scout brought out here right away."

PART SIX

Then out spake brave Horatio,
   The Captain of the Gate:
"To every man upon this earth
   Death cometh soon or late.
And how can man die better
   Than facing fearful odds
For the ashes of his fathers
And the temples of his Gods. . . ."

   —Thomas Babington Macaulay,
    "Horatio at the Bridge"

The evening sky turned to ominous gray, then, toward the west, to black as a late summer thunderstorm moved in. Those below the hill, beyond the creek, had sniped at the hilltop's defenders but had inflicted no serious damage throughout the afternoon. It was obvious to Hamilton, however, that the numbers of the wolf pack had been growing throughout the day. He had sent some of the Guardsmen to help Reuben prepare to defend his portion of the saddle, since he figured he could ill afford to lose such a strategic piece of terrain. By evening, however, all the Guardsmen had returned to their positions inside the perimeter.

As the light slipped quickly away, Hamilton stood behind a breastwork, gazing out a firing port through binoculars that helped amplify the light. What had appeared open terrain weeks before when he had come out to the farm with Reichert now seemed to provide discomforting opportunities for cover and concealment along depressions and ruts and among the patches of brush which dotted the hillside. More important was that nature had taken its course. The corn now stood over seven feet tall. The possibilities for concealment were endless among the acres of cropland that stretched below the hill to the creek.

Although this problem had occurred to Hamilton much earlier in the summer, he had decided that he could not afford to destroy the badly needed grain on the remote possibility of a large-scale attack on the farm. He cursed himself now for his decision.

As he studied the creek line, Rogers walked up to him. Throughout the day, it seemed that the two men had naturally gravitated together.

Hamilton turned to Rogers. "I don't mind telling you that I'm awfully damned worried."

"I can appreciate that," Rogers replied. "What do you expect them to do out there tonight?"

"Well, frankly I didn't expect them to go this far, but if they're going to attack, they'll attack tonight. Either their leader will get his shit together tonight, or he probably never will."

"Yeah. Whoever the son of a bitch is that's leading them is working with a rag tag bunch of new recruits, I expect. Probably a lot of them are former county jailbirds. I'd guess they're like a bottle of champagne that's just been opened. They'll quickly lose their fizz after they've been out for a while. So their leader had better use them now or he'll not have that crew later. They'll be wandering off in all directions.

"But you know, Jack, it's still not too late to think about just moving off this hill and fading into the woods."

Hamilton shook his head. "Even if I wanted to do it, I'd never be able to explain running away." After a brief silence, he turned to Rogers. "See that old cemetery down there?" he asked, pointing in the fading light. "That's where people in my family have been buried since this area was first settled. Captain William Hamilton was the first. He was ambushed and killed by Indians as he crossed that creek on his way home in 1786. His grandson, Jesse, who was my great-great-grandfather, died here from a saber wound he received while riding with General John Hunt Morgan in 1863. My roots are as deep in this soil as the roots of the oak trees at that cemetery." He looked down the hill to the dark tree line and, it seemed, beyond, and said, "Before that scum drives me off this hill, there will be one helluva fight."

As lightning crackled in the distance, Rogers and Hamilton could see intermittently the headlights of several vehicles beyond the creek. Wolf packs were obviously assembling for the effort. Voices and engine noises could be heard between the rolls of western thunder. Men and machinery were moving.

Oppressive twilight finally darkened to night. Suddenly the rows of trees, no longer visible, came alive with gunfire. "Here they come!" Hamilton bellowed to the twenty Guardsmen strung along this side of the perimeter.

The darkness barked with staccato bursts of rifle fire as

the attackers moved across the cornfield in a rough skirmish line. The earthen bank around Hamilton and Rogers thudded with bullets that struck below their intended marks. "Jesus!" Rogers cried, "there's gotta be at least a hundred and fifty of 'em!"

"Give me some light!" Hamilton screamed over his shoulder, and a flare quickly streaked heavenward. The white, parachute illumination flare burst a couple of hundred feet in the air and bathed the field and the surprised attackers below in an eerie, unearthly light that cast strange, distorted shadows across the area. Many of the stunned gunmen ducked for temporary cover behind the stone walls of the cemetery and whatever else they could find.

The first wave of rain from the approaching storm began to fall as men below finally started to drop from the Guardsmen's bullets. Yet the mass of attackers continued undeterred. Rogers fired a borrowed M-16 at the human targets before him. As the flare's light waned, he cursed the descending darkness, and just then another flare whooshed skyward.

Rogers dropped back and began changing the magazine in his rifle when he happened to catch a glimpse through the downpour of something moving forward from the creek bed. Quickly came the hammering report of gunfire unlike all other. "Jesus, Jack! What the hell is *that*?"

Hamilton hurriedly wiped the water from the lenses and pressed the binoculars to his eyes. Though visibility, even with the flare, was limited, he saw an old International Scout, sandbagged, with sloping boiler plate added to its front. A heavy Browning .50-caliber machine gun was placed on top of the vehicle, whose roof was partially removed. The Scout was rolling the gun directly up the hill—straight for them.

"Dear God in Heaven!" Hamilton whispered. The heavy machine gun rounds tore across the breastworks, penetrating the earthen walls in many places. Two Guardsmen screamed in agony as they fell back in the mud, blood jetting from their shattered torsos.

The armored vehicle lumbered on, straining under the weight of the boiler plate and sandbags. Behind it came a small horde of men using its mass for cover in their advance up the muddy hillside.

"You stay here!" Hamilton cried. He scrambled past Rogers down the breastwork, slipping and falling in the muck, shouting for Reichert. As he found his way to the man, Hamilton yelled, "Is everything ready?"

"Ready as can be, sir," Reichert reported calmly. "Whenever they get close enough."

"Then use your best judgment!" Hamilton spun and raced back to his position. Bullets from the Scout's machine gun and the weapons of those who followed it ripped through the air above him. The orange tracers flew across the defensive perimeter as the .50 caliber belched leaden death.

The Scout, motor roaring, crawled up the hill until it was about fifty yards from the nearest defensive position. Suddenly the earth moved. A tremendous explosion beside the Scout blew the vehicle, its occupants, and men nearby high into the air. The shock wave hit Hamilton as if he had been bashed in the face by some unseen fist.

The explosion cast the wolf pack into total disarray, and the screams of the wounded pierced the night.

Unfortunately for the defenders, several attackers had the presence of mind to run to the Scout lying on its side, and remove the machine gun. As they retreated with the rest of the attackers, the skies opened with even heavier sheets of rain and the full fury of the storm fell upon them.

While the men along the breastwork cheered and taunted the attackers below, Reichert, grinning broadly from ear to ear, ran up to Hamilton. "How'd we do, Major?"

"You did just great!" Hamilton slapped him on the back.

"Just thank the ammonium nitrate. But what're we gonna do for an encore?"

"We'll just have to wait and see," Hamilton said.

A blanket hung over the back doorway of the farmhouse, shielding the light of the candle in the kitchen from the darkness outside. Hamilton moved the blanket aside and slipped in from the pouring rain. He looked at Roseanna, Jennifer, and Kip, who were sitting together on the floor on the far side of the refrigerator, a spot they hoped was out of harm's way.

Chris was in the next room, the dining room, attending to the wounded. Roseanna had apparently stolen a few minutes from helping her to reassure the children that their father and the Guardsmen had things well in hand.

From a low ridge several hundred yards away, out of range of the Guardsmen's weapons, Hamilton heard the .50 caliber machine gun, back in action, being tested by its new, inexperienced crew.

"Mommy, I'm scared!" Jennifer cried.

"I know, baby," Roseanna replied, hugging her.

"If they just sit off a good distance with that damned gun," Hamilton said, "they can give us hell and we can't do a thing about it." He knelt down beside Roseanna and placed his palm against her cheek. "It would be a lot better if we moved the kids to the fallout shelter."

"Can't. It's already packed with women and kids."

"Well, we're going to be needing several of the women on the perimeter to take some of the men's places. We've got to try to take out that damned machine gun. I'm assembling a raiding party to go after it."

"A raiding party? Good grief, Jack! Are these guys trained for that sort of stuff?"

"Not really. They're artillery people. Gun bunnies, gun drivers and the like. I'm trying to remember a lot of half-forgotten procedures myself. Stuff I haven't used since OCS."

"Oh, Jack, it sounds so risky."

"Of course," he replied, "but when I consider the risks tomorrow morning with that gun still ripping us up, I don't think I have much choice. And tonight's our best chance. The last thing they'll be expecting is a visit from us. So, anyway, I just wanted to see you before we left." He pulled her close to him. "And I wanted to tell you that I love you."

Tears filled Roseanna's eyes. She leaned forward and kissed him, and whispered, "Jack, please be careful." Half smiling, she hugged him closer. "You know, I've gotten kind of used to having you around . . ." she said, and then broke into sobs.

Hamilton held her tightly, and then released her from his embrace. "I've got to see the wounded before I go."

He walked into the next room. Chris and two other women were bandaging a soldier's shoulder shattered from the devastating impact of a .50 caliber machine-gun round. Hamilton checked on the condition of each of the wounded, and with each man who was conscious, he spoke a few words of encouragement. Three of the wounded had died in the last hour, but their bodies had not been removed. He finally came to Ackerson who lay bandaged about his ribs, a new splint on his badly fractured leg. A heavy sweat covered his forehead and the exposed skin of his torso.

"How're you doing, Ted?"

"Not very good at all, sir," Ackerson whispered. "I guess I really blew it last night. Rode right into the ambush. Really took the bait, I guess."

"No more than I did. Nobody could have seen it coming." He patted Ackerson's arm. "You were just doing what anyone would have done," he said. He just wished someone would say that to *him* and mean it.

"I hear you really tore them a new asshole a while ago." Ackerson smiled weakly.

"Yeah, I suppose we did. I've got a few more surprises planned as well," Hamilton replied, returning the smile.

A glance at Chris told Hamilton he should leave. As he turned, Ackerson whispered, "Go get 'em, Mad Dog."

Hamilton circled his thumb and index finger into the "okay" sign and then walked quickly from the room, giving Chris an affectionate squeeze on the arm as he passed.

In the kitchen, he said to Roseanna and the children, "Time to go." He helped the children to their feet, and then said to Kip, "You be sure to take care of your mother, young man." It was clear that the boy was torn between wanting to cry and wanting to act bravely. He clenched his jaw and nodded.

Together, they ran out into the rain, which by now was only a drizzle, and quickly made their way to the fallout shelter in the barn.

Twelve men had assembled around Hamilton and were checking each other's equipment prior to beginning their mission. Many were dressed in civilian clothes to enhance their ability to escape detection and pass as wolf pack members. Even those in uniforms with pistol belts and ammo pouches would not be very obvious, given the amounts of equipment that had fallen into the wolf pack's hands the previous night at the armory.

"All right, you guys, now listen up," Hamilton said.

The plan was simple. Since, from the noises drifting to the farm from the distant encampment, the gunmen were likely occupied with drinking and hell-raising, Hamilton and his men would simply proceed out the defensive perimeter to a point where they made visual contact the heavy machine gun. An assault team would break off and move to position within quick striking distance, and on the prearranged signal, the support team would lay down heavy fire on the objective. At a second signal, the support team would lift its fire, allowing the assault team to close on the machine gun.

Hamilton made clear that the task of the assault team, and, for that matter, of the whole patrol, was only to remove the machine gun's backplate, and thereby disable it. Trying to pack the machine gun back to the farm under fire would only risk higher casualties. And attempting to carry back significant amounts of the heavy and bulky ammo was out of the question.

Hamilton designated a rally point at the objective, and a couple more along the patrol route where the patrol would regroup in case of ambush.

After establishing a password, and explaining how to disable the machine gun, Hamilton asked, "Okay. Anybody got any questions?"

"Yeah," Rogers said, stepping in front of a couple of soldiers. "Do you have room for one more?"

"This isn't your fight, Kurt. No need to risk getting your ass shot off."

"For the past three months, except for that incident with Chris, I've let the whole world go by and just tried to stay above what was happening. Until tonight, that is. But fight the bastards here or fight them at my place next week, what the hell's the difference?" He broke into a wide grin. "Besides, wasn't it Churchill who said something about there being nothing quite as exhilarating as being shot at—and missed?"

Hamilton paused for a second and then smiled. "Okay, it's your ass." To the others he directed, "You guys take ten minutes more to make final preparations. Sergeant Mattingly, check each of them out for loose gear or rattles."

As he finished, Hamilton saw Chris standing a few feet away in the darkness, and he stepped toward her. "What is it?"

"It's Ted, Jack. He's gone. I'm sorry, but there was nothing more we could do." She gently took Hamilton's hand into her own.

Hamilton had developed a real friendship with Ackerson despite the rocky start of their relationship. Lately, there had been almost a big brother–little brother sort of affection between them. The hollow feeling in his chest and the lump in his throat now prevented Hamilton from saying anything.

Finally, he squeezed Chris's hand tightly, and then slowly walked back to the patrol. Despite the feeling of monumental emptiness inside him, things had to be done now that simply could not wait.

The men in the patrol finished darkening their faces with sticks of camouflage paint. Last-minute questions were answered. Then each member slipped to the back side of the perimeter. They topped the breastwork, slipped through holes in the barbed wire and, one by one, quietly slid down an embankment to the firmer footing of the undisturbed soil below.

Reorganizing themselves, the men cautiously worked their way across the field, taking advantage of natural depressions, fence lines and brush lines for concealment. The heavy cloud cover, just starting to break up as the storm moved on, favored them by reducing visibility. They made no sounds to be heard above the katydid chorus and the drunken, raucous shouts, laughter, and braggadocio gunfire from the wolf pack's fireside festivities.

Hamilton cautiously checked the creek line for sentries. The smell of marijuana, accented by the cool night air, drifted downstream in the patrol's direction. After waiting for a minute or two in order to determine where the sentries were located, Hamilton heard bits and pieces of muffled conversation from men posted along the bank thirty yards upstream. They now seemed totally occupied with passing around a couple of bottles of bourbon, booty from a nearby distillery.

Nugent and the other point man checked out the far side of the creek, and the patrol glided silently through the roiling water of the rain-swollen stream. Finally, Hamilton stopped the patrol about a hundred and fifty yards from the scene of the gunmen's revelry, and then he moved forward with Nugent to peer at the wolf pack through the trees.

When he finally got close enough to get a detailed view of the spectacle unfolding in the clearing, Hamilton swallowed hard. Nugent whispered, "Ho-o-ly shit!"

A crowd of two hundred and fifty, including perhaps forty women, milled around a large bonfire. The atmosphere brought to mind a football homecoming Hamilton remembered from his college days. In other ways it reminded him of the revelry he'd observed in the infield of the Kentucky Derby the preceding year. Only this was revelry without the humor.

The men around the bonfire seemed hell-bent on consuming enormous quantities of liquor, and many of them staggered and reeled across the clearing. Occasional shots were fired in the air as the intensity of the debauchery escalated.

Suddenly, Hamilton saw one of the many women drunkenly wobble and climb her way to the top of a pickup truck's cab. The slender blond of nineteen or twenty attracted the attention of many of those around her, and she began dancing to the music provided by a nearby guitar player. Men crowded the "stage" like patrons in a topless bar, hopeful and demanding. "Take it off! Take it off!" they chanted. The young woman obviously relished the limelight. She played her newfound celebrity status for all it was worth, and teased the crowd to its limit for each article of clothing she slowly removed, molting to the music.

As she finally slid her panties to her feet and triumphantly and brazenly tossed them out to the eager men below her, the crowd roared fiercely with approval. Several gunshots were fired in the air. A raw, unbridled sexual energy pulsed across the clearing.

Then another woman, one with long, raven-black hair, cued on the blond's example and scrambled to the top of a nearby sandbagged pickup. She commenced the identical ritual, and the crowd moved immediately to the new dancer's position.

The blond, now abandoned, began to pick up her clothing in disappointment. Just as she located her jeans, three men approached her and began talking in animated tones. Finally, the nude woman walked away in the darkness, laughing, followed by her three admirers.

Hamilton turned his attention back to the raven-haired beauty who continued to enthrall the crowd. "Ki-ki! Ki-ki! Ki-ki!" they chanted in a pulsing, pounding rhythm that split the night air when she removed her bra and let her heavy, perfectly shaped breasts fall free.

As she started to play with the zipper of her blue-jean cutoffs, the crowd to her side suddenly began to part and to make way for a bearded figure who strode angrily toward the truck. Almost everyone around the man deferred to him, and Hamilton immediately deduced the man's importance.

The figure stalked up to the truck, grabbed Kiki by the ankles, and pulled her tumbling to the ground. The man then took her by the arm and marched away with the protesting woman in tow. No one was laughing now. Slowly, however, the frivolity began once again.

Hamilton noticed that the heavy machine gun had been remounted atop a '63 Chevy pickup. Dozens of people were scattered in the darkness around the truck, drinking from bottles of liquor, swapping tales of bravery that night, and promising to "kick ass" at the next encounter. Atop the truck a young man with an oily rag in hand slowly rubbed—almost massaged—the .50 cal's barrel and receiver, seemingly oblivious to the bacchanalia around him.

"There's our target," Hamilton whispered, pointing to the pickup with the machine gun. "Bring Mattingly's men up here and set up the M-60. Since we have no commo, you'll have to wait until you see a green star-cluster flare. I want the first bursts of gunfire to come from over here so it'll draw their attention from us. Just make sure that you clear those bastards away from that truck. Understand?"

Nugent nodded slowly. "No problem, Major."

"I'll bring the assault team up to that neck of the woods on the right. At the first flare, shoot anything that moves on the left side of the bonfire," Hamilton said, his right index finger stabbing through the night air for emphasis. "Make sure Mattingly has that straight. When you see the red star-cluster, you shift your fire to the left side of that truck over there while we then close on the .50 cal. Finally, when you see the white parachute flare that means we're clear and you should hose down anything that moves out there. Keep 'em pinned down for one minute exactly before breaking contact and haulin' ass back to the farm. Got it?"

"Got it."

The two men withdrew from their observation point and rejoined the patrol. After proper coordination, Hamilton moved out with the assault team and Nugent guided Mattingly's support team forward. In twenty minutes, Hamilton, Rogers, and the assault team were poised near the neck of the woods from which they would launch their attack.

The party was already beginning to break up, booze and fatigue having felled many of the gunmen. Hamilton whispered to Rogers, "Most of those guys out there are too damned drunk to hit a target even if they can find their guns." Turning to the others, still whispering, he said, "Remember, nobody moves forward for five seconds. Give Mattingly's machine gun time to rattle 'em. Don't bunch up, and don't go past the bonfire until the red star-cluster goes up, or you'll get greased by our own guys. Remember that.

"And in case I get hit," he added, patting his pistol belt, "the flare is right here. Also, remember that speed is essential. We're hardly in a position to stay around and shoot it out with these guys.

"And one last thing. If anyone does get hit, we're to do our best to help him, but the people back at the farm need us badly. We don't need four guys getting killed trying to drag back one guy who gets wounded. Take care of that machine gun first, and then get your butts back to the farm. Is that clear? All right. Now let's go out there and kick their fuckin' asses!"

Hamilton signaled the team to move out. Each man crept forward and moved to the edge of the clearing. Hamilton moved carefully through the wet leaves into the open, beyond the overhanging branches of an ancient oak tree. He removed the flare from his belt, and held it extended from his body after placing the cap into the firing position. He popped the palm of his other hand against the base of the device, and the flare roared skyward.

One of the gunmen whirled clumsily in Hamilton's

direction. The white of the man's eyes glinted in the firelight as he stiffened at the sight of the flare's fiery wake. He groped for the revolver at his side, bellowing, "What the fu . . ." as a hail of machine gun fire cut across his midsection. The few moments of life left to him were wasted in a futile attempt to gather gray-blue loops of intestine back into his abdomen.

After five seconds to allow Mattingly's machine gun to have its effect, the assault team rushed forward, automatic weapons raking the entire area. Pandemonium broke loose. A long line of orange tracers from Mattingly's gun passed back and forth over the surprised wolf pack. It hammered bodies backward, spinning and twisting them into grotesque heaps on the ground.

Hamilton led the dash, Rogers at his side. The assault team was quickly at the temporary boundary to no-man's-land. Crouching by the three trucks parked by the bonfire, Hamilton fumbled for a moment with the second flare.

Two men and a woman came running headlong at them from their left, firing shotguns. Rogers' Uzi cut them down. As the second flare finally burst overhead, Hamilton shouted, "Move it!" The team sprinted forward, rifles blazing, leaping over bodies sprawled in its path.

Rogers was first to the pickup, and he vaulted into the truck's bed and up to the waiting machine gun. Hamilton and the others dropped to firing positions to cover him, firing at any figure moving in the light from the bonfires. Most of the wolf pack, however, had headed blindly into the darkness in fear and confusion. But the few who made it to weapons were rallying, and bullets were crashing into the pickup. The clearing now reeked of cordite, fear, blood and death.

Rogers removed the backplate and tossed it down to Hamilton, who rammed it inside his shirt and shouted for the team to move out. Rogers jumped down from the truck and his Uzi began chattering as he covered the withdrawal.

"Haul ass!" Hamilton shouted, and the two men broke for the woods. Just as they reached the trees, the gas tank from the nearest truck exploded in a giant yellow fireball that mushroomed skyward. Both men instinctively rolled with the impact of the shockwave into the underbrush, then came up running. Hamilton immediately turned and popped the white parachute illumination flare back toward the area over the clearing, and then raced onward.

Two hundred feet into the woods, Hamilton felt a searing pain in his right thigh, and his leg buckled beneath him. Rogers, unaware that Hamilton had been hit, ran on.

Clenching his jaw, gritting his teeth in pain, Hamilton twisted to see three silhouettes coming after him. His heart pounding wildly, he took aim, pulled the trigger—and felt nothing. Quickly he tried to clear the weapon and found the bolt jammed with a cartridge improperly fed from the magazine. He hurriedly attempted to dislodge the round without success. He grabbed for his .45, but to his horror he found only the severed lanyard, his pistol apparently having been lost in his fall. In desperation, he grabbed the machine-gun backplate from inside his shirt and heaved it with all his strength into the wooded darkness.

As his pursuers closed in, he frantically continued his efforts to clear the weapon. The raw bone and flesh of his fingers seemed to be locked in a desperate struggle with the aluminum alloy and brass of the rifle's receiver and jammed cartridge. Suddenly, from almost directly over his head, came several bursts of automatic fire. A hand grabbed his right arm firmly, yanked him to his feet, and pulled his arm across broad shoulders for support.

"Now let's get the hell out of here!" Rogers yelled.

WEDNESDAY, AUGUST 21st: Early Morning, The Ninety-Seventh Day

Lacy tendrils of fog hung in the air, an aftermath of the evening's thunderstorm. Hamilton, feeling the mist on his face and hands, its feather touch on his camouflaged uniform, knew the fog had to be heavy over the lower field and creek bed. An M-16 was cradled in his arms, and his leg was elevated as well as he could manage. He sat with Rogers at a new position on the earthen breastworks peering into the night, listening for some evidence of movement below them. With the success of the raid, and after repelling the attack, he felt vindicated. The burden of the disaster at the armory did not seem nearly as oppressive now.

Hamilton's leg throbbed with pain only slightly, dulled by a shot of xylocaine Chris had given him. Its effects were fading, but he was needed too badly on the line, as was each man not severely wounded. "You saved my bacon out there, but you were disobeying orders, Kurt."

The remark amused Rogers. He feigned a quick search of his clothing. "Excuse me, Jack, but does this look like a uniform?"

Hamilton smiled in spite of himself and tried to shift his weight for a more comfortable position. "Damn!" Pain shot up his leg. "For a few seconds, I sure thought that I'd bought the farm. I was scared shitless. I suppose I owe you."

"Voltaire summed it up, Jack. 'Courage is not the absence of fear. It is the mastery of it.'" Don't worry, fella, you've got the 'right stuff.'"

"Well, I owe you, anyway."

"That's the wonderful sort of guy I am," Rogers replied in his best tongue-in-cheek tone. "But hell, we're not home free yet. Those people out there have become very quiet in the past half hour, so either they are moving away from us, which I doubt, or they are moving *toward* us like pissed-off bees from an upset hive."

"Well, they don't have much time. The light's increasing in the east," replied Hamilton.

Reichert made his way along the earthen wall and squatted beside Hamilton. "Everyone's on maximum alert, sir. Every round of ammunition we have has been handed out, or is being held at points along the positions for quick distribution. We're doing okay on rifle ammunition, but only if we make every shot count, and as long as we don't burn it up on automatic fire. We're awfully short on machine-gun ammo though, and we've just a handful of illumination flares left.

"I've been talking to Reuben on the land line, and he tells me his people want to try to hold their ground. I told him he'd be a helluva lot safer over here, but he's adamant about keeping the bastards off his property."

"Did you tell him he's the weakest link in the chain?"

"Held no water with him."

"That's Reuben," Hamilton replied. "Tough old buzzard. He may go down, but if he does, it will be with all flags flying. He's right from the tactical side, though. The bastards take Reuben's and we lose the advantage of our elevation . . ."

The stillness was shattered by two hundred or more weapons and the tremendous cheer from the wolves surging forward from the streambed. The Guardsmen returned fire to the edge of the woods flashing gunfire.

As he gazed into the darkness trying to get a fix on the attackers, Hamilton realized the wolves were swinging to his left. Something was wrong. "Christ!" he exclaimed. "They're going for *Reuben's!*"

"Sweet Jesus!" Dick Carlisle bellowed. "They're coming this way!" M-1 carbine in hand, he began to bang away at the sparks of gunfire from the advancing attackers. The pack wasn't circling any more. It was coming in for the kill.

Ken Fitzgerald hammered away with the other M-1 carbine from his sandbagged position at a nearby window. Reuben and seven others did as well as they could with a motley collection of bolt-action deer rifles, shotguns, and a few .22 caliber semiautomatic rifles. Crouching behind her husband, Fran Fitzgerald tried her best to make her trembling fingers force the bullets into the balky magazines Ken was rapidly—too rapidly—emptying through his carbine.

"For Christ's sake! Get it together!" he screamed at her.

"I'm trying my best!" she cried back at him. She continued to fumble with the bullets as the rifle fire crashed through the walls, spattering her with fragments of plaster and wood.

As the bullets ripped through the main farmhouse, Dennis Waters reeled across the floor. The back of his head was blown away by the impact of a rifle bullet. Helen Waters held his limp body in her arms, screaming for help from the others, though it was obvious they could give her none. And the wolf pack continued to advance.

Hamilton saw the line moving in fits and starts. The flashes of gun muzzles gave the attackers the appearance of a line moving accordion fashion, as the wolves sprinted forward, dropped for cover, fired, and then advanced again.

He was encouraged when the gunfire from the Cissell farm began to hammer at the advancing horde. At first, he heard only rifle fire from the defenders, and then came the very different reports of shotguns, and finally, pistols. Though the angle made it difficult, the guardsmen directed as much fire as possible into the advancing pack.

The pack, meanwhile, had not ignored the Guardsmen. A light machine gun periodically raked the breastworks, seeking any soldier who imprudently exposed himself to get a better shot.

Several small explosions came as the attackers apparently reached the bottom of the hill. It was impossible for Hamilton to tell which side had initiated them from this distance. "Goddammit!" he roared to Rogers. "They must be going through the wire." Turning back over his shoulder he screamed, "Give me some light over there!"

"They're at the wire!" Fitzgerald cried out to the defenders. As he spoke, a white parachute-flare burst in the air nearby, revealing the advance scouts blasting paths through the wire below. On their heels, through the large garden at the base of the hill, so painstakingly tended for the last few weeks, came heavy boots on two hundred pairs of callous, bellicose feet.

As the wolves poured through the gaps in the wire, two more men in the house slumped, lifeless. Fran's fingers froze on the magazine she had been loading. She stared at the contorted body of Ray Lyons lying across the floor in front of her. Was it her imagination, or could she really see in this dim light the dead man's eyes staring into her own?

From below the floor of the house there came screams of panicked children. They were protected by the heavy masonry foundation, yet found the events transpiring about them to be terrifying. Their cries brought Fran back to action, and she started jamming the bullets into the magazine once again.

Reuben finally screamed, "We gotta make a run for it, or we're all gonna die right here!" He rang the field-phone land line to the Hamilton farm in order to warn the guardsmen of their retreat. "We're coming over!" he screamed into the phone. "For God's sake cover us!"

From the Hamilton farm, several figures could be observed running toward the breastworks. Hamilton yelled to the men nearby. "Make sure who you're shooting before you fire!"

Bullets zipped through the air as the attackers moved around the Cissell farmhouse and outbuildings. The pack then turned its fire on the fleeing defenders. At Hamilton's direction, Reichert sent Nugent forward to help guide Reuben's people through the maze of wire and wooden obstacles in front of the defenses.

Fran's son, Michael, ran in front of her in the darkness. Had Cindy and Melanie not been clutching at her hands as she ran, she would have crossed herself. Dear God, she prayed, just let us make it to that farm! Bullets whizzed past her head. Others plowed into the ground around her. On she ran with the other women and children as the whooping and hollering to the rear increased.

Just as she reached the gravel road between the farms and was starting down the slight embankment, Melanie screamed, went limp, and fell to the ground. Fran stopped abruptly. She looked down in horror and saw that her daughter had been hit.

Pushing Cindy toward the wire, Fran desperately gathered up the unconscious child in her arms. She stumbled toward the protection of the Hamilton farm just as Reuben and the other men caught up with her.

Due to the intricacy of the barbed wire, the retreating group bottlenecked at the entrance of the passage. "For God's sake, hurry!" Ken Fitzgerald screamed as he ran up to the wire. He turned and fired a burst of bullets from his carbine toward the Cissell farm. Dick Carlisle turned, dropped to the ground, and began firing repeatedly at his pursuers.

"Go ahead, Ken!" Carlisle yelled.

Fitzgerald gave him no argument. He began crawling through the barbed wire toward the fortifications as rapidly as his knees, hands, and elbows could carry him.

Finally satisfied that everyone else had withdrawn, Carlisle jumped up and began running for the entrance of the wire obstacle. At the opening, he spun and fired the last of his ammunition, and then turned toward the breastworks and the safety beyond. A bullet immediately slammed into his upper back, throwing him lifeless onto the barbed wire.

Within a few seconds, the last of Reuben's group emerged from the wire, over the breastwork, and into the relative safety of the compound. Another illumination flare exploded over the attacking force. The few gunmen who had ventured beyond the buildings on the Cissell farm quickly withdrew, and the roar of battle was reduced to occasional gunshots as the wolf pack began regrouping.

Reuben jogged through the mud to Rogers and Hamilton, then leaned against the side of the earthen wall, breathless. "Damn those rotten bastards!" he exclaimed, wiping at his eyes. Bitter frustration and anger were evident in the old man's voice. "We had no chance at all once they focused their attention on us. We made them pay, though. But there was no way we could hold out any longer. We just didn't have enough fire power." He paused, and then added, "We lost five, *five* good men."

"You did your best, Reuben," Hamilton replied, putting his hand on the man's shoulder. "For now, take what's left of your people over to that far side. We're spread a little thin and could use your help."

Cissell nodded, and then dejectedly moved back through the mud to the remnants of his group, his age seeming to hang like a heavy mantle from his shoulders.

Across the hilltop on the other side of the saddle, O'Hara quickly moved through the ranks of the attack force, encouraging the men to make themselves ready for the final attack. Time was of the essence now. Dawn was already a red smear in the east, and the advantage of darkness would be lost soon. There was no way of knowing what efforts might be made by local people to help the Guardsmen when the new day came.

For now though, despite the casualties the gunmen had sustained, or perhaps *because* of the casualties they had sustained, as well as the additional impact of the ingestion of enormous quantities of Nelson County bourbon, these men were out for blood. They were determined to stamp out those who had hurt them so badly, who even now still stood in their way.

O'Hara hurriedly went among them patting them on the back and urging them to their utmost. Among them, that is, yet apart from them, for O'Hara never saw himself as one of them. Like oil and water, which can be mixed together from time to time, but never really become one, and eventually always separate, so it was here. These men were simply a means to an end, tools for the task. He detested their common and vulgar ways. Yet for the sake of expedience, he contained his feelings. After all, doing so was absolutely necessary if he were to obtain their cooperation in accomplishing his goal.

Huey approached O'Hara as his leader stood with Charlie Boy, talking with three men beside the barn. "Boss," he said nervously, "can I talk to you alone?"

With mild irritation, O'Hara concluded his conversation and walked over to the little man, saying, "What is it now, Huey?"

"Boss, I know what you said about them having all that gasoline, and stuff in there. But if they really have all that ammo and guns, they're gonna tear us to pieces out there, aren't they?" He stammered, "I mean that's *you* and *me*, too!" He braced himself for O'Hara's comeback, but was surprised at his leader's restrained tone.

"In the past few weeks I've done all right by you, haven't I? You can stay toward the rear in the attack if you like. Anyway, I suspect they're getting low on ammunition since their volume of fire has slowed considerably. Regardless, I'll be on the truck. So whatever happens, you just take care of yourself, little fellow, and don't worry about me. Now let's get going. It'll be light all too soon." He turned and called out, "Charlie, let's keep them moving!"

Huey stood there as O'Hara walked away in the darkness toward Charlie Boy and the truck he had referred to. A team of men was preparing the old Ford pickup sitting behind one of the barns. They were putting final touches on the "sandbags" which were fabricated from plastic garbage bags and which were placed around the cab and front bumper. Several crates of explosives were being loaded in the back of the truck. It was now obvious to Huey that this truck and its occupants were on a one-way trip to the

Guardsmen, who, O'Hara now admitted, did not have the massive quantities of ammunition he had been led to believe. For what possible reason?

O'Hara's inner peace caused Huey to consider one explanation. O'Hara, the primordial survivor, just might be bent on self-destruction. Exactly why, the little man could not be certain. He guessed, however, that it was some sort of self-inflicted punishment having some connection with events past and, perhaps, with one or more of the people among the defenders at the Hamilton farm.

Three hundred yards or so across the saddle, Hamilton was rising painfully. "I think it's time we walked the line again," he said to Rogers.

"Maybe you had better let Mattingly and Reichert take care of that and give your leg a break."

"Nope. I can make it. I need to see this for myself." In spite of near exhaustion from the last two nights' efforts, Hamilton walked with Rogers past each man's position, checking to make certain that they knew where to direct fire in the event of another assault. Hamilton limped up to a machine-gun position and tapped the gunner on the leg, inquiring as to his remaining ammunition.

The gunner was Sergeant Howard, the young NCO whose prisoners had "escaped." He looked at Hamilton and replied, "Not too good, sir. If you want to know the God's honest truth. I'm down to my last two hundred-round belt, and nobody's got any to lend. They're worse off than I am. I may have to pick up this gun and use it as a club before this is over with. I'm so damned scared you couldn't drive a needle up my ass with a sledgehammer."

"I don't think things are that bad. You just hang in there, Sergeant." Hamilton limped on with Rogers, using an M-16 for support.

"You know, Kurt," he said as he stepped around several empty ammo cans, "If anyone had told me three months ago that Jack Hamilton of First Fidelity National Bank would be sitting in a defensive perimeter defending his family from a band of two hundred gunmen, I'd have told him he was fair game for a mental inquest warrant."

"I suppose it was always the case that the wolf was just a few steps from our door, but we didn't want to believe it.

Maybe now, like Pogo once said in the comic strip, 'We have met the enemy, and he is us.'"

"Yeah. Something like that."

The two men continued around the positions, past Mattingly, Nugent, Brighton, and Reuben's people, until they arrived at a part of the perimeter occupied by a few of the women who were able to use a rifle. Hamilton kept walking until he found Roseanna, who was positioned near Cliff and Rick Sheridan.

"How are you doing, sweetheart?"

"I've never been so scared in all my life, Jack. I can't see anything out there, and I'm not sure I could hit it if I did," she said.

Just then there came a burst of machine-gun fire from the side of the perimeter nearest the Cissell farm. Hamilton spun and started back to his position until he heard Reichert bellow, "goddammit, Lucas! You're shooting at nothing! If you don't keep a little better control on that thing you're gonna wish you were dealing with *them* instead of *me*!"

After a couple of seconds there came the reply, "Damnation, Chief. I thought I saw something, I really did . . ."

After a few moments, Hamilton was satisfied that it was a false alarm, and he turned to Roseanna. "Well, it'll be full daylight in a bit. Maybe then everybody will get over the jitters. I expect the wolf pack won't want to charge across that ground in the light of day. So just hang on," He pecked her on the lips and started to move away.

"I sure wish that I'd paid a little more attention to those marksmanship lessons last year," she replied.

Hamilton continued around the perimeter with Rogers. He had just gotten back to his position when the sounds of motor vehicles revving their engines drifted from the Cissell farm.

Suddenly, a hail of gunfire came from the buildings and the wolf pack commenced its attack. A barrage issued from the defenders' positions. The machine guns commenced their throaty, staccato rhythm, which was distinctly audible above the raucous sounds of battle.

Hamilton fired an illumination flare, and another, and another to allow the defenders to spot their targets. He looked down the line and saw first one soldier, and then another fall back down the sandbagged breastwork, screaming in pain. Men nearby called for medics as the fight continued.

Rogers grabbed Hamilton and spun him brusquely to see the vague outline of five vehicles advancing in the increasing light. Protected by sandbags of sorts, they were moving abreast from the farm, though they were not as yet advancing a great distance. Hamilton groped for another flare, but there were none.

The attack continued for a few minutes while a group worked its way to the right of Hamilton's immediate front. Seeking cover in the small depression created by the road, its members took up firing positions along the ditch on the near side of the gravel and began pouring fire on the Guardsmen. They also began hurling small explosive charges at the barbed wire in front of the breastworks to clear paths through the obstacle.

The collection of vehicles sitting on the Cissell farm finally began its advance.

The trucks lumbered forward with their engines roaring and suspensions straining at the weight of their sandbags. Gunmen followed infantry-fashion as if behind tanks. They jumped out, fired, and then returned to cover behind each truck. Each of them, that is, except the center truck.

"Get your machine-guns on those goddam trucks!" Hamilton screamed to the men along the line.

A stream of orange light from each of two machine guns' tracers effectively decimated the two end vehicles. The thin plastic of the improvised sandbags and the thin ropes holding them in place yielded to the hammering machine-gun fire. As the sandbags ripped apart and spilled their contents to the ground, eliminating the drivers' protection, the vehicles stopped.

Hamilton noticed that the rate of fire from the Guardsmen had begun to drop off. He slid down from his vantage point and hobbled as quickly as possible to the nearest machine gun's position and beat on Howard's leg to get his attention. "What the hell's wrong, goddammit? Get those other trucks!"

"No more ammo!" Howard shouted. Before he could make further reply, he jerked abruptly and slid back down the embankment, crumpling to the ground, holding his chest which gurgled and foamed red between his fingers.

"Medic!" Hamilton cried, and a soldier and one of the women rushed to Howard's side.

Hamilton looked quickly to the other machine-gun position. He could see from the movements of the gunners that there was no ammunition there either. "Aim for the tires!" he yelled to those nearby. The trucks' machine guns, meanwhile, continued to rake the line with steady bursts of copper-clad death.

It was now nearly bright enough to see the details of the trucks, and the soldiers directed the fire from their M-16s at the tires of the vehicles. The small rifle bullets had been unable to penetrate the sandbags, but one by one they were able to puncture the tires of the trucks on the left and right of the line and to stop them about fifty yards from the breastworks.

The center truck, the truck from which none of the wolves sought cover, seemed to Hamilton to be in position to make a final run toward the fortifications. Strangely, the gunner jumped down from the truck, seemingly abandoning the attack.

Suddenly a bullet zinged past his ear, and several more ripped into the earth around him. Hamilton dove for cover, and shouted, "What the hell?" thinking that someone within the perimeter had shot at him, because that spot should have been protected from direct fire. It suddenly dawned on him, however, that with the increasing light, he had become a target for any sniper who might be on the barn roof or silo at the Cissel farm. From there a marksman would obviously have a commanding view of the defenses.

"Medic! goddammit, medic!" men were shouting along the breastworks. Hamilton scanned the positions around him and noticed that there was return fire from fewer than half of the fifteen men assigned to this part of the perimeter. Though he could see Cliff, Reuben, and Charlie rushing forward amid sniper fire to plug the gaps in the line, he knew the situation was now desperate. He simply had no more clever ploys or surprises to confound his enemies.

For the first time he considered that it might be necessary to evacuate the farm and make a run for it just as Reuben's people had done. If he didn't start things in motion, there might not be time to organize and execute a withdrawal—something which might become necessary within as little as a few minutes. Perhaps he ought to send a warning to the women and children in the shelter. The images racing through his mind of what might happen to them were not pleasant.

But as some of the gunmen bolted forward to the ditch along the road and assumed firing positions enabling them to place even more effective fire on the breastworks, there slowly became audible a pulsing, familiar rhythm.

"Thank God Almighty!" Hamilton cried, tears of joy and relief welling up in his eyes.

Two Huey helicopters thundered at treetop level toward the farm at attack speeds of one hundred and twenty knots. The choppers began raining deadly machine-gun fire upon the wolf pack on their first pass, and the pack immediately began to break and run.

"NO-O-O!" O'Hara screamed, reacting fiercely to this outside intervention. He jumped out of the cab of the center pickup truck, grabbed the machine gun, and ran across the field, encouraging those running past him to hold their ground.

Only Charlie Boy heeded his call.

"Oh, my God!" Charlie Brighton exclaimed. His finger pulled away from the trigger of his M-16 and refused to move. Indeed, it was as if his whole body were suddenly afflicted with paralysis.

Terry Rockwell's helo banked sharply and returned to make a pass directly at O'Hara. O'Hara stood defiantly with his M-60 machine gun at his hip and its ammo belt slung from his shoulder, sending a hail of bullets at the chopper thundering toward him.

Rockwell's doorgunner, Skeeter Mulrooney, quickly spotted O'Hara and swung his gun around toward the target. As the Huey swept forward, a surface-to-air version of "Chicken" evolved. O'Hara and Mulrooney refused to flinch despite the hail of bullets each was sending at the other. The orange stream of tracers gouged the dirt around O'Hara, then continued on, past Charlie Boy behind him, striking the truck and its cargo.

A horrendous explosion flung O'Hara and Charlie Boy churning through the air.

Blood rolling into his eyes from the Plexiglass fragments in his forehead, and hurricane force winds rushing at his face through the shattered windshield, Rockwell fought frantically to keep his chopper under control. The shock wave rocked the helo and sent it reeling like a feather in a whirlwind. Just when he though he had matters finally in hand, Glen Childs, his wounded copilot, grabbed him by the arm and pointed to the instrument panel. The bright yellow words MASTER CAUTION immediately grabbed his attention. His eyes darted to the pedestal between the two men, where a panel displayed more lights saying, XMSN OIL PRESSURE and HYD PRESSURE. The stiffening control stick confirmed the urgent problems.

O'Hara's bullets had found their mark after all. They had either destroyed the hydraulic oil cooler or ruptured a critical hydraulic oil line. Rockwell tensed. He knew it was a matter of seconds before the control servos to the rotor head locked up. The bird would not auto-rotate gently to the ground. It would not glide gracefully to earth. The Huey would drop like a rock.

Rockwell's nostrils flared broadly as he cried, "JEEE-ZUSS!" He quickly banked the aircraft, looking desperately for a safe place to land among the gunmen and guardsmen spread out before him on the ground. "I'm gonna try to make it to the farm!" he yelled over the engine's roar. "Hang on to your ass!"

It seemed to take twenty years, but it may have taken only twenty seconds for Rockwell to pass over the breastworks and to arrest his descent. He was coming in too fast about ten feet off the ground, when, suddenly, the blades froze. The chopper crashed to earth, crushing its skids beneath it, and sliding sixty to seventy feet along the farmyard on its belly before finally coming to rest on its right side. Miraculously, all of this occured without the aircraft bursting into flames, and without serious injury to its crew.

Rockwell and the crew evacuated the disabled Huey as quickly as possible, and left it a derelict in the middle of the farmyard. The attention of the farm's defenders was directed once again to the retreating wolf pack.

Charlie Boy vaguely sensed something wrong, but he was not quite sure what it was. As he lay sprawled on the ground, he felt no pain, just a comfortable, warm and sleepy sensation. He was vaguely aware of voices around him, though he could not understand them.

His mind was drifting . . . he had the handoff and he charged through that hole in the line . . . the field in front of him was clear . . . a coliseum full of people rose, cheering, to its feet . . . the 40, the 30, the 20, the 10 . . . and . . . touchdown! He flung his arms triumphantly into the air . . . he did his dance . . . and then he slid toward darkness.

Charlie Boy closed his eyes, slowly let out his last breath, and then died.

Charlie Boy's season was finally over.

In the confusion and the activity on the field between the two farms, little notice was paid to the small man who dashed nimbly among the carnage and quickly retreated with the body of the machine-gunner. Carrying the unconscious figure over his shoulder, the little man joined the others in flight as the remaining helicopter made yet another pass.

After drinking in the scene for a few minutes, Hamilton slid back down the embankment and sat looking up at Rogers and Reichert. Roseanna ran up to him, knelt down, threw her arms around him, and exclaimed, "You did it, Jack!"

"Yeah," he said. "With a little help from my friends."

PART SEVEN

Epilogue

No rumor of the foe's advance
Now swells upon the wind;
No troubled thought at midnight
    haunts
Of loved ones left behind;
No vision of the morrow's strife
The warrior's dream alarms;
No braying horn nor screaming fife
At dawn shall call to arms.

—Theodore O'Hara,
"The Bivouac of the Dead"

Hamilton stood at the entrance to the farm's breastworks. The compound had been open for the past three hours as the task of cleaning up the debris and rounding up the prisoners from the morning attack continued. He limped slowly out to the Guardsmen, who were checking the bodies of the fallen gunmen. Prisoners were being escorted to a holding area hastily improvised nearby.

Rogers walked up to Hamilton and stood for a moment watching the activity in silence. Finally, he said, "I suppose you can take a great deal of satisfaction in all of this. It's your victory."

"A victory, yes, but I really can't say that there's much satisfaction in it. Too many good men were killed. That takes the satisfaction out of it." He paused for a few seconds, watching the activity. "What in the world do you suppose caused them to attempt such a thing? Even though they almost succeeded, why did they risk paying such a price?"

"Greed. You had something they wanted. All the rules are gone. Now it's a 'me see, me want, me take' psychology. The right leader has always been able to direct basic impulses in some people for his own purposes, and apparently someone did here."

"I agree with what you say about the right leader and all. But greed? No. I think that the purpose had to be something else."

Two prisoners, both wounded, walked at gunpoint toward Hamilton and Rogers. Hamilton signaled them to halt and approached the first prisoner, a gaunt man with eyes set in hollow sockets.

"Who led you people, anyway?"

"A guy named O'Hara," came the sullen response.

"Where is he?" Hamilton replied, looking across the field and leaning on his M-16 for support.

"Dunno. Ain't seen him since them choppers came."

"What made you decide to attack this place?" Hamilton peered directly into the man's eyes, hoping for a truthful answer.

"O'Hara promised us more guns and lots of ammunition and gasoline. He said that if we did as he said we'd have anything we wanted after that. You know, booze, food, anything, I guess. I never met him until a couple of days ago, but the guy had a way about him. He could really whip up a crowd. After listening to him, man, you just *had* to believe. He was kinda strange in a way, though. Something just wasn't right in him. Like one of the guys said yesterday, the lights were on but nobody was home."

Hamilton paused for a few moments, and then stepped back, signaling the soldier to proceed with his prisoners.

Charlie Brighton walked slowly toward Hamilton from the debris of the destroyed truck. His face appeared flushed and tears painted his cheeks.

"What's the matter, Charlie?" Hamilton asked.

"That boy lying over there is my son."

Hamilton's eyes widened at Brighton's words, and after a few awkward seconds groping for a response, he said simply, "Damn, Charlie, I'm sorry."

"No need to be. Not your fault." His voice trembled and he spoke haltingly. "Thought it was him. Saw him just before the helicopter made the pass that blew up the truck . . . wasn't absolutely sure though. I could've picked him off, but something inside me froze, and I couldn't pull the trigger . . .

"There he was, one of the scum trying to overrun this place and everybody in it, and I couldn't make myself . . . do what needed to be done simply because he was my own flesh and blood. But then I guess I've never known what to do with him for several years now."

"Don't be so hard on yourself, Charlie," Hamilton said, placing his hand on Brighton's shoulder.

"Guess I'd better go break it to his mother." He started to walk toward the compound. "This is going to kill her."

Hamilton said nothing.

Finally, he and Rogers continued up the hill and met Roseanna and the children inside the breastworks.

"The little Fitzgerald girl you were asking about is hurt pretty badly, but Chris says she should make it," Roseanna said.

"Wonderful. At least somebody has some good news." A quizzical expression crossed her face.

Terry Rockwell, his head freshly bandaged, approached the group. Having hounded the remnants of the wolf pack for as long as practical, the other chopper had evacuated a load of the most seriously wounded to Frankfort, and had returned with another chopper. Now only one helo remained. "We'll be getting back to Frankfort now," he said. "We'll be taking the last of the badly wounded men with us."

With all of the confusion since the attack, this was his first real opportunity to talk to Rockwell, and Hamilton asked, "Did you guys come from Frankfort this morning?"

"No. Actually we landed last night at the armory. We found out what had happened there, and what was going on here from some of the people in town. But we figured that we couldn't do you much good until daylight."

A crew chief called to Rockwell from the remaining Huey. Rockwell turned and acknowledged the man, and then turned back to Hamilton. "Well, looks like they're ready. And since we've finally been able to tear Kip away from the controls of the helo," he said, smiling a little at Kip, "we'd better go on and beat feet out of here. See you soon, I hope." He popped Hamilton a quick salute and walked back to the chopper.

Several miles away, Huey and O'Hara sped along a narrow, winding road in a yellow Jeep CJ-5. O'Hara sat in the passenger's seat, holding his badly shattered left arm.

"Where we goin', Boss?"

"Just drive for now, Huey," replied O'Hara softly. "Just drive." The pain in his arm was horrendous, and he knew he was going to need expert medical attention. But for now, he just wanted to get far away from the scene of the morning's debacle.

"What about Kiki?"

"To hell with Kiki."

"Are we gonna try to round up any of the boys, or what?"

O'Hara grimaced as the jeep's suspension rebounded from the pothole in the road and pain stabbed at his arm. Looking straight ahead, he said, "It's not important to decide anything right now, Huey." He then added, "But like Charlie said his coach always told him, 'The opera ain't over until the fat lady sings.'"

The response puzzled the little man. He didn't press O'Hara further, but instead, shifted into high gear as he entered the straightaway and drove silently.

The helicopter slowly started to lift off. Kip watched as he and Jennifer stood between Jack and Roseanna. Skeeter Mulrooney, chewing a large wad of bubble gum, crouching in the Huey's door, blew a bubble until it popped, then waved to Kip. Kip smiled and waved in return.

The chopper continued to rise. It circled the area once, and as it came around, Kip waved even more vigorously. Mulrooney gave him a thumb's up and smiled as the helo passed by and headed toward the horizon.

Rogers wandered off to check on Chris, who was with the wounded. Roseanna looked out on the activity around her and said glumly, "Can we really have come down to this level? Killing each other over the control of a few rifles and bullets? Is four thousand years of civilization a thing of the past? God help us all if that's so."

"Hell, Roseanna," Hamilton replied, placing his hand on Jennifer's shoulder, "all of human history has been concerned with power, and the struggle for it. This is no different. It's just that here the struggle for us was more immediate, more personal. Civilization, or at least what we considered civilization, won't come to an end because people don't have cable television or presliced white bread for toast in the morning. And it won't end because two nations or two small groups of people do their best for a while to eradicate each other. The process might not be quick," he said, "but the odds are very high in our favor that we'll make it back in the long run—even if we do have to clear a lot of rubble out of the way first."

Hamilton watched the helicopter grow smaller, and disappear in the distance. He turned and pulled Roseanna closer.

"We'll make it, Roseanna. I'm betting the farm on it."

THE END

"It is not the critic who counts, not the man who points out how the strong man stumbled or where the doer of deeds could have done better. The credit belongs to the man who is actually in the arena; whose face is marred by dust and sweat and blood; who strives valiantly; who errs and comes short again and again . . . who knows the great enthusiasms, the great devotions, and spends himself in a worthy cause; who at the least knows in the end the triumph of high achievement; and who, at the worst, if he fails, at least fails while doing greatly, so that his place shall never be with those cold and timid souls who know neither victory nor defeat."

—Theodore Roosevelt

SOLDIER
OF FORTUNE
MAGAZINE PRESENTS:

BEETLE BAILEY

THE WACKIEST G.I. IN THE ARMY

☐ 56117-1	BEETLE BAILEY: LIFE'S A BEACH	$1.95
☐ 56118-X		Canada $2.50
☐ 56119-8	BEETLE BAILEY: UNDERCOVER OPERATION	$1.95
☐ 56120-1		Canada $2.50
☐ 56094-9	BEETLE BAILEY: TAKE TEN	$1.95
☐ 56109-0	BEETLE BAILEY: THIN AIR	$2.95
☐ 56111-2	BEETLE BAILEY: THREE'S A CROWD	$2.95
☐ 56115-5	BEETLE BAILEY: UNCLE SAM WANTS YOU	$1.95
☐ 56116-3		Canada $2.50
☐ 56164-3	BEETLE BAILEY #3: DOG GONE	$1.95
☐ 56068-X	BEETLE BAILEY #4: NOT REVERSE	$1.95
☐ 56086-8	BEETLE BAILEY #7: YOU CRACK ME UP	$2.50
☐ 56087-6		Canada $2.95
☐ 56092-2	BEETLE BAILEY #8: SURPRISE PACKAGE	$2.50
☐ 56093-0		Canada $2.95
☐ 56100-7	BEETLE BAILEY #10: REVENGE	$2.50
☐ 56101-5		Canada $2.95

Buy them at your local bookstore or use this handy coupon:
Clip and mail this page with your order.

Publishers Book and Audio Mailing Service
P.O. Box 120159, Staten Island, NY 10312-0004

Please send me the book(s) I have checked above. I am enclosing $_____
(please add $1.25 for the first book, and $.25 for each additional book to
cover postage and handling. Send check or money order only—no CODs.)

Name _____

Address _____

City _____ State/Zip _____

Please allow six weeks for delivery. Prices subject to change without notice.